RASTUS
On Capitol Hill

To Ernie
Best Wishes
[signature]
1 Nov 1993

RASTUS
on
CAPITOL HILL

Samuel Edison

Hunter House

The people and incidents in *RASTUS On Capitol Hill* had their origin and growth in the imagination and are not to be identified with any actual persons or events.

© Samuel Edison 1986
Cover © Hunter House Inc, 1986

All rights reserved. No part of this publication may be reproduced or transmitted in any form or by any means, electronic or mechanical, including photocopy recording or any information storage system without the written permission of the publisher. Brief quotations may be used in reviews prepared for inclusion in a magazine, newspaper or broadcast. For further information contact
Hunter House Inc., P.O. Box 1302, Claremont, CA 91711.

Library of Congress Cataloging-in-Publication Data:

  Edison, Samuel.
    Rastus on Capitol Hill.
    I. Title.
  PS3555.D49R3   1986   813'.54   86-21135
  ISBN 0-89793-045-2

Cover design by Qalagraphia and L. R. Caughman & Caughman Associates; cover illustration by Luis R. Caughman
Set in 10/12 California by Highpoint Type & Graphics, Inc., Pomona, CA; titles in Uncle Sam Stars
Printed by Bookcrafters, Chelsea, Michigan

Manufactured in the United States of America

9 8 7 6 5 4 3 2 1 First edition

For Carol Caldwell

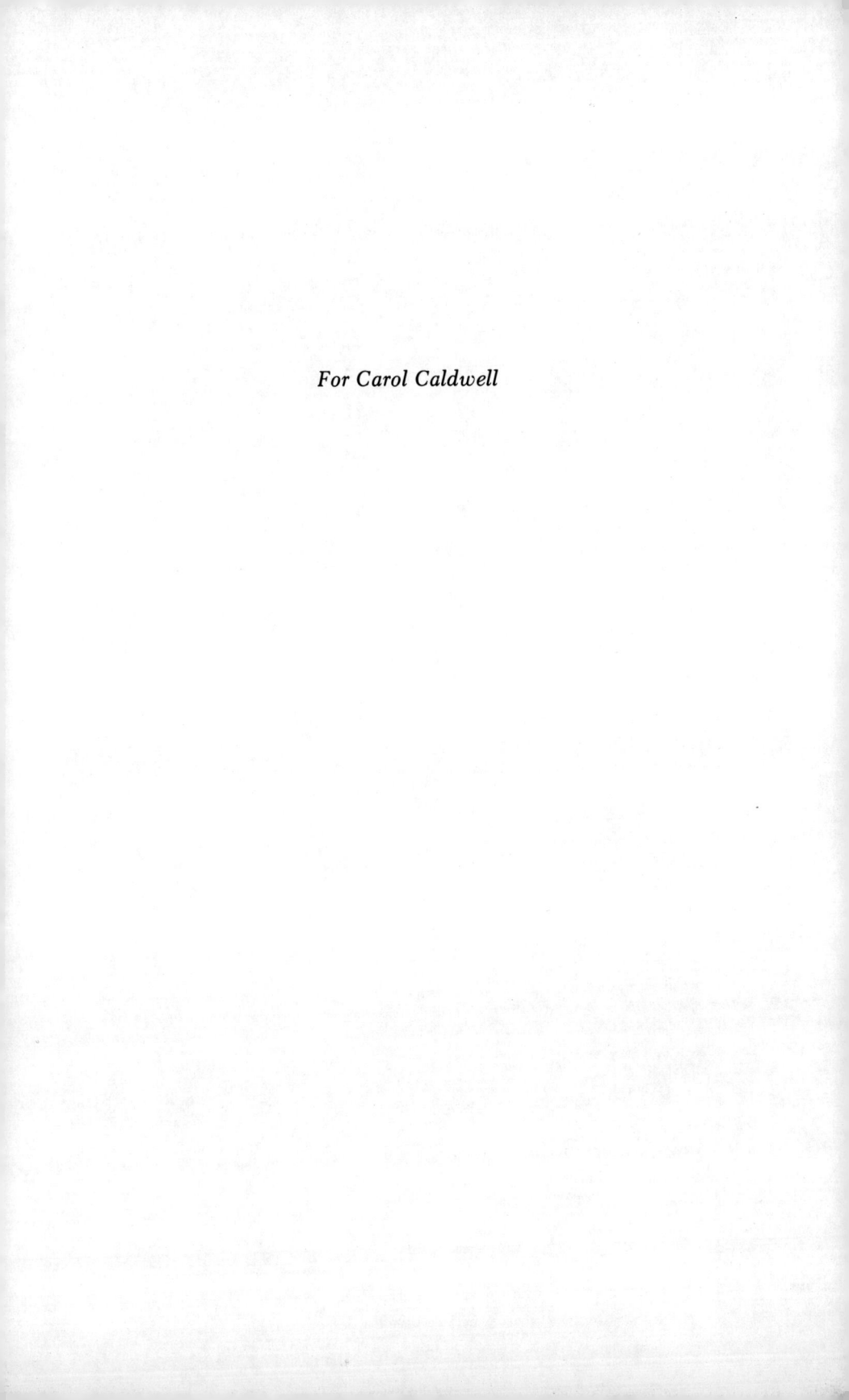

RASTUS on Capitol Hill

My name is Rufus Rastus Jackson all you assholes out there and don't nobody mess with me, man. I got a hangover, man, like my head is gonna explode, man. Any parts come flyin' outta my skull is gonna knock you on your ass and leave you for the garbage truck. Seein' as how this is the ghetto, that don't happen oftener'n once a month. I come to about an hour ago in this miserable hole of a house near the corner of 6th Street and G Street in the Northeast of Washington, the District of Columbia, the Nation's Capital and all that crap, and it ain't no place for a dog except I'm used to it. They's fuckin' roaches all over the place, rats been seen more than once, bloodsuckin' flies, the place stinks, why the hell ain't that bitch clean it up? Cause she gone. Took her clothes and a bottle of my gin and cleared out for good. No goodbye, no note, nothin'. Okay, she can't write no better than me. Which ain't much. Can't hardly read. Same with me. Can't hardly talk and make sense. Same with me. I am what comes out of puttin' time in the D.C. public school system: a big fat zero. Which is why I sound this way, say "shit" a lot and "fuck" and "you know." I say "you know" more than anybody on this block, maybe on Capitol Hill, which is where this part of town is located. When I say "you know" I surround it with a few words about what I'm tryin' to get across and hope for the best. Mostly I don't have no problem. The dudes I talk to, we about read each other's mind. About all is on it is booze and chicks and some place where I'm gonna live when I find the million bucks some cat leaves in my cab. I pick him up at National Airport, see, and carry him to the Washington Hilton up on Connecticut Avenue, a really classy joint where the call girls don't let you squeeze a tit for anythin' less than a hundred bucks up front. He in such a rush to get it on, he leave his briefcase with the million in cash right on the back seat. Dope money, probably, so I do him a favor not reportin' it to the fuzz. If I report it to the fuzz, the FBI be all over his ass like skin-tight pants on a 14th Street whore. Ain't it a shame I don't have me no whores? I should be a pimp, man, own me a dozen white chicks, call me sweetheart and big daddy and give me every last fuckin' dollar so I can have me a white Cadillac and a fancy penthouse up at the FoxDen Condominium on Massachusetts Avenue. Reason I ain't a pimp is because I didn't get no breaks in life. What do I mean by that? What I mean is skin black as soot, a nose so flat it's like pounded, and puffy lips turned up and down about an inch in each direction. You know why some blacks have fat lips, some don't? The thin-lipped had their great, great grandmothers raped down on the plantation a couple of hundred years ago and they been runnin' around ever since with all that white blood which makes you a tight, mean skinny mouth you can't do nothin' about. A lot of chicks go for that, strange as it may seem. Why I don't know. You ever been kissed, had your tits kissed, your cunt and everything else by a black stud with really thick lips? You probably couldn't stand it, turn you on so fast you just about die wantin' some huge black cock up your pussy. Yeah, I'm okay there, got me a big one, about the biggest one on the block if I do say so myself. Sanford, my downstairs neighbor, say *he* got one bigger but I see it when he do the gangbang last June after he stole the case of gin off National Beverage on 9th Street and he lie. Sanford work as a stock boy. Somebody wasn't too careful when they made up the order for this rich dude goin' out to Virginia with a trunk full of liquor and Sanford added a case before he roll his hand truck over to the parkin' lot and after he got him a dollar tip he went to his own car—a 1979 Buick—and put the gin inside. Hell, it ain't nothin' bad. National Beverage is owned by Hebes and they got so damn much money they wouldn't miss a case of gin more'n you'd miss somebody stealin' the *Washington Post* from your front door. Hey, I'm kiddin'. Them Jew bastards is the tightest, most hateful bastards in the world. Serves 'em right after what they did to Jesus Christ and my great, great grandfather. Okay, maybe not personally, but they the same kind of people spend all their time workin' and savin' and gettin' ahead the hard way. Don't hardly have time for the main thing in life which is gettin' a good glow on and gettin' your rocks off with some chick only too happy to spread her legs for a cat like me. And if she ain't happy it don't make no real difference. The girl Sanford brought down to the basement the day he stole the gin, man, she was *unhappy*. Like she didn't want no part of it. Like she didn't appreciate the clever way Sanford pick her up at the Greyhound Bus on New York Avenue. She was just standin' there on the corner of New York and 11th, with this dumb cardboard suitcase and a dress about as simple as a gunny sack and a crappy jacket like somethin' off the rack at Dart Drug and this scared look all them darkies has when they just off the bus from Niggerville, Georgia and gawkin' around like she don't know what to do next now she in Sin City on the banks of the Potomac River. Oh yeah, there's plenty to distract some dumbchick ain't sure about her next move. Down there they got them X-rated movies and dirty books and sex toys and even if you don't see nothing bad until you go in, there's these perverts sneakin' in and out and keepin' their eyes down like if any of their friends saw them they would about shit from embarrassment. I'm talkin' about white dudes, rich guys from Virginia and Maryland having 'em a little secret sin. It ain't no place for some dumb country cornball, no way. Sanford realize that right off. The hickchick's standin' there on the corner like she waitin' for a bus but at the same time careful of those creeps walkin' around loose, eyeing her some of 'em was, and God knows what would happen if some pimp should come by at that exact moment lookin' to entice some sweet young thing into the life where, once you gets into dope and booze, there's no way out. Man, it's a wrong number. So Sanford, he bein' your civic-minded solid citizen like he was a member of the Junior Chamber of Commerce, pull his car right alongside and toot the horn.

"Taxi, ma'am?" he say. "Where you wanna go?"

She look away, she turn around, she take off.

Sanford, he out of his car as quick as a hawk on a bunny rabbit, catch her before she gone twenty feet.

"Hey, wait a minute," he say. She stop, the dumbshit, and Sanford, he reach down for her suitcase and get his hand on the handle right next to where her own is, she holdin' it tight because the thing was loaded down with about everythin' she own in this here world, heavier than a son-of-a-bitch, and she tilted way over to one side just to keep the thing from bangin' the concrete. "Let me help you, ma'am," Sanford say. "Feels like you got a ton of bricks inside this thing. You in the brick business? Come all the way up north with a load of bricks, show your samples around, get you some business, is that it? Is that why you luggin' fifty pounds on a hot day in June without a friend in the world except me, a black brother gonna help you any way I can?"

"Mister," she say, "you just move yourself right along, you hear? Otherwise I'm gonna kick you in the shins and holler for a policeman both at the same time and you gonna end up in jail."

Sanford laugh right out loud. And he look this chick over and he see she somethin' he could have some fun with if he took the notion.

Had her pretty white teeth and some good-lookin', light-colored skin and kinda half brown, half blue eyes flashin' at him strong as stars. "Hey," he say, "you got me all wrong. I'm just tryin' to help."

"I don't need no help," she say. "You leave me alone. Go on about your business."

"Hey," he say, "I'm doin' my business. That my taxi," he say, pointin' to his car which don't any more look like a taxi than the white Cadillac I'm gonna get me one day looks like a beach buggy."

"Don't look like no taxi to me," say the chick. "Don't say taxi, don't say nothin'."

"Well," say Sanford, explainin' eveything with this sugary tongue he got on him, "that's because I'm off duty. But when it comes to good-lookin' young ladies newly arrived in Washington I gotta get back on duty right now. Otherwise I couldn't go to church on Sunday."

Sanford smile. He a smooth-lookin' dude, age of twenty-five. Got him a neat, old-style, close-cropped haircut with a part razored in and a skinny nose and his lips is thin and his teeth is on straight. He about the color of Potomac River mud which ain't black and ain't white, somethin' in between which means he is a livin', breathin' example of your American mongrelization. Oh, yeah, he is a mongrel, pure and simple, and some folks figure they better off that way. Me, I'm a genuine black stud, take me the way I am.

Okay, Sanford smile and commence tuggin' on the suitcase and the chick she still holdin' on too and before she realize it she right up next to Sanford's car. "Where to, lady?" Sanford say, nice and polite. "Just name it and you got it. It's all on me."

The chick didn't hardly know what to do. But Sanford talkin' so sweet and smilin' so pretty she figure maybe he on the up and up.

"I wants to go," she say, "to the YWCA. I wants to get me a room."

Sanford, he about die. Throwed up his hands, rolled back his eyes and shuffled a little dance step, like your old-time movie nigger can't quite believe his ears.

"What?" he say. "You're not jivin' me?"

"No, man," she say. "I wants to get me a room in a respectable place and start lookin' for work."

"Oh, Lordy," say Sanford. "You in the middle of your lucky day. You won't believe this in a million years but I live in the YMCA which is right across from the YWCA and you goin' my way so it ain't any trouble. The YWCA! Ooowee and hit dog! I knew you was a Christian lady the moment I laid eyes on you."

And with that he picked up the suitcase and put it on the back seat and before she realized what was goin' on he kinda maneuvered her into the space between the door and the car and nudged her a little and quick as a flash she was in the front seat with the door slammin' shut nice and solid. Sanford run around and get in his ownself, turned the key and took off. Right away he leaned over and got the door lock down, gave her tits some pressure with his arm on the way back and had his hand on her knee and was movin' her skirt up by the time she realized she had goofed real bad. She knew the only way was to appeal to his reason.

"Let me out of here, you motherfucker," she say. "I ain't what you think."

When Sanford hear that he put his right hand on her left leg and squeeze it so goddamn hard she just about scream and he say, "You open your mouth again, it be the last time." And he give her a glare and knotted up his forehead and begin to breath hard the way Sanford do when he mad and, good Lord, anybody be a fool not to pay him some mind because when you cross Sanford you takin' a chance with a man who lasted until the final cut of the 1978 Washington Redskins.

After that she don't try to argue none, only start bawlin', sayin' "Sweet Jesus, help me, help me" every now and then, thinkin' she could jump out when Sanford stop for a red light only if she do that it's goodbye suitcase and everythin' she own in this here cruel world. So after a while Sanford, he drive up in the alley where we is right now—757 6th Street Northeast in the heart of Capitol Hill—and stop his car.

"Why we stoppin' here?" dumbchick say, her tears still gushin' out good. "Don't look like no YWCA to me. Where the sign say YWCA? Huh?"

Sanford, he laugh. He home now and he got this woman where she can't do nothin' about it.

"Get your ass out of the car," Sanford say. "And hush up bawlin'."

"I ain't gettin' out," say dumbchick.

Sanford laugh again, evil-like. He get out, he go around, he gonna jerk that girl out of there so fast she be lucky her arm don't say "so long" to her body. Door won't open. Then Sanford remember he lock the son-of-a-bitch from the inside. Pisses him off. Goes back, gets in, reaches across, lifts the door-lock button and gives the chick a belt on the face with the back of his hand.

"How come you don't open the door when I pull?" say Sanford. He givin' her a real hard time. "You dumbasses from down South, don't you know nothin'?"

She bawl harder than ever, the water runnin' down her face like her eyes has got waterfalls. Sanford don't pay no mind. He get out for the second time, go around again, put his hand on the door and yank. What happen this time? Door won't open! The chick, she locked it the moment Sanford turn his back! Sanford, he about to explode he so goddam mad. He rush back to the left side, he gonna get in the car and beat up on the chick until she dead. What happen then? The left-side door won't open! The chick, she locked that one, too! And Sanford, his keys is inside and he don't have no spares in his pocket for just such an emergency. He about to go blind he so pissed off.

"You open the door, you hear me, you fuckin' little bitch," say Sanford. He boilin' hot now. He angrier than a tiger in a trap.

Dumbchick give him the finger. Sanford, when he see that, he start beatin' on the window and pullin' on the door handle and rockin' the car and swearin' all kinds of bad words. Didn't do no good. Dumbchick, she stick out her tongue, move her ass over to the driver's seat, turn on the ignition, step on the gas and start to back Sanford's car right the hell out of there. If she done that, God only knows what would have happened to Sanford. Because dumbchick, she would have yelled for help the first cop come across her line of vision and before long the fuzz be all over the place and Sanford be in bad trouble for kidnappin' the chick and beltin' her in the face. He can't complain she stole his car because he stole it first. Yeah, that's the truth. Stole it about six months ago offen a parkin' lot and he put in a minor tuneup and a paint job and two new tires and he be damn upset he lose his investment when the cops check up on his registration and driver's license and how come somebody been fuckin' around with the serial number?

Okay, this is where I come in. Just about the time the chick put the car in reverse, I drive my taxi up the alley right in behind. It's where I park when I come off duty, which I was, havin' done ten hours with not more than eighty bucks to show for it which ain't much when you consider I have to pay the cab company thirty a day and buy gas and oil. Christ, the chick and I damn near do a boompsie daisy with her rear fender and my front but I give her a blast with my horn and she stop at the last moment. I don't know what the hell is goin' on. Then Sanford's car go forward and I see Sanford off to one side and he yellin' "You trapped now, you dumb shit, get outta my car." He was right. She *was* trapped because with me behind her and six garbage cans and a refrigerator and a coupla bed springs and a washin' machine ahead of her there wasn't no way she could escape without crashin' me or them. "You hurt my car you be goddamn sorry," say Sanford. "You go to jail so long you be a grandmother when you come out."

Okay, I get out and walk up to Sanford and he shakin', he so worked up. I say "Hey, man, what's goin' on? How come you so uptight, man? Cool it, man."

So then he tell me all about it, exactly what happened, which is why I can explain it to any of you white folks out there don't know nothin' about the way it is down here in the ghetto.

"Okay, man, no sweat," I say. "I can handle it."

And I go over to Sanford's car and look in and see the chick, she cryin' her little black heart out, boo-hoo-hoo. This is where I come on strong with the charm. I say, "Hey, baby, open the door. Why you wanna stay in there? Heat gonna get you, heat gonna fry your brains to fritters. Don't you need to piss?"

She say, "Piss on you and that other guy and piss on this car."

"No, baby," I say. "Don't be that way. I your friend."

Okay, so we talk back and forth about a half hour and soon she got to piss real bad and she roll down the window and open the door and step out. What happens next, she squat down, snake down her panties and let it go. She been holdin' it so long it come out like a fire hose under pressure. Some of it bounce up from the concrete and splash against Sanford's whitewalls. Man, he is madder than a cockfight. He snatch her up when she done and knock her upside the head and toss her over his shoulder like she a sack of flour. Didn't pay no mind to her clawin' and kickin', jerked her suitcase out of the back seat and headed for the basement. I follow in the rear.

The basement is where Sanford live. Ain't nothin' to brag about. In the front room is the Savior on black velvet over the fireplace. On the opposite wall is about thirty square feet of tits and pussy cut out of *Playboy*. White chicks every one. I ask Sanford once, "Say, how come you got so many? Ain't two tits and one pussy enough to turn you on? Once you turned on, you on. Can't get no harder than hard, can't get no bigger than what you got." Sanford say, "If they was here I could handle them all. When I'm in the mood and I all the time am, I could fuck as many chicks as could squeeze in this room." *He* say. The rest of the room is your standard ghetto furnishings: a beat-up sofa the color of puke; two metal foldin' chairs the kind you sit on in the welfare office and if they ain't chained to the floor you can snap 'em together in no time and have 'em in your car trunk before the supervisor in charge realize what the hell is goin' on; a floor lamp with a shade say "Miller, the champagne of bottle beer. If you got the time, we got the beer, if you got the money"; a color TV set never once turned off in the three years since Sanford give twenty bucks to a friend who stole a few more sets than he had customers for; and a screen door with the screen pushed through so bad the flies and mosquitoes come and go like they friends of the family. And so on—no rugs, no plants, no flowers, no clock, no books, not even a calendar. Just your ordinary poor-folks house ain't worth shit. So why don't Sanford fix it up, make it look better? Hell, he have faith in the future same as me. Tomorrow or the next day or the day after he gonna win him a million bucks in the D.C. Lottery or the Irish Sweepstakes and live in style the rest of his life up around Massachusetts Avenue. So why bother puttin' any money in this hole when he just passin' through?

Passin' through the front room is what Sanford do next. He ain't in the mood to offer his best friend or his new friend any kind of refreshments. Dumbchick is ridin' on his left shoulder and his right hand drops the suitcase anywhere and he head straight for the back room. The back room is where Sanford sleep and fool around. He got him a bed and a radio box can play louder than fifteen jackhammers all goin' at once and more of them dirty pictures with the cunts lookin' at you like somethin' out of a book for doctors. In the corner is a pipe rack holds Sanford's clothes—his white Saturday-night suit, his red sport shirt, his blue polka-dot shirt, his yellow, his two pairs of pants, his one pair of Saturday-night shoes and his straw hat with the wide brim. Underneath is a pile of underwear and socks. About it. The rest he got on his body. Only not on his body very long because after he dump dumbchick on the bed he begin flingin' off his clothes. Dumbchick start bawlin' and carryin' on again. She yellin' "Jesus, save me, save me," like some born-again sinner at the Sunday morning revival. It don't do no good. When Sanford get buck naked he begin rippin' her dress and shoes and everything else. You gotta give her credit for puttin' up a good fight. She kick him and scratch him but he win in the end. After a while she naked as the day she left her momma and started out in this cold, cruel world. Not a bad-lookin' bod. Not as good as the stuff on Sanford's walls, bein' kinda medium in the tits and skinny in the ass, but fuckable if you ain't got nothin' better and it don't cost a dime.

"Okay, friend," say Sanford to me. "Get lost. I can handle it now."

So I turn around and go upstairs to my own pad where I am now and throw some baloney and mustard and ketchup and an onion on a bun and open a bottle of beer and that was my dinner. Too damned tired to fix anything else. Okay, I know what you thinkin'. You think I gonna stand by and let the chick get raped and don't do nothin' about it. You gonna hate me right off the bat, right? You gonna have a lifelong antagonism toward old Rufus when we just gettin' acquainted, right? Friends, it ain't that big a deal. You can ask dumbchick. Been goin' on in her family for years. Started with her great, great grandmother which is why her eyes is almost blue and her skin kinda in between, same as Sanford. And maybe her great grandmother and her grandmother though not necessarily by some white honkey. Plenty black men treat plenty black women like they is dirt and they used to it. Dumbchick can't be exactly surprised at what happens after she stupid enough to get in Sanford's car. Once she do that she layin' herself wide open. If it comes to trouble with the fuzz, Sanford can claim she acted like a downtown whore when he was mindin' his own business and she offered him her ass. Also, he ain't gonna hurt her bad. Nothing rougher than he already give her. Sanford brag he can go for hours but three minutes is his limit before he gets his rocks off and then he gonna sleep a long time innocent as a lamb. So she wasn't in no real danger. And Sanford, hell, he my buddy and is they any reason he shouldn't have him a little fun? Which was why after I finished eatin' I got in my sack and didn't worry no more about it. Must have slept maybe three, four hours. Woke up and felt somethin' ain't right goin' on. Directly below my back room is Sanford's back room and anythin' too loud down there I can hear it. What I hear wasn't Sanford and dumbchick screwin' but some other voices, maybe five or six. I realize then what's happenin' and I be goddamn mad. Jerked on my pants and went outta my front door and down the stone steps to Sanford's front door which is directly under mine. I barge in and rush back to the back room. Just what I expected: five dudes from the block—one fuckin' and four waitin'. Well, goddammit, I don't go for that kind shit one bit. Sanford by himself, okay, but invitin' in practically the whole neighborhood is another story. I know them guys. Skipper and Maurice and Leroy and Leroy's brother Walter was in line like they buyin' tickets at a picture show and Henry Hammond was in the saddle.

"What the fuck is goin' on?" I say.

"What the fuck you think is goin' on?" say Sanford. He sprawled on the floor and he drinkin' out of one of his bottles of gin. "We got us a gangbang. You want some? Be my guest. Only don't break in the line." He laugh. All them motherfuckers laugh. But I don't laugh, man. Not when I see dumbchick. Her face been hit bad, she bleedin' around her eyes, her lips all puff up, her tits is bruised and Henry Hammond is poundin' away on her like he churnin' butter. Man, I seen guys do a lot of bad things to women but this is the worst. The chick ain't sayin' nothin' much more than a moanin' sound and her eyes is closed and then they open for a second and she look right at me and they flash a sign: Help me or I be dead. Maybe yes, maybe no. Some guys say you can't screw somebody to death no matter how hard you try. More likely the guys tryin' it keel over from a heart attack. The thing was I didn't want to take any chances. If she do die, then they got to dump the body someplace, say out on the beltway, I-495. If it's a one-man job you can maybe get away with it pretty good. But when you got Sanford and five other guys, somebody gonna squeal for the reward money and the cops come around to the scene of the crime and sure as hell somebody gonna finger me though I am innocent as God in heaven. So I know what I have to do. I get my hands around Henry Hammond's neck and jerk him offa dumbchick and outta the bed and turn him around so he facin' me and raise my knee and jab him in the nuts. He scream, man. He say, "What you doin', man? You crazy?" I jab him another time and he fall to the floor but he still screamin'. I reach down for dumbchick and get my arms under her and lift her up. She is limp as spit and also a goddamn mess. Stinks from gin and piss and come and she either puke or somebody puke on her and I'm pretty close to heavin' my own self. I head for the door.

"Hey, man," say Sanford, real angry-like, "where you goin'? You can't do that. We ain't had us enough." And Maurice, he come forward and Skipper, he glide around behind and I can see them shitasses is gonna give me a hard time. I ain't worried. I put dumbchick on my left shoulder and hold her up there with my left hand. With my right hand I reach in my pocket and come out with my switchblade. Click and it's open and I cut the air about half a circle and them fuckers back off as quick as mice surprised by the cat. Because I been known to use the thing once I get in the mood. Okay, so we back outta there in a hurry and in no time we up in my pad and the doors is locked and I can dump dumbchick in the shower which may not be exactly what she wants but she smell so bad I can't hardly stand it. Anyway, she don't collapse and I scrub her up pretty good and dry her off and put her in my bed and she about the only woman ever in it that don't get fucked first before knocking off some Zs.

Next day we talk it over. She look better. At least she ain't bleedin'. She say she wanna go to the police, say she want Sanford and them other creeps arrested. "Nah," I say. "Only make it worse. They be out on bail in half an hour. Unless you figurin' on goin' back to Georgia before the trial they be threatenin' you all the time. Tryin' to scare you to death so you won't swear in the courtroom they did it."

"How they gonna do that?" she say. "They ain't comin' in the YWCA. Men ain't allowed."

I bust out laughin'.

"Why you wanna go to the YWCA? What's wrong with here?"

She look around. What she see ain't much different from Sanford's. Just your basic ghetto furniture—cheap, beat-up and grimy—plus a nineteen-inch color TV Sanford's buddy gave me a deal on. Also a record player but it don't work and the radio was stolen a coupla months ago by one of them neighbor kids wanderin' in and out like they own the place.

"Look bad," she say. "I left a shack in Georgia better than this. Don't you never open the windows, let in some fresh air? You got cigarette smoke been hangin' around for six months."

Her name is Celia and she a high school graduate, age of twenty, and she say she can type thirty words a minute and do file-clerk work and she come to Washington expectin' to get her a job with the FBI and rise to the top.

"Lookin' like you look, you ain't gonna get a job nowhere," I say. "You rest up here for a while and take it slow. Can you cook, can you do housework?"

She don't like the idea too good at first but I say it is the best thing for her and I go down to Sanford's place and get her suitcase and say, "Sanford, the chick is gonna stay with me and I don't want no trouble from you because I can turn you in any time for sexual assault. If I catch you foolin' around you gonna be a dead man."

Sanford say, "Okay, let's be friends. I ain't lookin' for no trouble."

That was in June. Me and Celia hit it off good right away. Good cookin', the house don't look so much like a pigpen and she ain't a bad piece of ass. I take her around, introduce her to the old folks upstairs, Mr. and Mrs. Dudley, been livin' there like twenty years, and to all my other friends up and down the block. After about two weeks she pretty well healed and talkin' again about gettin' her a job. I say, "No, baby, ain't no rush. To tell you the truth you ain't gonna get a job 'cause you don't have what they call job skills. You gotta talk smart on the telephone, spell good and type good. I see can I get you a typewriter." So I talks to my dealer, the same one who handles hot TV sets, and in a couple of days Celia have her an IBM Selectric. Wow! The son-of-bitch go like a machine gun! Knocks out words faster than a man can think! A cat could write a book! And she start practicin' and workin' on her spellin' and she start talkin' fancier. I feel proud I been such a good influence. And even though she still have a lot of down-south in her I begin to like her. I say to myself, "Hey, man, you thirty years old, about time you settle down and start goin' through life with some woman happy to spend the rest of her days makin' you happy." So I feelin' upbeat about the whole thing. Then a couple months go by and almost before I realize what happenin' she begin actin' uppity, actin' like I ain't good enough for her. Can you imagine? And about the same time she always be on the telephone when I come home and I too polite to listen but once I hear her say, "Black women been kicked around too long. We don't have to take this shit." Who she talkin' to? She ain't talkin'. And also she don't spend as much time in the kitchen or keepin' the pad clean and since I ain't about to lift a finger myself it beginnin' to look as bad as before. And another thing. When I come home from drivin' that fuckin' cab around all day and could use me a quick piece of ass to relieve my tensions, she say she got too much on her mind about the problems of black women in the District of Columbia and she ain't in the mood and I can jack off for all she care. Goddamn! Well, I don't take that shit from nobody even though I am patient where chicks is concerned because they just naturally inferior and don't know no better. So it come to the point where I was slappin' her around a little for her own good. Nothin' like that time down at Sanford's, but enough to make her realize I'm in charge and things better go my way or else . . . Only it don't get any better and we snarlin' at each other most of the time or yellin' when we ain't and yesterday afternoon was the final showdown. She say she had her a job startin' next week at the Building and Restoration Permits Office of the District of Columbia and she been taken around already and been introduced to everybody and she know she gonna make friends fast. They was the kind of high-class folks she wanted to associate with, she say, have 'em around for get-togethers and parties but she be ashamed to bring them here because to tell the truth I ain't nothin' but a semi-illiterate cabdriver in which *she couldn't take no pride at all!* Yeah, I know what you thinkin'. Treat 'em good and they treat you like dirt. "I be movin' out tonight," she say. "Goin' to the YWCA until I can find a place of my own." It ain't good news. "You're a no-good bitch," I yell at her. "You're a two-dollar whore ain't worth twenty cents. You *better* go because from now on you be as welcome as a boil on the ass." If I hadn't had to go on duty that very moment I'd have slugged her into D.C. General Hospital.

Okay, I got home about 1 A.M. and she has carried out her threat, took everything she own but the IBM. I knock off half a bottle of gin I feel so cruddy. 'Cause the truth is I missed her. Dumbchick for sure but I still missed her. Got me hooked and then give me the brush. Got me used to *her* and then didn't have no use for *me*. Got me thinkin' about *marriage*. . . Now ain't that stupid? Well, there be another one along one day, I ain't gonna worry about it.

Okay, now we about ready for the update. It's like ten o'clock in the mornin' and workin' through my headache is these strange voices, outside, walkin' around the property. Sounds like whitey to me. I step up close to the front window and peek around the shade.

A good-lookin' Mercedes is parked at the curb, about a 1982 model, twenty thousand bucks at the minimum, and between me and the Mercedes is Lucius Deepthroat from the rental agency and another white man and a real hunk of oustandin' blond chick. She wearin' . . . Well, I ain't good at describin' what chicks wear but a three-hundred-dollar call girl would give you an idea. The man been eatin' good all his life and he got him a three-piece suit must have set him back five-hundred bucks, a dark tie you could wear to a presidential funeral, a silk shirt with the cuffs peekin' out of the coat sleeves just enough to flash the gold-coin cuff links, polished alligator shoes when alligators been endangered in this country for years and you can't even buy 'em in Mexico for less than two hundred and fifty, and gold-rimmed glasses which if he wasn't wearin' 'em I'd be thinkin' about chargin' out and bustin' him one in the mouth 'cause what the hell is this cat doin' in my front yard starin' at my house? I wants to know. Only I ain't gonna rush out and ask questions because at the moment all I is wearin' is shorts and my eyes is red and I ain't shaved lately and if these folks should be from the D.C. Lottery or the Irish Sweepstakes come to tell me I is a million-dollar winner and would it be okay to take my picture I would have to say no. But Lucius is talkin' to the white folks and they listenin' and they ain't no reason why I can't tune in, too.

Lucius say: ". . . in 1866, right after the Civil War. Notice the beautiful way the bricks flare out at the roof line. Suggests a castle, wouldn't you agree? And look at the height and slimness of the bay windows and the lovely arc of bricks at the top and the lacy iron grillwork at the bottom. Isn't it elegant? And the stone steps, see how gently they've worn down through the years. The possibilities for the yard—why, they're just endless. Ivy, perhaps, and a small pond and a stone bench and a shrub high and thick enough to hide the fence because for a time there might be a smidgen of danger. Oh, but I just love it, love it. Anybody lucky enough to acquire this place will thank his lucky stars forever."

Did I tell you Lucius Deepthroat—that ain't his real name—is one of them Georgetown faggots been accused of comin' over on this side of town tryin' to get friendly with them young studs over at the Marine Corps Headquarters? He better not fuck around with me.

The white chick say: "Can we go in?"

Lucius say: "Oh, I'm afraid that's quite impossible. Sometimes the tenants are a trifle suspicious of strangers—I haven't the foggiest notion why—and it's in the lease we can't get in unless we're invited. Which, I'm sorry to say, doesn't happen very often although I'm happy to say you'd not be missing much in the way of furnishings. The ceiling height, of course, is something to marvel at and the mouldings—oh, God, I'm simply mad about good-quality mouldings."

The white man say: "Well, we'll have to see the interior sometime. When?"

Lucius say: "The end of October at the latest. The notices will go out next week and they'll be given a month."

The chick say: "How much?"

Lucius say: "It's a steal really when you consider it's only three blocks from where it's already happened. I think eighty-nine five should do it. If you act right away, that is. He who hesitates has to get a bigger loan."

The white man say: "We'll think about it."

Lucius say: "Oh, I envy anybody with the foresight and the courage to be the first. If you ponder it, it's like Dr. Livingston and Dr. Schweitzer going into the great African jungles and upgrading the quality of life all around them."

They stop talkin', climb in the Mercedes, take off.

Uh oh, God almighty and Heaven help us, that is bad news for sure. Sounds like they tryin' to bust the block, don't it? Sounds like the poor folks is about to get shafted again. Sounds like those white fuckers is fixin' to turn this black fucker out of his home sweet home.

Well, don't anybody count on it except over my dead body. This ain't exactly no surprise and I ain't gonna take it lying down. Right now I gotta consider what I'm gonna do next. For a while you gonna have to listen to somebody else.

But I be back soon. You can count on it.

Howard and Vivian Baltus, what a hook-up! Vivian's forefathers didn't come over on the *Mayflower*; they kicked the Pilgrims out of England! Vivian arrived in 1975 as an immigrant on a Boeing 707 fresh out of Oxford with a fancy degree in media communications. Her plan was to get a job in America that would make it possible for the Yankees to hear her beautiful British accent. Howard's ancestors came from the other side of the tracks altogether. His grandpapa Hyman arrived at Ellis Island in 1890. He couldn't speak a word of English, no trade, nothing—a poor immigrant of a Jew whose mother had been murdered in a pogrom and who had been smuggled over the Polish-German border in the care of a hopeful and desperate family taking the boat from Bremen to the Land of Milk and Honey. What propaganda! He was met at Ellis by his papa, who had come over two years before and made enough money to pay for Hyman's passage. Hyman was fourteen at the time, the perfect age to go into the garment sweat shops of the Lower East Side of New York City. He worked his fingers to the bone from morning to night, saving, scrimping every penny and plugging away at the essence of the American dream, Jewish version, which says that every immigrant who came off the boat inside of thirty years would be a regular titan in the garment industry. Didn't happen all that often, take it from me, but in Hyman's case it worked so well in only twenty-five years he was Chairman of the Board of Baltus, Nadelson and Rosenburg, known commonly as Banner Suits, Inc. It is still one of the biggest clothing manufacturers in the country. What Hyman accomplished was a kind of miracle. His son Samuel did even better. And why not? Private schools, prep school and a degree from an Ivy League college. Samuel was one smart kid. He would be a businessman (it was

Hyman's wish), and after he had his undergradute degree from Yale—he was third in his class—an MBA from Harvard was a matter of course. Every success followed. He did well at Banner because of Hyman but when papa retired Samuel went crazy with acquisitions. Not only in men's suits but every other thing a man could wear—plus hair spray and mouthwash and after-shave lotion. Every dollar he borrowed from the bank came back two. In the romance department also a success. Married five times, each one younger and prettier than the one before. His last marriage—he was fifty-nine, she was twenty-two—caused an uproar in the family. She was a shiksa! Why, after four perfectly normal marriages with bickering and nagging and all the rest that is standard equipment with a good Jewish marriage, did he turn his back on tradition? No comment was his only comment.

Howard was born from Samuel's wife number three in 1946. A nice kid, a good boy, a student like his father. A Harvard undergraduate and also an M.B.A. from Harvard but with a difference. He didn't want to make a lot of money. Grandpa, who passed away in 1960, left him a trust fund so that for the rest of his life Howard wouldn't have a minute's worry about paying the rent. Social justice was what he decided on. Which so often these days means something in Government. At Harvard he had fooled around with undergraduate politics. After graduate school he had volunteered for the political campaign of Richard M. Nixon, remember him? He was given his choice of several low-level governmental positions as a reward for his ability to raise money and he took a position in the Department of Commerce. He arrived in Washington in 1970, a serious, nice-looking young man, twenty-four years old, of medium height, a solid build, a strong Jewish nose, soulful brown eyes, wavy black hair, a conservative taste in what he wore, smart opinions on music and literature, nimble on the dance floor—a regular answer to prayers of maidens and non-maidens alike. He rented a beautiful apartment on Massachusetts Avenue, the same street where all the foreign ambassadors hang out, and the good times came his way one after another year after year. He gave a few parties, he went to a hundred. At Georgetown, Woodley Park, Cleveland Park, Foggy Bottom—nothing but the best. And he also took to hanging out at one or two singles bars in Georgetown, high-class in every respect and if you didn't satisfy the man at the door—I'm not talking tip, I'm talking appearance, *savoir faire*, do you look like you belong?—sorry, but the place is full. Try again in a month.

It was at such a place that Miss Vivian Eggleston Carstairs with the fancy name came into the life of Howard Baltus. Love at first sight as you wouldn't believe it. Somebody with a little finer taste, not in such a rush, at least take her outside, see how she looked under a strong light, wouldn't have jumped in like a crazy person. Howard, no. He was poleaxed with passion. Okay, she is a looker as nobody can deny. Everything the best: blond hair handled exclusively by Jean-Pierre, makeup by Elizabeth Arden, clothes from Garfinckel's, Saks and Lord & Taylor, shoes from Gucci, Pucci and Tucci. Eyes like sapphires. A nose so good she can pose in an ad for a plastic surgeon and teeth so perfect the same for a dentist. And skin, has she got skin! It figures, right? In England there is something in the air puts the peaches and cream in the face better than a marble statue in the Louvre Museum. And speaking of the Louvre, Vivian has a figure as good as anything that came from Greece thousands of years ago. Altogether she looks like a million dollars. That's not so much these days but even so . . . And don't forget her voice. Which is almost impossible if you have any leanings toward culture. Because WCLS, which is Washington's classical-music station, is where Miss Vivian Eggleston Carstairs is the star announcer. Her diction is so perfect, her accent so upper-British-class and her voice so persuasive and compelling that any time she takes on a new sponsor he has to put on extra help just to keep up with the extra business.

It was hot stuff between Howard and Vivian the second date. The first date he took her to dinner at Rive Gauche (eighty bucks at least), disco dancing at Pisces (another thirty dollars down the drain) and to his gorgeous apartment on Massachusetts Avenue where the Napoleon brandy (a hundred dollars a bottle and they went through half) loosened their tongues over a discussion that had a lot of jokey content but nevertheless got right down to the blistering issue of the day: Do you have herpes? Indignation, you wouldn't believe it. "No, no, no," they both said. "I've been celibate ever since *Time* magazine." Which wasn't exactly the truth but at least showed they had some awareness of the fact that if you want to try it with someone new these days you are just about taking your life in your hands. A week later Howard and Vivian took dinner at Dominique's, danced at La Rondelle, consumed the rest of the brandy in Howard's den and did it on Howard's bed. It was the most sensational sex in Howard's entire life up until that time. Okay, the kid hadn't had all that much. Maybe a dozen or so at most, starting with pimpled girls at Radcliffe—where sleeping with was what you did if you were going steady and your roommate was away for the weekend—and continuing through the years with secretaries and models and salesclerks and other nothing-special floozies hoping they could catch Howard when he wasn't paying attention and marry him for the rest of their lives. Vivian made them look like amateurs when it came to bringing out the beast in Howard. What made it such a big deal for Howard once it was obvious he would get some return on his investment was the way she put it.

"Darling," she said, "if you don't carry me into your bedroom straightaway, I will absolutely rape you right on the den rug."

Also, "Oh my God, darling, you should have warned me. I had no idea it was so huge."

Also, "Fuck me, you bloody bahstad! Fuck me!"

There is nothing terribly original in any of this, it must be admitted, but when it came out with this precise British accent it had a tremendous effect on Howard. Just think, he thought, from two to five o'clock this afternoon this same superior voice was heard on the radio by thousands and now it's all for me alone. His orgasm was so powerful he was sound asleep in seconds. Vivian was not so overcome and she got out of bed and went to the bathroom and splashed around with the equipment she had had the foresight to bring in her handbag. Vivian did not believe in taking unnecessary chances.

A month later they were united in Holy Wedlock in spite of objections from Howard's aunts and uncles and from Howard's father, Samuel. A Jewish boy marrying a shiksa, nobody approved. Times have changed but the suspicion lingers on. Even Samuel was against it even though he had taken on a cocktail waitress for his final marital fling. The difference, he said, was that from his last marriage there could be no children so nobody should get too excited. Howard and Vivian would be expected to have children. What religious education would they have, what country club, what loyalty and all the rest of it that goes with a mixed marriage? Think about it, they were told, don't be in such a rush. None of the arguments made the slightest difference to the lovebirds; they were stubborn as mules. The wedding was performed by Judge Russell of the District of Columbia Superior Court. A traditional Jewish wedding was out of the question. Rabbis can't unite non-Jews with Jews, period. Absolutely forbidden. So Judge Russell was given the work. He is a nice black man no matter what his color. He was invited to the reception afterwards which took place in Howard's apartment where Mr. and Mrs. Howard Baltus would reside after a leisurely honeymoon in the Caribbean Islands.

Well, really, why did they do it? For Howard, one, she was a beautiful shiksa and Jewish men, even though they should know better, have always had an itch to possess the wicked infidel. Two, his father had favorably impressed him as a successful womanizer and he liked the idea of showing him his son could do even better because between Vivian and the fifth Mrs. Samuel Baltus there was no comparison. And three, Howard was slightly tired of running around. He and his wife would go crazy over domestic bliss and happily settle down with each other forever. Hah!

Miss Vivian had her own reasons. She was descended from bluebloods all the way back to King Arthur and the Knights of the Round Table and if they didn't exactly hate Jews they didn't go around getting married to them either. Then Howard came along and was attractive in spite of a nose slightly larger than she liked. Falling for Howard went against her heritage and her instincts and gave her the typical excitement young people get when they are kicking their traditions in the face and at the same time thumbing their noses at mummy and daddy. (Actually, Vivian had neither at the time, both having died in an automobile wreck that, according to Howard, was caused by too great an affinity for British gin.) Beyond the exciting "defiance" aspects were the appealing facts that Howard was adoring, had a hairy black chest on which she liked to finger paint when they were showering together, and was good in bed. Looking to the future, he was also money in the bank. Her career was going well but it would go no further. She took home forty thousand a year from the radio station but she realized that the big bucks on TV would never come her way. It was her beautiful accent. Disembodied on radio it was fine. But if she had shown up on TV regularly, every American girl struggling for the same opportunity could rightly complain: How come this foreigner rates a job when there are plenty of American girls just as good? So she was very pleasantly stuck and one day her voice would age and crack and she would be out on her ass, which also would have also aged and become as little in demand as her voice. With Howard's trust from Grandpa, even if Samuel should leave everything to that fancy whore he married, Vivian and Howard would have more than enough.

Their marriage started like any marriage: screwing right and left and upside down and a lot of other crazy things newlyweds do these days, it's hard to keep up. After the hormones got a little worn down in six months' time, Howard one day looked at Vivian and realized that he and she should face up to the serious business of getting on with life. He also looked around his apartment: It was no place for an offspring and an heir. It was too frivolous: hi-fi stereo in every room; a bar stocked with thirty-five bottles of alcoholic beverages; paintings and photographs running a little too heavy to female flesh; soft lighting you couldn't tell where it was coming from half the time; shaggy rugs like something in a sheikh's harem; furniture so expensive that if you spilled a drink on a sofa you felt guilty forever; a gadget that dispensed perfume all over the place . . . well, you didn't ask for an inventory. All in all it was as immoral as a whorehouse, which, until his marriage, it had more or less served Howard as. Now, however, it failed to suit his new role as a proper husband and one day a father. Vivian and Howard would have to depart his pad and find something more substantial.

Possibly you have already figured out what comes next. Yes, it is the very house where the schwartze lives that Vivian and Howard decided to buy. Why there, of all places? Howard reasoned like this. One, it would be a tremendous experience moving into a depressed neighborhood where their prosperous presence would serve as an inspiration to the neighbors. Two, their restoration of the house would encourage their neighbors to do the same and so everybody's property values would be raised. Three, it would be close to Howard's office and Vivian's radio station. Four, it was a house, and a kid should be brought up in a house, not an apartment. And five, it would eventually be a very prestigious address: Capitol Hill. Better than Georgetown one of these days and a lot less expensive.

So they talked to real estate brokers and Lucius DeTroit, a lovely young man with a French background and impeccable manners, took them around one morning to the rowhouse at 757 6th Street Northeast. You know what rowhouses are? Just what you'd expect: houses all in a row with a common wall between adjacent properties. Maybe twenty feet across at the most, with a tiny yard in the front, a tiny yard in the back. Seven-fifty-seven is a little different because it's in the middle of the block with an alley running along one side. Otherwise an exact copy of the six houses attached to it. Dull, no? No. Those old-time architects of eighty, ninety years ago knew something about constructing a house in which the owner could feel a certain pride. Not your modern slap-dash out in the suburbs. Here everything was built to last. Well, not exactly everything, because when the whites, for whom the houses were built, began moving out in the twenties and thirties to bigger houses in the suburbs, the blacks moved in and rented. Your average black in those days had trouble enough surviving. Keeping the place looking good was the least of his concerns. In a matter of years what had been good, solid middle-class white neighborhoods became ghettos. The exteriors still had a certain style, a certain handsomeness, but the interiors went to hell in a hurry. You wouldn't want to live there under any circumstances, I assure you.

Fancy Miss Vivian had the same reaction the day she and Howard saw it for the first time. Howard was less squeamish. Jews tend to be less so; it is their liberal leaning. And also Howard's grandpa had lived in the Lower East Side equivalent in New York only a hundred years before. He could relate. Vivian of Berkeley Square was utterly repulsed and especially so when Mr. DeTroit insisted she and Howard step through the frazzled boxwood hedge that bordered the front yard so they could see at close range the intricate and delicate pattern of the window grilles, the floral designs molded into certain of the bricks, and the butt plates of the rods which had been inserted horizontally the width of the house during construction to provide strength and rigidity. Mr. DeTroit knew his houses, no question. What he didn't know was dog shit and when Miss Vivian stepped into some there was a big stink and not just from the poo-poo.

"My God, Howard," she said pretty heated because they were her new Tuccis and cost a hundred and fifty at least. "Let's go."

She turned away and headed for their Mercedes. She stopped at the curb and scraped her shoes back and forth and after she had finished she looked back toward Howard and Mr. DeTroit. The idea was to show by the expression on her face that she expected them to come to the car immediately and take her away from all this fetid squalor. 'Fetid squalor'? Not a phrase your everyday person would use but Miss Vivian Dainty thinks this way and so it must be put down exactly. It was while she was giving out with the dirty look that she saw Rufus Rastus Jackson, one of the tenants. He was peeking from around the edge of the venetian blinds, naked from the waist up, giving her the once-over and thinking dirty thoughts, no doubt. Vivian the Ice Maiden, when she realized what was going on, gave this Jackson person a very haughty stare and a glare, turned away, folded her arms and because Howard and Mr. DeTroit were still talking and by now she was really impatient and angry, stamped her foot. Again the dog shit!

Three days later, after much discussion pro and con, Vivian and Howard drove by in the Mercedes at five o'clock in the afternoon with Vivian at the wheel to take another look. Howard had suggested going in Vivian's little MG because it was less ostentatious than the Mercedes but Vivian said no, she wasn't about to expose the thing to baseballs and footballs in the streets, to dogs who couldn't wait to lift a leg on a new automobile wheel and to kids who, the moment the car was parked, would rush up and spray "fuck you" on it with red paint. Actually, they didn't park the Mercedes because all the spaces were filled. They simply double-parked, kept the engine running and peered out the windows. Howard regarded the place fondly; he could see the possibilities: an ivy-carpeted yard, a weeping willow, tan paint on the bricks, trim black shutters, a polished oak door with a solid brass doorknob and possibly next to it one day a plaque designating the place "An Historic Landmark." All Vivian the Finicky could see was soot-blackened bricks, the bashed-in front-door screen, cracked windows, a neglected hedge and a barren yard. And what she heard didn't help make a good impression. From the basement came this ear-piercing blast of rocket music. Why black people like it instead of a nice Viennese waltz or possibly something from *Fiddler on the Roof* is a mystery for which there is no explanation. Anyway, Howard and Vivian peered and discussed. Suddenly, like two animals escaping from a cage, out from the front door rushed Rufus Rastus Jackson and his neighbor from downstairs, Mr. Sanford Williams. Such a commotion! Screaming and pushing and shoving and finally wrestling on the ground like two gorillas from the National Zoo up on Connecticut Avenue. Suddenly, Mr. Jackson pulled out a knife from his pants pocket, pushed a button and quick as a snake out jumped a knife blade. Zip here and zap there and Mr. Williams was ducking and twisting and squirming all over the place.

"Oh, my God," said Miss Vivian of the Squeamish Nature. "Howard, do something. He'll kill him."

Howard is not crazy. "No way," said Howard, "let's stay out of this. One of the neighbors will probably call the cops."

"No," said Miss Vivian of the League of Concerned Citizens, "we've got to do something." And what *she* did was put her head out the window and say, "Yoo hoo, I beg your pardon. Could you possibly be of assistance? We're looking for 757 6th Steet Northeast." Which was exactly where they were as she well knew. But give her credit for getting their attention! Mr. Jackson looked at her and both men stopped fighting and Mr. Jackson closed his knife and put it away.

"Get the fuck out of here, you white bitch," Mr. Jackson yelled at Miss Vivian of the Shocked Expression. "And don't never come back."

And with that he reached down to the ground, found a lump of brick and heaved it toward the Mercedes. It missed by inches. But it got their attention you can be sure of that. Miss Vivian of the Perils of Pauline stepped on the gas and zipped out of there in a hurry.

"Howard, I do hope you're satisfied," she said when they had gained the safety of Constitution Avenue. "What a perfectly shocking incident. I'm in tatters."

"Don't let it upset you, sweetheart," said Howard. "I feel now more than ever that we should buy the place and restore it and move in. If nothing else we'll cleanse the neighborhood of murderers. The sooner we're here, the sooner there'll be a drop in the crime rate."

Hah! Poor Howard was a dreamer, as we shall soon see.

This here is Rufus Rastus again with the eleven o'clock news and I gotta tell ya, man, it ain't lookin' good. Like Sanford and me was horsin' around a couple of days after Lucius let them white fuckers tramp around the front yard and damn if that same green Mercedes don't roll up just as I was about to change Sanford from a tomcat to a capon. Well, hell, I can mess with Sanford anytime and when I sized up what was goin' on I dropped my knife and picked up a brick. Son-of-a-bitch, if that white chick hadn't taken immediate evasive action I'd have plugged her right between her beautiful fuckin' eyes. As it was I hit Mr. and Mrs. Dudley's old white Chevrolet, the one that ain't been driven for months, just sittin' at the curb all the time with a police boot on it and a bunch of tickets and a sticker on the rear window say "tow." Well, one of these days when the cops ain't got nothin' better to do . . .

After the Mercedes showed I figure things is startin' to get serious, only maybe Mr. and Mrs. Honkey don't realize it. If they'd had any sense they would have quit right then. Anyhow, nothin' happens for a coupla days. Then on the last day of September comes this letter. The postman says I gotta sign right here on the receipt. Fuck no, I say, I ain't about to sign no receipt and I ain't about to accept no letter which asks for one. Postman let me look at it and it's from the real estate office and rental agency which is supposed to be doin' somethin' more than collectin' rent for this hole but ain't spent a dime on it since the day I moved in. Ain't done no paintin', ain't fixed the plumbin' and the window in the back the neighbor kids busted last year is still lookin' for glass. I patched it with a page from the *Washington Post* and Scotch tape but it ain't much help because the gas heater don't put out more warmth than a candle. I lay all this on the postman even though I know he live down the street in a house just as bad. He say, yeah, it's the same with me. Then I tell him he can bring that letter around forever but I ain't gonna take it. Postman say, "It won't do no good. They gonna move your ass out in the end."

We see about that.

Okay, postman come and postman go for a month and I ain't signin'. I pay the rent so they can't get me for that. I slip into the rental office one mornin' about 7 A.M. when the only one in the place is the guard. He don't know me and at first he think I'm doin' an early-morning holdup. He surprised when I tell him I don't want any of his money, I want to leave some of mine. The dumb shit don't know nothin' about the rent receipts but I been in the place about a hundred times and I know where they are. He sign and I get my copy so I'm covered.

Okay, about 11 A.M. this morning right after I roll out of the sack there's this knock on the door. I go see who it is and damn if it ain't Mr. Lucius Deepthroat himself. The funny thing about Lucius is he ain't your swishy faggot at all. He got him a neat, blow-dry hair job and his moustache ain't allowed to have one hair out of place and he wearin' your standard three-piece gray suit and a blue tie with pretty little boats sailin' up and down and black shoes lookin' like they just came from a two-dollar shine. He about as sincere appearin' as an encyclopedia salesman. If you didn't know better you'd think his briefcase had his samples. "Good morning, Mr. Jackson," say Lucius when I get to the screen door. It was still warm for October and this hole ain't got no more air conditionin' than a pizza oven. The front door was wide open. "What the fuck you want, boy?" I say, givin' him a frown. Any chance I get I say "boy" to a white man. Payin' 'em back. Only it don't bother 'em none because they just look down their noses like I'm some dumb kid tryin' to get attention. They figure I can be ignored or brushed off until it's time for me to jump through the hoop. They *know* which one is the *real* boy.

Lucius smile the way college graduates smile at dumb black guys. It don't mean smile, it means look out. "I'd like to come in, sir," he say, smooth-like. "Something I have to discuss about the premises."

"It's about goddam time," I say, givin' him a really powerful scowl. "How come you ain't been here before?"

I push open the screen door and he walk in and right away I notice he take a deep sniff with his nose and hold it, like he decided he not gonna breathe for some time. Well, the place do smell awful and if he gonna pass out or get so sick he gonna puke, it just proves this dump is as bad as I been sayin' all along. If I was the kinda cat lookin' to make trouble I could go to the District of Columbia Health Office any time and have this place condemmed as unfit for human bein's.

"Back here," I growl at him, leadin' the way. He follow me, kinda cringin' past the sofa and the coupla foldin' chairs and the beer cans and the dirty dishes and then he be blinkin' his eyes and pressin' his lips when he see my good-lookin' nineteen-inch Sony TV and my IBM Selectric on the dining-room table because he be sure they stolen. "You know where I can get me a good insurance policy real cheap?" I ask him. "The neighbors they got around here, ain't nothin' safe." He keep quiet, only give me his tight smile and a little negative of his head and hunch his body and hold his briefcase real close in case somethin' should crawl out of the woodwoork and contaminate him forever. We go on, past the kitchen, where the roaches and flies are fightin' it out amongst themselves, and into the bathroom.

"You see this goddamn toilet?" I say to him. "It don't work for shit. And it don't work *on* shit—or for piss, either, very good. Look here."

I get in front of the john and winch it out and aim it. I got me a strong bladder and once the piss gets goin' I likes to back off as far as I can and still keep it splashin' in the water. That way I find out how far I could do some good if somebody should start a brush fire in my back yard. Movin' away means my cock has to be lifted a pretty good angle and anybody standin' off to one side like Lucius was gets a really outstandin' view of the thing. When the pressure began to weaken I eased back to the normal position right next to the bowl and milked out the last of the dribbles. A little more than was really called for—maybe five or six times altogether—and in a coupla seconds the thing began to rise up on account of the special attention I was givin' it. Oh, not a real hardon, not anything I'd be proud to show to a chick but it was enough for Lucius. The son-of-a-bitch couldn't take his eyes offen it. I am proud about what the Good Lord has seen to hang on me and I like to admire it myself. Only this time I was lookin' at Mr. Deepthroat. His eyes is glintin', his breath is gettin' strong, his mouth is loose and I can hear him swallow a couple of times and so fast it didn't seem possible a film of sweat forms on his forehead. It don't exactly surprise me none. Much as he fights it, a faggot cannot control hisself when he sees a really big one.

"All right," I say. "Now lemme show you how fucked up this thing is."

I pushed the flush handle on the john. The bowl took on maybe two or three inches of water, threw up a turd or two from the night before, swished around a couple of seconds, coughed once, hissed a little and didn't do a damn thing more. "Now that's how this thing has been for the last three months. What the fuck are you gonna do about it?"

"What?" say Lucius. My cock is still hangin' out and even though it had begun to shrink a little while I was explainin' the john problem, there is still plenty enough to interest Lucius. "What? Huh? Excuse me, sir, my mind was wandering . . ."

"Lucius," I say, droppin' the mean tone I has been usin' and gettin' all friendly and confidential, "tell me something." He looked like he all set up for what come next. "Which way you like it best? In the mouth? Or up the ass?"

Lucius about shit, he so embarrassed. "Mr. Jackson," he say, "I'm not accustomed to having perfect strangers relieve themselves in my presence. Which is what you more or less are—a perfect stranger. Yes, perfect . . . God, what am I saying?"

I tuck it back in my pants, go up to Lucius, put my arm around his shoulders, turn him around and head him toward the bedroom. "Lucius, old buddy," I say smooth as cat purr, "seein' as how I'm in a good mood and it's about lunch time and I got this feelin' you gonna get the toilet fixed and some paint put down, I'm gonna show my appreciation. I ain't givin' it away—can't do that, you wouldn't have me no respect—but you deserve a break today and I ain't talkin' about no lousy hamburgers at McDonald's. No sir, I'm gonna let you eat what you like best in all the world and if you do a good job—and I have this feelin' you gonna be the best—at the end you get to lick up all the sauce. That's what you want, ain't it, now tell the truth."

"Yes," he say, almost so low and sad I can't hardly hear him. "Yes, God help me, I'm afraid I do."

I laugh. "Well, God won't help you but I will."

We don't have to go into no gory details about what happened next, do we? We do? You ain't seen it in the porno movies? You ain't read about it the porno books? You ain't got a few friends go in for that sort of thing? No? Okay, you asked for it but don't complain if it turns your stomach. All right, I strip down and pump a little iron and pose one or two basic positions and Lucius is fascinated like I'm some kind of Mr. America. His eyes is all bugged out from takin' it in.

"Okay," I say, "sit on the edge of the bed and let's get it on."

He do. He don't like it that the bed ain't made and the sheets showin' some shit stains and some dream stains but he do it. I move in on him when he start reachin' for it but then I back off. Move forward, back off. Move forward, back off . . . Tease the shit out of him. "Please," he beg. "Please." Okay, I take pity on him finally and let him do what he wants. He puts his hand around it and works it some and in a couple of seconds it's as strong as pipe. Then I come right on up close and let him have one good suck. It ain't bad, but two lips and one tongue and one mouth is pretty much the same all over the world.

"All right, baby," I say, jerkin' it out. "That's it."

"What?" Lucius say. "What's wrong? Is something wrong?"

"Fifty dollars," I say. "My fee is fifty dollars. For a sample. You like it, you gotta pay another fifty bucks if you wanna taste the cream."

The fucker don't understand. He look bewildered, sad. "Mr. Jackson," he say, mournful like and the tears formin' in his pretty brown eyes, "I'm not accustomed to paying at all. Not with money, anyhow. I pay with my guilt."

"Tough shit," I say. "You cocksuckers think you can come to Capitol Hill and get us studs for nothin? This ain't Georgetown, friend. Around here you got to pay through the teeth. Only if I feel yours you gonna be sorry."

Lucius sigh, pull away, straighten up.

"I don't have a hundred dollars," he say. "I don't even have fifty. But much as I hate to admit it, I'm terribly attracted to you and I'd like to please you. I really want—well, to love you."

He shouldn't have said "love." I know what love is as well as the next man and gettin eaten ain't it. How could he "love" me?

"Motherfucker," I say. "You a no-good fucker. Not even fifty? You think I run my business on credit? Take VISA? MasterCharge? Shit, no. How much you got?"

"I'm not sure," he say, reachin' around for his wallet. "I'll check."

I snatch the thing out of hand and flip it open. A five and two ones.

"You dumb shit," I say. "Don't you know better'n to be walkin' around with no more than that? Ain't you heard about the muggers' minimum? You don't have at least twenty bucks, you gonna be cut or plugged. What the hell is wrong with you?"

He looks kinda crushed.

"Mr. Jackson," he say, "I guess this was a mistake. I better go now. I'm sorry."

"Wait a minute," I say. "If you can't pay you sure as hell ain't gettin' the benefit of my beautiful body for nothin'. Turn your back until I put somethin' on."

He do it like a good little boy and I slip back into my jeans and T-shirt. "All right, I'm keepin' the seven bucks and I'm takin' your watch and your ring. Is it from some dumb college? Looks like a ruby in there. Get it off before I jerk it off."

He take off his watch, he take off his ring. The ring say Georgetown University. "Tell me something, Lucius," I say. "How can a man with a college education be satisfied to fuck around with tenants? Can't you find nothin' better?"

Lucius put on a small smile. "Just a couple of years. I'm learning real estate. One day I'll use my experience to get into large-scale restorations."

When he say that it ring the bell on my problem. "What, like buyin' these old heaps and turnin' out the blacks and makin' another Georgetown? Is that how you gonna operate? Make your money offa kickin' out the poor people?"

He rise up, pats his pretty haircut and reaches for his briefcase. "Mr. Jackson, maybe we better go into the living room. There's something I have to tell you."

I know what it is but I let him talk anyhow when we move into the front room. He turn away when I offer him the sofa and takes one of the foldin' chairs. I can see he figurin' the steel can't hold bugs the way a dirty old sofa can. "It's up to you, Lucius," I say. "You never had lice and you don't want to take any chances now, right?"

He kinda shudders. "Mr. Jackson," he say, "before we start could I please have my ring back? The watch is cheap and if you need it, fine. The ring—well, it means a lot to me and it can't be replaced—not like the watch."

"Shit, man" I say, "I don't need your damn watch or your damn ring. Be my guest."

I pitch 'em over.

"Thank you, sir," he say. He put on the watch, he put on the ring, he open his briefcase and he bring out this long, legal-lookin' document. He clears his throat and he say, "I see you have ignored our attempts to advise you through the mail. But it doesn't really make any difference. The house has been sold and the fact that you have chosen not to respond to a notice to quit the premises has been legally noted. You and Mr. Sanford Williams and the Dudleys upstairs have thirty days. If you're not out by the end of November the sheriff will put your furnishings and everything else out on the street. The doors will be padlocked and that will be that. I'm personally sorry because—well, I've admired you from a distance in the several years I've been assigned to this property and you are something terribly splendid in the way of male physique and it will be a loss that I won't be seeing you again. And I also feel sad because I must tell you something about yourself you may not be aware of. I'm a homosexual and I accept it and I'm essentially out of the closet and I can cope with the help of friends and psychiatry and counseling and everything else available to somebody who can afford it. But you—I don't know if you've even thought about it, but after what happened a little while ago in your bedroom, well, you may not realize it, but technically you're just like me. Regardless of who sucks and who doesn't, when two men do it, they're both gay."

Shit, man, I hit him upside the head so hard he fall offen the chair. Then I kick him a coupla times and grab him up by the collar and punch him in the stomach, turn him around, drive him toward the screen door, get it open and boot him down the steps. "Man, don't you never say that again," I yell at him. "You hear me? You say that again and I'll kill you with my bare hands." It was the most angry I been in my entire life. Furious, fuckin' fumin'. Me, the super stud of 6th Street, accused of bein' a faggot! Hell, I'm the straightest cat in the world. Okay, I let the cocksucker eat me some but it was only to get the crapper fixed. Treat somebody good and they'll turn on you every time. You can't trust nobody!

After that I calm down and pretty soon come up with a plan. Sanford ain't home but I scrawl a note and I go up and tell Mr. and Mrs. Dudley and then I start goin' up and down the block, door to door, spreadin' the word like old Paul Revere hisself. Most folks kinda shake their heads, like they know this comin' sooner or later. But they say, yeah, we try to be there. I go all the way down to the corner and say "How ya doin?" to one of my buddies works there and he say okay. From noon to eight I gotta drive the goddamn cab but at eight-thirty I be home and ready to get started. I check with Sanford. "Sanford," I call through his door. "It's about time. You ready?"

Sanford come to the door. He ain't been too friendly since the time I catch him stealin' some of my typewriter paper and chase him into the front yard and was about to operate on him without no gas. But he open the door and he say, yeah, he ready. He ain't happy lookin' so I reach in my hip pocket and offer him a slug of my half-pint of bourbon bought for the occasion. "Now you sure you understand?" I say. "Any questions?" "No," he say, "it ain't no big deal."

So I mosey on down the block toward the far corner remindin' folks and I'm almost there when this son-of-a-bitchin' big roar comes from the engine, the siren starts to scream, the lights flash and out from Number 7 Hook and Ladder comes this big mother of a fire engine headed up 6th Street. It's around the corner of H Street in a flicker and I know we got at least twenty minutes before it be back home again. And I also know it wasn't goin' to no fire. Sanford had done exactly what I told him: drive to the phone booth in the farthest corner of the fire district, call in a fire, voice 'em a little panic so they know you for real and get the hell out of there. I pick the fire house because it's the only building on the block big enough to hold two hundred people and even then it got to be rid of at least one fire truck so there be room. It was the fire station lieutenant I was talkin' to earlier in the day and we worked out our plan so ain't nobody suspicious.

While the people is streamin' in I climb up on the ladder truck where everybody can see me. "Quiet," I yell when I figure all that was comin' had come and they hush up good. I look 'em over and they a lot like me: bus drivers, day laborers, security guards, janitors, maids, dishwashers, waiters and plenty of those other poor bastards that are the backbones and assholes of Washington. "First thing, somebody shut the big doors. This is a private meetin'." It wasn't, but I say that to give 'em the impression they was in on somethin' special. And for another reason you'll understand a little later on. "All right," I say when the doors is slammed, "let's not waste no time. That fire truck be back from that false alarm in fifteen minutes. Let's decide what we gonna do." Right away there was talkin' from all sides at once. I gotta tell you I was impressed with some of the unexpected ideas my neighbors come up with. Henry Hammond, for example. You remember him? He one of them fuckers that gangbanged my former chick Celia before I got to know her. "Let's torch it," he yell. "Leave it for dead. Ain't nobody gonna buy it when the floors is burned out and the roof is collapsed."

"Great idea, Henry," I say. "Thanks a lot. And just exactly where do you think me and Sanford and Mr. and Mrs. Dudley gonna live after that? You wanna take us in?"

Everybody laugh.

"And don't go thinkin' it's only my place," I say. "All you people is in the same boat. Once my house goes, the rest follow in no time. So it ain't just me. We got to save the whole damn block."

Voices come on strong. "Right on, brother" and "Yes, indeed" and "You right" and "Amen" and all the other things blacks say when they gettin' roused up behind a good cause. Then the voices die and it gets quiet for a second. I'm about to go on when some drunk asshole leanin' on the fire pole takes off his cap, throws up his arms and lets out "Hallelujah, praise the Lord." Everybody laugh again. That's one of the troubles with blacks; give 'em a chance and they be funnin' everything.

"Enough of that," I say, stern and serious. "This ain't no time to be callin' on the Lord. Maybe later we have to. Save it for then. All right, anybody else want to sound off? Only let's make it one at a time."

So everybody got a chance and pretty quick they talkin' about how they gonna "shoot any white honkey come around my place, you better believe it."

And they gonna "chain themselves to the kitchen sink."

And "once they start to fix the place up, we steal the new plumbin' as quick as they put it in."

And "we could buy us a whole bunch of D.C. Lottery and Irish Sweepstakes tickets and buy the whole damn block with the winnin's."

And "we got to go to the *Washington Post*, this ain't fair."

And "a march on City Hall, let them bastards know."

And they talkin' guns and rocks and bloodshed and lootin' the stores and startin' fires and Martin Luther King Junior and in no time at all they so worked up they about ready to take to the streets. That's good, gettin' worked up. But it's bad goin' off half-cocked. I hold up my hands and yell at 'em, "All right, that's enough. Calm yourselves down."

They don't want to. Once they get wound up like that, they go crazy gettin' it out of their systems. But I keep after 'em and since I'm the highest one in the place and also the biggest and strongest they begin to cool it. "Okay," I say when I see they losin' their excitement, "I know how you feel and you got some good ideas. Now how about you listen to mine."

They look up. They wait. They ready for somethin' powerful.

"We gotta fight this thing the same way whitey fights," I say. They like that. They nod, they said "all right" and "right on" and all the rest of it. Yeah, the way whitey does it is the best way. What's that?

"Anybody here know the name of a good lawyer?"

Well, they just laugh and hoot and jeer. Because it's your black experience lawyers cost money and ain't worth shit. Otherwise, how could Leroy Wilson, another one of them gangbangers, who didn't do nothin' more than knock off three banks without hurtin' a soul get eight years at Lorton Reformatory?

"Listen to me," I say. "It's the only way. We get a good lawyer we can fight and delay forever. Now who'll put up the first buck?"

No answer. Once you start askin' money from poor black people you in for a heap of disappointment. Everybody in the place kinda shake they heads and start for the door, the little door inside the big one. Thank the Lord the big one isn't still open, otherwise they be runnin' like mice hearing the cat bell. But I leap off the fire truck and press through the crowd and I get to the door before too many could escape. I hold out my cap and damn few of 'em don't put in at least a quarter and most a dollar and some two. By the time everybody trails off into the night my cap is heavy. But when I get back home and lay it all out on the dining-room table and count it, it only comes to eighty-seven dollars and fifty-four cents. Well, shit, what kind of lawyer would work for eighty-seven dollars? I don't know, only I sure as hell gotta find out. Tomorrow I gotta start lookin' for a cheap mouthpiece. See ya.

4

There is incontrovertible evidence that Geraldine Lance tried it with a man when she was seventeen and in high school and with a woman when she was nineteen and in college and several men when she was twenty-three and twenty-four and twenty-five in Georgetown Law School and several women when she was twenty-seven and just getting her law practice established and many men and women in the years that followed. She liked them all, that is the truth of it, she didn't love any, didn't want to marry, didn't want to live together, didn't want to be distracted from the main satisfaction of her life which was practicing law and getting all the pleasure she possibly could from her many erogenous zones. She liked to have sex immediately she felt the need. She would call the current favorite and if the favorite was not available or uninterested, call somebody else and keep calling until she found somebody who could come over right away. It could be either a man or a woman—it didn't make much difference which. Usually the liaisons took place in her small house on Columbia Road, in the northwestern quadrant of the District of Columbia, where the bed was rarely made and the dishes were as often dirty as clean. Her dog, Hardin, lived with her. He was part Great Dane and part German Shepherd and until he got to know you he could put on some terrifying expressions and bark and growl you into a state of advanced terror. Once he had checked out your intentions—a matter of two minutes at most—he would fall in love and if you didn't resist try to prove it. He would sniff you in the most intimate places front and back and if not told to "Stop, you over-sexed bastard" begin to develop an erection. Some dog fanciers in Miss Lance's social set said he was as good sexually as his mistress, although there was an apocryphal quality to such gossip and much of it should be discounted. Miss Lance herself denied there was anything special between the two of them. She did admit she had once defended in a bestiality case and had experimented with Hardin for the sole purpose of better relating to her client. Hardin had the run of the house and the backyard. If he wanted to dig unsightly holes in the earth he could do so or if he wanted to watch Miss Lance and her friends indulging in pleasure he was permitted to do that, too. The couplings didn't necessarily take place in the bedroom. Statues and photographs and paintings of riveting explicitness lined the walls of every room and it was Miss Lance's fetish to conduct her sex sessions near a particular ornament most felicitous to the mood of her and her partners. She had something appropriate for both the young and slim-hipped and the old and paunchy. "Look, sweetie," she might say, "there you are being ravished by the satyr. I can do just as well." And she did. She was equally facile at inducing and experiencing the ultimate sensation. When she brought you to orgasm it was always one of the best three or four of your life. You would yell and sweat and pant and dig your nails into whatever parts of her anatomy you could grab and eventually beg her to stop because "My God, I can't stand it. No more, please. Oh God, you're killing me. Stop, stop, stop!" and so on, which was a great exaggeration because no one had ever required as much as a ride in an ambulance though there were one or two occasions when momentary loss of consciousness could not be ruled out. She was just as enthusiastic when it was her turn to revel in the greatest pleasure God ever created, saying terribly flattering things like "You're absolutely the best lover I've had today" and "Oh, Jesus, your cock should be preserved for the ages" and "God, if I didn't have to go down to the D.C. jail and see a client in the next twenty minutes I would stay with you forever" and "Darling, how clever of you. I've never done that particular position before in my whole existence. Such originality!" Her face tended to the pedestrian but her body was something to regard with awe and wonder. She had taken on pudge at puberty and by the time she was completely developed she had a forty-six-inch bosom and a forty-eight-inch behind. But it was solid stuff, quite satisfactory to the touch, and universally admired. Her red hair was neither naturally curly nor wavy but it did have good body and a substantial oil content and when it was freshly washed and in the sunshine, the stuff gleamed in a very attractive way. It attested to her good health. A few freckles never did a woman any harm. Her nose was a nose, nothing special, hooked slightly though in no way extreme enough to suggest she might be Jewish. The lips were perfectly standard in appearance, neither particularly full nor thin. In practice they featured an unusual pneumatic quality, so when she kissed you or sucked you, you felt the pressure had been perfectly adjusted to do the very best by your central nervous system. Her grey eyes were her best feature: twinkling a lot and reflecting her usually happy mood. Her teeth were perfectly functional: she had them all and her sexy little nip was as good as anything you could get from a really high-class call girl provided you paid extra. Something kind should also be said about her chuckle. It had bubbles in a brook and the birds in the trees and the wind in the willows and a bunch of other nice qualities far too subtle for description. Her laugh was a different story: explosive and long-lasting as a roll of thunder. Clothes weren't something she paid much attention to. All she asked was that they emphasize her cleavage and be tight across her behind. In summer she affected a bikini. The first sight of her so adorned dropped many a jaw, though it was nothing compared to when she shed it in broad daylight under a strong summer sun. She did that most often on the houseboat of her partner, Audrey Copper, a woman who lived on the vessel year-round with her husband and kid. The boat was berthed at the Capitol Yacht Club, down on Washington Channel. Weather permitting, the owners, the kid, Miss Lance and seven or eight other jaunty types would ease out of the slip and head down the Potomac River for the weekend. It was fun to wave to the tourist boats and the sailboats and the mighty power cruisers requiring great wealth, all of which on a fair summer's day gave the good, grey Potomac a festive air indeed. Smoot Cove, an expanse of water given to underground springs and thus theoretically purer than the river proper, was the usual destination. The trip from the yacht club took an hour and as soon as the boat had been anchored at a remove of some fifty yards from any other, it was Miss Lance's wont to climb to the upper deck, fling off her bikini and shout, "All right, the rest of you candy asses, follow me." And she would take a dive. Oh, it was something to behold, let me tell you, this one-hundred-and-eighty-pound hunk hurtling through the air and busting the water all to smithereens. The impact was a sensation, so much water being splashed back aboard that the others not already stripped were wetted so thoroughly they might as well be.

 She tended to be a trifle coarse about her language. She would say "shit" when there was no reason for it. Or "fuck" when it wasn't even on her mind. Or "motherfucker" or "bastard" or "son-of-a-bitch" when "shoot" or "drat" or "gracious" would have been more than ample. She would be admonished from time to time by squeamish judges on those occasions when she forgot herself in the courtroom. It really didn't amount to anything serious and she had never been held in contempt. She had come closest the day she had prosecuted in a radical mastectomy malpractice suit. When it was time to make her final argument she had approached the jury box, picked out the best-looking man in the front row, reached out with her left hand, grabbed his right and before the poor fellow realized what was going on planted it on her left one. "You feel that?" she said in a very dramatic tone of voice. "You like that? You want to fondle that, right? Well, sir, you'd never want to do that to my client because that charlatan, that quack, that butcher sitting right over there with that smirk on his face . . ." and she turned and pointed to the defendant, ". . . that incompetent wreck of a sawbones has cut my client's femininity right down to her ribs!"

The judge chewed her out something awful and the defense counsel jumped up with a motion for mistrial. It was Judge Russell presiding and he had half a mind. But he was sensitive to the feelings of the spectators (who had just about burst into cheers over Miss Lance's performance), he realized where the sentiment lay in the case and he didn't relish being categorized on the editorial pages of the *Washington Post* as a legalistic nitpicker. In truth, he appreciated smart-ass shysterism as much as anyone and also he had been entertained at Miss Lance's more than once and hated to think he would never again get to fornicate beneath the painting of Zeus making out with an earthling. "Denied, counsel," he ruled. "Take your seat."

Her offices were in the Gondolph Building at 11th and K streets. The structure had been architected eighty years before by a man who had nothing against pigeons and through the years their droppings had mottled the facade's curlicues and ledges and gargoyles in a most unsightly way. It was not a prestigious address but since Miss Lance did not consider herself a prestigious lawyer it served her fine. You gained her establishment by ascending in the rickety elevator cage in which one Daisy Hatfield, a black septuagenarian, served as both operator and concierge. When you announced Miss Lance's floor, Daisy, if she hadn't seen you before, would likely say, "You in trouble, huh? Trouble with the law? Been caught doin' you some embezzlement? Been caught foolin' around by your wife? Been caught pickin' pockets? And you look respectable. Lordy, these days it's hard to tell." When she jerked the cab to a stop at Miss Lance's level and slid back the grille she'd say, "Down that way," pointing, and look you over disapprovingly until you gained the frosted door which announced that Lance & Copper, Attorneys at Law, were behind it. There might or might not be a secretary on the other side. Miss Lance and Mrs. Copper were not too proud to answer the telephone, they had mastered typing, and unless they were overwhelmed with business—and they rarely were—either would sit in the outer office and serve as receptionist. Mrs. Copper's private office contained a formidable mahogany desk once the property of her grandfather, an imposing collection of lawbooks and an awesome assemblage of Waspish forebears who looked down from the walls with such righteousness that a substantial number of Mrs. Copper's crime-tainted clients immediately said they had searched their consciences, realized their guilt and would just as soon be thrown upon the mercy of the court. Mrs. Copper said she would do her best. Thus was justice inexpensively and efficiently served.

Now your Miss Lance was a different type of lawyer lady altogether: casual in a certain way and flamboyant as we have seen and her office was an extension and reflection of her home—cluttered, disheveled, and you could never get your hands on the pertinent file without first pawing through thirty others that were on the beat-up desk or on the client's chair or on the carpet. Her lawbooks rested primarily on the bookshelves purchased years ago at Hechinger's Hardware and were installed beyond her desk chair, a piece of furniture terribly tired from the years of supporting the solid senior partner. Hardin, that great beast of a dog, was known to hang around the place on an erratic basis, earning his chow by serving as guardian. Many undesirable types could drop in unannounced at any time and his presence was justified.

It is truly hoped that nothing said about Miss Lance up to this point has given you the wrong impression. Screwing, yes, she loved it and skinny-dipping and the strong drink and all other various and sundry felicities the Good Lord put upon the earth to help our passage through it. Did it affect her abilities as a counselor? Never in a million years. She was a damn fine advocate and when you signed on with her you got a commendable representation. It is true she was not one of your gung-ho types who took the law more seriously than it deserved. It was her father, a fine Irish gentlemen now devoted to his memoirs, who had encouraged her to study the law and so make herself useful to society and who was responsible for her moderate attitude. He had applied the philosophy to his own profession, also lawyering, and it had given him a good living and his daughter an expensive education at Georgetown University. "Never forget," he had once said, "trying a case in court is a game. Some win, some lose and whichever you do is not important. What is important is finding a client who'll pay the entry fee for the next contest." So she had developed a laid-back approach, never chasing an ambulance and preferring as clients those persons who seemed to have some potential for sexual divertissement. She had reached the age of forty content with $35,000 per annum. This paltry sum required that she practice certain small economies and on the day she became connected with what has heretofore transpired these took the form of cleaning her office—dusting, mopping and running the vacuum. She had clothed herself in an ungainly smock and had kerchiefed her hair. She was alone except for Hardin snoozing under the desk. Mrs. Copper's kid had developed something nasty in the way of an intestinal upset and she was home on the boat ministering to him.

When the rap-rap-rat-a-tap-rap was heard, Hardin sprang up and sprinted for the front door of the offices' main entrance, barking and growling himself into something of a tizzy. Miss Lance followed at a more measured pace and with her Smith & Wesson .375 raised to the point where if someone were to burst in she would be ready to plug him. It is a sad commentary on society these days in general and on the quality of life in the District of Columbia in particular, but small law firms—indeed, small firms of any description—do well to keep a loaded firearm hidden on the premises but quickly accessible should the need arise. And it is a very good idea to keep the outer door bolted. Such was the rule at Lance & Copper and when Miss Lance got close and saw the muddled image of a large person through the rippled glass she wasn't about to go up, unbolt and say "Come on in."

"Who is it?" she said. "What do you want?"

"The lawyer," was the response. "Is the lawyer there?"

Now it didn't take Miss Lance more than a second to realize she was conversing with a black person. It's curious how they've kept their picturesque accent even though most are years from slavery and the Deep South and by now should be speaking English as perfectly as everybody else.

"What's your name? Do you have an appointment?" said Miss Lance. She would not be rushed.

"Hell, no, I don't have no appointment," the black man said. "Right here on the door it say 'Walk In.' Don't you mean it?"

Miss Lance thought it over.

"Wait a minute," she said. She fashioned a grip on Hardin's collar with one hand—the creature was still barking like crazy—stuck the revolver down her bosom with the other and unbolted the door. Then she dragged Hardin back three or four feet, retrieved the revolver, raised it so she was sighting right down the barrel and said, "Okay, you can come in now."

"Hell, no," the man said. "I can hear that hungry fuckin' dog. How come you don't feed the son-of-a-bitch? I could report you to the SPCA."

"Listen," said Miss Lance, "don't give me any smart-ass. The dog won't bite unless you ask for it. But I've got to tell you, one false move and you're hamburger."

"Listen, back. If that dog as much as scratches me, you gonna be the one needs a lawyer."

The door opened slowly and there in all his macho glory stood Rufus Rastus Jackson—tall, muscular, broad in the shoulders, slim in the ass, bulging at the crotch and as conscious of his physical perfection as was David when he posed for Leonardo. We're speaking from the neck down, of course. Above it, the nose was flat, the lips were gross and the eyes were full of suspicion. Such an expression seems in the poorest possible taste from a man who is, after all, living free in this most blessed of lands, praise be to God. He should be grateful. Miss Lance, for her part, lowered her revolver almost right away and let go of Hardin. Hardin took a shine to the man immediately. He stopped barking, wagged his tail, went right up to Rufus and sniffed him out.

"Who are you?" said Rufus. "I'm lookin' for the lawyer. You the cleanin' woman?"

"It all depends," said Miss Lance. "If you're selling really good mops and superior floor polish I might be . . . Of course I'm the lawyer! Who the hell are you?"

Rufus chuckled. "Okay, lady, don't get your ass in an uproar. Up 'til now I ain't had no need for a lawyer. So how the hell should I know they don't all look like F. Lee Bailey. You know F. Lee? Carried him in my cab one day. Five-buck tip."

"I think I've heard the name," said Miss Lance. "You need a lawyer, why don't you go to him?"

"Weren't you taught any manners in law school?" Rufus asked. "Aren't you gonna ask me in? I stay here at the door with the breeze blowin' through this drafty building the way it is I could get pneumonia and have to get me another lawyer to sue you for givin' it to me."

Miss Lance smiled a trifle.

"All right, come in. Hardin, stop giving the gentleman the impression you're gay. Get back to the office and go to sleep."

Hardin loped off and Miss Lance and Rufus followed. She cleared the client's chair of files, motioned Rufus to it, created a space on her desk, sat, reached for a pad of legal paper, cranked her desk-corner sharpener around a pencil and went to work.

"All right," she said, "I'm Geraldine Lance. What's yours?"

"Rufus Rastus Jackson."

"Got a permanent address?"

"Hell, yes. Whatta you think I am? Well, after that question I got an idea."

"All right, let's not get our feelings hurt. What is it?"

"Seven-five-seven 6th Street Northeast. In the District."

"Got a phone?"

"Sure."

"What's the number?"

"555-2743."

"You work?"

"I told you I drive a cab. Am I gonna hafta repeat everything?"

"Maybe. I like to double check. How about money. You got any money?"

"Not a lot."

"I don't do charity. Hardin needs a new collar and I could use a few new things myself. The cleaning woman! Jesus, I guess I've been letting myself go."

"Hey, I kid a lot. I didn't mean nothin' by it."

"Okay, I'm not going to charge you extra. Only answer my question. Can you pay?"

"I've got eighty-five bucks. How far will that go?"

"About twenty-seven more minutes. I charge a hundred and fifty dollars an hour."

"Then I better stop right now," said Rufus. "This thing ain't gonna be fixed in no half hour. I got the feelin'."

"There's a fifty-dollar minimum. You're already committed to that. That gives you twenty minutes. Sound off."

He did so—the house, the honkeys, the notice to get out, the meeting, the money, the fear that yet another old ghetto neighborhood was about to be busted into latter-day Georgetown.

"Wait a minute," said Miss Lance at the ten-minute mark. "Let me get this straight. You've been told to get out, right? But what about a chance to buy? When did that happen?"

"It didn't. Not that it makes any difference. Ain't none of us could afford it."

"That's where you're wrong, Mr. Jackson. It makes all the difference in the world. Who's the real estate handling the sale? You know?"

"I guess it's Capitol Hill Properties. That's where I been payin' the rent."

"Are you certain they haven't said anything about you having a chance to buy before it's sold to someone else? Sent you a registered letter? Spelled it all out?"

Rufus sighed.

"Miss Lance," he said, "I ain't gonna jive you. I refused to sign for any letters from them bastards. I figure I got to sign somethin' before they can go ahead and as long as I don't sign I got 'em by the balls."

"By the balls. Very graphically put. Mr. Jackson, I don't know where you learned your law, but you've got a good grasp of the fundamentals."

"That's what I said. Grasp 'em and don't let go."

"Uh huh. Tell me, Mr. Jackson, do you do anything besides driving a taxi? Numbers running? A little dope? Anything like that?"

"Hell, no. Too risky. What I'm loookin' for one of these days is a nice string of white chicks sellin' their ass up and down 14th Street. In the meantime it's just two-bit hackin'."

"Well, if what you're telling me is the truth you might come out of this smelling like a rose. Or even like a 14th Street streetwalker wearing a pretty good cologne. Or even possibly like an expensive call girl wearing Joy. I think there's reason to be optimistic."

"Oh, yeah?"

"It's a matter of the District of Columbia law. Section Six, I think it is, of the District of Columbia Real Estate and Housing Code. Wait, I can check it in a minute."

She put down her pencil, turned toward the bank of lawbooks behind her desk, studied the titles briefly and extracted a weighty tome. She opened it to the index. "Let's see," she said, "there's 'Notification before sale.' Very good. 'Condition of property.' Could be useful. Ah, here we are: 'Opportunity to purchase.' Page 310. Okay, let's see what the good people down at the District Building have to say about opportunity." She turned to page 310 and for several seconds perused it. "'Opportunity absolute . . . Sixty days . . . Must satisfy the housing code prior to . . .' Hey, get this: a fine of ten thousand dollars and a year in the pokey. Terrific. Couldn't be better. Mr. Jackson, you've come to me with practically an open-and-shut case. If the owner of the property hasn't given you a chance to buy it and has sold it to someone else without doing so, the law says you've got him where you want him. By the testicles, to use the flowery phrase lawyers are fond of, and to use yours, by the balls."

"You mean it?" said Rufus. "What you're readin' takes care of the whole thing?"

"Mr. Jackson," Miss Lance said, "yes it does. Just one small paragraph says it all. The law has been broken and when the law has been broken, somebody has to pay. And unfair as it may seem when such things are considered in the abstract, somebody gets paid, too. I'm talking about lawyers. You can't simply take this law book in your own hands. But I can—for a hefty fee. Given enough time and money I can prolong this thing for months if not years. Which is ultimately all you can hope for. Eventually you'll have to go. Get it?"

"Oh, yeah," said Rufus. "I ain't lookin' for no charity. How much?"

"I'll need five hundred dollars fairly soon—a matter of weeks."

Rufus whistled. "I'll have to do a lot of hat passin'. Or get the neighbor ladies to sell cookies. Or shortchange a lot of my customers."

"Listen, I want to make it clear about the money. I only count it—not trace it. But if you get the money illegally and are caught, don't come around and ask for help. I would have to charge extra for that and it would never end. Or it would end up with you in Lorton Reformatory. Right?"

"Oh, sure, I'll be careful."

"Not just careful—honest, too."

"Okay, I'll get it the hard way."

Miss Lance wondered. She was pretty certain this great black creature had never done anything the hard way. Not worked hard at school, not worked hard at any of the dead-end jobs she presumed he'd had through the years, not worked at saving money for his distant old age, not worked at anything much beyond getting drunk and getting laid. She did credit him with one thing: He hadn't come to her as a defendant in a criminal case. She saw a certain number of his black brothers in that respect. A few were brought in by parents or wives and when that happened she could nearly always count on a reasonable fee. More often she was assigned by the District Court to defend the penniless for peanuts. That's when she saw the muggers, rapists, burglars, murderers—"the despised, the discredited, the disadvantaged dregs of Washington society," to use a phrase she sometimes tried on juries. She gave them all the best defense she could, albeit through the years she had developed a hard-bitten attitude toward criminal-case verdicts. It didn't upset her if she lost; her client was probably guilty and so deserved to be put away. It didn't excessively please her if she won; her client was probably guilty and getting away with it this time would only encourage him to try again. The next time she'd have him as a loser.

"By the way," Miss Lance said, "how'd you get my name?"

"Daisy Hatfield who runs your elevator. She lives on my block. Says you helped one of her nephews when the police accused him of dealin'. He was—but you got him off. She been workin' for you for fifteen years."

"Not for me. The people who own the building. Was Daisy at the firehouse meeting?"

"Hell, yes. She don't wanna be on the street. She ain't trained as a bag lady. Prince Georges County? No way. She don't wanta live way out there. How come you don't pay her enough so she can live some place better'n 6th Street?"

"I don't pay her."

"That's the truth. Not very damn much."

"She doesn't work for me."

"Take her away from her friends, her church, her neighborhood stores and what have you got? Somebody ain't too long for this world. The bad thing is, we gotta pay you for help when it's people like you causin' all the trouble. Daisy ain't no dog, you know, Daisy work hard all her life and she shouldn't be treated like no slave. Daisy got rights but nobody don't give a shit . . ." Rufus was getting wound up and had not Miss Lance cut him off might have made a very impassioned speech indeed.

"Keep your pants on," said Miss Lance levelly. "I'm not representing Daisy. Not yet anyhow." She glanced at her pad. "Who did you say owned the property?"

"It beats me, man. I been there 'bout five years, payin' the rent regular and never behind more than a month or two at the most. In all that time ain't nobody come around to fix a thing. Ain't had no paint, the plumbin' stinks, some windows is busted . . . It's a mess. The only good thing is, I'm used to it."

"I can imagine. Well, you may not know who the owner is but it's no secret. All it takes is one little phone call."

She swiveled around toward the phone, checked her Rolodex and dialed a number. "How are you doin', you old bastard?" she asked when she heard a voice say "District Land Records, Callahan speaking." "Wait, don't answer that because I couldn't care less. A more important question is how an old Irish fart like you keeps his job. What are you, the token white guy the D.C. government keeps on the payroll to prove it's an equal opportunity employer?" Miss Lance guffawed at her wisecrack. "Faith and begorra and may the saints preserve us and the devil enrich us, would you be knowin' who this is? . . . Right, sweetheart, you got it right the first try: fightin' Geraldine Lance, the defender of the faithless, the champion of the chumps, the friend of the friendless and the pricker of pricks. Speaking of the latter, I need your help . . . No, not that way. Christ, I know you, Callahan, you haven't had it up since Christmas of 1955. . . Okay, okay, I apologize if I've hurt your feelings. Make it Labor Day, 1957. You feel better?" More raucous laughter. "All I can handle. What? I said handle, not candle. I haven't used a candle since before they invented vibrators. Or something . . . All right, enough of this blarney. The blessed D.C. government doesn't pay you to waste time talking dirty to respected members of the D.C. bar. So let's get down to it. Get your spectacles on and give me the rundown on 757 6th Street Northeast."

There was a two-minute pause. "Strictly speaking," said Miss Lance to Rufus, "you're not supposed to be given that info over the phone. But Callahan and I are old buddies. And also I slip him a fifth of Irish on St. Patrick's Day. Which would probably be enough even if we were deadly enemies . . . Hello? Yeah, I'm still here. What took you so long? My client says he's not going to be billed just because you had to go to the crapper . . . Listen, when you've had as many whores as you've had, you got to expect a little trouble passing your water. Which is why they call it the prostitute gland, right? . . . Up yours, too, buddy, which is where it is, I do believe . . . All right, okay, I will if you will." She poised her pencil. "Say that again—and spell it. H-a-r-r-i-s-o-n. Okay. And the first name? No first name. An initial? . . . J? Okay. A middle name? H-o-n-e-y-w-e-l-l. Honeywell. J. Honeywell Harrison? What the hell kind of name is that? J. Honeywell Harrison. Wait a minute, I think it's ringing a bell. Isn't he the minister of that fancy Afro-Episcopal Church up on the Gold Coast where resideth the blacks who have made it, baby, climbed out of the ghetto and gone to bigger and better things up around Rock Creek Park? I declare I am surprised the good reverend would have him a slum property in his portfolio . . . Well, we learn something bad about the good every day of our lives . . . Thanks, Callahan, keep the faith."

Miss Lance put down the phone and turned toward Rufus. "You heard that. Your house is owned by the Right Reverend Doctor J. Honeywell Harrison and I do believe the reverend is in a heap of trouble. Okay, I'll take it from here. Get the money. The sooner the better.

Rufus nodded.

"By the way," Miss Lance said, "I'm giving a small party on Sunday evening. If you've got a fare that takes you up around Columbia Road, feel free to drop in."

5

Washington is so refreshing, really. All terribly democratic about the mixing of the races and the religions and getting on with the melting-pot bit and all that sort of thing. One needn't feel the least bit self-conscious about letting practically anyone come into your life. Back home in England I'm afraid we're still rather on the formal side. Arabs and the black immigrants from the colonies are common as dirt but one simply looks right through them on the street and almost never sees them at parties. It is a bit snobbish, I admit, but we've done very well without them all these years and it is difficult to comprehend why they want to intrude where they're not welcome. In Washington it's different. The blacks have been here longer and many have done quite well. Some, it pains me to say, have not taken full advantage of the marvelous cultural and social opportunities. Rufus Rastus Jackson comes to mind. I was introduced to him as "Vivian Carstairs, of WCLS, surely you've heard her and heard of her," which is ordinarily more than enough to elicit a good deal of flattering commentary. Rufus Rastus Jackson merely looked me over and said, "I couldn't care less about that long-hair shit. How come you don't play no rock and roll?" Well, you see what I mean.

That small encounter occurred six weeks after Howard and I were very nearly stoned to death at the property on 6th Street. That was in October. In November Mr. DeTroit, from the real estate agency, called Howard, saying he was frightfully sorry but it appeared we should count on a fairly substantial delay in taking possession of the new house. Something about protecting the legal rights of the tenants. This was a distinct surprise because Mr. DeTroit had indicated most convincingly that they would be swept away without the slightest difficulty. "I don't understand," said

Howard. "We made a firm offer and you led us to believe it was acceptable to the seller, who, by the way, has never been identified. Who is he?" Mr. DeTroit said he would prefer not to identify him yet because the seller wanted to first take care of the legal questions raised by the tenants. "Legal questions?" said Howard. "You mean the tenants are raising a stink?" Mr. DeTroit said yes, the tenants had gone to a lawyer.

"Well, I guess *I'd* better get one," said Howard with some heat. "And you should, too, because I intend suing you and your company for all you've got. You told us the property was definitely available. We made a firm offer, we put down some earnest money and we want to take possession as soon as possible so we can get started on restoring the place. We need to move in in a matter of months. My wife is pregnant."

This was an exaggeration. I am *not* pregnant, though Howard has been working on it with enormous enthusiasm and he presumes if it has not actually happened this month it surely will next. Mr. DeTroit said congratulations on the blessed event but would we please not sue him because he had already suffered a *degrading humiliation* at the hands of one of the tenants and his nerves were absolutely stretched *beyond human tolerance* and if there was any more trauma in his life he simply *would not be responsible.* (Howard fancies himself as something of a mimic and in repeating Mr. DeTroit's half of the conversation he was pretty good at conveying Mr. DeTroit's feminine side.) Howard said it was not his nature to cause unnecessary hardship to anyone, but he had to protect his own interests. Mr. DeTroit asked for a little time. It just so happens, he said, that his social circle included the attorney representing the tenants and possibly something could be worked out on an informal basis. Howard said he would give him two weeks. Howard's threat to call in his attorney was not entirely serious because he would just as soon avoid trouble. Howard is basically a man of conscience and as much as he aspires to live in a beautifully restored house with a spectacular view of the Capitol he is not happy about booting out the renters. It is explained, I suppose, by his liberal inheritance and the fact he's a Jew—which may be a redundancy. Jews are sensitive that way—aspiring to the good things in life but feeling slightly uncomfortable about attaining them. It is as though any minute their prizes could be jerked away and they themselves could be sent off to a concentration camp. Really, this religious prejudice is a bore. I mean, look at me, I married Howard, didn't I? He is directly descended from Moses, I am certain, though he does not at all look it, being more like Paul Newman than anything. Does Paul Newman wear glasses? That is the only important difference. I tell Howard very often I love him and I am fairly certain I do. It is the primary reason I married him. The secondary reason is that he will someday inherit an enormous amount of money. One must be practical; female radio announcers fade out all too soon. You've noticed, I suppose, that the news is never read by anyone whose voice has taken on the scratch and gravel of old age. But to continue with the house. Or not to. Because at the end of the two-week period Howard allotted him, the news from Mr. DeTroit was not optimistic. Something about how the tenants were being inordinately difficult.

"Jesus Christ," Howard exploded, "I've just about had it with this deal. I want my money back."

"It can still be worked out," Mr. DeTroit said. "If you could see your way to make a small gift to the tenants, the thing might go more smoothly."

"What?" said Howard. "This an outrage. No way. How much?"

"Not a large amount," Mr. DeTroit responded. "I've talked to the tenants' lawyer and she has a figure in mind. Miss Lance is very reasonable. Not like a lot of lawyers one could mention, sucking up every penis—I mean penny—that comes along."

"What's her address?" asked Howard. "What's her phone number? I'll call her office."

"Not necessary," said Mr. DeTroit. "Miss Lance believes a casual approach would be best. She's giving a party on Saturday. I've been asked to invite you and Mrs. Baltus. The principal problem tenant will be there, the one who is being so obstructionist. Miss Lance thinks you and he could work out something informally—save a lot of fees and animosity."

Which explains why Howard and I were at Geraldine Lance's house on Columbia Road last Saturday night. I realized straightaway it was the sort of affair at which I must be extremely cautious. Because cocaine was much in evidence. I do it once in a great while with close friends and I have learned to appreciate the top-rank product. With strangers I must be cautious. One never knows who will squeal to that woman who writes the gossip column for the *Washington Post*. She can be a dear about an unimportant affair you might be having at the moment but when it comes to drugs she can be far too zealous. While I realize I am not exactly at the highest level in Washington name-recognition circles, I do believe I qualify as a celebrity second class, senior grade. As you can imagine, the station can be more than a little sticky about drug-related publicity and I have been warned once or twice to be careful.

There were perhaps forty guests altogether at the party and a typical Washington mix they were: sixty-five percent white, twenty-five percent black, five percent Oriental and five percent all-mixed-up and uttering the most incomprehensible and unidentifiable languages God ever created.

What the men wore ran the gamut:

Tuxedos: "We've just come from . . ., we're just going to . . ."

Three-piece suits: "I run the Zimbabwe desk at State. Terrible pressure, really . . ." ". . . practice medicine. Care to join me in a beautiful little wildcat venture out in Wyoming?" ". . . a broker. You interested in a stock that'll double in the next sixty days?"

Casual two-piece suits: ". . . a used-car salesman. Funny thing, people say I don't look too honest but I am . . ." ". . . a haberdasher. That's an interesting suit you're wearing. Some of those old-fashioned garments still look good on a certain type of individual . . ." ". . . pimp, man. Anytime you're down on 14th and U streets just mention my name . . ."

Sport shirts and trousers: ". . . residency at Georgetown University Hospital. No, herpes can't be cured. Why do you ask . . .?" ". . . dilettante sailor. Could I interest you in a cruise to Bermuda next summer . . .?" ". . . D.C. cop. Bank holdups my specialty . . ."

T-shirts and blue jeans: ". . . that office building going up at 15th and L, I'm the crane operator . . ." ". . . been laid off six months. You know anybody . . .?" "No speaka da English . . ."

Running shorts and track shoes: ". . . D.C. marathon. Finished one-hundred-fourteenth last year. How about you?"

The women wore the female equivalent:

Elegant gowns: ". . . as I was telling the President not an hour ago . . ."

Cocktail dresses: ". . . I represent the tenth California district. Yes, there's a rather large gay population. I happen to be one of them . . ." ". . . a model for a selective clientele. Certainly you may have my card. . . ." ". . . concentrating on my fifth divorce . . ."

Pants suits: ". . . my own beauty salon. Beautiful hair like yours needs . . ." ". . . a really dumb job—Pentagon secretary . . ." ". . . free-lance writer specializing in sex in the hereafter . . ."

Blouses and slacks: ". . . paint. My show opens next week. Care to come?" ". . . an old lover of Geraldine's before God entered my life and straightened me out . . ." ". . . high-school dietitian during the day and topless disco dancer at night . . ."

T-shirts and blue jeans: ". . . advertising. The left one is still available if you want to push anything . . ." ". . . good grass. Not any of that local shit grown in the bathroom . . ." "No speaka da English . . ."

Running shorts and sneakers: ". . . a body like a man's, right? Turns you on, doesn't it, sweetie?"

There was the usual buffet food: roast beef, ham, chicken, salami and cheese. I gave it a B minus. The best party fare comes from Ridgewell Caterers and when money is no object they will bring out all of the above plus people who will shuck oysters and do beef tartare and cook interesting small crepes. Their crew includes butlers for taking around champagne on silver trays and such ornamentation can make a marvelous impression. Geraldine's spread was nothing so glamorous. I imagine most of it came from the neighborhood deli, which is perfectly all right when you're playing around with a limited budget. She doesn't have a great deal of money, I could see that right off. The house is on the small side and the furniture has the beat-up look it gets after twenty years and then there is a resident dog. I must tell you about the dog! He's an enormous mixture of Great Dane and police. He barked at each new guest for a few seconds, then he was friendlier than the dickens. Well, more than just friendly. He nuzzles you all over and if you're not careful he'll jump up on you and immediately his thing emerges and he begins making these terribly gross pelvic movements. Honestly! Why Geraldine didn't banish him to the backyard I can't imagine. Possibly it was because certain of the guests seemed to take a perverse pleasure in stimulating the creature. But I must say it does distract one from the usual small talk of a party when there is a dog going around all over the place with an erection.

Only that dog wasn't the only distraction. My dear, the pictures everywhere! Human beings and animals consorting sexually in the most uninhibited way. It was terribly embarrassing. One could hardly bear to look, though there was a certain fascination at regarding sexual postures you might not have even thought physically possible. Howard was smitten, dragging me from room to room upstairs and down, and saying things like, "Wow, let's try that as soon as we get home!" Once the tour was completed and once we had taken on all the food and drink we cared to, we sought out the hostess. Geraldine had greeted us cordially enough when we showed up an hour and a half before, kissing me and saying something kind about my work and kissing Howard and saying "God, you're the best looking thing. I wish you were my client instead of that revolting Mr. Jackson." Which I'm sure she didn't really mean but it took the combativeness right out of Howard and showed she was pretty clever considering she is basically only an Irish-fishmonger type without the slightest refinement. A big, noisy, brash, back-slapping, whiskey-swilling wench is what she is and you'd do well to have her on your side. Still, it's difficult not to like her. Me especially, because I do have this certain built-in English restraint and a woman like Geraldine is a positive influence on my personality. When Howard tracked her down after our repast and tour of the premises she was holding forth at the front door, kissing some of the guests goodbye and squeezing and touching them a good deal more than was strictly necessary but nobody seemed to object.

"Well," said Howard, "thanks for the party. Sorry the other side didn't show up. I guess it will have to be in your office after all."

"That son-of-a-bitch," said Geraldine, very annoyed. "He promised me. And not just because of the chance to talk about the 6th Street property. He's been to parties here before and once he discovered I put out a pretty good spread he'd die before he'd miss one. Of course, he does have to drive the cab and maybe he had a trip out to Dulles Airport. This is a hell of a lot more important. But he ought to be here soon. Can't you stick a little longer?"

"I think we'd better go," said Howard. "The ambience of your house has got us all stimulated and we want to go home and try out some of the innovations so enticingly displayed on your walls."

"What? Is that all?" said Geraldine in a voice heavy on bray. "Hell, I can take care of that. Let me borrow your pencil and some paper." I don't know why she knew Howard is the sort of man who always has paper and pencil even at parties. It is the bureaucrat in him. He opened his jacket and from the breast pocket extracted a gold pencil and a notebook. "Good," she said. "Now I'll just make this strong enough so there won't be any doubt." And she scribbled "Get out of the room you miserable fuckers. Give somebody else a chance!" "There you are," she said. "Just present that at the front bedroom upstairs and you won't have a bit of trouble. You're guaranteed half an hour. Is that enough?" "Really," said Howard, "I think we can wait 'til we're home." "Ah, waiting, that's bad," said Geraldine. "Listen, what would you say to a little cocaine? Some say it's as good as sex, but I haven't made up my own mind about that."

Howard is a trifle stuffy about drugs. Alcohol, yes. With drugs he's frightened he'll become an addict. And he is diffident about group sin, which cocaine sniffing is definitely made for. He has confessed he has not participated in a single orgy in his entire life. Nor have I, for that matter, but I think one's husband should take the lead in such matters and I have so far deferred to him.

"No," said Howard. "I think not."

"Well, then," said Geraldine, "if you must."

She opened the front door to let us out and there, poised to either knock or knock the door down, was Rufus Rastus Jackson with his fist raised, the 6th Street ruffian and the cause of all our trouble.

"How ya doin', baby?" said Jackson to Geraldine. "I had to go to Dulles. I could have grabbed a bite out there but I figured, what the hell, I might as well freeload on my mouthpiece. Whatcha got to eat? Whatcha got to drink? Whatcha got to smoke?"

"Calm down, Rufus," Geraldine said. "This is Howard and

Vivian Baltus. I told you they would be here."

Jackson looked us over. "Oh, yeah, you the block-bustin' white honkeys. The guys gonna give me some money. You know what I'm gonna do with it? Trade in my beat-up old cab for a green Mercedes just like yours." He laughed, barged on through Howard and me to the point of physical contact and headed for the still bountiful buffet. Howard looked pained. I was frightened.

"He'll be all right after he's swallowed some roast beef and knocked back a few drinks," Geraldine said. "Why don't you freshen up at the bar and mingle some more. Twenty minutes should do it."

So Howard and I refilled our glasses, chatted a little, wandered here and there and eventually ended up at the door of the upstairs front bedroom. Howard knocked.

"Quit bugging us," a female voice said from within. "We signed up for twenty minutes and we still have ten to go."

"Oh, excuse us," said Howard. "No problem. We're just killing time."

"How many are you?"

"My wife's with me."

"Well, come on in. There's enough for two."

Howard turned the knob and we entered. Inside the room were the beauty salon woman, the California congresswoman, the medical intern and the cop. What they were doing was coke. It's a charming ritual, isn't it, on the order of the Japanese tea ceremony: the mirror-top table, the little cellophane bags, the careful tapping out, the ordering of the lines with the Ace of Spades, the rolled-up hundred-dollar bill, the snort, the rush . . . Geraldine had likened it to sex. It is far superior. The pleasure of sex is finite. With good coke there is sensation as good as orgasm and thrown in for good measure are rainbows and sunsets and sparkling wit and infinite wisdom and all the marvelous things that fill our daydreams but so rarely come to us in reality. And it goes on just as long as the snow is on the table and money is in your wallet.

"Want to buy in?" the beauty salon woman asked. She was dressed in an overly yellow pants suit, she was heavy with costume jewelry and her hair was coiffed in a manner which suggested it had been done by somebody partial to meringue and spun sugar. She did not appear entirely together but if her demeanor was more affected by coke than Canadian Club I couldn't say. "Cost you two hundred and fifty."

"No, thanks," said Howard. "We'll pass on it."

"What are you," asked Hair Majesty, "chicken or cheap?"

Howard chuckled. "A little of each, I suppose."

"This is good stuff. Worth every penny."

"Oh, I'm sure it is," said Howard. "Still . . . Uh, what would you say if we bought fifty to go. We'd rather do it at home."

"Fifty? *Fifty?*" the woman shrieked derisively. "Are you kidding? You some kind of cheap Jew Boy? What do you do, sell insurance? Had a tough week, did you? Why don't you try down on 14th Street?"

One rarely comes up against anti-Semitism at Washington parties. Elsewhere, yes. In the office, shops, the subway—one hears things. It is not always vicious; often it takes the form of jokes. Like the one about the young rabbi and the old virgin . . . Stop, they've got me doing it. At parties one ignores it or laughs it off or walks away. There is no profit in rejoining in kind. But Howard has told me often he doesn't take shit from anybody and the moment he had been insulted and without the slightest hesitation he pitched the contents of his highball onto the face of Hair-On-High. If the doc, the cop and the congresswoman hadn't grabbed her, Howard would have suffered a serious facial clawing but all she managed was a kick in the shin and a screaming tirade. The noise attracted most of the other guests and Geraldine and the dog and for a few minutes it was as exciting as a brawl in a bar. Then Geraldine climbed onto a chair and told everybody to cool it.

"All right," she said, "that's enough. I don't know whose fault it is and I don't care. I run disreputable parties and these things happen once in a while. I blame no one and you're all invited to the next. But for now I want you to put down your drinks, put on your coats and beat it. I can't stand the sight of you."

The guests groaned or laughed but there was a general flow toward the lower level. "Not you," Geraldine said to Howard and me. "Wait. The last time I saw Rufus he was putting the make on the disco dancer. We'll pry him loose and get on with our business."

We descended. Except for a couple entwined at the bar, the house seemed empty. "Anybody in the john?" Geraldine called. "In the kitchen? Let's move it troops. The party's over." There was silence except that the male half of the bar couple looked in our direction and said "Hunh?" It was Jackson. "What the hell you talkin' about? We ain't goin' nowhere." I could understand his reluctance. He was all wrapped up with the dietitian/disco woman and, to use Geraldine's quaint American expression, he was "putting the make on her" indeed. After his statement he reapplied his lips to hers and they continued kissing as freely and openly as teenagers. I must say they seemed to be enjoying themselves. Her body fitted against his as snugly as ivy on stones. His left arm was around her shoulders, his right hand had a grip on her right buttock and his groin was grinding away. She had short blond hair, an inadequate little nose, eyes of no distinction, thin lips around a small mouth and a muddy complexion. She looked like the sort of girl who had spent her childhood in an Alabama shack and her adolescence in a textile factory. It was easy to presume she had come to Washington on the strength of a job offer as a counter clerk at McDonald's. She did not appear to be the sort of creature who would enjoy being manhandled by a black gorilla but tastes are strange these days and one must not rush to judgment. Their kissing was almost continuous, though occasionally he would break away from her mouth and nibble her ears and her neck and while this was going on I am pretty certain he said, ". . . baby, let's you and me go upstairs and do it, whattaya say, huh, you want some big black cock up your pussy, baby, do you, want it bad, huh, hey, let's go up there, I know you want it, yeah, yeah, you can grab it, big ain't it, yeah, unhuh, oh, baby, but wait til it's in there, you gonna beg me to do it forever, be your big sugar daddy, oh, yeah, you goddamned hunk of white pussy you come up against a real man tonight . . ." Heavens! It was disgusting, really, but I am striving for accuracy.

"All right, Rufus," said Geraldine, "that's enough. Kiss your chick good night, let go of her ass and show her the door."

Jackson broke away from his work. "No way, Geraldine. This chick is gonna be my first piece of white pussy and I ain't givin' it up. Fuck off."

"Rufus, it's not that much different, I have it on good authority," said Geraldine. "But that is not the point. The party's over. It's time for business. Your friend goes, you stay, got it?"

Jackson regarded Miss White Trash. "Baby, this ain't the end. I got a lot of money coming from those fancy white dudes." He looked toward Howard and me. "And when I do, you and me gonna get together and get something going, okay? Now don't forget."

So we went into the study. One wall has a painting of a satyr being sucked by a nymph, another has a life-size drawing of a black male and a white female doing what is commonly referred to as sixty-nine and the third had a three-by-four-foot photo of Geraldine's dog doing it to a sheep. Is that possible? The remaining wall was covered with books and to give myself at least some chance to concentrate I sat in the small sofa facing them. Howard joined me. Jackson picked up a cane-bottom straight chair, twirled it a hundred and eighty degrees, sat on it backwards, rested his arms on the top rung, tilted forward to the point of balance and looked defiantly at Howard and me. Geraldine sat at her flat-top desk, an impressive mahogany structure featuring legs shaped like phalluses and an intricate frieze of intertwined genitalia in endless pursuit of each other around the perimeter. Where does she get these things?

"All right," said Geraldine, "the meeting will come to order. Perhaps it would be a good idea to begin with formal introductions. Mr. Rufus Rastus Jackson on the one side and Mr. and Mrs. Howard Baltus on the other. Mr. Jackson drives a taxi, Mr. Baltus does something important in the government and Mrs. Baltus is with radio station WCLS. She calls herself Vivian Eggleston Carstairs when she's broadcasting, Mr. Jackson, and I'm sure you've heard her or heard of her."

"I've heard her," said Jackson. "Ask her why she don't play some rock instead of that long-haired shit?"

"Neither that question nor its answer are in any way pertinent to this proceeding, Mr. Jackson," said Geraldine, her annoyance evident. "Please refrain in the future."

She gave him a very stern look and then turned toward Howard and me with an expression not much more benevolent.

"I want to make it plain to both sides," she said, "I'm in charge and don't anybody forget it. Speak only when called upon. No swearing or profanity. No racial or religious insults. No finger pointing. No threats. If we don't waste time this thing can be settled in five minutes."

I presumed this speech was for the benefit of Jackson. Howard and I are the sort of people who need no such coaching. Well, possibly Howard because he does have his excitable side.

Geraldine put on her spectacles, opened a manila folder on the desk top and became all lawyerly. "Mr. Jackson has the option to buy the place himself for the asking price of eighty-nine thousand five hundred dollars. Same thing applies to the other tenants. That's not likely to happen. But the law presumes there's a real possibility and Mr. Jackson has to be given time. I only represent Mr. Jackson, not the others. Mr. Jackson has informed me he speaks for the others and represents them. Since there are about thirty housing-code violations on the place, Mr. Jackson can insist that they be corrected before he makes a bid. This could run into months. The Baltuses want the place as soon as possible and they're willing, as I understand it, to ease the pain of Mr. Jackson's departure—which Mr. Jackson must realize will happen eventually no matter how smart his lawyer is."

"I'm ready," said Jackson. "But everybody better realize I don't come cheap."

"Mr. Jackson," said Geraldine, "you have not been recognized. If you wish to speak, raise your hand."

Jackson raised his hand.

"Please lower your hand, Mr. Jackson," Geraldine said. "We've just heard you. There's no point in being repetitious."

Jackson grunted.

Geraldine looked at Jackson very coolly and much the same way at Howard. "I think the bidding can start at either side. Mr. Baltus? Mr. Jackson?"

Howard looked at Jackson; Jackson looked at Howard.

"A hundred dollars," said Howard.

"Seventy-nine thousand dollars," said Jackson.

"A hundred and fifty dollars."

"Seventy-one thousand, five-hundred and no dollars."

"Two hundred dollars."

"Sixty-nine thousand, three-hundred-and-eighteen dollars and twenty-five cents."

"All right," said Geraldine, "This isn't getting us anywhere. If both sides are going to be unreasonable we might as well stop right now."

"I ain't bein' unreasonable," said Jackson. "If the motherfuckers don't wanta meet my price, it's okay with me. Screw 'em."

Geraldine leapt up from her desk, snatched up the cushion on which she had been sitting, strode to Jackson and whacked him briskly about the head and shoulders.

"One more remark like that and you'll be on the street. And if you think I can't do it on my own, let me tell you, Hardin can."

We have seen that Hardin would ordinarily rather make love than trouble but I am certain that if Geraldine said "sic 'em" he would so so straightaway. Geraldine, of course, is a mighty force unto herself. I would give her a domination rating of about ninety-six. The Head Of State Of A Powerful Nation might ignore her but I can think of no one else.

"I'm sorry," said Jackson. Jackson sorry? He did not strike me as a man who says that often. "Gimme a break."

"All right," said Geraldine, settling down at her desk again. "God, I love swinging a pillow. Takes me back to the old days at St. Agatha's School for overprivileged young ladies of the Catholic persuasion. Now, where were we? Oh, yes, the bidding. Mr. Baltus, your bidding so far has been insulting and facetious. Is this typical?"

"Miss Lance," said Howard, "this is a most unusual and irregular way to conduct business. It is certainly outside my routine. And I think it would be pointless to continue. I don't quite understand how I got talked into it in the first place." He gathered himself to rise. "Thanks again for the party. We'd better be going."

"Five thousand," I said. "Take it or leave it. It is our final offer."

Howard turned to me, taken aback. "What did you say?"

"Five thousand dollars. Gracious, Howard, it's nothing to

become agitated over. You can write it off your income taxes. And I'm certain Mr. Jackson would be grateful for our unexpected generosity. Isn't that so, Mr. Jackson?"

Jackson looked at me as though he had not been previously aware of my presence.

"And just who the hell are you?" he inquired. "Who asked you? This is talk between men. Now shut the fuck up."

"Yes," said Geraldine, "Mr. Jackson has a point. Each side can have but a single spokesperson. Of course, if Mrs. Baltus is to speak for the Baltus interests I have no objection."

"Objection," said Jackson.

"On what grounds?" asked Geraldine.

"General unfairness," said Jackson. "Two women against one man. It's got to be man against man or I get to bring in a chick, too."

"Mr. Jackson, I'm your attorney. Have you forgotten that? I'm here to protect your interests."

"Don't look that way. How come they sittin' on the sofa and all I got is this miserable chair?"

Geraldine sighed. "I have been patient so far, Mr. Jackson, but you are pushing me. You know perfectly well you may sit wherever you like."

"Well, how about something to drink? I came late. Everybody else got way more'n me."

"That's a laugh. You and your little floozy had almost drained the bar when I rescued you. I don't suppose she told you she has herpes."

"Herpes? What the hell is that?"

"Goddamn it, can't you read? Does no one ever leave a copy of the *Washington Post* in your taxi? You don't know about herpes?"

"Is it like the clap?"

"Worse. You can cure the clap."

"I only had the clap once. I use a rubber mostly." He scrutinized Geraldine; he scrutinized me. "You can't tell just by lookin'. Not at faces, anyhow."

"I've had about enough of this," said Howard, jumping to his feet all indignant and red-faced. "Vivian, let's go."

"Now hold your horses," Geraldine rejoined. "Give the man a chance to speak his mind. It's all part of the negotiating process. Mr. Jackson is not accustomed to attending parties where people are as dressed up and as high-toned as you and the missus. It makes him nervous. It's why he talks so dirty. And also so crazy. Seventy thousand dollars? You're out of your mind."

Jackson shrugged. "Hell, I can always come down. But first I have to be sure the other side is negotiatin' in good faith."

"Negotiating in good faith?" said Geraldine. "Now what the hell kind of lawyer's talk is that?"

"Yours. The last time I was in your office I heard you say it on the phone. Sounds good, don't it?"

"Not bad. And does it apply to you? Is your faith good?"

"Hell, yes. I came down from seventy-nine thousand dollars, didn't I? How about the other side?"

"Yes," said Geraldine, turning to me. "Is your faith good?"

"Better than Mr. Jackson's," I said. "We're offering five thousand real dollars. All he's done is take ten thousand dollars off a figure which is totally unrealistic. He's given nothing; we're offering a lot."

"Five thousand ain't a lot," said Jackson. "I could win that much in the D.C. Lottery and it wouldn't even be first prize. It don't amount to shit."

"There will be a brief recess," announced Geraldine. "Rufus, come to the bench."

So Jackson and Geraldine huddled and Howard sat down and he and I huddled. "Howard," I said, "how far are you prepared to go? How about ten?"

"No, that wouldn't make any difference. The guy's completely unreasonable. And not entirely sober. I think we should turn our backs."

"Are you certain? I can see how we're going to be terribly bogged down if this thing isn't resolved right away."

"Let's not look too eager. The best strategy at this point is to walk away from it."

Howard rose and cleared his throat in anticipation of an announcement but before he could get the words out Geraldine also rose and said, "Mr. Jackson has requested a delay to permit him to consult with his colleagues. The court grants his request that the hearing be continued to next Sunday night at the same time. Court stands adjourned. Anybody care for a drink?"

This smacked of something beyond the obvious, but at the time I was in no mood to ponder it. I was grateful that Howard and I could finally get the hell out of there, go home, fling off our clothes and still inspired by the artwork on Geraldine's walls get something going with the chandelier, the ironing board and a pair of skis.

6

You ever wanted to be a hero so damn bad you forgot your good sense? I'm tellin' you, man, I was learnin' about myself and it wasn't all good. I was ready to quit screwin' around with the Baltuses—then and there. If it wasn't for Geraldine askin' me to think it over for a week, I'd have told 'em to forget the whole thing, I ain't takin' no money. Not just because they wasn't gonna give me a good hunk of it, which they wasn't. I could see the way the man was nickel and dimin' he wasn't really serious. The chick, okay, she done a little better but it was about what you expect from a chick: chicken feed. I figure I could maybe hold out for fifteen thousand. But if I get it, what the hell gonna happen then? I would have to give twenty-five hundred each to Sanford and the Dudleys. Considerin' how I have taken on the responsibility for helpin' 'em out, it's only fair I should get a little extra. That leaves me ten. Not even ten when I gotta pay the mouthpiece. So what's comin' on next? Set me up a business? Nah, I don't wanna be in no business even if I could start one for eight or nine thousand which I guess ain't all that easy. Keepin' books, payin' taxes, answerin' the telephone, kissin' asses, regular hours—it ain't for me. With the cab I works when I want to. What cab driver don't? Only that wasn't the main reason I backed away at Geraldine's. Something funny hit me outside of the booze. I realized sittin' there that if I went along with the white folks—no matter how much money—I'd be a traitor to my class, I'd be turnin' my back on my own people, I'd be sellin' out on all the folks on 6th Street. Well, shit, man, you say why you talkin' that way? That ain't black ghetto talk, man, that be honkey talk. You got to look out for your own self, dumbass. You right. But I gotta let you in on a little secret. Remember when I was up on top of the fire truck at the meetin' and runnin' the show like I was Martin Luther King? And everybody lookin' up and payin' attention and finally, at the end, layin' money on me? Oh, yeah, I felt good, felt important. The people didn't see me as a dumbhead cabdriver. They see me as the leader of the *poor oppressed black folks on 6th Street!* I liked the feelin', liked it a lot. And I figure if I was gonna be a leader I had to start actin' and lookin' like one.

When I show up at Geraldine's the followin' Sunday night I is already beginnin' to see myself different. I look different, too. My tan corduroy suit is fresh out of the cleaners. Settin' it off is my yellow sport shirt with the long collar points and blue flowers runnin' all over and my brown belt with a shiny brass buckle say "The Best Part Of A Man" and an arrow pointin' down. Also a pair of new brown shoes. The kicks cost me close to a hundred bucks. Could have gotten a pair about as good for twenty bucks if I put out the word and be willin' to wait a coupla weeks. I didn't have that kind of time and also when you're buyin' hot shoes you don't have that much of a selection. So I go down to Hahn's and had the clerk bring me out six or seven different styles. He try me first on patent leather and then suede but I say, no way, man, they too flashy. Then he bring out a pair as plain as bedroom slippers only slim and trim and with a deep solid tone not really shinin' but not shabby neither. I don't like 'em but they about twins of the pair Howard Baltus was wearin' last week and I figure if I get the same kind, he and I be on the same footin'. After I buy the shoes I buy a haircut and two bottles of hair straightener. My hair is kinkier'n steel wool and about as tough. One bottle wouldn't do the job. Lady in the barbershop say did I want a manicure? "Mani what?" I say. "I ain't sick, don't need no cure." It ain't that funny but she laugh just to be polite. But they do be grimy and the nails is long so I ask her how much and she say seven dollars and I say how long does it last? She say a week. Well, hell, seven dollars a week is a lotta money but I ain't plannin' on it regular and I tell her to go ahead this one time. She do a good job, I gotta admit, and I tip her a buck after she points out that is the custom. "What you need now," she say, "is a sparkler. I know somebody." Nah, I say, I got my own man, figurin' the cat who got me the IBM could come up with a diamond with no trouble. Why should I give my business to some chick in a barbershop I don't even know when I can deal with the same outfit I been dealin' with for years? Maybe I could do a little better with the barbershop babe but I would rather mess with somebody reliable even if he don't say, "You got beautiful strong hands. I bet some woman just love to have your fingers do the walkin' up and down her spine." After the barbershop I call him and he say, "Yeah, man, I got somethin' in the shape of a horseshoe. You wear this mother you be lucky the rest of your life." "Do I get to try it out?" I ask. "See do my friends like it." He say, "Yeah, you give me a hundred on a money-back guarantee if they don't say you the most."

So that's the way I am at Geraldine's for the second party and business meetin' combined. Sharp, man, sharpest man in the joint. Even that stuckup Mrs. Baltus gimme a glance and mosey over where I am hangin' out, say good evenin'.

"How ya doin', baby" I say, reachin' out and givin' her a pat on the ass. "Ain't you put on a little weight since last week? Whatcha drinkin'?"

Them chicks with the foreign accents think if they tighten their lips, frost their eyes, raise their eyebrows and look down their noses you gonna whimper like a whipped dog and go hide in the corner ten minutes after which you say, scuse me, your highness, I didn't realize what I was sayin', will you do me a favor and have my head chopped off?

I just laugh at her, look her up and down, see where her nipples is located, see can I see down the front of the thin white stuff not workin' too hard at keepin' her from catchin' cold. Oh, it is a beautiful sight down there, no matter how many tits a man has seen in his lifetime. I remember such things and I know for a fact I has looked at 28-and-½ bare tits, the half bein' this one old broad about forty had her a cancer. It ain't bad once you get used to it. Particularly if you the kind of man who likes to have a finger on the love pimple and at the same time get both hands on the knockers. It ain't possible if there be two and you get accused of favorin' one over the other. If you only have the one tit, you can concentrate on it.

"You lookin' kinda peaked," I say to Mrs. Baltus. "You gettin' enough?"

The next thing I know she draws back her pretty little white hand and lays it right against my cheek. A real slap, what the gun molls in the old-time movies would hang on some gangster when their feelin's was hurt so bad they forgot all their manners.

I laugh again. "Baby," I say, "you answered the question. It looks like Mr. Baltus don't have the balls." And I wander off, givin' her an airy wave with my diamond hand and lookin' around to see is they anybody else I can shake up. Lo and behold, Nobaltus hisself is talkin' close up with Geraldine over by the pink marble statue of some stud pickin' cherries off a tree while this naked chick has got her legs wrapped around him. Geraldine is wearin' this bright green gown goin' from her neck to her toes but if it covers that much territory because it's supposed to be hidin' somethin' it ain't doin' a very good job. You can see she is mother naked underneath—we all are but with her there wasn't any doubts—and her knockers is stickin' out plump as cabbages. The crack in her ass—goddamn, it is an open invitation to give her a goose. Only I don't because she has a serious discussion goin' with Mr. Noballs. Noballs is wearin' a light tan suede jacket, a beige shirt with pink pinstripes, a chocolate tie with a mess of stunted watermelons and brown gabardine slacks breakin' just perfect over the same shoes he wore last week, twins of mine.

"How they hangin'?" I ask Smallballs. "The little lady don't wanna complain but she sent me over as an old friend of the family. You tried ginseng? Ginseng is good. You tried dirty books? Nothin' wrong with dirty books. Triple-X movies? You tried 'Deepthroat'? Deepthroat maybe turn her on, turn you on, too. But hell, man, you standin' right next to Geraldine Gorgeous, this year's Miss Tits and Ass of Columbia Road, and if she don't get you stirred up nothin' will. How you doin', baby?"

Geraldine, she got a great sense of humor, don't let nothin' bother her, give me a whack across the shoulders, a smack on the lips and a laugh strong as a sonic boom.

"Rufus," she say, "you're terrible. Now be a good boy and buzz off. Mr. Baltus and I are discussing the property situation. I'll call a meeting the moment the last guest leaves, collapses or rents a room for the night. In the meantime, go charm the other guests the way you've charmed poor Mr. Baltus and try to keep your drinking down."

"Okay, baby," I say to Geraldine. "And okay to you too, buddy," I say to Beebee Balls. "You better have your checkbook warmed up. I'm gettin' more expensive by the minute."

By then No-Balls-At-All is frowning so bad it gonna permanently damage his face and he lookin' at me like I'm a piece of shit but he don't say nothin', only turn away with a sneer on his mouth and a snort on his breath.

So I wander off into the crowd, see if I can put a little life into the party. About forty people millin' around, about as many as last time, and they the same crazy mixture of colors, ages, voices and outfits. Some is wearin' blue jeans and T-shirts. About what I had on last week myself. Last week it seemed okay. This week it looks bad, kinda mean to Geraldine. I mean, she puttin' out all the grub and booze the least people can do is dress up proper, show her a little respect. I mean, if I can take the trouble, why can't everybody else?

Lucius Deepthroat sure as hell had. I spot him over at the foot of the staircase and it looks like he is headin' for a climb to a bedroom with this rough-lookin' character in a studded black leather jacket and cowboy boots. Lucius is wearin' everythin' purple: dark purple shirt, light purple bow tie, medium purple pants, pale purple socks and regular purple shoes.

"Hey, Lucius," I yell at him from across the room, "wait a minute." And I work my way through the crowd, rubbin' up against an occasional ass and elbowin' a tit or two and sayin' "'Scuse me, sorry, 'scuse me, sorry" as I go so it don't look too deliberate. "Lucius," I say when I finally reach him, "how the fuck are you?"

Lucius cringe, like he don't know me but I don't let him get away with it. I grab his hand, give it a shake like to crush the bones and a thump along his shoulders about collapsed him. "You lookin' good, man," I tell him, "the best lookin' queer in the place. Who's your friend?" Lucius gulp, turn red, turn away and pull away but I hold him tight as a handcuff. "Hey, I know you're in a rush to get it on with leather cock here, but you and I ain't had a chance to talk in weeks. When you gonna get my crapper fixed? The turds is still floatin'."

I know I am even worse than Geraldine say, but I'm gettin' away with it because I'm a guest at a party. If I talk like that out on the street I better be ready to defend my mouth with my knuckles. Here they so dammed stiff and proper they ain't about to throw no punches. "Mr. Jackson," say Lucius, "honestly, you are mortifying me to death." I can see that; the tears is startin' to form. "If you want to discuss your plumbing problems, I'll be glad to come around at any time. Would tomorrow be satisfactory?"

"And let you fuck around again?" I say, lettin' my voice rise up a notch. "No way. Send a plumber. That's what I need. Not a cocksucker."

Lucius, he about bawls. I don't think my voice is carryin' all that much but you know how it is at parties, people begin prickin' up their ears and movin' closer (or farther away, dependin') when they hear dirty talk and four or five come right up to get a good view if there is gonna be a fight. This black-leather dude step toward me like he gonna save Lucius from further humiliation but, shit, he only six feet tall and about one ninety and when he realize he up against three more inches and thirty more pounds about all he leads with is a dirty look. I laugh. Hell, it seems I ain't done nothin' *but* laugh since I arrived but I feelin' so doggone good I can't help it.

So I drift off, spreadin' my charm all over the place, slappin' backs, praisin' the ladies, tellin' jokes and generally makin' a marvelous impression. Okay, three or four guys look at me like they don't believe it, but several sweet-lookin' foxes didn't have no trouble with starin' me straight in the eye and fussin' with their hair. And you should have seen Hardin, the horny hound dog! He real happy to see me, jumpin' up on me like we goin' steady and movin' his ass back and forth like my pants is in heat. If I hadn't brushed the son-of-a-bitch off, he'd have unloaded somethin' disgustin' on my leg. Well, movin' around as I was, not stoppin' too long at any one place, I begin to get a grasp of how a fancy party works. The number one thing is don't get there right on the button of the startin' time. The best-lookin' people come exactly forty-seven minutes after. Two, don't sit down. Somebody sit next to you and talk your ear off and you trapped. And three, don't under no conditions put any food on those little plates. You put food on a plate it'll slow down your consumption somethin' awful. Grab at it right from the servin' tables is what I do. First the shrimp, heavy on the sauce. Then the roast beef, don't fuck around with no bread, fills you up. Turkey, three or four slices with pepper is nice. Salami, make sure it ain't baloney. Cheese, watch the cheese, bad on your digestion. Egg rolls, chicken livers wrapped with bacon, meat-filled lumps of dough avoid like poison. Fattenin' every one. Cucumbers, cauliflower, radishes, cole slaw, potato chips, forget it. Why waste your space with that cheap stuff? For dessert, go for the strawberries dipped in cream or sugar. It ain't bad. The funny thing about strawberries is six or seven somehow settles your stomach, makes more space in your belly and you can go back for a coupla more hunks of roast beef if you ain't quite filled. Drinkin? Well, as for drinkin' you got to learn you a taste for white wine. It ain't real good but some of your chintzier hostesses try to save a few bucks and that's what Geraldine was doin'. You don't wanta complain about the booze if the food is okay. The food is the main thing. You can always get smashed somewheres else.

About ten o'clock the crowd begins headin' for home. Early to break up a party I'm thinkin, 'cept most of them look like they have to get up every Monday mornin' and go to work. Us cabdrivers can stay out all night and sleep all day. Course, if we *do* sleep all day then we gotta work all night. Once National Airport closes down at eleven, there ain't a lot of steady business out there. Yeah, you can cruise Georgetown waitin' for the drunks to come out of the discos and sometimes I do that. You gotta be careful about drunks, particularly somebody give you an address in Anacostia or where I live, on Capitol Hill. Half them mothers has Saturday Night Specials. If you let 'em in your cab you takin' your life in your hands. If you refuse 'em, they turn your number into the Hack Office for racial discrimination. It ain't racial, believe me. None of them guys outblack me a bit. What they really complainin' about is how I'm deprivin' 'em of their livelihood. Which is mainly pushin' their piece into your neck and takin' every fuckin' cent you got.

Okay, the party is grindin' down and Geraldine is kissin' and gettin' thanked and kissed at the front door and after a while the only people left in the livin' room is me and the Baltuses and Hardin who is lyin' in the middle of the rug lickin' his cock. If a man could suck his own cock, you figure that would be the end of the queers? If I had the right connections I could get some money from the Feds and make a study. Speakin' of a study, I know that's where court will be in session and I head for it when the last of the guests is linin' up in front of Geraldine. Over in the corner is this wooden chest with orgy carvin's on the top and sides. The funny thing, after you see as much screwin' and suckin' and assholin' as there is at Geraldine's you almost lose interest. The front of the chest is mainly two tits, one on each door. If you press a nipple, then take your hand away, the door springs open. Behind the left one is brandy; behind the right is . . . guess what? Milk. See, it's a refrigerator on the right side and besides milk there's soda and ice cubes and ice cream. None of that crap for me. I bring out the brandy and pour out a pretty good slug. Funny thing, the bottle say Napoleon. Which is news to me because I thought he was a general, not somebody in the liquor business. Then I take a seat on the sofa and drop my feet down on the coffee table. Now don't get excited. Maybe I done one or two things tonight ain't exactly kosher but dammit I know enough to take my shoes off first. Which I did, though keepin' 'em close by in case Baltus should do the same and maybe they would get mixed up, seein' as how they be the same style though mine are 12E and his can't be more than 9B at the most. He probably got him a little pecker, too.

When the Baltuses and Geraldine come in, Baltus sits in that miserable straight-back thing I was put in a week ago and the chick pulls up a round leather tuffet like a doughnut without the hole alongside Baltus and squats on it. For a second I get a flash up her legs and had the light been a little better I might have actually seen right down to her precious pussy. Presumin', of course, it wasn't wrapped up. Which ain't likely. Ladies like her don't believe in bein' free and easy like Geraldine who, praise the Lord, sashayed in from the last of her guests with everythin' shakin' and jigglin' and makin' me think, goddamn, I'm gonna get me some of that before this thing is all over. Do a good job like I know I'm capable of and maybe she give back some of her fee.

"God, I'm tired," she say the moment she slump to her desk chair. "And broke, too. You freeloaders can really pack it away. But why complain, it's all tax deductible. Oyez, oyez, court is now in session. Remember, everybody is still under oath. Mr. Baltus, I believe you have the floor. Pray proceed and please be pointed."

Baltus reach into his pretty suede jacket, come out with his glasses and a notebook, put on the first, open the second, blink his eyes, clear his throat and say, "We are willing to upgrade substantially our previous offer. I think Mr. Jackson will be extremely impressed with our generosity."

"Out with it, man," say Geraldine. "Don't keep us in suspense."

"Twenty thousand," say Baltus. "It's incredibly, unreasonably, absolutely way too much but we are offering it nevertheless. We are expected at another party and there is no point wasting time. Can we shake hands on this so we can be on our way?"

"Where's the party?" I say. "Can Geraldine and I go? Ain't neither of us had nearly enough to drink and the night is still young. Geraldine, whattaya say?"

Geraldine spring out of her chair like she some kind of Jackie in the pulpit, reach back for her cushion, draw back her arm and fling it right at my head. My reflexes are still as good as they were when I was the star forward for Eastern High School a number of years back and I duck without no problem. The brandy glass didn't have my style and got hit and got broke. Brandy is all over the place.

"All right," I say to Geraldine, "that's gonna cost you. Mr. Baltus, could I trouble you for a page out of your notebook and your gold pen? I ain't leavin' the room so you don't have to worry. Thank you, sir. Let's see now. Cleanin' the suit, seven dollars. The shirt, three dollars. The belt and buckle, buck and a half. Items not visible to the naked eye, five dollars. The shoes—well, you about totaled the shoes so I got to charge you full price, a hundred and fifty dollars. Then there be wear and tear from goin' to the cleaners and the shoe store and loss of income from the taxi and gas and oil and loss of party time because this be my best suit and until it's cleaned up I be ashamed to go anywhere in public. Let's see—zum, zum, zum, carry two, zum, zum, zum, carry three. Uh oh, I figure you into me for about three hundred dollars."

"Mr. Jackson," say Geraldine, "I must warn you. You are dangerously close to being held in contempt of court. I will tolerate it only so long. All right, you heard what the man said. As your counsel, I recommend you accept it before he changes his mind. What's your decision?"

It was time to get serious. Okay, up to now I been horsin' around cause the black imp inside me got to have *some* fun once in a while. Now I got to stop actin' the clown and face up to the main fact—which is what I say the next time I open my mouth is gonna make a big difference to a lot of black asses over on 6th Street.

"Miss Lance," I say, "Mr. and Mrs. Baltus, the answer is no. Twenty thousand ain't nearly enough. A hundred thousand wouldn't do it. Not even two hundred thousand. I 'spect I give you the wrong impression the last time we was sittin' around. See, what I forgot, probably cause I was drunk more than I should have been, it ain't just me. Since last time I been elected President of the 6th Street

Association for the Resistance Against Sticking It To Us—RASTUS for short—and we can't accept anythin' less than goin' on the way we has. What we want is to stay in our homes and pay the rent and that's all we want. Anythin' else, forget it."

There's a long sigh from Baltus and an angry look on Geraldine's face and a kinda growl from way down her throat she probably pick up from Hardin. Her teeth is showin' and they is awful close together like she already bit down hard on somethin' she don't want to swallow.

"Mr. Jackson," she say, "what in the goddamn hell is wrong with you? Take the money, pay me my fee, take a percentage of the gross as your commission on behalf of your association—RASTUS you call it? Sounds familiar—and distribute the remainder to your followers as you see fit. They should be grateful. It shouldn't be necessary to remind you because I thought I made it clear all along. You've got to go sooner or later, the same with the other tenants and the same with everybody else on the block. There is no way you can win."

"Who said anythin' about winnin'?" I say. "Winnin' would be if the honkeys left us alone. What we're gonna do is hang in there. And if we hang on long enough—well, some of us will die and go to Heaven from a room where we been sleepin' in a bed all along. If you gotta go that's the best way. Even honkeys can understand that. And if we do a really good job of hangin' in, maybe you'll lose interest. There be a lotta ways to get that to happen we ain't even talked about. Oh, yeah."

See, I'm tryin' to put up a good front. In the first place there ain't no RASTUS beyond how I dreamed it up on the spur of the moment. It ain't bad, though, right? In the second place, you put out a few unspecified threats and take on a kinda grim, serious look—which I did—the honkeys don't know what to expect next. Fire, bullets, sticks and stones, all those things flash through their minds. Gives 'em the heebie-jeebies.

"So if you white folks want to keep on, don't say you wasn't warned."

Nobody didn't say nothin', just peerin' at each other back and forth, right and left, didn't know what to say. So I say somethin'.

"Geraldine, how come I ain't had the pleasure of showin' you my hustle? Let's shake it, whattaya say?"

The next day I go by the fire station and ask the station chief would he let me know the next time his boys be out on a little job. Wednesday night the phone rings about nine o'clock and he say, yeah, the place be half empty did I want to use it. I yell for Sanford and Mr. and Mrs. Dudley and we head down the block knockin' on doors and anybody we see on the street say, Let's go, man, RASTUS is meetin' right now in the fire house. They didn't know what the fuck RASTUS is but seein' as how most of 'em wasn't doin' much more than watchin' TV or goin' to the liquor store a pretty good crowd follows us. I get up on the driver's seat of the hook and ladder—that thing is so shiny and bright I feel like a king on a throne—and when everybody who was comin' had, I ask first off is they any objection to my bein' elected President For Life to RASTUS, which I explained what it was. There wasn't no objection so I was swept in by acclamation. After that I figured I owe 'em a little speech. I promise 'em that their faith would not be trampled upon and their trust in me would be rewarded and we all in this together, forever, and we would win in the end. Most of 'em clap and cheer and whistle but one smartass yell, "Talk straight, man. You a black man and you gonna be one the rest of your lifetime." I ignore him. Don't give him the satisfaction of arguin'. "All right," I say, "now we got to get down to the nitty-gritty. I been to a lawyer and she can't do us no good. They is no way we can stop the honkeys. Sooner or later they gonna own every house on the block. Only thing we can do is make it hard for 'em as long as we can. Not by doin' it alone. Unh unh. We got to get us some committees. Sanford, I want you to take on general harassment. Okay? Henry Hammond, I got you down for plumbin' and wall paperin'. Daisy Hatfield, you here? Okay, you the garbage dumper. Mrs. Dudley, I'd like you to take care of landscapin' if you don't mind. Mr. Dudley, can you handle a flooded basement? . . . Great, I knew we could count on you. Maurice Parsons, you the mail slot specialist . . ." And so on. Damn near everybody got an assignment, makes 'em feel important. As for myself, I ain't sayin. But I got a plan, man. Only my time is up. Somebody else got to have a chance to talk, too. Fair is fair.

7

My name is Howard Baltus. I have always had a decent respect for money. I am adequately salaried and there is a monthly reminder of the generosity of my grandfather for which I am grateful. I am surprised when my own largesse is spurned. Mr. Rufus Jackson, of whom you are already aware, turned down twenty thousand of my dollars. It's hard to say why. He claimed it would have been disloyal to his neighbors but can you really believe that? Everybody connected with the situation knows that progress for 6th Street cannot be delayed forever. But that is Mr. Jackson's problem, not mine.

After Miss Lance's last party I finally began to get the show on the road. First there was the matter of the housing-code violations. You will remember that it is necessary to clear them up before the current tenants are formally given an opportunity to match my offer of $89,500. Fat chance. There is no question that the responsibility for the repairs to the property lies with the owner, one J. Honeywell Harrison, minister of the Afro-Episcopal Church on Colorado Avenue, a very fashionable black neighborhood just off Rock Creek Park. It is interesting how difficult it was to obtain that information. I must have called the District of Columbia Land Records Office ten times before I was able to run it down. I heard "You got the wrong number" and "Sorry, he be at lunch until three o'clock" and "She just stepped out of the office, hard to say when she be back" and "This here is the Dog Licenses, not the Land" and "Mister, we closed for the day, try tomorrow" and "Ain't nobody here by that name, you a bill collector?" and "Sir, don't raise your voice to me. You got any complaints you can write directly to the Mayor's Office" and "That number has been changed, the new number is . . ." and "Not over the phone. If you want to, you can come on down here and stand in line" and "You a lawyer? Can't give it unless'n you a lawyer.

Or a real estate agent. Same difference." I had, of course, asked Mr. DeTroit, of Capitol Hill Properties, for the owner's name a number of times prior to the last Lance party without success. His reluctance was never explained. But since I had become friendly with Geraldine Lance, who is a lawyer, albeit an eccentric one, I tried her. She knew.

The Reverend Doctor Harrison is the sort of person I admire. I imagine he is a tall, slim, distinguished gentleman of about sixty much loved by his parishioners for his emphatic preaching style, his utter devotion to the teachings of the Bible and his generally infinite wisdom about matters both secular and spiritual. I say "imagine" because I never actually had the pleasure of meeting him. Pressures of the pulpit, he said, and the needs of his flock left him little time for mundane business matters.

"Well, Reverend," I said to him over the phone, "there is the matter of the twenty-seven housing-code violations on the 6th Street property. They have to be corrected before the house is offered for sale to the tenants."

"Absolutely," said the reverend. "No question. The great mystery is why the property was permitted to deteriorate so badly in the first place. The property managers should have never let it get in that state. It is an abomination before God when His children are reduced to living in a house where twenty-seven housing violations have been permitted to build up through the years when there is no excuse for it at all."

"Right," I said, although I suppose if the property had been better maintained I wouldn't be able to buy it for a lousy eighty-nine five. "I'm sure you made it clear all along that certain of the rental income was supposed to be plowed back into caring for the property. I know that's the only way you'd want it."

"Oh, absolutely again. If only God would permit it. Unfortunately, some of my brethren in certain parts of our great and beloved city have not kept pace with others who through the dint of hard work and an utter devotion to the teachings of our Lord Jesus Christ have managed to leave the ghetto and come to the Gold Coast. I wish I had the time and the energy to counsel with my tenants who take a perfectly beautiful dwelling and in a matter of months turn it into something awful, something dreadful, something unfit for human beings so that in time they are hardly human beings themselves, more like apes some of them, utterly gross, incapable of taking care of another man's property which he has generously let them use through the years for practically no profit at all, as a matter of fact cost him money out of his own pocket and so on. If only I could get my hands, if only I could . . . Excuse me, Mr. Baltus, sometimes the strain of being a property owner and landlord overcomes me and I permit myself to carry on in a way which can only cause my old heart unnecesary hardship. It is also why I have reluctantly decided to let the property go for a whole lot less than a hundred thousand dollars, its true worth I do believe."

After this outpouring, reflective as it was of the good reverend's concern, it was evident I would have to wait a lifetime before he spent a dime on curing the housing-code violations. What the hell, he is a minister doing the Lord's work on the other side of the fence as far as a Jew is concerned but they are good works nevertheless. I imagine his total yearly income doesn't exceed $35,000 which these days isn't very much and why quibble over a few thousand bucks? I figured that would be more than enough to cover everything. The repairs would have to be made as part of the restoration project anyhow, so why not get it over with?

I must confess I was surprised when the list of deficiencies was presented. The man from the Housing Office who made the inspection had been nothing if not thorough. He objected to the wear in the stone steps leading to the front entrance; he discovered a crack between two bricks on the back side twenty feet up I couldn't even see; the floor in the second-story bedroom tilted more than he liked although I have always felt a little floor tilt is a good thing and part of the charm of an old house; he was fussy about the stairs between the first and second floors saying they might collapse at any moment (though they had apparently held up well enough for almost a hundred years) and he was grim about the possibility of the place being struck by lightning because somebody sure as hell had ripped off the lightning rod years ago and the house had been dammed lucky not to have been demolished by fire many times, wouldn't want that to happen.

I turned the entire project over to Hilltop Home Improvements, Inc., a firm heartily recommended by Capitol Hill Properties. A Mr. Archibald Dumfries, representing Hilltop, showed up at the property one day accompanied by Lucius DeTroit. Mr. Dumfries' face bore the satisfied expression one sees on a carpenter about to do business with a man who has distrusted all hammers since the day one crushed his thumbnail. Mr. DeTroit's face bore the satisfied expression one sees on a man who is probably going to be favored with a percentage of the gross. I was uncomfortable about being there myself because I didn't know but what I might run into the obnoxious Jackson, a man I would just as soon avoid. Actually, and you may not believe this, but this would be my initial visit to the interior. Vivian and I saw the outside for the first time last July and it is now December. Thus slowly goes time when a lawyer and the

District of Columbia bureaucracy are given a chance. As it turned out, Jackson was at home when we arrived and, considering his habitually unpolished manners, was as cordial as can be.

"How ya' doin', Howie?" he said. "And Lucius, old buddy, how you doin'? Who you got there, the plumber? Comin' to work on the john, are you? I knew if I was just patient and put my trust in my good buddies, everything would work out. Step right this way to the crapper."

Mr. Dumfries turned up his nose at that remark and turned it up again when we were escorted to the bathroom. God, it was foul-smelling and awful-looking. But we need not dwell upon it. As former Vice President Agnew so succinctly and accurately put it some time ago, once you've seen one slum you've seen them all. Mr. Dumfries hardly glanced at the room, just took out a notebook and wrote: "Bathroom, rip out and replace everything."

"Everything?" I said. "Now, wait a minute. What about the bathtub? That's an antique you're talking about. Those feet in the form of claws, that's real craftsmanship. We've got to save that."

Mr. Dumfries shrugged. "No sweat off my ass. By the time you undercoat the tub and resurface it and screw around with one thing or another it'll cost as much as a new one. But if that's what you want . . ." And he wrote: "Save the tub. Refurbish completely. Do a good job on the claws."

And so we toured the house, Mr. Dumfries thumping the walls, twisting the water pipes and electrical fixtures, testing the hot-water heaters and the heating ducts, jumping on the floors at various critical areas, shaking his head a good deal more than I personally thought was necessary and taking scores of notes. Jackson, who tagged along throughout, said "Right on!" or "Oh, yeah!" or "You right!" every time Mr. Dumfries would record yet another deficiency. Why, I don't know. Okay, the place would be spruced up some, but he would benefit only until I am the owner at which time he would be out on his ass. On the whole my own reaction to the dwelling was positive. I could see the potential readily enough. Indeed, I began to sharpen my vision about how it would look when the restoration was complete. The nursery, for example, would be the bedroom now occupied by the Dudleys. They were upstairs, old people in their eighties, wrinkled and faded but alert, and as polite as can be. Mrs. Dudley offered us a cup of tea. I turned it down out of a possibly exaggerated fear that the cup had not been properly washed. Mrs. Dudley was not offended. Mr. Dudley, thinking I was probably accustomed to something stronger, said he had a bottle of sloe gin and he would be happy if all of us joined him. I and Mr. Dumfries declined but Jackson said "Hell, yes, let's get us a buzz on to celebrate how this dump is finally goin' to get some money spent on it." Don't you just hate it when somebody is casual about your money? Mr. Dudley poured for Mrs. Dudley, himself and Jackson and while that was going on I drifted toward the front-room window and had my first look at the Capitol as seen from the room that not far in the future would be the Baltus' master bedroom. The Capitol is a magnificent edifice, no question, but its grandeur is never properly appreciated unless it is regarded through the window of your own home. Right now it looked almost as though it were an extension of that home. It gave me, as it would any American, a very warm feeling. You may think me excessively sentimental but that's the way I feel. I am a patriot and I don't apologize for it. Let the others bitch about how the country is far from perfect. Not me. I thank God every day that it permitted my great-grandfather to become a citizen and his descendants to prosper. Truly, only in America. I turned away from the stunning view eventually and joined the others. Mr. Dudley was relating his personal history to Mr. Dumfries and Lucius DeTroit. He said:

"Born in 1896 in Roanoke, Virginia. My daddy did share croppin'. Me too from the time I could carry a hoe to the time I came to Washin'ton in 1913. First job I shined shoes down on 12th Street. Second job I was a busboy in the old Willard Hotel. Third job I was a porter at Union Station. Fourth job I was a janitor at the Pentagon. Fifth job . . . fifth job I lost my fourth job and went back to shinin' shoes in the Pentagon barber shop. Sixth job . . . well, there wasn't no sixth job. Mrs. Dudley and I were married in 1918 There are somethin' like forty-three grandchildren, hard to know the exact number, it changes so fast. They good children, help us considerable. We live on the Social Security as much as we can. Been here about twenty-five years, I reckon. Don't know exactly where we gonna go when our time is up. I ain't gonna let it upset me none. The Lord will provide."

The thing I liked about Mr. Dudley was how he kept it right down to the bare bones. Anybody else, just because they offer you a drink they think they have the right to bore you to the back teeth. Okay, so his existence wasn't all that tremendous. But he could take credit for leading a good, industrious life and if he didn't make a lot of money . . . well, what the hell, money isn't everything. The way he and Mrs. Dudley had maintained and furnished their place deserves a lot of credit. Nothing fancy, you understand, but consistent with their conservative lifestyle. Jackson should have used them as a model. Where he had let everything in his place go, the Dudleys had at least kept their furniture looking reasonably good, considering it was threadbare. As a matter of fact I wondered if they were aware that the front-room loveseat had an elegant solid cherry frame which, in the hands of a competent upholsterer, could be converted into something I would be very proud to possess. Possibly when the time comes for them to go I might make a generous offer for it. I really mean that. I'm not going to take advantage of people who are down on their luck.

Sanford Williams down in the basement was a different story. The sooner his kind pack their bags the better off the neighborhood will be. He let us in with the greatest reluctance. If Jackson hadn't told him it was okay I doubt seriously we would have been permitted entrance. "No sweat," said Jackson, "This ain't no plain-clothes fuzz lookin' for dope. You got any?" Sanford said, "Hey, man, don't joke like that. You can't tell. What's goin' on?" Jackson explained. Sanford was not convinced. I gave him five dollars; he was convinced. We entered. As soon as we had I was almost sorry because the front room contained as disgraceful a display of human concupiscence as I have ever seen. Pictures of bare-breasted and bottomless women covered an entire wall—which was bad enough—but across from it a velvet Jesus Christ viewed the blasphemy with the forbearance for which He was rightly famous. Okay, it's only pictures and a painting but can you imagine anything more distasteful? Hey, don't get me wrong, I'm not a prude. At Geraldine Lance's, you may remember, I showed a lot of interest in her sex art. Only there at least it *was* art. In gilt frames and everything. Here it's hardcore porn. Now I could understand why the Reverend Doctor Harrison inspected his property so infrequently.

Sanford's basement will be devoted primarily to the Baltus' rec room. I know some rowhouse owners like to rent out the basement for the extra income. Fortunately that is not necessary in my case. What I foresee down there is a mahogany bar—something on the order of fifteen feet—and a Bosendorfer baby grand and a billiard table. I play neither piano nor billiards, although the kid that Vivian and I are striving for with everything we've got will be tutored in the former when the time comes. The billiards table will serve as the focal point of our parties. I earnestly believe casual dress has been tolerated way out of proportion at parties these days—Geraldine's comes to mind—and I envision our black-tie Sunday evenings as curbing that trend. We will be served a delicious dinner in the dining room—currently Jackson's bedroom and a place where from the looks of it eating of all styles has been common—and afterwards the company will drift downwards. The ladies will adorn the bar and the men will light cigars and sight down their cue sticks. Brandy will be in crystal snifters; cigar smoke will be in the crystal chandeliers. If someone wants to drift over to the piano and impeccably render

"Melancholy Baby" or "Starlight Melody" or "God Bless America" they have my permission right now. Okay, I know you're laughing. You're thinking, "What a square!" You're thinking, "Is this guy for real?" Okay, maybe I'm tending toward the old-fashioned but it's in keeping with the character of the house. If we just wanted to swing the rest of our lives, Vivian and I could stay in the Massachusetts Avenue apartment house where such things are common.

Mr. Dumfries' listing of the basement deficiencies almost wore out his pencil. He cursed evidence of a leaking brick wall, he was horrified at the creakiness of the doors, he took a dim view of the dim view through the windows, he was terribly put out that the chimney showed no evidence of a recent sweeping, he was aghast that large sections of plaster had departed the walls and ceilings and he had a two-minute head shake over the kichen stove. "That stove, Mr. Baltus, that stove is a ticking time bomb. You see that fitting there, right under there? No? Bend lower, sir. There. If that fitting should go with the condition it's in, you'd have a gas explosion would wreck this building from one end to the other. Thank God I came by when I did." There is a lot of the dentist in Mr. Dumfries, wouldn't you say? Nothing prior pleases him.

Nothing pleased Sanford, either. For a man so young he showed an unbelievable resistance to change. He said the place was fine the way it was; why did we want to come in and fuck around and make it so neat he wouldn't feel comfortable any longer? Had I answered that question candidly he would have accused me of being racist and I am anything but. I said it was a matter of the law; the law required a certain standard no matter how inconsistent it might be with a tenant's more casual approach. "Fuck the law," said Sanford. "The law ain't payin' the rent. I pay the rent." It was pointless to debate him and I did not try. He would be gone soon enough, probably to one of the public housing apartments over by the Anacostia River. Let him grind that down as he had ground down mine. The D.C. Government lives with that sort of thing all the time and is used to it. Not this kid.

Mr. Dumfries said he would come up with an estimate in a couple of days. I impressed upon him that all I was looking for at the moment was something to satisfy the housing code; if he did a good and reasonable job, the major features of the restoration—sanding the floors, painting and papering the walls, outfitting the bar, fabricating three or four closets, installing the chandeliers, putting in a circular staircase, replacing all the doors and God knows what else—might possibly come his way. "We don't cut corners, sir," he said. "We are too careful of our reputation to do anything like that." This was an understatement of the first rank as I subsequently learned. The estimate arrived three days after our inspection visit. Hilltop Home Improvements, Inc., it said, would be pleased to undertake the below-listed work for the Total Sum of Six Thousand Five Hundred and Twenty Three Dollars, with One Thousand in Advance and Periodic Payments as the Work Progresses. Barring an Act of God, it said, or Labor Unrest or A Severe Shortage of Materials, the Project would be Completed in Sixty Days or The First of April, whichever came Last. I am not exaggerating. It really did have all those capital letters and there was a nice touch at the close: "Respectfully submitted. I remain, Sir, your most Humble and Obedient Servant, Archibald Dumfries, Prop." Charles Dickens, thy legacy hath descended to avaricious craftsmen with a genuine feel for the literary.

I signed a contract and wrote out a check. "Keep me informed," I said in a note I attached. "Speed is important. That does not mean I am willing to pay for overtime." For a week I heard nothing. Then one morning my secretary told me a Mr. Rufus R. Jackson was on the phone, was I available? I groaned, I said yes.

"How ya' doin', old buddy?" Jackson began. "Hey, I didn't know you couldn't be talked to unless I talk to your secretary first. But that's okay, she got a nice, polite, kinda deep high-class voice. Do you know is she married? What does she look like?"

"Mr. Jackson," I said, "I am a very busy man. Is there something I can do for you?"

"Hey, buddy, it's the other way around. I'm callin' to do something for you."

"Really? And what might that be?"

"You know my crapper? The trouble I've had with my crapper? How the turds don't go down?"

I sighed. "Yes, Mr. Jackson, I'm aware of the problem."

"Well, Mr. Dumfries is here and he say the thing can't be fixed nohow. He say it is too goddamn old, seen too much shit in its lifetime."

"Yes, well, that is very sad."

"He say you gotta put in a new one. He say it's the only way."

"Well, what's the problem? Mr. Dumfries knows he can go ahead with whatever is necessary."

"Right. The only thing is, what color? Now I know all this expensive fixin' up is to satisfy the law, but one day after my black ass is gone, your white ass is gonna be where my black ass has been so many times and the question is, what color commode would move you the best? Personally, I like to shit on something white and since I'm the one has to be satisfied—the housing code and everything—I guess I could just tell Mr. Dumfries to go ahead with white. But I ain't gonna be here forever and you gettin' to be my good buddy so I figure what the hell, why don't I give you some input? If you want grey or pink or green or even purple—boy, I betcha Lucius Deepthroat would go for purple—we can discuss it man to man. I don't wanna be unreasonable."

I slammed the phone down. I gave explicit instructions to my secretary about future calls. I called Hilltop Home Improvements and left word that Mr. Dumfries was to get in touch the moment he showed up. I stormed around my office five minutes. I said, "That son-of-a-bitch, oh, that son-of-a-bitch." I made two fists and punched the air. I calmed down. I vowed I wouldn't let him upset me again.

And he didn't until his letter came a couple of weeks later. It said:

> Buddy:
>
> You okay? Haven't seen you around the premuses in a heck of a long time. Nothing wrong I hope. I am typing this on my typeriter I got some time ago for a chik turned out not to be so good a chik as I hoped. That is the way it goes somtime and I am sure it has happened to you. Buddy I have to tell you my feelins been hurt a whole lot because you wont talk to me on the telaphone. Your secreatary say you put out the word. How come? Is it somthin I did? I axed your secreteary. She says she cannot discuss personal matters between you and me. Well you aint put out nothin about me and her and I think we got somethin goin. Tomorrow night I is pickin her up after work in the cab. Gonna have us some McDonalds if she is black and some ribs if she is white. I aint sure over the phone but I figure she probalby white because you look like the kinda cat feel happier if he got the same color skin keepin creeps with different color skin from botherin him on the telephone. Same here, Buddy. Buddy, the reason I has take my pen in hand at the tiperiter is that Sanford caracter live down below. You remember him? Kind of a dumb guy, always standin in the way of progress. I dont trust him one bit. You heard him when you was here last time. Dont wanta change. Dont appreciate what you doin for him—new kitchen stove and new kitchen sink and new linoleum over that hole in the corner where the rats been comin in. You know what he said the other day? How come

he didn't get no new refrigerator? Yeah, thats what he say.
Can you believe it? I told him there wasnt nothing wrong with
the refrigerator he had. Clean it up once in a while, I told
him, and throw out that baloney and hot dogs been hangin
around so long the cokroches cant resist no longer and is
movin right in with the icecubes. He is a mess is Sanford. A
born troublemaker for sure. And the Dudleys upstairs,
remember them? Another problem. They look sweet as an ad for
a nursing home but let me tell ya somethin they be up to no
good. Mr. Dudley come knockin on my door yesterday night
wantin to know is I aware that the paint in the bedroom over
the new plasster is givin Mrs. Dudley a headache? Hell no.
Why should I be aware? It ain't me responsible. Only I didn't
say that. I say thats too bad, I am sorry about that. Then he
say well he thought I was a good buddy of Mr. Baltus and I
better tell him before he report the problem to the Public
Health Department. Can you imagine? Some people dont have no
sense of gratitude right? Well I just thought you ought to
know whats goin on around here. Nothin you should worry about
too much except when the morale is bad you never know what
might happen next. If it were my place I would spend a few
bucks on a trusted friend who can make sure his old buddy
dont get taken advantage of. Of course it is only a
suggestion and you can do whatever you want. In the long run
I think you will find my rates reasonable. After so much has
been done on the place so far by Mr. Dumpfrees and his crew
of workers it would be terrible to get anybody riled up. They
could wreck the joint and you be right back at square one.
Lemme know through Miss Cynthia Anderson your secrethairy. In
the meantime hang in there.

    I remain, sir, your very humble servant,

                                   Very truly yours,

                                   R. Rastus Jackson III

8

This here is Rufus R. Jackson speakin' out of turn. I know I been hoggin' it more than my fair share and I is sorry. But what I got to say is awful important and I figure you got the right to know it without no delays. The thing is, Howard Baltus tried to kill hisself. Yes, incredible as it may seem, the man who was dedicated to upgradin' the quality of life on 6th Street Northeast has just about give up his own. It happened about three weeks ago—the exact date was February 13—on a Friday night, and was the direct result of his failure to attend the Friday Night Services which I happen to know is a requirement layed on all Hebes just like I'm supposed to go to church on Sunday. If he'd been there prayin' up a storm and askin' for forgiveness for what he and his brothers did to sweet Jesus Christ it would have never happened. But, no, he played hookey and came over to the property. Only it wasn't no social call to see how me and the others is bearin' up to the certain knowledge that one of these days we is gonna be out on our asses with no roof over our head. What he was comin' for was to look at the damage. Yeah, I am sorry to say there has been some bad things goin' on at 757. Even though Mr. Dumfries and his crew from Hilltop Home Improvements had been slavin' away five days a week they didn't seem to be gainin' on it. Like a month ago they brought over a new hot-water heater for my place and the next day they come back and discover it have a hole in the side. Why? Hard to say but the bad workmanship comin' out of factories these days could be the answer and it don't help none when they claim the Limited Warranty don't apply to somethin' been bashed in with a sledgehammer. Or the new kitchen sink down at Sanford's. Installed one day and gone the next. Sanford really pissed off. Good thing they left the old sink. Sanford put it back in place as best he could though he ain't had no plumber trainin' that amounts to anythin' and it's leakin' pretty bad all over the new linoleum. Bad news up at the Dudleys', too. Lightin' fixtures is the problem. They put in all this expensive fluorescent stuff, the kind you see when a movie star puts on her lipstick, you know. It didn't last more'n two days. Vandals from God knows where came in while the Dudleys was sleepin' and attacked everythin' with a baseball bat. They know it was a bat because when the Dudleys called the police it was right there in the middle of the glass. Mr. Dudley said it was from the old days when he used to play on the Union Station team. Shortstop, with a .285 lifetime average. The bat been put away in a closet these many years say Mr. Dudley and if Mr. Dumfries' workmen hadn't been screwin' around where the roof has been leakin' it would be there to this very day. But no, they had pulled everythin' out and no wonder the vandals found it because it was right out in the open just beggin' to be used. Mr. Dudley said he had saved the bat through all the years on account of he hit a home run with it in the eleventh inning in a game between Union Station and the Pullman Porters in 1927. The police put all this down but I personally doubt very much they gonna solve the crime. The police gotta lot of black brothers these days and they know what the hell is goin' on as well as you and me.

Okay, there was a few other minor items hardly worth mentionin'. Like the screen been ripped out of the new screen door. Why somebody would do that ain't easy to explain because it is only March by now and the mosquitoes and flies is still a long ways off. Also some dumb fool with absolutely no sense splashed a bucket of green paint all over the new drywall in my bedroom. Hard to do unless it's deliberate and I ain't namin' no names but it wouldn't suprise me none if those guys workin' for Dumfries hadn't did it out of sheer spite against Dumfries bein' such a hardass and also so they could get a little extra money doin' the whole wall over. The new back steps—well, you wanna be damn careful if you comin' to vist me that way. The thing is, they covered with crankcase oil and be more slippery than a riverboat card shark. I didn't find out how bad it was until Baltus fell on his ass goin' down. See, the moment I got home from drivin' the cab that Friday I could tell the place didn't look right. The screen door and the green paint was the worst but there was also one or two other things that don't amount to shit but ain't good news neither. Well, hell, I thought, this is something my old buddy Howard ought to know about right away. So I call him up on the telephone. Tried to break it to him gentle like, tellin' him it wasn't anything couldn't wait until mornin'. "No," he say, "I'll be right over." And in about twenty minutes the Mercedes pulls in behind the Dudleys' old Chevy and Baltus runs up to the front door and knuckles it real hard like he lettin' everybody on the other side know he gonna get to the bottom of this right now.

"Now slow down, buddy," I say when I come to the door and see it's him and not some bill collector tryin' to catch me unawares. "Don't get your balls in an uproar. It ain't worth it."

Only he barges right on in like he own the place and heads back toward the bedroom where the paint has made such a mess on the walls. Looks a lot like green flowers, with the petals formin' where the splash was strong. Some of it dripped on down and made these funny-lookin' puddles on the floor and since I didn't realize they wasn't dry when I first saw them an hour before, I may have edged up a little too close. That would explain why there is green footprints in just about every room you go into. Does resandin' a floor cost a lot? It was sure gonna take somethin' like that to make the joint look presentable enough to please Mr. Baltus. 'Cause when he saw the way everythin' was, he gets pretty excited—breathin' deep and grindin' his teeth and shakin' his head and rubbin' his chest with his hand like he in some pain right around his heart. And he say "goddamit" a lot and "Jesus Christ" and "somebody will pay for this" which was surely the truth though at the time he probably didn't realize he the one. It was on the tip of my tongue to say this could have been avoided if only he be willin' to hire a live-in nightwatchman but I can see he ain't in the mood for logical thinkin'. So I just hush up, only shakin' my head when he shake his and cluckin' every once in a while when he find some new discovery give him a lot of hurt. Like the hole near the hot-water heater. Damn if some meathead ain't fucked around with the pipes so bad they is a hole right down to Sanford's. A big hole—big enough if I want to yell down to Sanford to let him know what's goin' on I can do so and save on the telephone. And speakin' of the telephone, the thing rings right about then and when I answer it who could it be but the Missus.

"Oh, Mr. Jackson, how are you? This is Vivian Baltus. Is my husband there?"

"Hi, Viv, babe," I say, "how you doin'? I caught you this afternoon on the radio. This fare said he didn't like soul, would I mind switchin' to rock and roll? You was in the middle."

There wasn't nothin' said for a coupla seconds and I figure she waitin' for a compliment because if you be a public performer there is no limit to the number of times you want somebody to say you is the greatest even if it comes from some ghetto no-account whose opinion ain't worth shit.

"Is that so, Mr. Jackson?" she say finally. "I hope you didn't find me too hard to take. My kind of music doesn't appeal to everybody."

"Hey, baby, that's where you're wrong. That Beethoven got him a good strong beat—especially toward the end. And now that I got your number and seein' as how we're practically gettin' to be good friends I'm gonna play you all the time."

She laugh some. "Well, that is very kind. I hope my program has wide appeal. We don't want it just for highbrows."

If I was the kind of thin-skinned person takes offense easily I could let myself get insulted after that. Okay, I *know* I ain't no highbrow but I don't like to have it pointed out so sneaky.

"Oh," I say, "I know what's good for me. Maybe you can teach me a few things. And maybe I can teach you a few things. I got me a few basic skills don't hardly show when I'm drivin' the cab, you know what I mean?"

You can read into that whatever you want. What I don't have to take is cunts like her puttin' me down. She don't say nothin' for two or three breaths and then she say, "Uh, Mr. Jackson, is Howard there? I think I'd better talk to him."

"No sweat, baby," I say. "I'll get you another time."

See, I could say things like that because Howard wasn't even in the room.

"Howie," I yell out, "get your ass in here. It's the missus on the phone."

Where Howie has been during the above conversation was in the bathroom. And when he come into the front room he is carryin' one of those bathtub claws he is so crazy about. Ordinarily if you carryin' a claw you carryin' a tub, because they be welded to each other tighter than ink on paper. In this case the claw was by its ownself, cut off from the tub by somebody who knew how to use a hacksaw. Anybody who could've seen the expression on Howie's face wouldn't have done it. He is so mad the veins on his head is standin' out and throbbin' and his face is red and he is damn near foamin' at the mouth. He jerks the phone out of my hand.

"Wait, Howie," I say. "Calm down first. Don't let the little woman hear you when you so upset. Tell her you call back later when you more your normal self."

He don't go for that, good advice though it be.

"Would you mind leaving the room?" he say. His teeth is all gritted together and he be huffin' and puffin' like he just done the hundred-yard dash and I figure I can't reason with him so I go back to the kitchen and get me a cold beer. Cold beer is good when you has finished your day's work and you know you has done your best and nothin' bad is on your conscience.

I am too polite to listen in when I been sent out of the room but I could hear poor Howie layin' his problems onto Vivian, which was dumb because they ain't a thing she can do about it. Then he come back to the kitchen and I say does he want a beer? No, he says, does I have anything stronger? I don't like to waste the good stuff on anybody that ain't a chick but I get down under the kitchen sink and bring out my bottle of Harry's Rare Blended Bourbon Whiskies, Aged In The Cask Since Nineteen Seventy-Seven. I give him a good snort and he knocks it back and says can he have another. Oh, hell, yes, Howie, only watch it because you got to drive way up to Massachusetts Avenue and it would be bad if you got arrested for drunk drivin' mixed up with high blood pressure.

So we sip a little and eventually he calm down and say "I want to make it plain I don't intend putting up with this a bit longer. Not one bit."

And I say, "Well, just a little bit because there's somethin' else I gotta show you outside."

He give me a sad, kinda miserable look and he say, "I can't stand anything else. I am about at my limit."

"I ain't gonna lie to you," I say. "It ain't good but it won't cost much to fix. On the way out you can see the new back steps."

I turn on the back porch light and we go out the back door. The new landin' and steps is there, all good-lookin' pine and a sure big improvement on the rickety heap been there so long it looked like a pile of kindlin'.

"After you, sir," I say, nice and polite. "Go right on down to the ground and then I'll lead the way."

He do so. Step one, no problem. Step two, movin' good. Step three, steady as a rock. Step four, pow! bang! crunch! It was step four that done it, the step that had been oiled even more than the others and was slicker than twenty-five banana peels. Lucky for Howie, though, step four was almost at the bottom and while he bounced right smart against the railin' and the wall and the steps—grabbin' and clutchin' and tryin' to keep his balance any way he can—he only actually falls a foot or two before he hit the ground. He be messed up pretty good even so. His pants is showin' an ugly smudge on the seat and his hand is sure as hell bruised where he put it up against the bricks to brace hisself. His jacket . . . well, his jacket got snagged on some nails those Dumfries shitheads hadn't pounded into the railing deep enough and he be lucky if they accept it at the Salvation Army. And also he must have taken on some serious other injuries I couldn't make out because he was lyin' there yellin' and moanin' like some little kid beat up in a street fight.

Seein' the danger, I was too smart to follow. I just swung my bod over the railin' at the landin' and glided right on down. Did I tell you I was the star high-jumper at Eastern High at the same time I was also All-City on the basketball team? No? I am too modest for my own good. Anyhow, I land light as sunshine and go over to Howie to see if I can help him in any possible way. He is okay except as I already said.

"Howie, dammit," I say, "what the fuck is wrong with you? Drinkin' and goin' down steps don't mix, everybody knows that. Now you better shape up and quiet down or some of the neighbors is gonna call the cops on account of you is disturbin' the peace."

Then I help him to his feet and brush him off, bein' careful not to come in contact with the oily parts which was widespread. Once you get near crankcase oil it goes right for the fingernails and you're in for one of those expensive manicure jobs before you realize what the hell is goin' on.

Howie stagger around some before I be satisfied with his condition but I finally figure he be ready for the next event.

"Okay, buddy, it's right around the corner."

Right around the corner puts us into the alley where I parks the taxi. Only it's not the taxi I want him to look at, it's the wall of the house. There ain't much light but anybody can see what's on it. Part of it is in red paint and part is yellow and part black and there is a dab of green at the lower right-hand corner. It all adds up to something grabs your attention as strong as a police siren. It's an announcement and what it says is:

DEATH TO THE JEWS!

This black swastika is off to the left, the words is in the middle in red and off to the right is this Jew star in yellow. The green was for the signature of the artist except he can't write too clear because I couldn't make it out at all. The letters and the other things is about five feet tall but not too far up and it looks to me like the responsible person done his thing standin' on the ground.

"That's good, Howie," I say to Howie. "This way we don't have to use no ladder, maybe break our necks in addition to the other things you still smartin' over."

Howie don't say nothin', just look at it for a while. I ain't no mind reader so I can't say what he's thinkin'. Seems real unhappy and puzzled, though, like he can't understand how this kinda thing can happen in a civilized country like the USA. Then he starts shakin' his head and mutterin' somethin' under his breath about maybe Hitler didn't lose the war after all. This is when I get the feelin' he pretty discouraged, don't feel like goin' on. A man that upset could easily cut his wrists or take the gas or jump out a window. So I'm damn happy we can do our work from ground level. I go back into the house—through the front door, you can be sure—and find a bucket of green paint and a coupla paint brushes. I hand one to Howie, keep one for myself.

We start slappin' it on. I am kinda slow and deliberate on my side because to tell you the truth the perpetrator of the crime had a real artistic ability—shadin' the letters and the swastika and the star in a very professional way and givin' everything a beautiful 3-D effect so it stood out—and I be sorry it has to be covered up even though it is causin' Howie so much grief. Howie, on his side, is sloshin' paint on right and left and if you don't give a shit the way he didn't, pretty soon' you pretty green yourself which was what happened. He was still bleedin' a little from where his head had made contact with the railin' and his right hand was beginnin' to puff up from where it banged against the bricks. Altogether he is a mess, which don't seem fair for a man who could easily afford to have somebody else swing a paint brush back and forth even though it be mornin' before he could get estimates and sign a contract and get the project under way. He couldn't trust the Dumfries mob to do it; I sure as hell wouldn't. Them sons-of-bitches will never get my business no matter what. I have seen at first hand how they will drag their feet on a job if you give 'em the slightest encouragement.

We quit finally. It don't look too bad. I am almost proud of my half, gave me confidence that if I ever get tired of the transportation game I could probably make out okay as a house painter. I say to Howie, you done pretty good, let's go in and have a drink. We go in, we sit down at the kitchen table, we pour out the Harry's and we drink it until there isn't none left.

"There be a liquor store right down on the corner," I tell Howie. "Seein' as how you outdrank me about two to one, how about you goin' on down there and gettin' us a refill?

Howie don't say nothin' because he in no shape to say much about anythin'. The paintin' has got him plastered, which when you consider they go together ain't surprisin'. His eyes is not makin' any sense at all, his hair is all messed up with green spots so he look like somethin' out of Halloween, his mouth is slobberin' spit and his nose is leakin' pretty bad, too. Every once in a while he raise his hand and sight down his finger at me like he gonna make a point but the words don't come. The fucker can't hold his liquor, I be thinkin', the fucker ain't half the man I is.

"Howie," I say when I realize he ain't gonna be the generous guest, "either you get your ass outta here or you gotta crash. Us cabdrivers can't sleep late on Saturday like some folks I know. You wanna stay, you can have the front room sofa."

That gets his attention, gets him on his feet, gets him lookin' for the front door. I could see what he was thinkin': it's okay to get drunk with some black dude when you really need it, but as for actually spendin' the night in his rat-infested, flea-ridden, roach-crawlin' house where the toilet has a bad history, forget it. No way. Impossible. I wouldn't be caught dead. How could I explain it to my friends? So he lurches out the front door, staggers down the front steps, finds the Mercedes, fumbles with the door key, lucks out finally, settles himself in and turns on the ignition.

Now this is where I say Howie Baltus tried to kill hisself. And it is also where maybe I didn't do my duty as a public-spirited citizen. See, I could have reached through the door and grabbed the keys and put 'em in my pocket where no guy the size of Howie had a chance in hell of ever gettin' 'em out. If I do that, the poor bastard is trapped for the night. He'd have to crash with me even if he despise the thought about as much as God despises sinners. Callin' a cab wouldn't do no good. This block is my territory and if he call the cab company they say, "Man, what's wrong with you, you callin' from a taxi driver's house right now" and hang up.

So I don't do nothin' and when Howie pulls away from the curve and guns the Mercedes down toward H Street at about sixty miles per hour I know he is headin' for his doom. Can't nobody drive that fast drunk and live to tell about it. Sooner or later he gonna murder some innocent tree and by the time the guys in the ambulance pick up the pieces he be dead on arrival for sure. So long, Howie, it's been good to know you. Now maybe we get a little peace and quiet down on 6th Street.

Well, shit, old Howie must have credit up in Heaven you wouldn't believe. He didn't kill hisself at all. How do I know that? Account of what happened the followin' Monday morning. I get up at the crack of ten o'clock and damn if I don't hear this barkin' sound out beyond the front door. At first I think maybe Geraldine Lance and Hardin has come to pay a social call. Okay, I been freeloadin' at their place more than I should and I figure they come around for hominy grits and country sausage and homemade biscuits with the honey from my own bees and the morning glories on the table just like I was some cultivated person capable of puttin' down somethin' better than cornflakes and coffee. Only it ain't Geraldine and Hardin, no siree. I get up and poke my head outside and I be goddamn if out on the sidewalk there ain't the biggest, meanest-lookin' police dog in the entire world barkin' his lungs out right in my direction. And that ain't all. Holdin' the son-of-a-bitch is the biggest, meanest-lookin' son-of-a-bitch in the entire world and he lookin' at me, too. At first I think he be a policeman but then I see he ain't. He wearin' a uniform, okay, but when I size him up I see he sportin' an emblem on his upper arm say "Special Police." Special police, shit. He ain't nothin' but a security guard, the kind they got in every office buildin' in the city on account of if they don't, there wouldn't be a single typewriter in the place come mornin'. This one is a black brother but he regardin' me about as friendly as a snake do a rabbit. Same to you, buddy.

"Hey, man, you some kind of a posse?" I yell at him. "What the fuck you doin'?"

"What the fuck you think I'm doin?" he yell back. "I'm guardin' the place."

"Guardin'? From what, man? This ain't no jewelry store. What the fuck you guardin'?"

"You," he say. "I'm guardin' you and the property."

"You crazy, man," I holler. "You makin' a big mistake. I don't need no guardin'. This place don't need no guardin'. Get your ass and your dog's ass offen my property."

"Fuck you," he say. "We ain't on your property and it's not your property and we on the public sidewalk where we gonna stay. You don't believe it, read this."

And the mother reach in his pocket and pull out this legal-lookin' document about two feet long with a red seal on the bottom. If it's got a red seal on it you better pay it some mind. So I walk on down the front steps and up to this dude and he hand it over.

"Can you read?" he say. "If you can't read lemme know."

Can I read? Of course I can read. I don't do it too much on account of there ain't no need. Radio and TV keeps me informed about everythin' important goin' on in the Nation's Capital and nothin' important goes on anywhere else. Oh, yeah, we Washingtonians is conscious of the unique role we play in the scheme of things. (I heard some congressman say that on the TV and he been elected to fourteen terms so he must know what he talkin' about.) About the only serious readin' I do is street signs when I take a fare somewhere. And *Playboy*. I can read the pictures in *Playboy* without even moving my lips.

"Don't be no smartass," I say to Hired Gun. "And hold that fuckin' dog. If that dog bites me you gonna be sued for every dime you got now or any time in the future."

I reads the document. Not all of it, not all the fine print. But I get the main idea from the big letters up at the top and what they say don't leave much doubt: Authority To Protect Against Malicious Mischief, Petty Larceny, Simple Vandalism, Unlawful Appropriation, Unauthorized Use and General Ripping Off. Under that it says 757 is now under the protection of Capitol Security Corporation and It Is Empowered To Take All Necessary Measures. It didn't take me long to put two and two together. Mr. Howard Baltus, bein' aware of the piss-poor performance of Hilltop Home Improvements, has taken legal steps to ensure that those guys shape up or ship out. Good for him and also good news he is alive and kickin'. I may have said somethin' nasty about him a while ago but God is my witness I didn't mean most of it.

"Well, great, man," I say to Pistol-On-The-Hip. "No problem. Welcome aboard. Can I get your little dog some water?"

"Water? This dog don't drink water. This dog don't drink nothin' but blood. You wanna donate?"

After that I figure I better go back in. I call Geraldine right away and lay it on her.

"Geraldine, what the hell is goin' on? They can't do this, can they?"

"Oh, yes," she say. "New law just in effect. Paragraph 27, Section 14B of the Prospective Buyers Protection Statute. Any person who has indicated his intent to purchase can invoke it. And Howard has, as was his right. Sorry about that."

"As long as the dog don't shit on my front walk and the guard don't piss on my front hedge, it don't make no difference to me. Don't tell me they can come inside."

"No, but you better watch yourself. I saw the Baltuses at a party Saturday night and he's on to you. Which explains why you're surrounded front and rear."

She is so damn right. I hang up and go out the back door and I be go to hell if there ain't another vicious dog and another vicious keeper patrollin' the alleyway.

"How ya doin'?" I say, nice and friendly. "Can I get your little dog some water?"

"Water? This dog don't drink water. This dog don't drink nothin' but blood. You wanna donate?"

I ain't no business man with a staff to train and supervise but I do know one of the things bosses is always lookin' for is gettin' everybody to react the same way in certain common situations. Like those two guys.

Okay, they be some changes around here after 757 becomes a concentration camp with the Gestapo on duty twenty-four hours a day. Can't nobody go in, can't nobody go out but what the guards is writin' it down and the dogs is barkin'. If you carryin' somethin' they gotta know what it is, pokin' in all the boxes or paper bags you might be usin' for your laundry or your groceries or anythin' else of a purely personal nature. Naturally, this creates an unfriendly mood around the premises and any old buddies who might be wantin' to drop in for a chat or a beer find they got more important things elsewhere. See, I likes a lot of company and when my friends can't come by to discuss what's goin on I begin to feel I don't have my finger on the pulse of the neighborhood. As you know, I am tryin' to establish myself as a force for improvement and good.

I gotta admit the Hilltop Home Improvements crew starts gettin' their act together. In about two weeks everything is about done and one day about noontime I drive the hack home to discover that there is a goddamn standin' committee. Sanford has got in touch through the cab dispatcher, says it's an emergency. What we have is Howie hisself and Viv and Lucius Deepthroat and Geraldine Lance and Hardin and Sanford and Mr. and Mrs. Dudley and Mr. Dumfries and the inspector from the D.C. Housing Code Office and a coupla cops sittin' in a D.C. police car and them fuckin' guards and their man-eatin' dogs. The Baltuses and Lucius seem to be kinda dressed up, like they on their way to a public hangin'.

"Hey," I say. "What's comin' off?"

"You and me and the Dudleys," say Sanford. "This is it."

Okay, I let everybody in seein' as how further resistance would be foolish and in about twenty minutes the housing-code inspector has seen enough and he is satisfied. He signs this big old form and hands it to Howie and Howie the moment he has it turns to Lucius and he say, "The premises now meet all the housing-code requirements as stated in D.C. statutes. I offer eighty-nine thousand five hundred dollars for the property, which is the asking price. It is necessary, I believe, that the tenants be given an opportunity to match the offer. Mr. DeTroit, as the agent for the seller, would you please apprise them of their opportunity."

Lucius do so.

"Uh, Mr. and Mrs. Dudley, Mr. Sanford Williams and Mr. Rufus R. Jackson, It is my duty to advise you that . . ." And he drone on for a while, tellin' us what we already know, that we got to get it up or get out.

"Now, Rufus," say Geraldine at the end, "you and the others have forty-eight hours to match the offer. Do you want the time?" Except that she has a briefcase you would never know Geraldine is a lawyer. She is wearin' a skimpy white blouse strugglin' to do a decent job of containin' her boobs and a red skirt slit up the sides and it is so tight across the ass it's a wonder she can fart. She looks like a lady wrestler tryin' hard to establish she is a woman.

Sanford shake his head and Mr. and Mrs. Dudley do the same and I get somethin' collected from the back of my throat and arch it at Howie's shoes. They are black loafers with tassels and I wonder how they would look with my tan corduroy suit, in tan, of course, with a nice spit-shine to bring out the significant values. Significant values? What the fuck is goin' on? I never used to say things like that, but just a few parties at Geraldine's is gettin' me away from all that ignorant jive talk used to be my limit.

"Fuck no," I say, "why would we want any more time? We wasted enough time as it is."

As soon as I say that, Howie whips out his wallet and from his wallet whips out a check and lays it on Lucius.

"A certified check," he say. "Can we get on with the paperwork?"

There is a frenzy of paper signin' between Howie and Viv and Lucius and even me, the Dudleys and Sanford. What we sign is somethin' say we had our chance and turned it down. After that Howie and Viv and Lucius get this shit-eatin' expression on their faces like all their problems is finally over with. Oh, yeah . . .

"Seven days," say Lucius. "I'm sorry, but the tenants must be out by next Wednesday noon at the latest."

The Dudleys nod, they be gonna live with some of their many children, and Sanford say okay, he gotta place over in the public housin' at Anacostia, he be gone by the weekend.

"Sooner than that for me," I say. "You can start evictin' me any time. This afternoon if the sheriff and the marshals ain't got a previous engagement."

This little announcement catch everybody by surprise.

"What?" say Geraldine, showin' puzzlement. "Are you sure?"

"Shit, yes, I'm sure. I'm only askin' one thing, that the job be finished by four o'clock."

"Rufus, what's this all about?" say Geraldine, her wheels spinnin' every which way. "What are you up to?"

"Hey, how come y'all so suspicious? You got what you want and I'm goin' along."

Everybody look like they don't believe me. But they see I'm serious when I say 'scuse me and go into the back room and start puttin' my clothes and my shoes and my coupla sheets and blankets into the boxes I been collectin' from the supermarket against this very day. It don't take more'n a few minutes. Then into the bathroom for my shavin' gear and one final crap. Another few minutes. Then I drag everthin' into the front room and alongside the pile I put my TV and my IBM and my radio box and that be that. It take so little time everybody still standin' there, still don't know what the hell's goin' on.

"As soon as I can get this stuff in the cab I be on my way," I tell 'em. "As I was sayin', I'd appreciate it if you have the furniture and the rest of it on the sidewalk by four o'clock. Sanford, buddy, if you could just put some of that on your back, we can be outta here in no time and leave the new owners in peace."

Sanford pick up a load and me too and we move to the cab. By the time we get everythin' in, about the only room left for fares is for somebody don't mind crouching on the edge of the right front seat.

"And where exactly are you going?" Geraldine wants to know. She has followed us and she is standin' off to the side with her arms folded across her knockers like a drill sergeant catchin' some recruit about to go AWOL. "Some motel? The YMCA?"

"Got somethin' better," I say. "This may come as a surprise, Geraldine, but I'm shackin' up with you. You gonna give me a key now or you gonna meet me there? Or you wanna wait 'til you through for the day at the office?"

Geraldine bust out laughin'. "Super," she say. "I know I'll never get my fee in money. This way I can take it out in trade."

"Hey, I mean it. Listen, you owe me. You said you could delay this thing damn near forever and all you did was five months."

"Now wait a minute," say Geraldine, like she done been promoted to a judge and can dish it out tough all over the place. "I never made any promises. Lawyers don't make promises. If lawyers made promises they would spend all their time defending themselves in malpractice suits."

"I got a case. You been consortin' with the enemy. A little bird told me you was at the same party the other night. How come you didn't take me?"

"And why would I do that?" she say, drawin' her head back and gettin' haughty. "You'd only make a pass at every chick in the place. I'm seeing changes for the better in you all the time, Rufus, but you're still pretty crude. I hope you realize that." Then she smile her natural, good-natured way. "But if you really want to stay with me you can. Not forever. And with no promise of hanky-panky. That's another thing I never promise."

"Geraldine, honey," I say, "you're gonna be beggin' me. But I can wait. You don't have nothin' against me jerkin' off once in a while, do you, in the meantime?"

Geraldine got a laugh on her explosive as a stick of dynamite. When she thumps you across the shoulders you gotta brace yourself to keep from collapsin'. Both together is a force powerful enough to keep peace in the Middle East forever. "Come around at five thirty," she say. "I'll prepare the guest room. Only don't consider yourself a guest. I expect to be paid. And I mean money."

The time is fine with me because I have to make a few phone calls and also hustle my ass in the cab to make up for what I lost bein' officially told I is a displaced, homeless person. Just about four o'clock I have my quota for the day and can drive by 757 to see how things are goin'. They goin' fine: the marshals is carryin' out the last of the furniture and the other crap which all of us collect in a lifetime, ain't it the truth, and the neighbors is already startin' to run off with it. Even some of the block's finest citizens is involved. But I don't chase after 'em or give 'em hell. I just park the cab in the alley, stroll out to the front and stand around with what's left of my lifelong possessions lookin' as miserable as I can. Before long this young black dude with a notebook and another black dude with a coupla cameras strung around his neck come up and the first guy says, "How ya' doin? We're looking for Ralph Royce Johnson, do you happen to know him?"

One of the most important things they teach in journalism school is to get the name spelled right. I know that for a fact, and when this young cub starts out with the wrong spellin' I is irritated. Only I try not to show it.

"Son," I say, "you wouldn't be meanin' Rufus Rastus Jackson of 757 6th Street Northeast, would you?"

The dude checks his notebook.

"Oh, yeah, right. Rufus Rastus Jackson. Uh huh. The reason I thought Rufus was a mistake is we don't see much Rufus these days. Nor Rastus either. A lot of Jackson, of course, and a lot of Johnson, too. Sorry about that. You him?"

"Yeah. What's yours?"

"Abligandas Ali Mohammad. And this is Kashiri Ayatola."

I should have known. Hair in dreadlocks, feet in sandals and ratty-lookin' beads over baggy-lookin' ponchos. Ain't ponchos but sure looks like 'em.

"Listen, lemme ask you one thing. Don't you guys waste a lot of time repeatin' your names and spellin' it all out? You ever think of goin' back to Al or Jimmy? I mean, it is America. You were born here, right?"

The dude with the notebook ignores me. The other dude takes my picture.

"Okay," I say. "I can see you ain't from the *Washington Post*. Which is it?"

"*Afro-American Tribune*," say Notebook. "Only six years old but our circulation is already up to thirteen hundred and fifty. You ever read us?"

"Hell, no. Listen, this is a big story. I don't know if I can afford to let some small-time outfit in on it. Maybe you guys better step aside until the *Washington Post* and the TV stations show up. Would you mind?"

"Big story?" say Brother Cub. "My editor says you've been evicted. It happens every day. What's so big about it?"

"Friend, there's a lot more to it than that. This story has far-rangin' social significance as well as human interest out the ass. This is a big story. The guy that gets this story is a cinch for a prize and a raise."

"Uh huh," say Poised Pen. "Okay, I'll listen. But keep it short. I've only got ten inches."

So I lay the whole thing on him: the Baltuses, Capitol Hill Properties and Capitol Security Corporation. "Vicious, man-eatin', probably rabid police dogs barkin' all night and snappin' all day. And today was the end. Right there is the last of my fast-disappearin' furniture. You better get some pictures because the neighbors is takin' it away as quick as they got the strength."

Snap Chap shoots a few of me beside the sidewalk heap and in front of the house and then I take 'em around to the alleyway and show 'em the taxi.

"Now this is your angle right here. Because this ain't no ordinary cab and this ain't no ordinary alley. This here is the home of the dispossessed person Rufus Rastus Jackson, one day soon to be famous as President Forever of the Resistance Against Stickin' It To Us, RASTUS for short, and right now a martyr to the cause to which he has dedicated his life."

If I was a newspaper reporter as Junior Journalist was supposed to be, I would be writin' all this down fast.

"Wait a minute," say Obbligato. His face puckers and he looks like he ain't heard good. "Let me get this right. You've been kicked out of the house because it's been sold. And you intend living in your taxi? Why?"

"Hey, Obie," I say, "you missin' the point. It ain't just livin' in the taxi. It's where I'm gonna park it every night after I quit work. Right here. Right where I been parkin' it the last six years and where I has the God-given right to park forever."

"Oh, yeah?" say Oblongato. "Won't the new owner complain? Aren't you on his property?"

"Hell, no. This alley ain't no real alley. It's a street. Belongs to the city. What with the junk scattered all over it, it ain't been open to traffic for years. But it's still a street and anybody can use it. The owner can't say shit."

Obie-Ahbie-Oobie thought this over. "Yeah, okay, but so what? What are you trying to prove?"

"Obie, man, get with it. Ain't you been listenin'? This taxicab is about to become the headquarters and shrine of RASTUS. Right here—and you better write this down—is where the fight began that will ultimately end with the destruction of the white honkey block busters and the eventual victory of the poor, downtrodden blacks who have been abused all these years but who still cling to their ancestral homes with all the tenacity of some poor lonesome sheepherder defendin' his hut against the onslaught of a hungry wolf."

Quite a mouthful, right? Took me a day to write it and two days to memorize it. But it was worth the trouble. Oh, yeah.

9

This is the mouthpiece speaking, finally able to get a word in edgewise in her own defense. They are a long-winded, hoggish lot, I'm sure you've discovered by now, and prone to stay in the spotlight as long as the director will tolerate them. If I were in charge I would limit them to five minutes a crack and insist upon strict adherence. The penalty for disobedience would be banishment from these pages forever. I am sure the more reasonable characters would respond in a mature and intelligent way, though there is one who has been indulged out of all proportion and is probably beyond any meaningful restraint or correction. I refer, of course, to Rufus Rastus Jackson, the rapscallion rogue formerly of 757 6th Street Northeast and now at an undisclosed residence on Columbia Road. The man has been getting away with murder and I mean that almost literally. You have seen how he taunted poor Howard Baltus to the point where Howard was beside himself from aggravated prejudice and harassment. To Rufus it's all a big joke, but a man of Howard Baltus' tender sensibilities takes such things very seriously. As should we all.

It is undeniable that Rufus has been treated badly, too. What is amazing is how adroit he has become at publicizing it. The day after he was interviewed by a reporter from the *Afro-American Tribune* the story appeared. Not on Page One exactly, though not buried in the classifieds either. Actually it would be difficult to bury anything in the *Tribune* because its total length is only eight pages, the last three of which are devoted to legal notices. The story on Rufus was headlined "Evicted Black Tenant Pledges Fight" and there was a subhead which said "Middle Name Takes A Stand." A picture of Rufus alongside his meager household possessions had a certain power. Rufus, as has been pointed out by Rufus and others, is ugly as an ape but he does have a splendid physical presence and he had stripped to the waist before posing. This was explained in the text by a quote from Rufus: "They took my house but I still have my beautiful God-given body. Praise the Lord." This a *non sequitur* of the first rank and shows the outrageous and unprincipled lengths to which Rufus will go for a little free publicity. Not that I blame the man but I do not have the slightest doubt that the RASTUS movement is doomed.

All right, enough of this stuffy analysis. You would just as soon move on to the juicy parts, right? Like what's going on personally between me and Super Stud? So far, damn little. Because Rufus is taken with his resistance effort far beyond anything I would have imagined. After the *Tribune* story he repeated the phone calls he had made the day before and damned if he didn't talk the *Prince George's Gazette* and the *D.C. Daily* into sending reporters to the alley at 757 a few days later. Rufus met them there at four o'clock and repeated his tale of woe: how he had been evicted from the property and was now living in his taxicab in the alley and would continue to do so until something was done for the poor, oppressed people of 6th Street. The man from the *Gazette* said he didn't think his editor would go for it because it was getting warm and nobody could freeze to death in a taxicab. But the *D.C. Daily* sent a photographer along, and his picture of Rufus huddled under a blanket on the back seat was truly touching. The paper put the picture and the story in its City Life section the next day. The headline said, "It's In The Back For Evicted Black." All well and good. Except that what the poor trusting readers of the *D.C. Daily* don't realize is that Rufus isn't living in his cab one bit beyond the time it takes to be interviewed and photographed. As soon as he quits driving for the day he drives here. After the three interviews and the two stories, Rufus settled into a routine which has persisted now for better than two weeks: Every morning he calls the papers and the TV stations and every afternoon at four he drives up to 757 and waits for somebody to come around with a notebook and a camera. So far there has been no further interest but Rufus says it's only a matter of time before the *Washington Post* and the *Washington Times* and the TV people get with it.

I have been extremely generous about Rufus' accommodations. I gave him the front bedroom, the one where Howard was insulted by one of the participants in a coke snort. It has a decent bed, an adequate chest of drawers, a full-length mirror and a very fine old painting of Leda and the Swan. It shows the two combined in a most intimate and imaginative way. I don't imagine many people have considered the technical problems an artist must overcome in showing a swan screwing a woman but he has managed the thing very nicely and should other of his works come on the market I would be be pleased to consider them. A grizzly bear and an Amazon, for example. What would you think of that? No? It doesn't interest you? Very well, I force my tastes on no one.

Rufus dominated the room and the rest of the house immediately and completely. "Geraldine," he said, after he had installed his typewriter and his minimal wardrobe, "you is one sweet momma for lettin' me crash. But I gotta make it plain I don't want the maid or anyone else messin' around with my things. I be doin' a lot of writin' now and I can't have my papers get all screwed up by somebody with a dust rag and a vacuum cleaner."

"Maid?" I said. "And just what gives you the idea this place has a maid? If you want your room cleaned, do it yourself."

"And another thing, if there is any phone calls tell 'em you ain't seen me in a week. I ain't supposed to be spendin' the nights anywhere but in the taxi and if the word gets around I be here it could destroy the entire RASTUS movement."

"Anything else?"

"Yeah, when does you turn on the air conditionin'?"

"Anything else?"

"You got a small desk anywhere around? It ain't easy typin' on the floor."

"Anything else?"

"A better readin' lamp?"

"Rufus, you can hardly read. No. Anything else?"

"Is it okay if I help myself to the refrigerator? When I come in at night I like a little snack—coupla eggs, six strips of bacon, toast, coffee. It don't amount to much."

"Rufus, let's get this straight. If you want to stay here okay, but you can't freeload. With breakfast and your little late-night snack the price is a hundred bucks a week. Cut out the food, the price is fifty. Either way I'm giving you a bargain. Take it or leave it."

Rufus yelped. "Geraldine, you takin' advantage of me. But you got me over the barrel. Okay, I'll sign up for the food included."

It is interesting how a landlord-tenant relationship can color any other. I don't think either Rufus or myself has had any particular difficulty with the lawyer-client situation; my advice has been sound and if Rufus has chosen to ignore it, that is his problem. As for something sexual between us, his live-in status seems to have produced a surprisingly discouraging atmosphere. You may have gathered I would not be exactly averse to something springing up between us. I was serious when I told him that shacking up with me didn't mean he could count on having my great statuesque body whenever he chose. But I am accustomed to getting full benefit from it and at first there did not seem to be any compelling reason why it should be deprived the sensational pleasure I know goddamn well Rufus could provide. His brief presence has already had an inhibiting effect on my usual routine—which is to invite somebody over several nights a week or an occasional afternoon when it is quiet in the office. But when Rufus is there or when he may barge in at any moment, it definitely detracts from the easygoing mood I like when I am doing sex. Since he is both the cause of the difficulty and an obvious solution, I did not really expect that much time would elapse between his moving in and our making out. Strangely, the way it has been around here so far I wonder if it will ever happen. Because the truth is I am becoming terribly conscious of the economics of the situation: the heat, the hot water, the air conditioning, the telephone, the consumption of food and the general wear-and-tear on the premises. I resent it all to hell. Feeling that way, the idea of giving even more to the guy is the last thing on my mind. There is also the matter of the usual frictions that arise when two large people and one large dog occupy one small house. It is one reason, I suppose, I have never actually lived with anybody. I consider myself remarkably generous to my friends and God knows I have wined and dined and partied them far in excess of any reciprocation. Fine, it gives me a good deal of pleasure to do so. But I have the feeling that Rufus is taking advantage of me and that at the first opportunity he should be booted out on his ass. It is not just the money, although I realize now I did not accurately estimate the costs; he uses the utilities with the abandon of an oil sheikh creating a demand for his product. I will be patient another month at the most and then he must go. There are plenty of reasonable apartments in far-out Anacostia and Rufus must be made to understand he should rent one as soon as possible. Seven Fifty-seven 6th Street Northeast is gone forever. In the meantime, in case you may think I have been coy and evasive, I have not. Neither Rufus nor I have made a pass at the other. I for the reasons stated and Rufus because—well, it's hard to say exactly but I suspect he feels a certain timidity and lack of confidence when it comes to seducing a white woman. If it were rape, no problem. But making love—ah, a black man can feel guilty about that: he is the descendant of slaves; I am the descendant of slave owners. Well, I am not literally, but you get what I mean.

Cancel some of what I said. Yes, since I wrote the above the week before last there has been a change in the relationship. It sounds more significant than it really is in my opinion but I suppose the jury will decide. It stems from what happened last night, a Saturday. Lucius DeTroit threw a party at his place in Georgetown and Rufus and I went. Lucius lives in a rowhouse on P Street. Forty years ago it wasn't much different from the 6th Street house before the restoration process began. Now you couldn't touch it for less than three hundred thousand bucks. We were both specifically invited: me directly by invitation and Rufus by a postscript that said if I knew how to get in touch with Rufus he was invited, too. I understood, of course, that if I wanted to bring another man as a date that was fine. I am careful about going to parties with an escort because I never know but what I might find something there that captures my fancy more than the guy that brought me and so would prefer to take the former home. Or be taken home. Though not often. My place is more conducive and also there are sex toys in some number. I don't think this has so far been mentioned but it is true. I have a goodly supply of vibrators and dildos as well as a few whips and several pairs of patent-leather high-heeled shoes for those who are bored with the mundane and seek the exotic. It is a sad commentary on our society that straight fucking is pretty much discredited. Eating is the big thing these days, as I'm sure you know, but there is a sameness even there. Isn't there something better? Must we be content with thirty-second orgasms the rest of our lives? Can't the thing be extended indefinitely? What lies beyond the horizon? Surely American technology is capable of improving on the basic built-in central nervous system which has come down through the ages hardly changed at all.

I went to Lucius' party in my restored Jaguar XK-12, the most phallic car ever built, and Rufus in his cab. I arrived at about nine. It was nearly ten when Rufus showed up, after work, in a very good mood and looking quite presentable. He was wearing a tan corduroy suit and it was apparent he had shaved and bathed in a lot of my expensive hot water. Lucius' place is typical Georgetown gay: plenty of trendy paintings, antiquish furniture and about fifty plants. The way you can tell it's a gay's place is because there is never any bathroom freshener in the bathroom, gays being of the belief that their shit doesn't stink. Another clue is that a blown-up copy of the Declaration of Independence hangs on the wall above the bed. And yet another clue if you still have doubts is that photographs of Mother When She Was A Young Woman are all over the mantel or the piano. They're supposed to have despised their mothers but hate to admit it. Thus do they show a false front to the world. Lucius' place is unusual in that he has a painting of a nude woman in his bedroom but it is only old September Morn testing the waters and she is about as sexy as a sardine. Lucius is currently living alone. I could tell that because when Lucius has a live-in lover he goes to some lengths to conceal that fact. The usual way is for the lover to arrive late at the party through the front door and to leave early, with much small talk between the two as though they hadn't seen each other in simply ages when in truth they probably spent half the afternoon arguing about the menu. It would very often descend, I imagine, to sophomoric exchanges on the order of, "Well, if you don't want ice cream, it's perfectly all right with me to let 'em eat cake. Or cock, as the case may be." Great peals of laughter following such repartee, undoubtedly.

Rufus' good mood was the consequence of his having used his sob story to good effect on a fare. He said he had picked him up at National Airport, took him to the Madison Hotel on 15th Street—one of the more expensive places—and on the way asked him if he was an editor, a reporter or a TV anchorman. Because if he was, Rufus was available for interviews on a story of tremendous importance. The man said no, he was only the president of an oil company but he would like to assist in any way he could and would fifty bucks help? Rufus took it. As we are seeing more and more, the man is utterly without shame.

He brightened even brighter when he discovered an important editor was at the party. The guest list was made up largely of Lucius' fancy neighbors. It included a couple of congressmen, a United States senator, a cabinet secretary, somebody on the President's staff, two lobbyists, several of my colleagues at the bar and a Formerly Very Important Person. There is nearly always one such, a man who was Big in the Roosevelt Administration and who takes the most comfortable chair in the place and holds court. They are harmless, these old parties, but they have a grip like a trap and if you approach intending only to shake hands and be polite for a moment you may find yourself stuck a long time. It is no use saying "Excuse me, there's an old friend on the other side of the room I haven't seen in ages." They are invariably deaf and are likely to respond with "Wages? Yes, that was a problem in 1939 but this is how we solved it. . ." and you are stuck for another ten minutes. My strategy is to avoid them at the outset and keep moving. The bar is the safest place because most are too feeble to totter even that far and must have their drinks brought to them. But not by me. It was at the bar that I bumped into Horace Endicott. Yes, I did. I stumbled after my third small scotch was served and I am afraid Mr. Endicott got badly splashed. He was a good sport about it and when I offered to have his suit dry-cleaned he politely declined.

"Oh, I've heard of you," he said when I introduced myself. "You're the attorney who let some guy in a jury box feel her up." That was a long time ago and it is only rarely that somebody remembers. "I don't wonder that you won your case. Anybody not favorably affected by handling those babies would be impartial and fair beyond all reason." He looked them over. "Horace Endicott," he said. "Dirty old newspaperman."

Horace Endicott is the Roving Editor of the *Washington Post*. The Roving Editor ranks well below the Executive Editor, the Managing Editor, the Deputy Managing Editors, the Editorial Page Editor and the Deputy Editorial Page Editor but is definitely superior in authority and prestige to the Assistant Managing Editors, the National Editor, the Area Editors, the Columnists and all the Reporters. The Roving Editorship is the common reward for a good and faithful servant not destined for the top but worthy of flattering recognition toward the end of a career—albeit without any more money or a bigger office. Endicott is your typical Ivy League graduate, Washington version, always slightly rumpled in the suits and not terribly well combed but lean as three miles of daily jogging can make and confident beyond belief. He is getting on toward age fifty I would imagine, though a lifetime of the best food and drink and a tendency toward the inscrutable have kept his face from developing the wrinkles a lesser-nourished or more-expressive type might have to suffer. He is good-looking on the order of a young William Holden or an old Richard Burton, which is to say he is a beautifully bland WASP type whose features will remain nicely proportioned forever. Have you noticed how the Jewish and Irish nose tends to expand with age? Not Horace Endicott's. They have always bred for beautiful, straight-edged noses in his family and his is the perfect example of what can result if one is careful about such things.

There is a directness about journalists which in some circles has given them a reputation for ill-bred nosiness. I don't mind. When Horace wanted to know the state of my practice, the location of my residence and the extent of my social life I told him. Small talk is a prelude to intimacy and is quite necessary if the social forms are to be observed. I mean, you simply can't leap into bed with someone without having spent a decent prior interval inquiring about the other's favorite food and restaurant and movie. To do so smacks of gross carnality. I think the quickest I have ever done it was forty-five minutes after introduction, which is certainly rushing things but which is explained by the fact that the other party was a deaf-mute while I have never gotten around to mastering sign language. What else could we do? With Horace I didn't imagine the interval would be very much greater. My decision to screw or not screw is usually made in ten minutes, a time necessary to ascertain if the subject is healthy ("Jog? Swim? Tennis? Boomerangs?"), interested ("Would you mind telling me something? You strike me as a person desperately in need of relief from sexual tension. Am I right?"), and available ("You say that slim and lovely creature in the designer dress engaged in intense conversation with Senator Hastings is your wife? Too bad. I've had my eye on the senator the whole evening").

Horace passed my test with the highest marks and also satisfied me on the little extra query required by the times. I learned it in *Time* magazine and what you do is lightly put your fingers on the wrist of the subject, look into his eyes and murmur, "You'd better tell me the truth before it's too late. You've got herpes, haven't you?" A guilty expression and a sudden surge in pulse rate should not be ignored. Horace said he hadn't had a blemish in that area since diaper rash. I was satisfied. Still, I didn't say "Let's get out of here as soon as it is politely possible." No, my loyalty to clients does come first in spite of what you may have read elsewhere and I realized that my new friendship with Horace could help Rufus. Rufus had greeted me on his arrival in a manner somewhat outside his ordinary. There was the usual pat on the ass and the "Hiya doin', babe?" but after that he leaned toward me and gave me a kiss on the cheek, a sign that Rufus is making some progress at sophisticating his manners. Do you suppose the day will ever come when Rufus will eschew ass patting entirely and limit himself to "So nice to see you," "You're looking well" and "That dress is a dream. You're absolutely adorable"? It would be nice, wouldn't it, to see that hulk show some of the refinement his ancestors achieved when the top few were excused from the fields and taken up to the big white-columned house, there to be trained as genteel and obsequious butlers and parlor maids. That is an aspect of slavery which has never been given its due.

After Horace and I had felt each other out, I looked around for Rufus. He wasn't on the ground level but the back garden is a big attraction in Georgetown houses and with Horace in tow I headed for it. The garden couldn't have measured more than fifteen by fifteen feet and featured those ornaments which are *de rigueur* in Georgetown: a statue of a little kid pissing into a pool, a stand of bamboo trees, a fruit tree, a bed of flowers whose sunlight requirements are minimal (because privacy is very big in Georgetown and the cedar fences are high) and a small wrought-iron table and a couple of iron chairs.

Now you may not believe this and I am humiliated to be in any way connected, but on one of those chairs—which at best was designed for a husky hundred-and-twenty-pound faggot—stood Rufus, and I'll be goddamned if he wasn't making a speech. You can imagine what it ran to: "the poor, oppressed people of 6th Street, the honkey white block busters, the absentee black owners and we got no place to live in but taxicabs." Honestly, I was embarrassed as can be—which is admittedly not much by the usual standards but still I reddened more than a little. Had it been my home and my party I'd have slugged the son-of-a-bitch. I looked around for Lucius, who if he were a real man (but of course he isn't) wouldn't have permitted such outrageous behavior one minute. I'll be further goddamned if he wasn't right up in the front row hanging on Rufus' every word. Hell, he wasn't the only one; they all were. Everybody in the garden was totally mesmerized. Okay, there is the novelty and shock aspect which accounts for some of it. Georgetown parties are strong on politeness and a variety of points of view and if you keep your voice down and don't drink to the point of obnoxiousness you can say almost anything without causing the slightest unease. But here was this great gorilla carrying on like a soapbox preacher at Dupont Circle, a park-like place with a fountain and marble benches where tolerance for Washington weirdos is high beyond belief. Only Rufus wasn't just being tolerated, they loved him. The words poured out of him, the sweat poured out of him and the charisma poured out of him as powerfully as from Martin Luther King, Jr., on one of his better days. Then he stepped down to cheers and applause and if I hadn't caught his eye and given him a really serious frown I think he might have passed the hat.

"Rufus," I said, barging through those who remained for the question-and-answer period, "could I pull you away from your admirers a minute? There's someone you should meet." And I grabbed an arm and worked him off toward the corner of the garden where I had momentarily planted Horace. "For God's sake," I said on the way over, "this is supposed to be a party, not a fund-raising. Okay, they liked you but tommorrow they'll forget you. Now this man has the power to generate more than a few cheap cheers."

I made the introductions and said they both looked a trifle thirsty, I would bring something from the bar. Horace showed a flicker of annoyance. I mean, one minute he had his hand on the hand of his next conquest and the next he was having it crushed by this towering monster who wanted to conquer him. Yes, that is the confrontational impression Rufus so often gives, more is the pity. He would do much better to emulate his cap-tipping forebears. Rufus said, "Double scotch. Dewar's White Label if they have it. Nothing lower than Johnny Walker Red." Oh, God, he is superficial beyond belief. Horace said, "White wine, a glass of Perrier, anything. It doesn't make much difference." I like a litle indecision in a man, it does humanize him. Would that Rufus were more like that. I traipsed off to the bar and placed my order. Lucius was there, telling one of the two bartenders to go into the kitchen and help the caterer with the serving of supper, and it was apparent Lucius had been doing spot checks on the stuff he was serving his guests way more than was strictly necessary.

"Lovely party, Lucius," I said. "Or it was until Rufus showed up. What got him started?"

Lucius drinks—has that been revealed earlier? He has to go to the dryout farm several times a year. Lucius is wealthy. Has that been revealed? His great-grandfather was a railroad and steel tycoon. Inherited money allowed his parents to send him to an exclusive young men's boarding school and to a very fine university, Georgetown, and to work or not as he wishes. Lucius is gay. Everybody has revealed that, I'm sure. It stems from his time at boarding school where he learned masturbation, assholing and cocksucking. And Lucius is something of a weak-kneed ninny.

"I beg your pardon," said Lucius, who was in his cups to the point of nonrecognition and incoherence. "Who is it? Anybody I invited? Not that it's important. Now that you're here we can be friends even if you've lost your way looking for a better party down the street, right? How about it? Are you my friend? Are you?" He made a supreme effort at focusing. "Of course, Geraldine, it's you, darling, so nice of you to come. How have you been, darling? I can't tell from looking at you. It seems so dark in here, terribly dark in here for only ten-thirty at night, which is what it's supposed to be if you can believe this cheap watch." He contemplated his wrist. "Now this watch, this very cheap watch, once played a part, a very cheap part, in an encounter I once had, an encounter of which I am not proud at all, not at all, and which I thought I had swept from my mind until this very night when the other party, this person who took my watch—did I tell you he took it?—well, this very same person, whom I have avoided all these past months except where business required and then only briefly, well, this very same person, this other party I'm referring to, this man, yes, he is a man, God is he a man, well this man, this god I invited out of some minor need to see him again, well, this goddamned god asked me for a little time to talk to the guests about something he was sure would interest them and I said well, why not, why don't you just step right up on this chair and I will ping a knife against a glass to get their attention and you can go right ahead, say whatever is on your mind because, well, the way I feel about you there is nothing I wouldn't do to please you and he did, he got up there as you have seen and I did try to fight it, I have always fought it though why should I fight it, what is the point and when he was up there looking so big and powerful and dynamic, he is dynamic, wouldn't you say, probably one of the ten most dynamic men in this city, God, I realized I wanted him, wanted him more than ever, wanted that goddamed big cock of his up my—in my

—wherever the hell he wants to put it and the moment the last of you goddamed freeloaders got the hell out of here I would have done it, I would have sucked that lovely thing to death, its death, my death—Oh, God, do you realize what's happened? Do you? Do you know what's going on right this minute in my own garden, right over there by the cherry tree—there, right there where I'm pointing—that goddamned Horace Endicott is stealing the man I love."

Gays do run to excessive jealousy, that is a documented fact. They are suspicious of the most innocent encounters. I wouldn't touch one in the presence of the other with a mustard plaster. You can get your eyes pulled and your hair scratched and it simply isn't worth the trouble. The trouble, of course, is very often handsome, trim, witty and an excellent dancer. I do not have any difficulty in attracting straight men, but once in a while I do make a minor-league effort to entice some beautiful hunk of an aberration. The idea is to straighten him out—in more ways than one—and to condition him so his orientation toward females becomes manly and aggressive. It is the sorority instinct in me. It never works. It has been said often but I will say it again for the benefit of any dedicated but naive women who are trying to make born-again men out of hard-core cocksuckers, you are wasting your time. Speaking of cocksuckers, I wonder why it's perfectly fine to have your cock sucked by a woman who does not see her dentist regularly and who may not have brushed her teeth since the day before yesterday while a really substantial segment of the population gasps with horror if it's done by a man who brushes after every meal and is a conscientious flosser? Can the cock tell the difference?

"Lucius," I said, "for God's sake stop worrying. Horace and I were fooling around at the bar a little while ago and I assure you he is not interested in Rufus. At least not the way you are. If he looks slightly erect—and yes, I think he is—it's only the residual effect of talking to me. Well, I better not let him shrink too much more."

I returned to the garden with the drinks. Rufus was smacking his left hand with his right fist in a most emphatic way and Horace was taking notes. All newspaper people carry notebooks; it is a rule.

"Here we are, gentlemen," I said. "A lovely hemlock and soda for you, Horace, and a double Chivas Regal for you, Rufus. It's not what I ordered but the host interceded with the bartender and this is what I was handed. Drink up because a buffet will be emerging shortly."

"Hemlock?" said Endicott. "What have I done to deserve this? I thought Lucius liked me."

"He does ordinarily," I replied. "But there are special circumstances which apply. Like this rabble-rousing brute on my right.

Rufus, hemlock is not the latest thing in recreational drugs in case you were feeling neglected. And it isn't in Mr. Endicott's drink. I made a small joke to make a point."

"Yes," said Horace, "And I get it. I hope you reassured Lucius. I'm completely hetero—though not quite so much as when we were rubbing around at the bar."

"Listen," said Rufus, in that overwrought way so typical of him, "if that fuckin' Lucius invited me to this party so he could suck me off, go tell him to forget it."

"Rufus," I said, "you are embarrassing Mr. Endicott and me. In polite society one does not refer to it as sucking. Sodomy, possibly, or oral sex. We deal in euphemisms—and one day when you learn the meaning of the word, you should too."

"Euphemisms my ass," said Rufus, scornfully. "I calls it what it is. If you wanna call sucking a cock sucking a euphemism, it's okay with me. But I ain't gonna do it."

"All right, Rufus, don't. You should stick with whatever makes you feel comfortable, no matter how uncomfortable you make everybody else."

"Listen, man," said Rufus, "I ain't been trained to be no diplomat. Like right now I'm gettin' goddamn hungry. When are we gonna get some chow?"

Yes, we could all stand some food, no question, and immediately after Rufus asked, Lucius, at the back door, answered "Now." Horace and I turned toward the house right away—"Come on, Rufus"—and were able to get choice locations at the head of the line forming around the dining-room table. It was not that we were all that nuts about what was displayed—your standard ham, turkey and roast beef, salad and rolls—but Horace and I had counted the guests and counted the chairs and realized that between the two there was a deficiency of fourteen. Such is the typical situation at such parties and leads to a fairly spirited version of musical chairs. While some people are content to picnic on the rug and others can cope with a knife, a fork, a plateful of food and a glass of wine while standing, I can't. Under my well-upholstered ass I like to feel a well-upholstered seat.

So Horace and I found comfortable chairs near the fifty-seven-leaf rubber tree which filled most of the bay window in Lucius' living room. Gays are as solicitous toward their house plants as parents are toward their children. Lucius has told me seriously that he budgets twenty minutes a day to their care and feeding. The rubber tree is his favorite and he actually does keep track of the number of leaves. Someone told him that once the tree has a hundred leaves you can tap it for rubber sap and sell your entire output to

Young's Rubber Company, which will convert it into Trojans. "The money is not important, but it's for a good cause," Lucius confided once. "Just another way I can contribute to zero population growth. Really, we gays have never been given the credit we're due for that."

While Horace and I worked our dainty way through the repast, Rufus, who had disdained to join us, sprawled on the majestic Persian rug which is the dominant feature of Lucius' living room and in his inimitable way proceeded to gorge himself and insult the rug maker. The man can consume food more swiftly than a garbage disposal unit in a kitchen sink. It stems, I suppose, from eating on the run while driving a taxi. It does not make for eating neatness, and soon Rufus' area was littered with small samples of everything on his plate. Why he does not use a fork is something I can't explain. He employs a two-handed approach: while one hand grabs at the food and raises it and stuffs it, the other is loading up. It is fascinating in a disgusting sort of way: the left hand rising, the right hand falling, the right hand rising, the left hand falling, the right hand falling, the left hand rising . . . and so on.

"I think he's a mess," I said to Horace. "What's your opinion."

"A mess, at least. But in truth I can't say I think that highly of him. What's your connection?"

"Strictly business. He's my client. He came to me when his house was put on the market."

"Ah, hah," said Horace. "And was it your idea to sic him on the distinguished Roving Editor of the *Washington Post*? With the hope, of course, that a sympathetic front-page story would be forthcoming?"

"No. Well, not exactly. Rufus doesn't have any trouble in attracting attention. A couple of the smaller papers have done him."

"Have we? If we have it's escaped me."

"Unh unh. Rufus called your city desk several times but nothing has come of it."

"Good. I must compliment the city-desk editors. If we responded to every kook that called to complain about some grave injustice we would never have time to cover the grave injustices that result from something done by the President or the Congress—or the thousands of other meatheads in and out of government who have a penchant for screwing the public. Speaking of screwing . . ."

"Certainly. Yes. But before we get around to the logistics, it really would be nice if your paper helped Rufus. He's a barbaric slob, I admit, but he's getting the shaft."

"Okay, I took a few notes. A reporter will get in touch. Now what was that about the fine print? My car or yours? Or shall we form a convoy and concentrate on following license plates?"

Now ordinarily I would have said, fine, let's finish the grub, thank Lucius and get the hell out of here, you follow me. But I suspected that Rufus' presence in the house would not be conducive. I hadn't heretofore told Horace that Rufus was my boarder and telling him now would probably inhibit the hell out of the poor man. And possibly me, too, though the thought of working out something orgiastic did momentarily flash across my mind. I dismissed it.

"Look," I said, "I'm not putting you off, becuse I'm sincerely interested. Tonight is simply not convenient. Tomorrow is. Here is my card. Come at one o'clock tomorrow and we can have lunch and each other. All right?"

Horace was crestfallen. Ah, it is flattering to see a man who's crest has fallen but who's cock is still on high. I checked his crotch. Yes, there was a good strong bulge. Tomorrow we would give it a workout.

I left the party twenty minutes later and just before I did I told Rufus he ought to think seriously about doing the same. "The longer you stay here the drunker you'll get and the more likely you'll be approached by Lucius. Maybe you wouldn't mind and maybe it would be worth it. As you can see, Lucius has influential friends."

"No way," said Rufus. "If that guy as much as smiles at me I'm gonna call the D.C. vice squad. You ready to go? I'll race you home."

I beat him by twenty seconds. Happy about that and also pleased that Handsome Horace would be coming tomorrow, I invited Rufus into the study for a nightcap. He poured himself four dollars' worth of brandy; what he left in the bottle for me wouldn't have stimulated a fly. I took off my shoes and flaked out on the sofa; Rufus took off his jacket, his shirt and his shoes and sprawled on the rug, his head supported by a needlepoint pillow depicting a shepherd, a shepherdess and a sheep engaged in pastoral orgy. It cost me two hundred bucks and I had certainly not bought it with the idea of having it cushion some kink-dome. But Rufus snatched it from the sofa, pitched it down and settled it under his head before I could complain. The thought of his greasy mop tainting my work of art sickened me more than a little. Does he ever wash his hair? The pillow will probably require an expensive cleaning. I am not all that ultra-fussy ordinarily but it is another example of how the Rufus occupancy has cramped my usual carefree approach to life. The man must go.

"Listen," I said after we had settled down, "I would appreciate it very much if you didn't show up here any earlier than six o'clock tomorrow afternoon. I'll be entertaining from about noon on."

Rufus laughed in a most salacious way. "That honkey from the *Washington Post*? You gonna go wild with him?"

"I was thinking about it, yes."

"No problem as far as I'm concerned. Hey, baby you done good. He practically guaranteed me a reporter tomorrow afternoon. If you wanta screw him, I sure as hell ain't gonna screw it up."

"Yes, well, I feel the need. My sex life has suffered since you've been here."

"Ain't it the truth. Mine, too. I ain't been laid in—well, jerkin' off ain't the best but that's about all I'm gettin'. I been tryin' to knock it off in the back seat of the taxi with Howard Baltus' secretary. So far she been deprivin' herself."

"The taxi? Really, Rufus, that is insulting. What does she say about a motel?"

"Nah, she say that too deliberate. Like I'm thinkin' she some kinda whore."

"A person of real sensitivity, obviously. Though what's wrong with God's good green earth?"

"Geraldine, I do not screw under Heaven. God can see."

"God can see you no matter where you screw."

"No, man, not though a roof. He's not Superman."

We went on in this unproductive way for twenty minutes. We said nothing profound or even terribly entertaining. It was merely post-party rambling, the time when the mind is not sharp and too much inclined to give utterance to any dumb idea that flits across it. I finished the piddling portion of brandy Rufus had left for me and opened a new bottle. I poured a little; he poured a lot. We drank, we dreamed, we hummed snatches of tunes long tucked away. We came to the time when it was necessary to make a decision: either we would roust ourselves and repair to our respective bedrooms or we would sleep the night through just where we were.

"How much you weigh?" said Rufus. "About a hundred and eighty? A hundred and eighty-five?"

"Huh?" I said. "Rufus, this is no time to be telling me I should go on a crash diet. I couldn't do very much by tomorrow afternoon anyhow."

"Nothing like that. I was just wonderin' if I have the strength."

"Strength for what? You want to carry me up to bed?"

"Baby, you jus' read my mind."

And where a moment before he had been somnolent, Rufus suddenly heaved up from the floor, came over to the sofa and snatched me up. It was caveman and Tarzan rolled into one.

"Auugh!" I shrieked. "What the hell do you think you're doing? Rufus, put me down."

For a second he looked at me the way King Kong looked at Faye Wray when he got his mitts on her the first time. Then he dumped me back onto the sofa—a good four-foot free-fall with two bounces before I settled.

"Well, it was a good idea," Rufus said. "Only I realized the moment I felt the full effect of your tonnage I couldn't get you across the room. As for the stairs, no possible way. Listen, you gotta be closer to a hundred and eighty-five than a hundred and eighty, you know that?"

I lay there all spraddled. "Rufus, my God, what's come over you?" It speaks well of my sudden poverty of expression to give utterance to a cliche. A brighter mind would have come up with something smart and memorable. "Are you out of your mind?"

I was in a rut. And I suspected Rufus wanted to.

"It ain't that. What I had in mind was—well, we both kinda zonked out from too much drinkin' and all. What I'm thinkin' is a nice hot shower. Fresh us up and make us feel better."

"Well, go right ahead. Only watch it on the hot water—which is something I've been meaning to talk to you about."

"Right, I know I been wasteful. That's why I'm talkin' about doublin' up. Two for the price of one. I'll scrub your back. And I promise I won't lay a finger on your front."

I laughed—a dismissive laugh, a drop-dead laugh, a you're-kidding laugh, a don't-be-ridiculous laugh, a laugh designed to put an end to all this nonsense right now once and for all. Then I stopped laughing and started considering. Why the hell not? What was the harm?

"I need two minutes to pee. And a minute to get my clothes off. I'll meet you in the shower in three minutes."

"Don't I get to pee, too? And I'm wearin' underwear, which is more than I can say for you. So I gotta have extra time for that. Make it five minutes and you got a deal."

We met under the pouring water right on schedule—two big people and a medium-size bar of soap—and we went to work on each other. I did his hair and his back and his chest and he did my back and my arms and my legs.

"You want me to do your face?" he asked presently. "Some chicks don't like soap on their faces. You one?"

"I don't mind. Go ahead."

He did my face—and my neck and my shoulders and since it would have meant an incomplete job otherwise, my knockers and my belly and the rest of it more or less hidden away. What the hell. I mean, what the hell. In a lifetime of observing male horseflesh, I must say that Rufus' body is a standout. He is spectacular when aroused, his thing being thick as my wrist and as elevated as a cannon. It pulsates as though it is conducting music. Not that it got to the point of internal crescendo and finale. I grasped the thing, true, and Rufus may have presumed I was going to guide it in. I didn't. I wasn't quite ready for that. But I soaped it generously, brought him close, kept him panting and moaning for a minute or two, realized that the hot water bill would be higher than ever if this continued much longer and gave him the final, triggering caress. It was a good, rousing orgasm and he was grateful. "Baby," he said, "baby, you the first white woman ever jerked me off. Oh, yeah." I've had better critiques but if it wasn't poetic it was at least heartfelt. Sincerity is important in such matters and I was pleased. And his hair was washed. Not that it changes anything. The man still has to go.

10

That awful black man can scream and curse and threaten all sorts of wicked mischief but I have paid dearly for the privilege of making an absolutely necessary statement at this point in time and I will not be denied. This will not take long. All I want is to defend myself and Howard against the vicious slander currently appearing on the pages of the *Washington Post*. I'm sure you saw the story in last Thursday's Metro section in which that Jackson creature was quoted as saying his eviction from the house on 6th Street was "heartless, cruel and utterly inconsistent with the democratic principles upon which this country was founded but which have never been fairly applied to blacks." Now who do you suppose wrote that? Not Jackson himself, surely. The last time I saw him he couldn't string two words together without interjecting "you know" between them. Disgusting American habit. I suspect it was one of the hack reporters at the *Post*. I have it on very reliable authority that they will create a quote if none is voluntarily forthcoming. I'm not at all surprised because you will recall that nasty business of several years ago when they had to return a Pulitzer Prize because the winner had fabricated a story out of whole cloth. Geraldine says don't blame her; she is not Jackson's writer. Geraldine says she still considers herself his attorney but only in the most casual way and just for the record. Geraldine is not to be trusted. I called her at home last week to invite her to a small party and when the ringing stopped and the phone was lifted, no voice was heard but I am very certain I heard Hardin's bark. I said "hello" several times only to be hung up on. I dialed again thinking I possibly had a wrong number. There was no answer and I know for a fact Geraldine uses an answering machine when she is not at home. Something quite strange is going on there and my feminine intuition tells me that awful Jackson is involved.

But to get back to the *Washington Post*, that bastion of yellow journalism. The Jackson story did not limit itself to an objective display of the facts, heavens no. For no good reason, both Howard and I were identified as the buyers. That alone is nothing we can complain about—it is a matter of courthouse record—but we do take the dimmest view of the way we were characterized. Howard came off as the "grandson of the founder of Banner Suits, Inc., and the son of Samuel Baltus, Chairman of the Board of Banner Suits and a member of the board of thirteen other corporations." The implication, of course, is that Howard is the pampered heir to great wealth and can write out a check for whatever he wants. Well, what if he can? Does the *Washington Post* have the right to comment on it? Is that serving the public? Whose business is it? I was identified as "an employee of classical-music radio station WCLS." I am definitely not an employee. The woman who mops the ladies' room is an employee. I am a staff announcer with broad discretionary powers in reference to program content and almost invariably I play whatever I please. There wasn't a single word about my voice being one of the most recognizable and distinctive in the entire Washington metropolitan area, not a word about my program's 30 share and not a word about its stranglehold on the listening habits of anybody in town who has the slightest inclination toward culture. I was that annoyed!

But that's not all. On Sunday there was an editorial. Frankly, I rarely bother with them. Howard likes to make love on Sunday morning before we play tennis. We have a long-standing reservation at Woodmont Country Club, a fashionable Jewish institution, for ten o'clock. Howard programs the morning to ensure we are always on time. He awakens at precisely eight o'clock without benefit of an alarm clock. He spends ten minutes in the bathroom and fifteen minutes making us breakfast. He brings it to bed and we have twenty minutes in which to consume it. Ten minutes are devoted to Howard's washing the dishes. That takes us to 8:55. Since dressing requires eight minutes and driving to the club another seventeen, we have exactly forty minutes in which to screw. Howard believes in prolonging sex as long as time permits and he has not the slightest difficulty in staying erect thirty-nine-and-a-half minutes. At thirty seconds before 9:35 he thrusts hard five times and erupts. Sometimes I am satisfied by then, sometimes not. Either way, we are at the court at ten o'clock on the dot. Howard's game is pretty good but mine is better and our score so far this year is seven matches to three, my favor.

I had dabbled with the paper last Sunday during breakfast and Howard's attendant chores, giving the Style and Show sections a quick skim. Neither mentioned me or anyone else I know and I put them aside after a few minutes. I do not read the comics, an American institution completely misnamed. I *did* read the front-page headlines but none of the stories because the radio station gets the entire wire-service output and that is enough for me. Howard brought the breakfast to bed just as I was finishing up the Sports section. Are you surprised that I am keen on sports? Actually I am quite athletic—tennis and swimming—and am disappointed that Howard is not more so because, frankly, it is something of a bore to beat him so regularly. He should spend more time at the Nautilus Club and get his body in better shape. I do appreciate a male body that is developed to its full potential, don't you? Broad shoulders and bulging muscles are not everything, of course. Any woman silly enough to be swayed by physique alone is asking for trouble but since it happens so often I suppose there is an inevitable quality about such things and one can fight it just so far. Not that I am in any way tempted. I can't think of a single man I know who has a knockout body. Well, that odious Jackson creature does seem exceptionally well-endowed the little I've seen of him but blacks are only recently out of the trees and that explains it. Now where was I?

Oh, yes, we had sex, played tennis, lunched at the club and returned home. I picked up the paper now sprawled about the bed and flopped down to give it a little more attention. I like to look at the clothes ads in the *Post* and to read what its columnists have to say about the new frocks. The editorial page somehow surfaced in the middle of my wandering and there it was:

A Continuing Injustice

The gentrification of slum neighborhoods has become so commonplace in Washington that it seems almost pointless to comment negatively on the process. Georgetown, where minions of the lowest economic strata once abided, is fashionable and expensive beyond belief. Foggy Bottom, where ugly gas tanks and an odiferous brewery dominated not many years ago, now ranks only a step lower than Georgetown but is many steps literally closer to the State Department, the World Bank, and the Kennedy Center and is consequently much appreciated by its well-to-do residents. Capitol Hill, once run down and shabby and still largely inhabited by working-class people at the lowest economic rung, is being rapidly upscaled, too. It does not quite have the variety of Georgetown nor the proximity of Foggy Bottom, but it boasts a certain charm and it is not surprising that people of means are choosing to live there. This is laudable. Not only do restored houses strengthen the District of Columbia's tax base, but it can be persuasively argued that when better-educated, more prosperous people move into a neighborhood it cannot help but have a beneficial effect upon the less fortunate who remain. It is sad, of course, that the poor people who are uprooted may have a difficult time in finding quarters as convenient and inexpensive. But progress cannot be stopped—nor should it be—out of individual considerations. The displaced eventually find other places as adequate as those they lived in before they were forced out and so suffer no permanent loss.

Recently, however, we have learned of a Capitol Hill resident determined to resist the conventional sequel to loss of house and home. He is Mr. Rufus Rastus Jackson and he is not going quietly. As recounted in these pages last Thursday, Mr. Jackson was forced out of his 6th Street Northeast dwelling after its sale. But Mr. Jackson, unlike the other renters in the house, is fighting his ouster in a most unusual way. He is a taxicab driver by trade and he has made his old taxi his new home. Where? Not in some dank garage or public parking lot but in the very alley adjoining the house where he for so many years parked when he was through for the day. And what does he hope to gain from this unconventional behavior? As Mr. Jackson so eloquently put it, "this property has been lived in by black people for almost sixty years and it is as precious to me as every arid acre to a Palestinian forced to move from it by ruthless Israelis. I am going to fight to regain it with every fiber of my mind and body."

It strikes us most emphatically that the intensity of Mr. Jackson's feeling should not be ignored. While we take a dim view of his declaration to "fight . . . with [his] body," the potential for violence in such cases should not be underestimated. Mr. Jackson and his neighbors are being violated every day and it behooves the D.C. Government and other appropriate agencies to take ameliorative action. It is a difficult situation and no obvious solutions present themselves. But something should be done.

Well, there you are, the knee-jerk, bleeding-heart liberalism of the *Washington Post* exposed for all the world to see. Oh, it it gives the appearance of being fair but it fools no one. Honestly, this town cries out for a newspaper with a realistic point of view. The

Washington Times is not the answer. I could never take seriously a paper run by the Moonies in spite of their professed hands-off policy because I have it from an unimpeachable source—Geraldine herself—that they have the oddest views about sex. Did you know that ninety-seven percent of the marriages in that great mass wedding they did several years ago in Madison Square Garden have not been consummated? Yes, they are all running around as virginal as babies and just about as unlikely to have any. The Reverend Moon has to approve personally before anything happens and he rarely does. I think he first requires that the couple bring in $50,000 from door-to-door sales. Honestly! The three percent who told him to go f—— himself were booted out of the church and were assigned directly to hell. Well, if they couldn't fornicate before, they were more or less in it anyhow so I see no great difference.

Heavens, I find myself nattering away as much as the others in spite of my promise to be brief. All right, I will now get on with it. As I said earlier, Howard and I were distressed about the unfair criticism directed against us but our consciences are clear and we are proceeding on schedule. Since the house became ours, the final restoration work is going quite well. We did feel it was necessary to take an exceptional precaution against any repetition of the sabotage that occurred earlier, and sturdy chain-link fencing has been erected around both the front and back yards. It is not attractive and once we are established and accepted within the neighborhood it will be removed. But until that happens there is the matter of the threats from Jackson. While I do not take them too seriously it would be foolhardy to ignore them entirely. Thus the fence. The publicity he seems capable of generating so easily will make no difference in the long run. Howard and I are the legal owners and that is that.

So I was not immediately upset when I first saw Jackson at the house the day before yesterday. It was after my 1 P.M. to 4 P.M. stint at the station. The decorator wanted me to make a decision on the wallpaper for the bathrooms. I parked my MG in the space once occupied by the Dudleys' old junkheap, went in, looked at the samples, made up my mind and left the premises. Just as I was shutting the front door, who should drive into the alley but the obnoxious you-know-who. He got out of the taxi, saw me, waved and yelled, "Taxi, lady? I got about fifteen minutes before my appointment. Where you headed?"

My instinct—and it is awful how that man can affect me at the most elemental level—was to respond with "None of your bloody business." Instead I said nothing, went down the front steps, walked the length of the front walk, walked the length of the sidewalk to the alley, turned left, walked up to Jackson and said "None of your bloody business." I mean, really, there are times when you had better say what pops into your head straightaway or to your undying regret you never will.

There is a raucous, whooping, go-to-hell quality to the man's laugh and with it are intermingled ad libs and sidebars—"ooohwee" and "oh, lord" and "ain't it the truth"—so you get not only the expulsion of a lot of air from a big chest but commentary as well. It is the most unsophisticated thing imaginable and I would not want to hear it often. But I can understand how its exuberant, supremely confident and almost overwhelming tone could make some people think he has the world by the short hairs with a downhill pull. A disgusting phrase but so apt in his case.

"Baby, you give me the best laugh I had today," said Jackson. "Tell me somethin', how come you always so pissed off at me?"

If he doesn't know by now, nothing I can say will make any difference.

"Mr. Jackson, honestly, Howard and I have been patient. But we can fight back. Don't push us."

"Hey, baby, I ain't pushin' at all. I'm just lettin' the people know the bad things been goin' on around here. The people got the right."

"How about the people's right to know you're a phony?"

"Me a phony?" A taken-aback, essence-of-innocence expression appeared. "Whattya talkin' about? I'm just a natural man, tryin' to make it the best way I can."

He said that with the disarming air he can affect on occasion and if I didn't know the truth about him I might have been taken in. I was not for a moment, I assure you.

"Mr. Jackson, you're not only phony but greedy and unreasonable as well. Instead of complaining to the newspapers about how the country hasn't been fair to blacks, why in the name of God haven't you done something to improve your lot on your own? If you can believe the newspapers—and I don't necessarily—you are almost literate. If you try hard, apparently you can speak proper English. What I don't understand is why you're content to drive a taxi. I am sure there are plenty of blacks no more intelligent than you who have struggled and climbed out of the ghetto. Why the hell haven't you?"

That was a pretty little speech, the delivery of which gave me enormous satisfaction. There is nothing better for generating a feeling of righteous superiority than telling somebody what he should do for his own good. We must exercise a degree of restraint where our friends are concerned, of course, otherwise we would soon have no friends. But when it comes to a sworn enemy who has left himself wide open, stating the truth of the situation no matter how much it may offend the recipient is tremendously gratifying. Except when it's someone like Jackson. The man obviously cannot be insulted. He laughed again.

"Viv, I gotta hand it to you, you one smart cookie. Only you wrong about one thing. It don't take workin' to get out of the ghetto. You honkeys think workin' is the answer to everythin'. It's the answer only if you can't do nothin' easier. Me, I'm on to somethin' give me a shortcut. See, the newspapers are gettin' behind me, the TV next, the important folks realize they got to take a position on this—well, in no time at all this cat gonna be famous. When you famous, somebody come around and say can you write a book? Can you be on the talk shows? Can you rouse up the folks so they demand it, won't take no for an answer, you gotta run for public office, maybe mayor, maybe congressman—oh, yeah, they's a lot of possibilities when you the voice of the poor oppressed people of 6th Street."

I don't know about you, but I've heard that line about the poor oppressed people of 6th Street to the point where I am going to draw blood if I hear it again. There are poor oppressed people all over the world but we're not subjected to a never-ending harangue about them. We who have achieved a measure of success don't need to be scolded. It's the poor who need a good talking to, though it can all be boiled down. There are only two bits of advice which the poor need and they are well known: work harder and breed less. If I had my way, breeding wouldn't be permitted unless one or both had at least ten thousand in the bank. Work first, I say, then fuck.

There is no profit in debating with Jackson—as we all know, he is monumentally stubborn and unchangeable—though the pleasure I derived from telling him off a trifle was not diminished just because he did not have the sense to agree with me. Since further dialogue would have been nonproductive I dismissed him with a what's-the-use expression and my sniff which, when well executed, can convey displeasure as effectively as any words. My contempt and disdain must have withered the fellow but I did not wish to remain for an observation of results and I turned away and headed for the MG. I hadn't gone more than a few steps when into the driveway came this enormous TV van and right behind it a car and out of the car stepped Sarah Lou Sampson, the star reporter of Channel 8.

I know her from watching television, I know her from parties. She and I have developed a long-standing, low-key friendship. I always praise her work; she always praises mine. There is a lot of the good-natured casualness of Pearl Bailey in Sarah Lou. She is black but not excessively so and her features are regular and pretty and somebody has done wonders with her hair. She is always impeccably turned out from one end to the other. I know for a fact that TV stations budget a lot of money for clothes for their major personalities and I have always regretted that radio stations are not equally generous. Okay, I can do my show in blue jeans and sometimes do, but I would not think of appearing in public that way. As soon as I open my mouth almost sixty-five percent of total strangers will recognize me, so I must always look my best. Which is about as good as Sarah Lou at her best.

Sarah Lou affects a rapid-fire speaking style and she has a reputation for skewering the phonies of Washington with the intensity of Mike Wallace pouncing on some malefactor during "Sixty Minutes." "Hey, Vivian, baby, what the hell you doin' here? Your station send you to do an interview? You offen the music? Would you mind tellin' me where you got that yummy sweater? I'm having a few people around next Friday, how about you and Howard? You got time for a drink in twenty minutes? Say, you're not part of the story by any chance are you? They told me to look for a big black cat in a taxicab. You know him? Oh, okay, I see him now. Unhuh. You involved with him? Messin' around, are you? How's Howard? Howard know about it? Give me a dollar and I won't tell Howard a thing. That Howard is somethin' else. How come you cheatin' on that sweet man? Listen, if you and Howard are splittin' would you do me a favor, give him my telephone number?"

As you can see, Sarah Lou is something of a tease and I do not take her seriously. Actually I laughed—for two reasons. First, that quasi-black street talk Sarah Lou affects is for show. When the camera is on, her speech is essentially standard English though she is not beyond giving it a touch of ghetto so her audience can relate a little better. Second, the idea that there could be something between me and Jackson was comical in the extreme, which is why she said it, I suppose, because outrageous provocation is her method. Once she gets you upset and off-guard you'll say things you would give your life to recapture but by then it's too late because the TV cameras have done their work and the next thing you know you're on the six o'clock news looking foolish.

"Sarah Lou," I said, "so nice to see you. Yes, that's your subject. No, I'm not messing around with him. Friday is fine. Must dash. Goodbye."

"Now wait," said Sarah Lou, blocking my path. "Just hold it right there one goddamn minute. How come you rushin' off so fast, huh, how come you so urgent about gettin' the hell out of here when I ain't laid eyes on you for weeks. Where you been keepin' yourself, huh? God, you the best lookin' thing. It ain't fair that you so slim and slick when I got to work my ass off to keep it off my ass. Feel that." And she reached out for my left hand and pressed it to her right buttock. "I got more lard on me than a fifty-pound pig. Terrible. Now you wait right there, you heah? I'll do this mother in no time at all and then you and I can go have a cold one. Take a deep breath, place your hands on your hips and don't breathe and don't move until I come back."

By then the cameras and the sound equipment had been taken out of the van and somebody with the fussy look of a producer had approached Jackson and was getting him lined up for the first shot. It didn't take a lot of imagination to see the possibilities and by the time the cameraman said he was ready and the sound man had his equipment balanced, Jackson was posed between his old taxi and my new house ready to hold forth about either. Then Sarah Lou advanced on him and began her interview. I thought I might as well eavesdrop, not that I expected to hear anything new.

Jackson: ". . . right here in the back seat. It's the same sleepin' bag I used when I was in Vietnam. Oh, yeah, I'm a veteran. I don't make much of it because I'm not lookin' for a lot of unjustified sympathy."

Sarah Lou (looking skeptical): "Uh huh, can you get comfortable in there? You got enough room in there?"

Jackson (just telling it like it is): "Well, let me just show you. (He opens the door, climbs in.) There are three main positions (demonstrating): my legs draped over the front seat, my legs through the window, and my knees bent so I can keep everythin' on the back seat. It is all painful but I am not complainin' because it is for a good cause. I can stand it as long as necessary if it will only help the poor oppressed people of 6th Street. The poor people been shafted too damn . . ."

Sarah Lou (cutting him short): "What about cooking? You can't cook in there, can you?"

Jackson (just telling it like it is some more): "I have a charcoal grill in the trunk. (Out of the back of the taxi and opening the trunk.) Good for hot dogs, hamburgers and steak. Only I never have steak. (Small-joke chuckle.) Can't afford steak on a taxi driver's take-home."

Sarah Lou (more skepticism): "You don't exactly look undernourished. You getting help from your friends? They ever invite you?"

Jackson (self-effacing and diffident): "Oh yeah, but I turn it all down. If I started acceptin' favors from people, it wouldn't look right. See, I'm on a kind of hunger strike except I'm not exactly hungry because it wouldn't do any good."

Sarah Lou (not pleased with that): "How long are you prepared to continue with this? A week? A month?"

Jackson (long-suffering): "As long as it takes. RASTUS will stand firm as long as it takes."

Sarah Lou (I don't get it): "Rastus? Who's Rastus? According to my notes your name is Rufus. What are you, some kind of stand-in? Where the hell is this Rastus?"

Jackson (the moment for his big line has arrived): "Rufus and RASTUS are one and the same thing. RASTUS is short for The Resistance Against Sticking It To Us. Organized for the sole purpose of combattin' the unconscionable onslaught by rich white people against the dwellin's of the poor oppressed people of 6th Street."

Sarah Lou (losing patience): "You already said that. Why are you repeating yourself?"

Jackson (as to a child): "For emphasis and also so the people will know where to send the money."

Sarah Lou (boring in): "Money? What money?"

Jackson (times are tough all over): "These things take money. Lawyers cost a fortune. So RASTUS is forced to ask for contributions of any size, large or small. I have it on advice of counsel that it is all tax deductible. The address is right here—757 6th Street Northeast, Washington, D.C., zip code 20002."

Sarah Lou (scoffing): "But that's the address of the house—and you don't live there any more."

Jackson (gotcha on this one): "No problem. Just put on the envelope, care of the RASTUS taxicab. The postman and I have got it all worked out. He hides it under a garbage can."

Sarah Lou (going for the jugular): "Mr. Jackson, I'm going to level with you. I think you're pulling something here. Before I put this story on the air I'd want to be convinced you're honest. Does this RASTUS of yours keep books? Are there elected officers? Does the District of Columbia know you're soliciting funds? You got a permit? Who's your attorney? Mr. Jackson, just who the hell do you think you're fooling?"

Jackson (his composure and his dumb little speeches collapsing all over the place): "Huh? What? Now wait a minute. You ain't supposed to give me no cross-examination. You supposed to let me tell it in my own way. Free speech and everythin'. Hey, you sound like some District Attorney . . ."

Sarah Lou (impaling him on a pin): "What do you know about district attorneys? You got a record? You done time in Lorton? You been in the federal pen in West Virginia? Don't lie to me. I got ways of finding out."

Jackson (regaining his composure a fraction but inserting a measure of whine): "Miss Sampson, you're comin' at me like I'm the guilty party. You want to be accusin' somebody, how about your honkey white friend right over there? She's half responsible. Her husband is the other half responsible. Why don't you talk to her?"

Sarah Lou (getting her back up): "Sir, I'd appreciate it very much if you wouldn't tell me who to interview. My editor told me you been pestering the hell out of her to get some publicity. Now are you going to answer my questions or not?"

Jackson (subdued and contrite): "I don't have no record. Nothin' that amounts to anything, anyhow. Drunk drivin' once or twice and speedin'. Show me a cabdriver that ain't. (Brightening.) But I ain't spent a day in jail. How about you?"

Sarah Lou (magnanimous): All right, let's cut the comedy. (Turning toward me.) Vivian, run a comb through your hair and check your makeup. You're gonna be on the six o'clock news."

I know I should have fled to the MG or back into the house except that a shot of me running away to avoid confrontation would have looked cowardly. I could plainly see that no good could come from a debate in an alley. On the other hand it is almost impossible for me to resist the opportunity to face a microphone. It is, after all, what I do. So I primped a little and when I was satisfied I said, "Sarah Lou, if you want my side of it, would you at least pose me someplace else. I would prefer not to be associated with that damnable taxicab."

"Sure," said Sarah Lou, "why not. Fellas, let's move it out of here and get set up over by the front door."

The front door couldn't make a better background. The thing is a masterpiece of brightly varnished oak and gleaming old brass and it looks as solid as a drawbridge in an ancient castle. It is terribly British, somehow, and is a most satisfactory reminder that I am descended from a people who, until the Americans and the Russians got into the act, were admired and respected above all others. Howard was assured by Mr. Dumfries of Hilltop Home Improvements that the door once guarded the inhabitants of a "mansion of the kind we don't see anymore these days what with the high cost of labor and everybody charging a fortune for home maintenance. It's a crime is what it is." He should know. He told Howard that he would never regret spending twelve hundred dollars for it because it "would enhance the value of the property out of all proportion and also discourage anybody who is thinking of attacking the place with anything less than a battering ram." Goodness. Well, whatever its fiscal and defensive advantages it is marvelously suited as a backdrop for a slim, blond type who often regrets she did not give greater consideration to a life on the stage. Ah, the dreams of youth . . .

Sarah Lou (businesslike): "You ready, fellas? Okay, here we go. Now Mrs. Baltus, you've heard Mr. Jackson criticize you and your husband for buying this house and evicting him from it. What's your response?"

Me (sweetly reasonable): "Sarah Lou, you wouldn't have believed this place if you had seen it before. It was unsightly beyond description. Mr. Jackson and the others who lived here neglected it so badly it is a wonder that the health authorities hadn't condemned it as unfit for human habitation. It was terrible, really—an eyesore and a pestilence."

Sarah Lou (that bad, huh?): "A pestilence? You mean it had rats and everything?"

Me (earnestness in every word): "Oh, I'm certain it did. Because of the garbage. I'm pretty sure the residents never wrapped their garbage. Or curbed their dogs. Uncurbed dogs—well, they weren't just uncurbed, they were running free most of the time and you know as well as I that when proper precautions aren't taken, we see the creation of too many animals that nobody wants and nobody takes care of. That's the history of this neighborhood, I'm afraid—too much creating and not enough thought about what happens when everybody descends to the level of animals. I assure you that when my husband and I live here there will be real discrimination about such things."

Sarah Lou (not happy about this): "Now wait a minute. You're doing a lot of accusing there. Where are your facts and figures?"

Me (primly triumphant): "I only need one. Look at Mr. Jackson. A prime example of what happens when nature is permitted to run wild. I'm sure there hasn't been any thought-out, goal-oriented planning for the man since before he was born. Certainly not since."

Sarah Lou (pressing for motive): "Hey, let's slow down. You sound like you're getting racist on me. If you are, I gotta stop right now. We don't do racism on Channel 8 unless it's the other way around. If you have something nasty to say about whites maybe I can keep it in. Otherwise forget it."

Me (armed with truth): "I am not racist a bit. My husband is not racist. If we were anti-black we would certainly not be moving into the neighborhood. But our buying the house serves two good purposes: It will mean its restoration and it will eventually rid the neighborhood of a man who made the restoration necessary. If Mr. Jackson had maintained the property properly the old owner would never have sold it. Mr. Jackson has no one to blame but himself."

For an ad lib I thought it came off very well. I mean, I do feel comfortable with the English language. I looked into the camera as steadfastly as the President facing the nation over some dread crisis and I was genuinely satisfied that I had scored effectively against the rabble-rousing Jackson. And particularly because I hadn't descended to histrionics or name-calling or sloganeering or any of the cheap tricks Jackson is dependent on. I had used an irrefutable argument stated simply and precisely and I had won. I knew that Channel 8's six o'clock news would make me look good and I don't mean just in appearance. You couldn't blame me for looking forward.

My God, you'll never believe what happened next. Suddenly and without the slightest warning, that barbaric Jackson, who I hardly realized was part of the group and who I most definitely had not invited onto my property, swarmed up the front steps, clutched me about the waist—yes, actually put his filthy hands on me— snatched me four feet off the ground, ignored my shouts of "Let me down, you black bastard," moved to the new wrought-iron railing which had been installed at the sides of the landing, swept me over it and lowered me to the ground, none too gently. Then he turned back toward the camera, which you can be sure was still running, raised his fists, took on this horrifying expression and began screaming. Yes, screaming, like some gorilla in a zoo who thinks if he raises a ruckus and shakes the bars he will somehow escape.

"Don't listen to that bitch, how come you listenin' to that bitch, how come you let her talk that way, tell lies, what the fuck is goin' on? This is my house, this always been my house, don't nobody understand that? This house is where I was born. I was a little kid right here. My motha and fatha died right here. God damn! You wanna know why my motha died? Died of the cold. Died of the pneumonia. Yeah, they turned off the heat cause one winter my fatha was in Lorton doin' time. How could he pay from Lorton? So they turned off the fuckin' heat and my motha got sick—damn if she didn't get sick—sick so bad . . ."

His voice trailed off and his fists came down and he gulped a couple of times and he sighed very deeply and he began to cry. Yes, the great hunk actually broke down, lost his composure completely and cried like a baby. God, it was awful. I actually cringed to be part of it. And for what? I mean, why get so frightfully worked up over a silly old house. It's just a place with a roof and walls. Something you buy and sell. Why take it so seriously? But seeing Jackson so overwrought, for a few seconds I was very nearly sorry for him. But not long, because the moment I recovered from the brutal shock of being lifted, swung and dropped, I centered my necklace, straightened my sweater, smoothed my hair and ran up the steps to the landing. Jackson was in pitiable condition, still crying, with his great ugly head buried in his hands and these awful sounds of self-pity oozing from them. I didn't let myself get deterred by any of that, you can be certain, and when I struck him I gave it everything I had. My right arm, I am happy to report, reflects the strength developed from the tennis and the swimming. God, it was marvelous.

Sarah Lou Sampson and the producer pulled me away immediately after the blow landed and once they did I succumbed to the emotional release which I had held in check to that point. I burst into tears, but between the sobs I managed to say what I felt: "You bastard, you terrible, terrible creature, you scum, you filth, Oh God, you are the worst person, I hate you . . ." I went on that way for nearly a minute, not at all conscious of what the camera might be seeing and not caring. And so for a while there was the strange tableau of this great black man and this beautiful white woman crying their hearts out. Honestly, this stupid house had caused more trouble. I wonder how much it would bring if it were put on the market?

11

This situation has deteriorated into very nearly farce: my wife breaking down, Jackson breaking down, the whole bizarre episode on the six o'clock news and again on the eleven. Just because I have been restrained and dignified so far does not mean I am accepting all this with equanimity. I intend throwing out a few complaints of my own. In the first place I strongly resent it that I have become an object of ridicule. This I blame completely on Vivian. Because of what Vivian did on TV I am being talked about behind my back and you better believe I am angry about it. I have become so adversely affected that I find myself suffering from a marked diminution in my ability to cope effectively at the office. I have been careful not to bore you with the minutiae of my career and I do not intend to do so now. Suffice it to say my recent work has not been productive. This is particularly bad because as has been explained by others I do not serve in the government for the money. The money is the least of it. If I don't perform competently the President will ask for my resignation. I am a political appointee and he has the power. Being asked to step aside by my President is not something I could simply shrug off. I am a dedicated and committed public servant and hope to remain so for my entire working life. Being kicked out because I couldn't hack it would be an enormous blow to my pride. It isn't as though compassion should be shown because I might end up on welfare. That happens so often in Government. Some incompetent bastard can't cut the mustard any longer but he's kept on so his wife and kiddies won't sufffer. My wife wouldn't and I don't have any children so I could be fired without anybody's conscience being bothered one small bit. As for my wife suffering a little, at the moment I heartily approve. Vivian has been given strict orders to keep her mouth shut from now on. I am beginning to wonder about her. What in the world possessed her to submit to that interview? If anybody should know better, it should be she. I must tell you that the whole recent history has meant some serious trouble for the marriage. A real coolness has developed and I am beginning to regard her with a substantial degree of distrust. She did not approach the purchase of the house with my enthusiasm, I am well aware, but it seems to me that any normally supportive and loyal wife would back her husband much more strongly. Oh, I realize she presented a good argument on TV but did you notice how little she emphasized the gains to come out of the restoration and how strongly she dwelt upon the shortcomings of Jackson? She seems to be eternally confronting the man. From the very beginning there has been an excessive antagonism and I don't wonder that Jackson is resentful. If she were only not so goddamned high-and-mighty, so self-conscious about being this superior WASP person I am sure she wouldn't be always sniping at the man. In spite of my certainty that Jackson was responsible for the sabotage during the early work on the house, I refuse to hate him. Besides, he has for all practical purposes lost his battle. All he's doing now is fighting a losing rearguard action—for which in a theoretical way I do not blame him—but now that the house belongs to me I am hopeful he will soon accept the *fait accompli* of the situation and move his ass out of the alley.

In the meantime he does persist in the most annoying way. He has incited the neighbors to picket the place. From morning 'til night they parade back and forth in front of the house carrying threatening posters. "The RASTUS will win in the end!" one says. Another says, "This is a pure black ghetto. Let's keep it that way!" And another says, "We got enough black trash as it is. White trash ain't welcome!" The most arresting is "Don't mess with our houses and we won't mess with your spouses!" What a racist threat that is, this reference to the age-old myth that white women are somehow attracted to black men because of superior sexual performance. What decent white woman would want to sleep with a black? It would be like enjoying rape, which if you enjoy it isn't any longer rape, and if you did how could you live with yourself? I don't want to sound stuffy, but there are limits. I know dating between the races is fairly common and some relationships end in marriage but have you looked at the statistics lately? Very negative. Only a handful actually do marry, which proves there is a self-limiting factor one should not ignore. If mixed marriages were so great, if blacks made such great lovers, everybody would be doing it, wouldn't they? But as long as blacks are unwilling to make the great sacrifices and the great efforts they will always be looked down upon. I know what I'm talking about. Didn't my own grandfather come over from the old country without a nickel and no education? He worked and rose above it and my old man did even better. And I'm pretty effective, too—Harvard and everything—and making a real contribution in Government and married to a stunning woman who at the moment I'm hardly on speaking terms with but who is nevertheless the greatest piece of ass I've ever had in my entire life. Though lately, what with my upset over the house, I haven't exactly given it the attention it deserves. Or maybe it's the other way around, maybe Vivian hasn't shown an awful lot of enthusiasm. It's hard to say exactly . . . Well, once this house thing is settled and we're in it and all the furor dies down I'm hopeful Vivian and I will be as nuts about each other as we once were. I know she is basically crazy about me. Not that I want to take undue credit. I had a few breaks so I'm at the top of the economic and social heap. If your average black had done half as well he could be married to some high-class WASP just like me. That way he could have the guilt by association as well as the pleasure.

But to return to the posters. I don't take any of it too seriously because it is democracy and free-speech at their best and in truth it doesn't make all that much difference. Nobody is going to back down just because of a bunch of lousy posters. Certainly not me. It is simply a good way to let off steam without hurting anybody and I approve. As long as it does not interfere with the work still continuing in the house I couldn't care less. The workmen come and go without restraint, the new furniture and furnishings move inward in a steady stream and the house is rapidly nearing completion. Did I mention that two guards with police dogs from Capitol Security Corporation still maintain a twenty-four-hour surveillance? Now, of course, they are on the inside of the wire fences. The dogs patrol them as though they are assigned to a concentration camp. Their mouths can't penetrate the linkage enough to bite but they often bark and growl and snap and lunge at the fence. I confess it gives me a certain amount of guilty pleasure when the picketers rear back suddenly or shy away.

I went to the house yesterday after work. It is looking beautiful as indeed it should considering the expense. I am particularly proud of the marvelous work Mr. Dumfries and Hilltop Home Improvements have done on the fireplace. The bricks are perfect. The grime from the days of the old tenants has been completely removed and now the bricks stand revealed in all their splendid simplicity. But it's not just that. Mr. Dumfries has actually enlarged the mouth so that it is twice as wide as the old opening and though this modification required extra bricks, the new ones blend so perfectly with the old that even I can't tell the difference. There is a manorial flavor now which can only serve to enhance the burgundy velvet sofa and the velvet side chairs and the paintings. I discovered three old landscapes in a Georgetown gallery. They are by a painter not quite of the first rank but I think they are lovely and I was happy to get the three for only $11,500. They hang on the wall opposite the fireplace. Directly in front of the fireplace I intend putting down the bearskin rug from the apartment. You recall it was on that rug that I realized how important it was for me to possess Vivian and for sentimental reasons it will be in the new place.

The dining room is lifted far out of the ordinary by the crystal chandelier—all teardrops and spheres and elongated triangles—and it casts a glow more elegant than anything in the finest Georgetown restaurants. I should praise the bedrooms, too. The master bedroom has a new Louis XIV–style queen-size bed. I don't believe in beds too big. Too big and you can rattle around and there is a feeling of sleeping on a playground and though it is to be a playground of sorts I like the necessity for snuggling . . . (Jesus, Vivian and I haven't done it in a week. I hate to jerk off in the shower but until I get a little more contrition out of Vivian I'm going to deny both of us.) The walls and the ceiling are covered with tapestries depicting hunting scenes from the time of Louis. Again Georgetown and again a bundle. But what you can't tell and what is supposed to remain a secret even from Vivian until the right moment is that the tapestries have control cords. If you pull them, the tapestries are drawn like drapes and the mirrors are revealed: floor-to-ceiling on both sides of the bed and wall-to-wall above. So you won't think we're some kind of tapestry freaks, the wall behind the bed is covered with the standard and beautiful drawings and prints and paintings that are *de rigueur* for a restored house in Washington. Why you can't put up the parents and the old aunts and uncles I don't know but no one ever does. It is not chic and chic is king. Hung upon the wall into which the bedroom door is set is another collection of serious art. It emphasizes the historic aspects of the house: a photo of the corner firehouse with a horse-pulled wagon out in front taken in 1900, another of a bunch of scraggly black kids posing for a baseball team photo in 1927 and a third showing the Dudleys posing at the dwelling's front door when they had just moved in in 1952. You remember the Dudleys, they used to live on the second floor? They were receptive to my offer to buy some of the photos they had collected through the years as well as their beautiful cherry-wood loveseat. I did not take advantage of them. I had the chair appraised by an antique dealer and gave them ten percent more than the appraised value. The same for the pictures. I had a few words with them the day they moved out. It was the same day Jackson's things were piled up at the curb when he was evicted. Him I avoided. But I made a point of wishing the Dudleys well in their new quarters and expressed the hope that they would be coming back to the neighborhood when the house was restored so they could see the difference. I would have slipped a few bucks into Mr. Dudley's hand to help with the cost of moving their furniture but one cannot do that sort of thing these days without the recipient becoming highly insulted and I would not have that happen for the world. I respect Mr. and Mrs. Dudley an awful lot, really, and I am sorry about how things worked out for them. The Dudleys had the misfortune to be born fifty years too soon. They believe in honest labor and keeping a low profile and not hoping for the receipt of something they haven't worked for. I would not be surprised to find Mr. Dudley, if he were thirty years old today, working as a bank teller in one of the local banks. I know I'd be happy to keep some of my money there by way of encouragement.

As for the lower level where Sanford Williams used to live, it will be everything I hoped for: the magnificent bar, the billiard table and the outsize baby grand. Beyond those amenities are the horse paintings and the countryside scenes and a very good leather-upholstered sofa and a few leather-upholstered easy chairs done in a style that is a nice complement to the bar stools. It will have the exact mood I'm looking for: sophisticated casualness or casual sophistication, whichever you wish to call it. I suspect it will be the focus of the party. Not that I will object if they want to stay on the main level but most of the food will be down here and, frankly, some of them may not be too comfortable with the furnishings up above. Down here if a drink is spilled or some food is dropped it won't make that much difference. Down here I have decided on carpets. Upstairs it will be Persian rugs and French lamps and Irish cut-glass ashtrays and on the bedroom level in the room designated the den will be the Sony TV, the Betamax, a few first editions, an old mercury barometer and a globe of the world. These could be easily damaged if the guests were careless or obstreperous, so they will be encouraged to come down here to the lower level. To minimize any threat to the billiard table it will be covered with a heavy quilt I had made for the purpose and on it will rest a slab of heavy wood and the buffet. There will be two bartenders behind the bar and a paid piano player at the piano. I would just as soon the guests didn't play it that night in spite of the likelihood that there will be some among them with the facility. You can never be quite sure if strangers will appreciate a Bosendorfer and they may be careless about spilling drinks on the harp. To help with that little problem I will make certain the piano player understands that the piano's lid is to be down always.

What's this about a party? I don't want to make a big deal out of it but I have definitely decided to give a party for everybody on the block—both sides of the street—as soon as the house is completed and furnished. I've been working on the speech for the occasion. I prefer not to tip my hand quite yet because a lot of the content depends upon the situation as it will be then. I mean Jackson, of course, and how things stand from the point of view of the newspapers and the TV. You can rest assured, however, that I will say the appropriate thing. I feel a fine speech could do wonders toward ingratiating Vivian and myself with the neighbors. If we can't do that, then the purchase of the house and the additional expenditure for restoration and new furniture will have been in vain. The new house will be marvelous, I know, but if we can't be accepted, then the whole project won't mean a thing.

Along those lines I went out of my way the other day to shop at the liquor store on the corner. It is an unprepossessing place, heavy on beer and on heavy iron shutters that guard it when it is closed for the night. I would imagine it was built at the same time as the other structures on the block, about the turn of the century. I suppose it once served as a grocery store. It is the only business establishment on the block. One wonders why the District of Columbia zoning laws permit a liquor store so close to residences. Some money changed hands down at the District Building very likely. It is popular, judging from the number of customers in it the day I was. I don't imagine the neighborhood has ever stopped to think that it is unseemly for a liquor store to be situated where young children pass by every day going to and from school. Perhaps later on I can play a part in getting the neighborhood to petition for its removal. For the present I can give it some of my business and be well thought of for so doing.

"Can I help you, buddy?" It was this white man behind the counter. He had greying hair barbered in the crew-cut style preferred by retired Marine Corps master sergeants, small blue eyes a trifle strong on the side of suspicion, an unlit but well-chewed cigar and the surging belly of a man who has spent too much time drinking beer and not enough time performing the athletic wonders beer TV commercials associate with their product. His T-shirt carried the legend "I root with the Hogs. Go Redskins!" The Hogs are what some sportswriter with a taste for the picturesque has dubbed the offensive line of the Washington Redskins, a football team representing the city in the National Football League. "Got a special on Coors Beer. $9.33 a case."

I drink beer only after a hard-fought tennis match at Woodmont Country Club. Vivian is a very fine player, a superiority I attribute to the fact that she has more time to devote to it. While I must put in an eight-hour day, she never spends more than four hours at the station and so gets to polish her game as much as she wishes. The club pro says she could be the club champion if she only worked slightly harder. Vivian also drinks beer afterwards. She limits herself to half a glass. I am saturated with sweat from my exertions so I drink five times as much. I feel I am living up to the expectation of the beer commercials when I do, although I wonder if there isn't some kind of inconsistency here: the tennis burning off the calories, the beer putting it right back on.

"No, thanks," I said. "But I might buy a few bottles of wine. Anything on sale? I'm just a poor man so every cent I can save is important." I said that facetiously because if you look at my clothes and my hair styling you'll know immediately I'm far from poor. I said it as a joke. The man behind the counter didn't get it. "No, sir, we don't have no specials on wine this week. Last week we did. A jug of Gallo red was only $3.49. This week it's $4.79. Still a good buy."

I do not drink cheap red wine or any cheap wine unless it is at one of those wine and cheese affairs that are sometimes unavoidable in Washington. They are often put on by book authors whose publishers are too cheap to throw something better or anything at all. If the publisher won't spring for a decent party you can be sure he brought out the book because he figured the author's friends would buy enough copies to make it worthwhile. It's not a bad risk, since the average man by the time he has written and sold a book has three close friends and four hundred acquaintants. A little luck with the review and a possible mention in a gossip column and the publisher has made expenses. Your average small-time author is only too willing to plow his advance back into any unsold copies and if that happens the publisher comes out of it with a profit. Not to mention the purveyors of wine and cheese.

"I rarely drink jug wine," I said. "Is that all you have?"

"No, sir," the man said. "We have a good selection of imported wines. Right over there in that tub. Help yourself."

I went to the tub. There was Liebfraumilch and Zeller Schwarze Katz and Niersteiner Gutes Domtal and several other German wines priced at $2.99 a bottle. They are sugar-doctored specimens I wouldn't buy if they were giving them away.

"Not quite what I had in mind," I said. "How about Château Margaux 1980?"

Château Margaux is a moderately priced French Bordeaux in the $25-a-bottle class. The man behind the counter deserted it, advanced toward the tub and shuffled the bottles. "No, sir, I guess we're out of it. Don't get too much call for anything that costs more than five bucks. I could put in a special order."

"No rush," I said, "I'll let you know. By the way, my name is Howard Baltus."

"I figured," the man said. "Heard some talk about a man with that name. Heard him described. My name is Henry Wallace, call me Hank."

"Oh, you've heard about me? What have you heard?"

"You're the guy restoring 757, ain't you? Lotta talk about that."

"Really? And what's it run to?"

Mr. Wallace surveyed the premises. At the far end of the store where the help-yourself cooler was loaded with beer, two black men were engaged in a fairly spirited discussion on the relative merits of Miller and Miller Lite. Up toward the front Mr. Wallace's colleague, a black man with a neat Afro and an orange and yellow dashiki—vivid, really, and so perfect with black skin—was waiting on a young black couple who were not sure if they wanted a pint of sloe gin or a fifth of vodka. Another couple perused the wines in another tub, a collection labeled "Cheap Wine—Your Last Resort Til Pay Day" and two elderly black women near the liqueurs were arguing about whose turn it was to buy the blackberry cordial. "It's your turn because last time I bought two bottles with the money I won on the lottery." "And would you mind telling me who loaned you the money to buy the tickets in the first place?"

"If I was you," said Mr. Wallace, his voice dropping to a level almost conspiratorial, "if I was you, as one white man to another, not that I'm prejudiced or anything, but you're gonna be in the neighborhood and a customer and everything, if I was you—well, if I was you, Mr. Baltus, yessir, I would be goddamn careful."

My gut knotted the way a gut will. Why? Why does the gut tighten up when the ears get the bad news? Why does the pain and the fear and the tension settle right down there where the sulphuric acid is waiting to etch a whole series of ulcers? Why? You tell me.

"What do you mean? Why should I be careful?"

A black woman in her fifties entered the store before he could answer and approached the counter. Behind it were the pints and half-pints of the bourbon and scotch whiskies blacks seem to find most appealing, not realizing possibly that buying in the larger fifth and liter capacities is definitely more economical. Perhaps that disadvantage is outweighed by the smaller size which permits the stuff to be conveniently carried in the handbag or even the pocket if it is a man. A man who carried a pint in a pocket would be oblivious to the danger of what might happen if he skidded on the ice and fell.

"Excuse me, Mr. Baltus," said Mr. Wallace. "This will only take a minute."

He went behind the counter, reached up for a bottle of Virginia Gentleman Bourbon, put it in a brown paper bag, took a five-dollar bill from the woman, went to the cash register, rang up the sale, brought back the change, handed it over, handed the bag over and said this:

"How ya' doin'? Doin' okay? Want a lottery ticket with your change? How about I keep the change against the next time? You sure you can make it? You ever think about not drinkin' for a couple of weeks? You wanta wait 'til there's somebody goin' your way? No? Okay, be careful on your way out, don't forget there's a step."

This little exchange ended, Mr. Wallace returned to where I was still stationed at the wine-bottle tub.

"I don't know if you noticed it but that woman was not exactly sober. I ain't supposed to sell if they're not sober. So I use them questions to cover myself. Kind of like a cop reading his rights to somebody he just arrested. This way I can't get blamed."

"Well," I said, "that's decent of you. You have mostly black customers, I take it."

"Yeah. Sometimes a white guy but that's usually some cabdriver just happens to be in the neighborhood."

"Been here long?"

"Oh, about ten years. Since I retired from the Marine Corps. It's a good little business."

"Any trouble? You ever been held up?"

Mr. Wallace laughed softly. "Are you kiddin'? Of course I've been held up. Three times this year so far. There ain't a liquor store in the District of Columbia that ain't been held up at least once. Most of 'em way more."

"That's terrible. You ever been hurt?"

"Hell, no. I don't do anything that would get me hurt. They show the gun and I hand it over."

I shook my head sympathetically and tch-tched twice to show my concern. "Isn't it expensive? Insurance? The loss of a day's receipts?"

"Nah, it ain't really that bad. The Brinks comes around twice a day so there ain't a lot of money in the till. And when I call the cops and they show up with their sirens blowin' and all, it attracts quite a crowd. So I get some business out of that. Any guy that comes in here with his ski mask and his Saturday Night Special probably lives right in the neighborhood and after what he did he could use a drink. When things calm down he probably comes on back as his regular self and buys a couple of bottles so he can celebrate with his friends. So I get some of it back that way. I don't worry about it. It's kid stuff and I can live with it." He paused. "But you, Mr. Baltus—well, I don't know. What I hear ain't kid stuff at all."

Have you noticed how a certain kind of person loves to dramatize everything? Make a lot out of nothing? Read into it what isn't there to be read? Get everybody excited when there's no need? Gossips and alarmists is what they are and we should thank God for them because if you can arm yourself against every dire threat these people visualize you'll be prepared for anything.

"Mr. Wallace, I realize there's a degree of hostility in the neighborhood toward me. Not surprising. But the pickets and the posters are a nuisance more than anything and I try not to take it too seriously. Once we move in they'll learn to like us. As a matter of fact, we're planning on a great party for the neighbors. Give me a good deal and you can have the liquor order."

"Very nice of you, Mr. Baltus, and I appreciate it. I'm sure we can work something out. Only if I was you I'd be thinkin' about something stronger than liquor. Like rat poison, maybe, or something good against roaches."

Mr. Wallace is like so many people—impatient and too swiftly inclined to the violent response. There is no need. Nearly everything can be worked out.

"Why, Mr. Wallace, how uncharitable of you." I talk that stuffy way probably more than I ought but sometimes it is a convenient shield behind which I feel protected. It is the educated person's way of glossing over reality. If I had said, "Hank, goddam it, you are right, them motherfuckers ain't to be trusted one fucking bit" I'd have been committed to take an action entirely unsuited to my temperament. "Entirely unsuited to my temperament." God, what an expression. But it hides the truth, the truth being that if there's going to be trouble down the road I am already prepared to be scared shitless.

"Mr. Baltus, I know these people and what they're talking is nothing you should turn your back on—unless you're prepared to get your ass shot off."

I would have debated the pros and cons of the situation at some length, treating it dispassionately and intellectually because when one does the menace seems less real. But just as I was marshaling my thoughts, the door of the store opened and in burst the great shaper of 6th Street thinking, Rufus Rastus Jackson himself.

"Hiya doin', everybody?" he said as he crossed the threshold. "Hiya doin'?" It was the entrance of a star from the wings, sure in the knowledge that he'd be recognized as such and that all the characters assembled before him would turn as one, expectant that his great presence would have some profound effect on everything. "Don't nobody forget the meetin'. Tonight at the firehouse. Eight o'clock sharp." He spoke his lines like a town crier who is more than a little tired of putting out the same speech again and again but who knows that repetition is the big thing for ensuring a good turnout. That explains, I suppose, why he stormed in and sounded off without really checking his audience. Because he didn't see me right way and when he did I got the feeling that his invitation to "the meeting" didn't exactly include me but that I was somehow connected with it. A meeting in a firehouse? Well, a firehouse is a public building and since I intend involving myself with neighborhood affairs I decided right then and there that I would go.

"Sure," I said to Jackson, advancing toward him. "Is it the firehouse at the other end of the block? Casual dress, I suppose? Will there be refreshments? If so, I'd like to contribute. How about a case of beer? Or if that won't do it, how about a keg?"

This frontal approach is not really my style. I would prefer to work behind the scenes and through a lawyer. But I'll be goddamned if I'm going to let Jackson and the neighborhood plot against me without doing something about it. And if I didn't sense a plot, my built-in Jewish sense of paranoia had failed me completely.

Jackson seemed flustered but only for a second. "Howie, baby, how the fuck you doin'?" He was wearing a green leather cap of the style where the visor and leading edge almost touch, a white T-shirt emblazoned in red with "RASTUS RULES!" and blue jeans held up by nothing but hips. One of the really unfair advantages blacks have is their naturally athletic bodies. If Jews were born with bodies like that they'd be as dominant in professional football and baseball as they are in literature, theater and banking. If the Washington Redskins had a Jewish quarterback they could raise their prices twenty percent because if there is one thing Jews do well it is support their brothers. Did you know The United Jewish Appeal raises better than $80,000,000 a year, the bulk of which goes to Israel? What black national charity is there? None. With blacks they always look to the Government. Which means tax money, my money. Oh, I don't begrudge them something but it seems they could do a litle better on their own.

"Fine, Mr. Jackson," I responded. "How about you?"

"Hangin' in there, man. Hey, man, the meetin' ain't nothin' would interest you."

"Really? How so?"

"The meetin' is just for tenants. Owners would be wastin' their time."

"Oh? How so?"

"Owners ain't welcome."

"Aren't welcome? Why?"

"Hey, man, can't you figure it out? This is a meetin' for the neighborhood. What we're gonna do is figure some way to kill all the guys buyin' up the property."

Jackson said that with a perfectly straight face. For a second or two nothing happened except that fifty thousand volts surged through an electric wire in my gut. Then Jackson laughed, as though what he had said was funny beyond belief.

"Since you're one of 'em," he said, "it wouldn't be no surprise if you was on the agenda. Only you got to wait and see."

Jackson laughed some more and so did the eight customers. In the course of the dialogue between Jackson and me they had formed a circle around us. There is something terribly unsettling about the Black laugh—cackling and at the same time mocking and at the same time primitive and at the same time ominous. It is a laugh that can grow out of the most terrible situations. It is what erupts from two black teenagers after they mug a grandmother and escape down the alley. That's what was coming from the customers. Only not just laughing. As if on cue they all pointed their fingers at me and one or two crouched suddenly, as though they were about to attack a tackling dummy, and the biggest man outside of Rufus put his hand into his pants pocket and I had the distinct impression he had gripped a knife. It was unbelievable, like something out of a dream or an inferior movie. Then Mr. Wallace, who was still at the wine tub where we had been talking, left it and with all deliberate speed went to the cash register, turned its key, reached under the counter and came up holding a double-barreled shotgun.

"All right, enough of that," he said. "Let's break it up."

They fled like window-breaking kids confronted by a pissed-off householder. Out the door and down the street whooping and hollering, some with one bottle, some with two.

"Hey, look," I said to Mr. Wallace. "Was all that paid for?"

"Hell, no," said Mr. Wallace. "Thieving bastards. But I know 'em all. The next time they come around I'll just give 'em a hard look and add it to the bill. They'll be back. Ain't another liquor store in this area that handles Goforth's Gin, a family favorite since 1978."

12

Okay, this is Rufus in control again and tellin' it the way it is, man, not a whole lotta dumb bullshit like what Vivian and that lily-livered Howard puttin' out every chance they get. What happened at the house with the TV, it wasn't that way at all. Don't believe it, man. There are some goddamn funny tricks can be played after they take them cameras back to the studio. Came out I was cryin'. Cryin'? Man, I don't cry. Okay, I was maybe kinda choked up on accounta all the shit they been pilin' on me, can't nobody blame me for that. But cryin', bawlin' like Vivian was, no way. The thing is they got Vivian's voice mixed up with mine so it makes me sound bad. But don't you worry about it none, I sure ain't.

Anyhow, coupla things happened last week put a whole new ballgame on what's goin' on. The first item was that bitch Celia. Remember Celia, the one that got gangbanged down at Sanford's? I be go to hell if she don't come up to the cab right about the time I pulled into the alley for my daily fifteen minutes of waitin' around in case somebody wantin' to do an interview. Say "Hello, I been hearin' about you." Well, big deal, everybody in town been hearin' about me.

"Well, well," I say, gettin' outta the cab, lookin' her up and down. "See who the cat dragged in. What's on your mind?"

She wearin' a white dress ain't a bit like that gunnysack which was about all she had the first time she come to Washington. Looks pretty fine, I gotta admit. Her hair is straighter and she smell good and any damn fool can see she come around tryin' to make a good impression. It don't really surprise me too much. When you startin' to be famous everybody wantin' to get in the act. Lotta cats got the idea that suckin' up to success is a good way to get there. But I ain't gonna give it away. That bitch walked out on me once. I ain't forgot that.

"Rufus, honey," she say, "long time no see."

"Fine with me," I say. "Let's keep it that way."

"Rufus, how come you actin' so uppity? I come here to be your frien'."

"Frien'? You ain't no frien' of mine. Unless you bringin' a donation for RASTUS. In that case maybe somethin' can be worked out. Dependin' on how much. How much?"

"Is that all I mean to you, Rufus, money? Money ain't everythin'. I miss you."

I look her over pretty careful and she showin' some upset inside her, some of it damn near leakin' out her eyes and bitin' at her lips and makin' her look kinda miserable at the same time you wanta almost pat her, you know what I mean?

"Big deal," I say. "I ain't forgotten how you used to complain I wasn't good enough. And also how you took off in the middle of the night like you owed on the rent. Runnin' out like that spoiled my chance to say 'so long' proper. But I can say it now: Fuck you."

"They ain't no need to talk dirty," Celia say. "You ain't on the TV. If you was on the TV all that would come out would be a mess of bleeps. Be ashamed of yourself."

I looked at my watch.

"Celia, or Delia, or Ophelia or whatever the hell your name is, why don't you just buzz the fuck off? I expectin' a reporter any minute. I don't want him thinkin' I'm associated with somebody don't look like they part of the neighborhood. The way you look, somebody think you slummin'. How come you got all those fancy clothes? You turnin' tricks?"

She kicked me in the shin, hurt real bad.

"No, I am not turnin' tricks. What's the matter with you? Don't you have no manners at all?"

"Hell, no. I say what I got to say, lay it on the line."

"You don't sound that way on the TV. I heard you on the TV, you sound almost high-class. You been goin' to school, takin' lessons?"

"No, I ain't takin' no lessons. Only when I ain't workin' my ass off for RASTUS I be friendly with a different class of people now. Like my mouthpiece. Like the guy that bought the house. Like my editor buddy. you don't know about him because you probably never read the paper, but I am on a first-name basis with the Roving Editor of the *Washington Post*. I could have dinner with him several times a week. I could have a nightcap before goin' to bed if I wanted to. I could discuss a certain lady we both interested in if I wanted to.

The thing is, I am too much a gentleman and it would only make him feel bad, makin' comparisons and everythin', because as you may recall, back when you was feelin' grateful when I saved your ass from further wear and tear not to mention the rest, I was givin' you about the best screwin' one man could give to one woman. You gettin' much lately? Don't look like it. Don't look like you been laid in a month. I can tell. A woman ain't been laid in a long time show it in a lotta ways. Quit lookin' at my crotch."

Kicked me again the bitch. Then tried to knee me. Oh, yeah, tried to get me in the balls. Well, shit, I grab her arms and push her away and shake her some. Goddamn if she don't start bawlin'.

"What the fuck you bawlin' about?" I ask her. "You feelin' guilty? Guilty chicks is pretty good at sheddin' water and carryin' on."

She don't say nothin', just sprinkle all over, make a mess of the stuff she got on her face. When chicks go to pieces like that the best thing is give 'em a good slap across the mouth, bring 'em to their senses. Only I don't do it, as much as I wanted. Bein' a public figure and everythin', I can't take no chances. The word gets around that I beat up on women all my credibility on behalf of RASTUS is gone. "Credibility?" Oh, yeah, just another one of them fancy words I picked up shacked up at Geraldine's.

Finally Celia slow down, get a grab on herself. "Rufus," she say, "is there someplace we could be alone? I got somethin' I want to tell you."

If she was gonna have a baby she couldn't blame me. Been too long. If she needed money she has come to the wrong place. I got too many RASTUS expenses. If she lost her job and needed her a place to stay—well, I could possibly consider the trunk for a month or so until she finds somethin' else. I mean, the trunk ain't bringin' in any income anyhow. It could be fixed up . . .

"Whattaya want?"

"I don't wanna talk out on the street. Can we get in the cab?"

"In the cab? You wanna go some place? You got the fare?"

"I wanna talk, Rufus. Serious talk."

"That's all? Just talk?"

"I been missin' you."

"Uh huh. I get it."

"Just five minutes."

"Uh huh. So we get in the cab. And we can get it on in the cab. Is that what you had in mind? As a matter of fact I could use a little dark meat. Been doin' it with . . . Never mind. Okay, get your ass in."

She get in the back seat, I get in the back seat. I have one hand up her dress and on her pussy and the other hand grabbin' tit and my tongue on her tongue and I gotta say it, black girls is hotter than any white stuff and fast on doin' what they wanna do. Maybe she don't realize what that is right off but with a little promptin' turns out she wants to unzip me and haul it out and eat on it. Okay, baby, if that's your desire why should I stand in your way especially since I ain't standin at all, worked around so I'm on my back and my poker pointin' to the ceilin' and Celia gorgin' on it 'til the thing explodes. It only took three minutes at the most and I be damned relaxed after that and ready to listen to Celia, see what she got on her mind.

"Rufus," she say, "I been hearin' some bad things down at the office. You in trouble."

"Trouble? How could I be in trouble? I don't work there. Don't even know where it is. Or what it is. What is it?"

"You forgot? Building and Restoration Permits of the District of Columbia. Anybody wants to restore they got to get our okay."

"Oh, yeah, well how come you didn't throw no monkey wrench about this place? I know you didn't give a damn about me when you took off, but you could have screwed it up a little. Or did you forget me that bad?"

"Rufus, don't go on about it. I had to move out so I could establish my own identity."

"Establish your own identity? What kind of talk is that? You sound like me on the TV. You been goin' to school?" Mimickin' her I was. "You been takin' lessons?"

"I work with white folks and educated black people. I try to sound like them so's I can get ahead. Next month I be up for promotion. If I don't talk nice before the board I won't get it."

"Far as I'm concerned, I hope you ain't. A bitch like you, handlin' the government's work and not lookin' out for a man what made it all possible, it's bad news. No way I want my taxes goin' for somebody don't care shit about the taxpayers. What's the name of your supervisor?"

"Rufus, hush up. Listen, you know the Hack Office, the one that keeps tabs on the cabdrivers?"

"Yeah, what about it?"

"It's right across the hall from mine."

"So?"

"I got a girlfriend there."

"So?"

"She told me somethin' be a lot of interest to you."

"What? She heard about me? She wants to meet me?"

"No, but she saw you in the paper, on the TV. She say you some kind of hunk."

"Ain't it the truth. She say anything else good?"

"You want it straight?"

"I sure do. Take me a few more minutes. You wanna help? Grab onto it, only be careful."

"I ain't talkin' about that thing. And I ain't grabbin' it. That thing can take care of itself for all I care."

"Yeah, it's a good one. Best on the block." I look at it. It look mighty fine, startin' to spring up now that it was the topic of conversation. "Hey, you better go. Some other chick in the neighborhood might be wantin' to visit me any minute."

"You don't want to hear about the Hack Office?"

"Okay, for Chrissake, let's hear it. They thinkin' of makin' a donation to RASTUS because I'm makin' all the other hackers in town proud?"

"Rufus, they gonna take your license away. You gonna lose your livelihood."

I sits up; my cock sits down. Cocks react right away to bad news.

"Huh? What the fuck you talkin' about?"

"Your hack license. You gonna lose it."

"No way. I ain't done nothin' wrong. No way I could lose my license. What did I do wrong?"

"You probably ain't done nothin' more than any other cabdriver in town—a little overchargin', a little takin' the long way, a little more swearin' than is called for. You could lose your license for any of that."

"No way. Ain't nothin' serious."

"The Hack Office thinks it's damn serious."

"Nah, they overlook it. They got to. If they grounded every cabdriver that broke the rules there would be too damn many people walkin'."

"Maybe so. But they ain't gonna overlook it no more. Not in your case, they ain't."

"Oh, yeah? Why not?"

"You a dumb shit, you know that? You think you gonna get away with stirrin' up things on the block? You think your dumbass RASTUS is gonna do any good? You think the people who're trying to buy property—and don't forget those who're tryin' to sell it—are gonna let you win? If you think you can win, man, you been dreamin'."

I put out some poo-poo on that remark. "Whattaya mean I can't win? If bein' in the papers and TV ain't winnin', what the hell is? It gets you things down the road."

"Down the road? If you lose your license, you won't even be on it."

"So what? I can do more than drive a hack. Screw the hack. I ain't plannin' on bein' a hack driver much longer no way. I got big plans."

"You better have. Because accordin' to my friend in the Hack Office a lot of pressure is comin' in. The real estate people ain't at all happy with you and real estate in this town has got power to get what they want. They ain't gonna let some smartass black guy stand in the way of progress."

"Oh yeah, well what exactly are they gonna do?"

"Act on the complaints, that's what. Overchargin', refusin' to pick up blacks—the usual. You got a few in your file, same as every other cabdriver. But that ain't the only part. They're settin' you up for somethin' a hell of a lot more serious. Like you been propositionin' your women customers. Like foolin' around with your women customers. Like rape."

I give out with a snort. "The first two maybe, but there ain't no way I could be set up for rape. I ain't that dumb. Any woman complains about rape in my cab has gotta be thrown out of court. Because I got the perfect defense. Everybody in town knows I'm crazy about women. And they crazy about me. Rapers hate women."

"Yeah, that's what it says in the book I got out of the library after Sanford and those others hurt me so bad. Only what the books don't explain is how sometimes they can hate and sometimes they just hard up."

"There is a fine line between, no doubt about it," I say. "In my case it ain't never come up. I am so in demand I can't hardly keep up with the chicks that are beggin' for it. I wouldn't hardly have the time to bother with somebody ain't interested." I put that out as serious as a church sermon because it is true.

Celia hit me. Doubled up her little fist and drove it into my rock-hard belly. Hurt herself bad.

"You think you're hot stuff, don't you," she say, her voice angry and her face all tight and pissed-off. "You think you're the greatest. Let me tell you somethin', you ain't no big deal. Why I come around here and be sweet to you and warn you, it beats the hell out of me. But I ain't doin' it no more."

After that she fuss around with her dress and her hair and move her good-lookin' ass outta the back seat. Slam the door once she on the outside, put on a mean face and take off down the street like she was finished with me forever.

Okay, it ain't nothing worth getting excited about. Chicks like Celia is born losers. They is here to be taken advantage of although I still have a soft spot for her on account of our early times before the RASTUS movement give me a chance to be somebody.

After the blow job and everything, I figure a little snooze is called for. When I wake up I turn on the dispatch radio, lookin' for Dulles Airport out in Virginia or BWI Airport up toward Baltimore. They is about the best runs in the business. Good for thirty bucks at least. They wasn't anythin' like that comin' over so I heads downtown. The Mayflower Hotel on Connecticut Avenue gets a lotta tourists from out of town and they be glad to ride in a taxi instead of that damn subway workin' hard to put the cabdrivers out of business. By the time I get to the Mayflower it is almost six o'clock and gettin' dark and some wind and rain has come up. Guys lookin' for cabs at the Mayflower is decked out in raincoats and umbrellas and the doorman is rakin' in tips for blowin' his whistle and probably gettin' more than usual because when it rains at rush hour in Washington the taxicabs got plenty to do and they can pick and choose. Like if I see some black dude looks like he wants to go to Anacostia, it's fuck you buddy, I ain't takin' no chances on gettin' a gun on my neck. So when I cruise up toward the Mayflower I was lookin' for somethin' good. The Hack Office don't like that. You supposed to take everybody. Only I been known to go suddenly blind when I don't approve of what's wavin' at me. But I be go to hell, what's standin' right behind the Mayflower doorman is this really good-lookin' blond chick. I cut off some amateur driver in a Yellow and ease in toward the curb and further go to hell but who should be thankin' the doorman for openin' the door and handin' him a dollar tip but Miss Vivian Eggleston Carstairs Baltus, the beautiful hysterical lady I had dealt with so masterfully the day the TV people came to get the lowdown on the situation as it exists at 757.

"Where to, lady?" I say nice and polite and at the same time steppin' on the gas because I don't wanta give her a chance to leap out in case she's thinkin' she's made a mistake. "Home? The radio station? 757?"

"Oh, God," she say. "It's you."

"Hell yes it's me," I say. "I got this funny feeling about ten minutes ago that you was lookin' for a ride in a nice safe taxi where the driver don't use no bad language. Not like some cabdrivers where they can't drive two blocks without sayin' 'fuckin' tourist' or 'goddamned red light' or 'asshole of a cop.' Nothin' like that with me. How the hell you doin'?"

"I'd appreciate it very much if you wouldn't talk that way," she say. "Unless you want me to get out at the next stoplight. If I do the Hack Office will hear about it as soon as I can get to a phone."

The Hack Office? How come everybody talk so much about the Hack Office? This book is supposed to be about me, not some creeps in the District of Columbia building got nothin' better to do than give a poor, hardworkin' cabbie a bad time. For all I care, they can take the Hack Office and shove it up its ass.

"Okay," I say. "I just said it to see if we on speakin' terms again. I hope we is because I has pretty much forgiven you for what you said on the TV. I don't hold no grudge."

"Forgiven me?" she say, all huffy. "You're absolutely insane. You should consider yourself enormously fortunate that I didn't have you arrested for assault and battery."

I like to be around her, I gotta admit it. The fancy way she talks, that's helpin' me a lot on the way I talk. She be a real good influence on me and I be the first one to give her credit.

"Could I ask you a couple of questions?" I ask her. "The first is, where do you want to go? And the second is, if you ain't in too goddamn big a hurry, how about you and me stoppin' off some place and havin' a drink? I'll pay. Or if you don't want to take nothin' offa me, you can pay for your own. Or if you're feelin' generous because I am a man without a home except for the moment you're in the bedroom of my temporary residence, I ain't gonna insult your charity. If you wanna pay for both I won't give you no hard time about it."

I'll be a son-of-a-bitch if she don't laugh. Yeah, laugh right out loud like she thought maybe I said somethin' funny. Like I was a comedian on TV, puttin' out wisecracks one right after the other, and gettin' maybe a thousand dollars a joke minus what I has to pay the writers.

"Well, why not?" she say. "Provided it's not more than a quarter of an hour. I'm due home in twenty minutes."

"No sweat. Where you hang out?"

"The FoxDen Condominium, on Massachusetts. I suppose you know where it is."

"Oh, hell yes. I been eyein' that place ever since it was built. One of these days I'm gonna have me a penthouse up there. Soon as I can get my call-girl business established."

She laugh again. "Mr. Jackson, my instincts about you have been correct from the beginning. Your professed devotion to the 6th Street house is all sham. Why do you persist?"

"Ain't you been readin' the papers, ain't you been lookin' at the two of us on the TV? I is the head of RASTUS and RASTUS got to give the right impression. I gotta think of my constituents."

"Your constituents? You sound like a congressman."

"I got to start somewhere. Start at the bottom, work hard and everything, maybe one day I sound like you. I gotta say it, you talk good."

"I didn't mean that way. I didn't mean the sound of the words. I meant the content."

"You sound good, you gets believed. That's the main thing."

"The main thing, I believe, Mr. Jackson, is to tell the truth."

"Hey, would you mind cuttin' out that Mr. Jackson shit? I ain't Mr. Jackson to my lady friends. They either call me 'Rufus' or they call me 'lover.' Okay, you ain't exactly a lady friend, but, hell, we seein' a lot of one another. There ain't no reason just because we don't see eye to eye about some things we can't get personal. Where's your favorite bar?"

"I don't have a favorite bar, Mr. Jackson, and I'd prefer to call you that if you don't mind and even if you do."

"Suit yourself. We're coming to the Diplomat Hotel. They got a bar there that ain't too fussy about what you got on. Whattaya say?"

"As long as we don't have more than one drink or stay longer than fifteen minutes, I couldn't care less. One bar is much like another. I frequent them infrequently."

She "frequents them infrequently." How about that for class?

I park the cab out in the front driveway where a sign say "Reserved for Taxis." Strictly speaking I shouldn't, seein' as how I'm not on duty, but I be go to hell if I'm gonna go in the parking garage where they would charge my ass for a whole hour even if I might stay as little as fifty minutes. Which I figured was gonna be the case with me and Vivian because when I get a chick in a bar where the lights ain't too strong and I blend in good and can turn on the charm, nobody can get away with less than two drinks and forty-five minutes of gettin' somethin' started. The cellar bar is the one we went to. It's the one where guys go after work with their secretaries or somebody's secretary, chicks who ain't accustomed to bein' shown off at the upstairs bar where the prices is higher and the lights is dimmer and even the classier call girls ain't permitted. In the downstairs bar, call girls as well as common street whores is welcome. As a matter of fact there is a bank of six telephone booths along the back wall and if you dial the number of the bar it is fixed just like a modern office so if the first booth is busy, it rings in the second booth and if that one is busy it rings in the third and so on down the line. It's somethin' the management has arranged to accommodate the call girls. There is this system whereby they take numbers like at a butcher's counter and answer the phones in order. Anybody jumpin' up and answerin' the phone out of turn can get her eyes scratched out and also be barred from the bar for periods up to sixty days dependin' upon how many times in the opinion of Bertram the bartender you been tryin' that shit.

Bertram is big on keepin' the bar orderly because he did some time in Lorton a few years back for dealin' dope and he learned his lesson. Also he knows that if he keeps the place friendly and don't charge too much for the drinks, he gonna get all the business and free pussy he can handle. He is nothin' special to look at—skinny and bald and on the short side, got bags under his eyes and creases and wrinkles all over his face and his teeth ain't too good. He is an old guy, maybe fifty years old, but it don't stand in the way of everybody likin' him. When you come in and he say "How you doin', man? You doin' okay?" and he reach across the bar to slap five and say "Aaaall riiight!" you know you got a frien', which in these hard times is worth a lot of money even if you got to spend a little. I lead Vivian to a table in the corner, across the room from the jukebox, where it ain't so noisy and pull out a chair and push it in when Vivian's sweet, round ass has settled down.

The bar ain't a big place—maybe ten bar stools and seven or eight tables—and the only thing that makes it different from a lot of other bars in Washington is the blackboard right alongside the juke box. How a blackboard came to a bar I don't know. But there it is, a big mother, maybe three feet by five feet, with a ledge to hold chalk and an eraser just like the third grade. Only it ain't for lessons. It's for the homos. There is a bunch of 'em living near the Diplomat, which is right close to Dupont Circle. Now it's a fact that your gays and queers and other weirdos got a gift for drawin' pictures better than the straight people. I don't know why. Maybe God did it so they would feel better on account of they don't get no satisfaction from puttin' a cock into a pussy the way God intended. Anyhow, they got in the habit of comin' into Bertram's bar and drawin' on the board. Anybody wants to can step up to it and put down whatever is on his mind. Bertram provides the chalk, includin' colored. In my time I seen some really good drawin'—naked ladies and all—but some of it looks like a nightmare and some of it looks like somethin' out of a garbage pail. The thing is, nothin' shows very long. Bertram's rule is that anybody who steps up to the board gets thirty minutes without interruption. After that the artist is guaranteed up to five minutes of whatever the customers want to say about it. After that the next artist can take over, erasin' the previous stuff all to hell and puttin' his own shit up. I've heard some pretty good things said. Like "lyrical synthesis of the highest order approaching the finest work of Picasso, Renoir and Vincent Van Gogh." And I've also heard a bunch of complaints. Like "totally lacking in the most basic and fundamental understanding of the medium" and also "Stinks," "Lousy," "Rotten," and "You asshole, whatever gave you the idea you can draw?" Okay, if you don't want to look you don't have to, ain't nobody forcin' you. The way I see it, the main thing in a bar is to get a good glow on and start settin' up the chick. Which is what I do with Vivian.

Gettin' Vivian settled down wasn't no hit or miss thing. I maneuvered her so she is facin' away from the blackboard. Sometimes, even though it is strictly against Bertram's rules, creeps has been known to write things like "Kill all the blacks and whites and leave the taxi drivin' to the Vietnamese" and "Heat your building, burn Jews" and "Down with the Spics, them no-good motherfuckers is greasy as french fries." If you get caught, Bertram will kick your ass out of the place forever. But when the joint gets to jumpin' late at night and the jukebox and the gin is doin' the work of the devil, he can't keep track of everybody. That's when some guy who don't care beans about law and order may try to start a race riot. I personally have been involved in some pretty good brawls, my favorite bein' the time I sent three white guys and a Korean whore to the hospital. The three white guys had broken ribs and the whore had a bad case of clap. I knew about the whore before the fight started and when the ambulance drove up, I threw her in because she don't speak much English and would never have gone on her own. I pinned a note on her dress: "My pussy is in bad shape, needs medicine. Anything you can do I will be happy. Give you a blow job right away or a free fuck as soon as my pussy is better." They cured her without no trouble at all. Which proves, I guess, that an ill wind can sometimes make you well. Or to put it an other way, sweet are the uses of graffiti. (I know that sounds pretty fancy for a ghetto gorilla, but I remember some things from high school.)

Naturally, I wouldn't want to expose a fancy chick like Vivian to such trashy language. Only they wasn't no problem when we sit down, she facin' the bar at one side of the square table, me at right angles. When you sittin' that way, you can drop your hand down onto the chick's knee easier than when you across. Though with my long arms I been known to make contact from even that distance. There was a dude at the blackboard doin' his thing. It was just a bunch of circles and squares and straight lines and wavy lines all mixed up like they had spent five seconds in a Waring blender. I couldn't make no sense out of it. Vivian look over her shoulder at it a few seconds and say, "Some Joseph Stella there, and some Gene Davis, but it's a mess mainly." I couldn't agree more, even if I knew Joe and Gene, which I don't.

"What'll you have?" I say to Vivian when the waitress come over. The waitresses wear bunnies and are polite and young. Accordin' to them, they all go to George Washington University, which is in the neighborhood, and work in the bar for $3.50 an hour plus tips to help Mom and Dad who have to get it up $14,000 a year to keep them in college. "You want a martini? Whiskey sour? Scotch on the rocks? You name it."

"Ah, I think I'd like sweet vermouth on ice," she say. "With a twist."

"What the hell kind of drink is that?" I say. "With a twist? What does the twist do for it? Tie you in knots?" I laugh a little at how cute I am and also to get Vivian goin'. That's the way you warm up your audience. Get 'em laughin' right at the start, break the ice so to speak and thaw 'em out right in the palm of your hand. The rest is easy. Only she don't laugh a bit, don't even grin. Okay, it needs work. Even Bob Hope didn't build Rome in a day.

"It is a very civilized drink," she say. "Possibly a trifle sweet for your tastes but I like it." The way she say it, it sounds like it ain't too sweet for me, more like I ain't sweet enough for it. Like I couldn't appreciate it. Like I ain't refined enough for anythin' but beer. Like I'm shit. Oh, yeah, it was a put-down all the way.

"Well, if you like it, I could probably learn to," I tell her. "And if I don't, I'll transfer it."

"No, thank you," she say. "One's enough."

That's what she say but that's not at all what she mean. I could see she was thinkin', anything that touches his lips first sure as hell ain't gonna touch mine second. Well, baby, I think right back, the way I'm plannin' it, you ain't gonna get anythin' from my lips secondhand. Firsthand is what I had in mind!

"Miss Bunny," I say, turning to the waitress, "bring us two large sweet vermouths on the rocks. Twist it for the lady and keep it straight and narrow for me. If I don't like it, I'm gonna trade it in for a double scotch."

Miss Bunny smile. "No trade-ins, Rufus," she say. "Maybe you better stick with the scotch. You always like that."

Remind me to give that chick a good tip. A scotch drinker, oh yeah, that's what I like to be known as. Not your gin or vodka like a lot of black types ain't accustomed to drinkin' anything better.

"No," I say, smooth as butter on biscuits, "the lady here is just an amateur and I'm gonna join her in somethin' ain't too serious. Maybe later we switch to the real stuff."

So then I turn to give the lady my undivided attention. Shit, she is prettier than a pinup, except she has all her clothes on. The funny thing, she looks good even without all the paint and earrings and stuff around her neck a lot of chicks show off when they all dressed up and tryin' to make a good impression. Which is nearly always, that bein' the way it is if you goin' through life tryin' to get ahead and gotta improve on the way God made you. Considerin' that God is supposed to do perfect work, how come he goofs so much? Like what he did to me from the neck up. I has every right to be pissed off. I ain't though. I got my great body, that's enough. Praise the Lord.

Vivian is wearin' . . . . Wait, I don't do that stuff. It looks like costs a lot and it fits like somethin' on a store-window model. I ain't gonna go beyond givin' it an A plus. But I look it over real steady and careful, thinkin' about all the good things hidden away, out of sight, nobody gets to look at 'em but that shithead Baltus. My cock startin' to grow, standin' up, lookin around, see what all the excitement is . . .

"Mr. Jackson," say Vivian, "I think you and I should have a serious talk."

See what I mean? Set 'em down, order 'em a drink, look 'em over cool as rain in November, like you own 'em already, and right away they want to talk serious. About what? About gettin' it on, about makin' out . . . What the hell else could it be?

"About what?" I say, sort of superior and big-shot. "I didn't come here to have no serious discussion. You wanta dance?"

There is an open area maybe six by six next to the jukebox. Dance if you got a quarter. I is somethin' to marvel at out on the floor. Can do the boogie, the boogaloo, the bungalow, the bongo, the bingo, the Bing Crosby, the cross-buck, the buck and wing, the Wing and a Prayer . . . you name it. Back in Eastern High School I was not only the star forward but Best Dancer in the Year Book. If I didn't have to go to work at an early age supportin' my momma, I could have been a big-time hoofer on the stage and in the movies. Of course, general ugliness had something to do with it, too.

"No, honestly," say Vivian. "I think we should talk. We may not have another opportunity."

Uh huh. Get that? She wants to work out the details now, not over the phone when God only knows who may be tappin' the line.

"Okay, baby," I say. "Lay it on me." I reach under the table and put my hand on her knee, give it a squeeze. "What's on your mind?"

Her knee jerk away and she rise up outta her chair and her hand come across the table faster than a rattlesnake snappin' at a field mouse. Whop, right across my chops. Repeat whop, comin' from the other direction.

"Hey, baby, hold it," I say, scrapin' my chair back out of range quick as I can. "We gonna go through this again? I thought we was buddies."

"Mr. Jackson, you have thoroughly misunderstood me," she say, her eyes flashin' and her breath goin' in and out like she just done the one-hundred-yard dash and her tits bobbin' up and down the way they do when the lungs is workin' overtime. "You are disgusting.

Honestly, you are so black, it is unbelievable. No wonder your race is still despised."

Now hold it right there. Just because I may be gross as an orangutan is no reason to condemn a whole lotta innocent people got nothin' to do with it. Lashin' out the way she was, right and left, without no cause, what the hell kind of carryin' on is that? Absolutely uncalled for. I give Vivian a really dirty look to show her remark was not appreciated one little bit.

"Vivian," I say, tryin' to keep a hold on myself because there is no point in lettin' your anger get away from you when you dealin' with a white honkey of the foreign kind, "you sure gotta lot of nerve. Only Americans can talk that way to me. You a limey, ain't you? You don't have the right."

"I want you to take me home," she say. "Straightaway."

Her look is as stern as a fifth-grade teacher discoverin' who wrote "Fuck this school" on the blackboard.

"In case you aren't aware, it means immediately."

About as pissed off as the high school principal lookin' at the kid who got caught.

"Right now."

As mad as mama when she gets the letter sayin' her guilty little chile is suspended.

"Aw come on, Vivian," I tell her, "I didn't mean nothin' bad by squeezin' your kneecap. It wasn't as though I put my hand on one of your boobs. Nobody could see."

Vivian does not have the best sense of humor sometimes and she don't laugh. Hell, no, looks madder than ever. Rises up, grabs up her pocketbook which she has parked on the table and swings it. You ever been hit in the face with a lady's handbag?

"What the hell you doin', woman?" I ask her. "Don't you realize that thing is full of keys and money? What the hell is wrong with you?"

Vivian don't say nothin', just swung the bag again, hurts like a son-of-a-bitch. "You are scum. One should strike out at scum until it is exterminated."

"Vivian," I say, "I already said I was sorry. I'll say it again. I'm sorry. Now please sit down before Bertram sees what's goin' on and asks you to leave. Once that happens you don't get back any time soon. How would you like it if it was spread all over town that you been barred from Bertram's bar for sixty days?"

Vivian thought it over. She realized there was no way she could get gentlemanly treatment from me and also that she had made her point and also after what happened she needed a drink, which Miss Bunny was at that very moment bringin' to the table. She sat down.

"Rufus, that'll be three dollars and seventy five cents."

It gives you an idea of how classy a joint Bertram's is when there's a sign on the bar mirror says "Please pay when served" and they mean it. No exceptions even for a good customer like me been givin' the place my business for years.

"Sure thing," I say, reaching into my hip pocket for my wallet. I open it. Nothin' there but a lottery ticket that missed it by one. "Uh oh, I don't have a dime." Gassin' up on the way down to the Mayflower had taken it all. "Stony broke. Guess I'll have to leave my I.O.U."

"Uh, I'm afraid not, Rufus," say Miss Bunny. "You know the rules. No credit. I'm afraid I'll have to ask you for your watch."

I couldn't believe my ears.

"What? What watch? What the hell are you talkin' about?"

"I'm sorry, but Bertram says if you can't pay, something must stay. Here's the schedule."

And she hands me this five-by-seven card. At the top it say, "Schedule of What's Owed Versus What's Kept" and under it is two columns. The one on the left say "You owe" and the one on the right say "We keep." The left column has amounts. Like "Under $5" and "Between $5 and $10" and "Between $10 and $15" and so on. The right column has the punishment just because you is a little short. Across from "Under $5" is "Any wristwatch, even Timex if in good working order." Across from "Between $5 and $10" is "Any wristwatch, except for Timex." Across from "Between $10 and $15" is "Good wristwatch, accurate to within plus or minus three seconds a day." Across from "Between $15 and $20" is "The keys to your car." And so on. Son-of-a-bitch, that Bertram has had the last of my trade for a long time!

However, rules is rules and I be the last person try to tell some guy how to run his business. Same with me. If some guy don't have the fare, I ain't beyond takin' a watch my ownself. Which is why I had a few watches on my body at the time. I pull out what was in my left jacket pocket and pick out a Timex, a pretty little thing I could easy raise five bucks on at the pawn shop. I wind it up and the tick is good and strong, the sort of thing you can count on if you tryin' for a miniature time bomb.

"Okay," I say to Miss Bunny, "here it is. Your tip gonna have to come out of that. Keep the change."

And I was just gonna hand it over when Vivian say "Stop."

"Stop," she say, "that won't be necessary. I don't approve of paying for drinks with stolen merchandise. I'll take care of the check."

Now what gave her the idea I had a hot watch? It is terrible the way that woman keeps insultin' me. However, seein' as how she was gonna pay, there didn't seem to be no point in raisin' a stink. I can take a lotta insults providin' the price is right.

Okay, after that we more or less bury the hatchet, settle back down like human bein's and drink our drinks. Vermouth ain't bad. Not as good as scotch but better than pink lemonade, though not by much. It's one of them sneaky drinks, got more deviltry than you think. After a couple of good strong gulps I am feelin' right calmed down, ready to start at Square One with Vivian again. Only she don't give me a chance to think of a good openin' line. Beats me to the punch.

"Mr. Jackson, I submitted to your invitation to join you for drinks because I saw it as an opportunity to discuss the situation at the 6th Street house. That was the only reason. Is that clear?"

"Clear as hell, babe," I say, though I ain't ready to give up on my dirty plans that fast. "Anythin' you say."

"What's happening at the property is causing Howard a great deal of anguish. The pickets, the general unfriendliness of the neighborhood, that idiotic RASTUS movement—or whatever you call it—the whole thing has gone on quite enough."

I don't say nothin', keep my mouth shut, take another swallow. Let 'em get it off their chest.

"What's so outrageous is that I'm convinced you don't really care about the house or the block or the neighbors. You're using the whole thing for personal gain. Deep down you're probably glad you had to get out."

"Huh? Why would I want to do that?"

"Because you saw it as an opportunity for publicity—something you could use as a springboard. In a way I can understand. Because you don't strike me as the sort of man who would be content to be a cabdriver the rest of his life."

I knew it, I knew it all along. Vivian sees me as somethin' and sees somethin' in me. Way to go!

"Well, you right about that," I say. "I got me lots of plans—call girls, standup comic, city councilman . . . Oh, yeah, they be a pile of opportunities comin' my way . . ."

"Excellent," she say. "Very commendable. I can help."

"Now you talkin'." I lean forward, give her a good look in her pretty blue eyes, give her a good look down the front of her dress. "What did you have in mind?"

"Money. A large sum of money. A sum of money so large you will cheerfully dissolve the RASTUS, call off the pickets and spread the word in the neighborhood that Howard and I are to be welcomed with open arms."

"Oh, Vivian, shit. Is that the best you can do? Money? You know I can't take money."

"Why ever not?"

"We been through that before. At the meetin' at Geraldine's. I can't be turnin' against my friends for money."

"That is ridiculous," she say, tossin' with her head and scoffin' with her throat. "The situation back then no longer exists."

"How come?"

"Back then you thought you might win in the courts or that we would be discouraged. It didn't work."

"Hell, it ain't. It's workin'. You gonna find out not so long off."

"Oh, don't be absurd. In a matter of days we'll be living in the house—and once we do the fight will be over."

"Oh, yeah, well if the fight'll be over, how come you wanna lay some money on me?"

"For Howard's sake. It's not enough that we own the house. He wants to be loved by the neighbors."

"You wanna be loved by the neighbors, you gotta love the neighbors. Ten Commandments. I think. You got a Bible on you, we could check it out."

"So if it were made worth your while, you could change the atmosphere. Nobody would blame you. You tried hard on behalf of your friends but now you should be thinking about yourself."

"I try to do that. Only I don't like to trample on my good buddies. They poor and ignorant, not like me, don't have a chance to break out into the big time."

"I don't blame you for your loyalty but you have your own future to worry about."

"Right. Just what I been sayin'."

"You know, Mr. Jackson, I've developed a certain respect for you in spite of myself."

"Glad to hear it. Same goes for me."

"It isn't every black person who would put up the fight. You deserve much credit."

"Thank you, ma'am, I'll take it. And speakin' of credit, since they don't give any here, would you mind payin' me for the ride right now? Either that or you're gonna have to buy the next round, too."

"Don't concern yourself with trifles. Let's get back to the main issue. How much would it take to buy your complete cooperation?"

"A lot and not a whole lot. The money, forget it. If I took money I would still feel I let my friends down. I couldn't do that. But there is somethin' I want awful bad."

"What's that?"

I look her over. She looks suspicious, but she usually does when she sees me. She looks slightly drunk; that vermouth is tricky stuff, no question. She looks gorgeous, one of the finest-lookin' foxes in the entire District of Columbia.

"You don't know? You sittin' right across from me and you don't know? Vivian, what the fuck you think I am? Some kind of queer? You about the most desirable white woman I ever had a date with in my life. Best talkin'. Best clothes. Prettiest round ass. Prettiest tits. Sexiest, even though you ain't exactly respondin' to anything I've tried so far. What I'm after should be clear as the Washington Monument. But if it ain't, you could put your hand between my legs and that crowbar up there would give you an idea. So what I want don't cost a lotta money and it ain't complicated. All I want is to get your clothes off somewhere, bed ain't necessary but it ain't ruled out, and fuck the shit out of you. That's all. You willin' to come across, things could be worked out on 6th Street in a flash."

I plant my feet for a fast getaway in case she screams and I put one hand down on the table in case she was gonna tip it and I had the other hand ready in case she was gonna go for my eyes. She didn't do nothin', just sat there, givin' me this very cold look and shakin' her head like some disappointed mama don't understand how her kid could turn out so bad. Then she sigh, pick up her vermouth drink and swallow it all down in one gulp.

"Mr. Jackson, thank you for the drink. Even though I paid for it, I can appreciate the sentiment behind it. I really must ask you to deliver me home now. Howard will be wondering."

Isn't that the shits? Woman been given the opportunity of a lifetime and she comes out with this dumb little speech like she never even heard it. If my cock didn't itch for the bitch so bad, I'd forget her. However, cock got a mind of his own and if he don't get what he wants, cock gonna be so hard all the time he ain't gonna be able to pass water. If that happens it's uremic poisonin' in no time. How come I know that? My daddy died from it, that's how I know.

"Okay, Vivian, okay. If that's the way you want it. No hard feelin's. Uh oh, I shouldn't have said that. And we ain't even touched. Unless you wanna count that split second I had my hand on your knee."

"I do count it, Mr. Jackson. I assure you you will never have another opportunity."

"Tell *me* somethin', Viv, was it really that bad? About the worst thing that happened since you realized you had somethin' between your legs guys like? I mean, it ain't the first time somebody made a pass, is it? The way you jumped, it was like your sugar was about to be sucked on by cockroaches."

"Tell me something, Mr. Jackson, why do you feel it's necessary to use such coarse language? I know you're capable of better."

"Viv, ain't it the truth. Okay, I'm gonna make an effort. And how about you doin' somethin' for me?"

"No. I'm not interested in doing anything for you. Asking you to watch your language is for your benefit, not mine. Shall we go?"

So we get up and get goin', out to the cab and in it and headed up Massachusetts Avenue. I feelin' pretty good because even though I didn't get too far with makin' out and got a chewin' out besides, I figured I'm beginnin' to turn her head in my direction. Remember, she said she had "developed a certain respect" and I "deserved much credit" and I was "capable" of doin' better with the way I talk. She be interested, no question. Keep up the good work, buddy, and you gonna score. The good mood gets me hummin' a little tune I composed a coupla days ago. You didn't know I had that talent on top of everythin' else, did you? It's called "RASTUS On The Rise." You wanna hear a few choruses? Okay, it goes like this:

RASTUS ON THE RISE, OH YEAH, RASTUS ON THE RISE,
RASTUS GONNA WIN YET, RASTUS GET THE PRIZE
RASTUS BE THE WAY TO GO, GOIN' ALL THE WAY
RASTUS BE YOUR SAVIOR ALL THE LIVELONG DAY
SO SING IT UP FOR RASTUS
SING, SING, SING
SING IT UP FOR RASTUS
LET YOUR VOICES RING
FOR RASTUS IS A COMET FLAMIN' THROUGH THE SKY
RASTUS IS YOUR LEADER 'TIL THE DAY YOU DIE.

Peppy, wouldn't you say? Got a real beat, right? Get the Supremes recordin' it with me doin' the lead and it would be in the Top Forty in no time at all. Oh, yeah.

We pull up in front of the FoxDen. It's exclusive. To give you an idea, it's the only condo in town where the doorman makes so much money he gives Christmas presents to the tenants.

"Here we is all safe and sound," I say. "That'll be seven dollars and eighty cents, Vivian."

"I beg your pardon," says Vivian. "That couldn't possibly be right."

I turn my head and look her over. Goddamn, there she is in my temporary bedroom where not three hours before I had let that Celia bitch get it on. Oh man, I wanted her.

"Oh, it's right, Vivian. I picked you up in the rush hour, remember. I get an extra buck for that. And it was rainin'. Another buck. And stoppin' on the way. Two bucks waitin' time. Plus the regular fare. So it all adds up."

"Two dollars waiting time?" says Vivian. "You're insane. It wasn't my idea to stop. Why should I pay?"

"I know it," I say, "but you didn't turn it down when you had the chance. Once you went along, I have to charge you. Hack Rule Number 27. You could look it up."

"Honestly, Mr. Jackson, you are out of your mind. Is this some kind of a joke?"

"Nah, it ain't no joke but it could be a deal."

I get out of the cab and go around and open the passenger's door, right side. Only I don't hold the door so she can get out. I slip in quicker than a burglar with a passkey, put my arms around her and before the cat has a chance to take evasive action plant my big, thick, ugly lips on hers. Press hard a second and back off. Get out of the cab, hold the door, put out my hand and slip her out of the back seat as smooth as a doorman with a uniform. Vivian flashes her eyes but she don't say nothin' and she don't swing nothin' and there is this look on her face say, God, it was awful but not that awful and at least I am escaped from this maniac and if I can rush up to my apartment and rinse my mouth out with double-strength Listerine, maybe most of the germs will be killed on contact. But, God, I have been kissed by a black person and I will never be the same again.

13

The man has a genius for fucking up. I'm talking about that scamp, scoundrel and ne'er-do-well each of us, in his or her own way, has learned to detest. As was predicted by other participants in this tasteless saga, Rufus was called down to the Hack Office and threatened with the loss of his hack license. I have better things to do with my life than spend most of it defending a man who is probably guilty of everything the Hack Office complained about and who also ought to be penalized for the general shambles he has created in my house and in my sex life. It is bad enough that he is using a scandalous amount of hot water and is foraging regularly in my refrigerator in spite of my well-publicized position against it. What irritates me even more is the entrenched quality of the man's existence. It's as though he has been in my front bedroom since its construction and intends staying there until it crumbles. Not that he confines himself solely to his bedroom, the kitchen and the bashroom. (I realize I have just uttered a typo, but if it displeases the compiler of this trash let him expunge it; I have a sufficiency of responsibilities as it is.) He seems to feel that we have somehow become co-owners of the place and is not the least inhibited about lounging about in the living room and the bar and the study. He makes occasional forays into the other bedroom—events which require no elaboration at this time—and apparently believes his success there entitles him to take his pleasure throughout the premises. I have not acceded to his selfish behavior without protest and just because he is about the most sensational hunk . . . Stop. I promised myself I would not go into that so you must content yourself with thinking the worst—or the best, depending upon your point of view in such matters.

"They're pickin' on me," said Rufus after the Hack Office called him in. "But I ain't worried. You can get me off."

"Absolutely not," I said. "I don't want any part of it.

"Oh, come on, Geraldine," Rufus said. "You due to win some time. Okay, you failed me on the house but your luck is bound to change. I'm gonna give you another chance to prove yourself. Only this time please try and do better."

The man is a master of the illogical thought process, as you can see. Not that I am any slouch. If I had as much control of my mind as I should, I would never listen to him. I suppose in some way I feel responsible for the creep. He didn't have my advantages, of course, but it is remarkable how successful he has become in using those who have. Rufus' manipulation of Horace Endicott, of the *Washington Post*, is a prime example. The paper still occasionally editorializes against gentrification and urban renewal and Rufus has been referred to as "the man who once lived in a townhouse, now lives in a taxi and, through his RASTUS movement, seems destined to play a prominent political role on behalf of his victimized brethren." Horace and I are each other's steady piece of ass and it is going very well. While Horace and I screw primarily at his house in Georgetown, I must occasionally invite him in for sex at my place lest he feel that his bedclothes are taking the wear and tear out of all proportion. As he has pointed out, there is also the matter of laundry expenses as well as expenses incidental to the consumption of toothpaste and toilet paper. He is not an ostentatious skinflint by any means—he takes us to dinner at restaurants which are on par with the places I select when it is my turn—but there is a certain Yankee parsimoniousness in his nature that requires him to be careful.

I am happy to say his slightly Puritan attitude toward money is not matched by any similar reserve in bed. He is a good, selfless, completely reliable practitioner who knows his business. He never permits himself to come before I do and, indeed, ordinarily induces so many orgasms in me that by the time he is satisfied with his own exquisite performance and thus earned the right to his own explosion, I am too exhausted to do much more than fake it. But, hell, I can do that so well only Dr. Masters or Dr. Johnson could tell the difference. I must confess that once in a while a fake is about all I am capable of throughout. It is when we are working out at Columbia Road. Prior to, I always tell the boarder in no uncertain terms that he better not show his ass around the place during the designated period. In spite of my explicitness, he has been known to practically barge right on in when Horace and I are knocking it off in bed or in front of the fire or on the bar stools or God knows where. I don't see any reason why I should stammer or curse or shriek in my own house. Horace does not quite have my sang-froid and it has upset him a number of times. It is amusing that Horace is not a bit upset if Hardin should observe us at play. I think he would welcome something involving the three of us but I am putting that off until such time as Horace and me become slightly bored with what we can work out together. Actually, Hardin is about as well hung as Horace and if Horace should see Hardin with his best hardon it might have an unsatisfactory psychological effect upon his own organ, a thing in no way exceptional though, as I have already said, quite serviceable.

I have told Horace that Rufus' presence is explained by my kindness in letting him rent my front bedroom so that he may have an office for RASTUS. Horace does not believe it for a moment but he is so nuts about me that he has suppressed his reporter's instinct to get to the bottom of it. At the moment my own generous bottom is bottom enough. Nevertheless, the possibility that Rufus might come upon me and Horace doing it and before we can say a word slap the uppermost of us on the ass with the *Washington Post* does have an inhibiting effect and explains why I fake it once in a while. The realization that Rufus might walk in at any minute would dilute anybody's concentration. Horace, for his part, suspects the truth about me and the stud but since the truth occurs so irregularly and Horace is in no way neglected, there seems to be no reason why we should not continue indefinitely. The continued reference to the RASTUS movement in the *Post* is explained by Horace's feeling that his ongoing success with me is dependent upon his being good to Rufus. I suppose I may have given that impression, another example of how cleverly RASTUS bends us on his behalf.

He sure as hell bent me toward defending him at the Hack Office hearing. We went down there last week. The hearing examiner is Wally Winston, a political drone with white skin and a black heart. He also runs the Hack Office and it is manifestly unfair for him to be both accuser and judge but the D.C. Government can't afford both so it takes the chance that nobody will push this thing right up to the Supreme Court. He conducts hearings in the same office in which he conducts the routines of hackery: a cluttered, filthy, threadbare cubicle which in many ways is reminiscent of my own just before I do my monthly cleaning. Wally is not accustomed to having the miscreants represented by council.

"Well, Miss Lance," he began when Rufus introduced me, "I can't tell you how honored I am. An attorney, a woman attorney and a beautiful woman all wrapped up in one. The Hack Office is charmed." The man runs to greasy black hair, black suits, a black pipe and black-framed glasses. Someone who required a favor once told him he was a cross between Rudolf Valentino and Cary Grant. What a laugh. A head waiter at a hamburger joint crossed with a used-car salesman is more like it. His complexion is loathsome. The man is forty at least but he's loaded with more pimples than a high school sophomore. They say jerking off causes it. I can understand why Winston would resort to it because no self-respecting woman in her right mind would want to spread her legs for that creep even with the knowledge that if she did it might reduce his pustules to an acceptable level. "Such pleasures come our way all too infrequently. If you'll just let me dust this chair . . ." And he whipped out his handkerchief and pushed it against the grime. Grime fadeth not. Counsel sitteth nevertheless.

"Would you care for some coffee?"

"No, thank you," I said. "Coffee would make me too alert. I wouldn't want to take advantage of you, Mr. Winston. I can defend Rufus against your trumped-up charges with my eyes closed. If I drank coffee I'd be so aggressive I'd probably bring action against you for depriving Rufus of loss of an hour's work—which is about as long as this hearing should take."

Winston blinked his beady little eyes. Winston coughed. Winston rubbed his hands together. Winston sat behind his desk. Winston patted his greasy locks. Winston scratched his left cheek with his right hand. Winston looked like he was about to lose a sale and be denied a tip.

"Well, Miss Lance," he said, this dumb little laugh preceding, "I hope you're right. It is never the intention of the Hack Office to deprive anyone of their livelihood. But as a government office with the statutory duty to make the city's taxi fleet the best in the country, we must take seriously any complaints against the drivers. Otherwise the fleet's fine reputation would be damaged irreparably. Once the fleet no longer has the confidence of the people, the people will take to the subway in ever larger numbers. Once that happens, the cabdriving industry will go into a severe decline, the poor cabdrivers will be forced onto the welfare rolls and the economical fares which are the hallmark of the city will disappear forever. As I was saying to the Mayor just the other day . . ."

"Cut the bullshit," I said. "You're not running for office. Let's get on with it."

Winston pursed and glared. And coughed, of course. Petty functionaries always cough when they are covered with confusion. Tough shit. Coughing followed by gasping followed by choking followed by extinction on the spot would be fine with me. I can't stand those toads. "Very well, Miss Lance. If you don't have time to be civil to a civil servant, I will not insist upon it." He opened the folder lying on the desk—a ratty, fly-specked folder and a ratty, fly-specked desk. "Here are the complaints."

"Wait a minute," I said. "Where the hell are your witnesses? I want to cross-examine the witnesses."

"There are no witnesses," Winston replied. "We don't require the complainants to appear personally. We accept their statements."

"Well, shit, buddy, over my dead body," I came right back. "We don't accept that. We want their asses in here where we can poke and probe and get to the bottom of this thing."

"Miss Lance, if I may be so bold," Winston said, "this is not a courtroom. This is not a trial. I am following the procedures spelled out by directives emanating from the City Council. We accept the statements in good faith. Now, if your client wants to object he will have ample opportunity to do so."

"I object," said Rufus. "Accusee gets the right to be confronted by the accuser. Article Three of the Bill of Rights. Them motherfuckers is lyin'. I ain't done a goddamn thing."

Winston opened the folder and commenced to leaf through the contents. "I'm afraid yes, Mr. Jackson. Seventy-three complaints. Every one has the ring of truth."

"All right," I said. "trot 'em out. But I want the record to show we object, take exception to and are thoroughly opposed to this entire proceeding."

"First violation," said Winston. "Overcharging. Eleven complaints. Average overcharge, twenty percent. Biggest overcharge, twenty-three dollars for a seven dollar trip. The date is October 17, last year."

"Statue of limitations," said Rufus. "Too far back. Can't nobody remember that far back. No way. Case dismissed."

"The statement is signed and notarized. A foreigner on business. Says you took him from National Airport to the Washington Hilton. Something here about you offering to send a girl to his room. Not material to this complaint except it may help you remember him."

"Fuck no. Too many of them out-of-towners wantin' to buy some of our good local pussy. Can't recall 'em all."

"Says he handed you some foreign money in payment. Says he didn't know what it was worth exactly but was sure it was enough."

"Hey, man, I ain't in the money changin' business. If the cat don't hand me dollars I ain't responsible for figurin' it out."

"Nobody said you were. But you should know there's a money exchange booth in the hotel lobby. You should have taken him in and helped him."

"Whaaaat? You crazy, man. I don't have time to look after some dumb immigrant. Show me where it says I got to baby the mother. Show me."

"He says he handed you the foreign currency and while he was registering he saw you at the money exchange booth. Right after he checked in he went there and checked on the exchange rate. That's how he knew you had robbed him."

"Robbed? Hell, man, I was takin' a big chance. Suppose the rate had dropped overnight? I'd have been skinned."

"As I said, the overpayment amounted to twenty-three dollars. Mr. Jackson, aren't you ashamed?"

"Hold it right there," I interjected. "Don't answer that, Rufus. The question is leading and it presumes guilt. Mr. Winston, if you intend browbeating Mr. Jackson on every little complaint I can see we'll get nowhere. Would you please lay out your perjured statements without elaboration."

"Miss Lance, I am perfectly willing to do so. That is, if you can possibly keep your client quiet."

"Rufus, shut up."

"I ain't gonna shut up. The fucker is out to get me."

"Well, somebody should. You deserve it. Now shut up or I quit."

"Geraldine, impress on him, I ain't just some common ordinary fuck-up. I am the RASTUS."

"Quite. Okay, Winston, let's hear the rest of your list."

It was goddamned impressive both in size and variety. There was Failure to Pick Up Blacks (16 complaints), Taking The Long Way (14 complaints), Multiple Passengering (8 complaints), Failure To Reduce Radio When Specifically Requested (13 complaints), Swearing (5 complaints), Taking Undue Liberties (4 complaints) and Miscellaneous Discrepancies (2 complaints).

"I can read the individual allegations if you like," said Winston. "I can assure you there is enough to put Mr. Jackson out of the cabdriving business forever. Which is what I'm afraid we must do. Sorry."

"Mr. Winston, tell me something. How much would it cost to have Rufus here knock you on your ass?

"Miss Lance, if you or your client wish to make a statement, now is when the rules say you have the opportunity. Do you wish to take advantage?"

I suppose I could have put Rufus on the stand. But it would have meant a stream of long-winded, fanciful denials larded with complaints of persecution because of his "vigorous fight on behalf of the poor and the down-trodden." The man would convince nobody. Or I could have persisted in my demand that witnesses be brought in. Or I could have spouted twenty minutes of legal mumbo-jumbo. Or I could have thrown Rufus on the mercy of the merciless. Which is what I did.

"Winston, what's your price? Is it a thousand? Is it a week in Florida? Is it a month's supply of whores? Is it a year of booze? How much does it take?"

"On the basis of the record, Mr. Jackson should be denied a license for the foreseeable future."

"I don't doubt it for a moment. Please answer the question."

"I have never been vindictive," said Winston, leaning forward so that his elbows were on the desk and his smug, phony and pimpled puss rested on his knuckles. "The city needs its good, experienced drivers. Frankly, and off the record, letting in Africans and Spics and those people from Southeast Asia is a mistake. They will never understand the city the way the natives do. They simply don't have the feel, the authority, the rapport with the great monuments, the latest White House thinking on any number of international problems, the advice based on countless encounters with the great and near-great, the wisdom acquired from short but meaningful relationships with people from all walks of life, the . . ."

"Hold it, Winston, you're not guest of honor at the annual cabdrivers ball. But you've made your point. You like Rufus and you're going to give him a break. We appreciate it."

Winston smiled. Have you noticed how a political hack will try to deny his venality by a shit-eating expression? It fools no one. Winston's face conveyed the classical greed you can expect in a ten-year-old at Christmas.

"Miss Lance, when I'm confronted with malefaction as serious as Mr. Jackson's I am truly torn. God knows I would like to keep him on the streets because that's where he belongs and that's where he's happy. But God also knows the man is guilty of very serious offenses, some of which are punishable by a stiff term at Lorton Reformatory. I'm a Christian and I listen to the voice of the Lord. And the Lord tells me that justice would be best served if Mr. Jackson were forced to hand over his license. I honestly wish there were some other way . . ."

"Praise the Lord," said Rufus. "Somebody say Amen."

"Amen," said Winston. "Brother, I am glad to see you are a fellow Christian."

"Hallelujah," said Rufus, "Let's hear it for the sake of sweet Jesus Christ."

"Enough already for the sake of sweet Jesus Christ." This was from me. "Christians, let's not get away from the business at hand. Which is an attempt to put a price on Mr. Winston's generosity."

"My dear couselor," said Winston. "I am afraid there is a serious misunderstanding. I do not take. I am fairly paid by the D.C. Government and my personal needs are modest. Any money, any gifts that come my way are turned over to the many organizations in the city designed to help the needy. That is the law, as you well know. Naturally, somebody responsible for upholding the law could not very well break it."

"Heavens, no," I said. "God forbid."

"There is nothing, however, to prevent public-spirited citizens who appreciate the conscientious efforts of the Hack Office from sending a little something to a favorite designated charity."

"A favorite designated charity. Of course."

"When it's designated, they always send a little card so I can tack it to the bulletin board. That way the staff gets the good glow from knowing they are responsible."

"The good glow. Certainly."

"The Old Hackers Home For The Aged And Infirm. I suppose you've heard of it."

"I can't say I've had the displeasure."

"Or Cabdrivers Anonymous For The Early Detection And Treatment Of Chronic Alcoholism."

"I'll drink to that."

"Some are partial towards the Taximan's Benevolent and Discretionary Fund. Just last week some people from the Capitol Hill area came by and wondered if I could help with the mailing address. It's not generally known."

"I can imagine. 'Of no known address.' Sure, too much publicity and everybody would be coming around for a handout. You said Capitol Hill. I have friends there. Anybody I know?"

"Oh, I couldn't possibly divulge. It would be breaking a confidence."

"Absolutely. Still, it's interesting. Most of the people from the Hill don't strike me as the kind who would be putting it out for charity. Rufus, for example, lives there and I have the feeling he hasn't put anything in the pot since the day his mother gave him a nickel to get a pencil from the blind man."

"Leave my mother out of this," said Rufus. "She dead."

"I'm terribly sorry," said Winston. "Was it recent?"

"So if capital is coming from Capitol Hill," I went on, "it's probably not from the residents. It would have to be business interests. And what kind of business interests? Interestingly enough, real estate interests just happened to pop into my mind. Could I be right, Winston?"

"My dear lady, you are clever. A very sharp mind, indeed. I can understand how you chose the pursuit of the law as an outlet for your talents."

"Winston, your sarcasm is appreciated. As is your cunning way with a circumlocution. 'A favorite designated charity.' Christ, why don't you just call it the Winston Fund For The Relief Of Wally Winston and get it over with?"

Winston gave me a dirty look which was not in any way remarkable because he looks dirty all the time. The man cries out for the best from a good dermatologist and Elizabeth Arden. "Look," he said, "I don't have an awful lot of time this morning. But I admire your spirit and your candor and I am not immune to the curvaceous way you occupy the visitor's chair. And Brother Jackson is a brother, if not a soul brother, and I am willing to work out something. What did you have in mind?"

"Not a lot of money, you can be damn sure. Rufus doesn't have much and will have even less by the time you take his cab off the street and put him on it."

Rufus made his little contribution. "Better than money, I could promise never to do it again. See, one of the things ought to be taken into consideration is this is the first time you guys ever complained. I've been drivin' for six years and nobody ever said shit before. So how was I supposed to know you don't like the radio turned up?"

"Yes," I said, "Rufus has a point. This sudden interest. But that would be explained by the sudden interest from the real estate types on the Hill."

"Maybe it would help if you understood that Mr. Jackson's suspension need not be forever," Winston said. "I have the impression that if Mr. Jackson were sidelined for a month, those public-minded citizens who have gone out of their way to bring his violations to my attention would be more than satisfied. For that short period the charities wouldn't feel comfortable about taking anything of real value from you."

"Oh? What would make them comfortable?"

"Miss Lance, I am a man of simple tastes. Possibly too simple. I suppose that's because I have spent most of my working life in the hacking industry. It is not an experience that makes one worldly. Not like you, an attorney, with your contacts and your wealthy well-connected friends. I suppose you make more money, have more fun, go to more parties in a month than come my way in a year."

"Mr. Winston, you probably overestimate my income and underestimate my lifestyle. I have more pleasure in my life in a week than comes your way in a lifetime. So what?"

"Lately I have felt the need to enlarge my horizons. My mother passed away recently and I no longer feel so constrained to follow her teachings."

"Well, what is it? You want us to buy you a piece of ass? If that's all it is I'm sure Rufus could get somebody over here in twenty minutes. Right, Rufus?"

"Oh, hell, yes. Of course, I personally couldn't go for any chick costin' more than fifty bucks. You want something better, the counselor would probably get it up for the remainder. Seein' as how often I get it up for her."

"That's enough, Rufus. Don't bore Mr. Winston with exaggerated personal revelations."

"It ain't exaggerated. I'm talkin' about payin' the rent and all you charge for those lousy litle snacks. Oh, I'm into you more ways than one."

"Rufus has a way, Mr. Winston, of putting the most prosaic arrangements in sexual terms. Please ignore him."

"Are you and he . . .? Excuse me, Miss Lance, I'd heard you were adventurous. I had no idea. But it gives me one."

"Now wait a minute. Let's not jump to conclusions."

"Your parties. I've heard about your parties."

"Good things, I hope. We try hard."

"Your house. I've heard about your house."

"A nice little house. Not for sale."

"Your furniture, your paintings, your sculpture. I've heard about them. Tell me, is it as exciting as it sounds?"

"Worse," said Rufus. "It's people and dogs screwin' all over the place. As a Christian, I have to close my eyes just to go to the crapper. Even there it ain't safe. The shower nozzle is in the shape of a cock, "hot" and "cold" are an open pussy and a closed pussy and the wall paper is the devil screwin' his girl friends. No two alike."

"Rufus," I said, "I'm sure you have disgusted Mr. Winston. I have the feeling he would be less offended if you referred to the penis, the vagina and sexual intercourse."

"Not at all," said Winston. "If you're not I'm not. Fascinated more like it. I don't suppose it could be arranged for me to have a guided tour."

"Okay, let's go for a deal. You limit Rufus' suspension to thirty days and I'll invite you to the next party. Bring your own coke. No cameras or recording devices and your stay is limited to an hour. You stay longer and some of my friends might think you're my friend. Can't have that."

Winston faced Rufus. "Mr. Jackson, it is my duty to inform you that your license is revoked for a period of thirty days effective from 5 P.M. this afternoon. Your company will be notified later today. Please leave the license with the clerk on your way out. Miss Lance, if you could just favor me with your address and the date and the time I will record it in my social calendar right away."

"My address is in the phone book. For the rest of it, all in good time. These things have to be arranged."

"I'll be looking forward. Would you object if I brought along a friend?"

"If you can find one between now and then, why not?"

Rufus and I rose and got the hell out of there. There is a dingy, noisy cafeteria in the basement and we went down for lunch. Rufus chose a bowl of soup, two hamburgers, a large order of french fries, a salad, two pieces of apple pie and a pitcher of beer. "This may be the last good meal for the guilty son-of-a-bitch," said Rufus, "in a long time. Could you pick up the check? I gotta save every penny for what I owe you on room and board."

He ate hugely of everything I paid for, including about half of my own french fries and both the tomato quarters in my salad. I don't know why they even bother sending those tasteless gassed things up from Florida. Rufus gulped them down. "I ain't gonna let 'em go to waste. Those two tomatoes, they may just give me the extra strength I need to get through the terrible days ahead."

"I hope you realize how lucky you are," I said. "They could have killed you."

"No big deal. I knew you could handle it. That's why I give you all my business."

"Listen, stupid, I had nothing to do with it."

"Oh, I can make a good impression when I have to. Up front and all out and everythin'. When he saw I was a good, God-fearin' Christian he didn't have no choice."

"Rufus, you have missed the entire point. Nothing you said, nothing I said, that party invitation—none of it made a bit of difference."

"How come you say that? If that's so, how come we just didn't do the whole thing by writin' each other letters? I had to shave."

"Can you write?"

"Damn right I can write. Only you the mouthpiece, and if you don't have a chance to mouth off you get mad. I know you, Geraldine, you like to get it up in the spotlight."

"What has apparently escaped you, my dear Mr. Jackson, is the fact that the real estate interests and Howard and Vivian Baltus want you flat on your ass for the next thirty days. Well, not so much flat on your ass as out of the alley. Don't you get it? You won't have the taxi after today and without the taxi you won't be the persistent symbol of resistance to block busting. With you gone, the hope is that the picketing will stop, the neighbors will become resigned and the Baltuses can move in with the realization that they've won the battle. The lucky part is the thirty days. Which proves somebody on the other side has a soft spot for you. Otherwise, you could have lost your ticket forever."

Rufus let it sink in, thought it over, cleared his throat and opened his mouth.

"RASTUS on the rise, oh yeah, RASTUS on the rise
RASTUS gonna win yet, RASTUS get the prize
RASTUS be the way to go, goin' all the way
RASTUS be your Savior all the livelong day."

"Huh," I said. "What the hell is that all about?"

"A little tune I wrote for the folks on the block. You like it? You think it could make the Top Forty? Got a beat, don't it?"

"Listen, Rufus, if I were you I would forget RASTUS right away and start looking for a job. Is there anything you can do? How about driving a truck?"

Rufus drew himself up in that haughty way he so often affects when he is the object of good advice.

"Geraldine, the President For Life of The Resistance Against Sticking It To Us does not drive a truck. He does not dig ditches. He does not swish mops. He does not wash dishes. What he does, if he's got a little backin' from people who appreciate a good opportunity is go into business for hisself. Okay, it's a sick wind, ain't it? Might as well take advantage. What would you say to settin' me up as the pimp of Columbia Road? I been lookin' it over and it's ripe for development."

I laughed.

"I ain't just jivin'," said Rufus. "Up around 18th Street they's a few hookers but they ain't doin' too good. The reason is, too many of them hot-blooded Spic chicks in the neighborhood is givin' it away. If we could stop that, get 'em under contract, we could have us a gold mine. The start-up costs don't amount to shit. It's telephones, mostly, and a few office supplies. I could work outta my bedroom so there wouldn't be no extra cost for that. You bein' a partner and everything, you'd have to pay half the rent. Which means I could save a few bucks right off. Whattaya say?"

I laughed again.

"I say you're out of your mind but I've said that before. Speaking of the bedroom, you'd better understand that if you can't pay me for it you're out on your ass."

"Ah, Geraldine, you couldn't do that. You got too much of a conscience against turnin' me into somebody who lives on the heat grate. No way."

Rufus' martyred, wounded look is pretty good. More than a few people would respond sympathetically. Not this kid. This kid does not fool around with studs who don't pay their own way. This kid . . . Besides, I made it with old reliable Horace last night and he had done his usual workman-like job for the usual twenty minutes, at which point he said he had to be in the office early and would I excuse him from anything further. Of course, sweetie, no sweat. That was the actual truth because it takes at least half an hour before I begin to really perspire and throw off water in sufficient quantities for it to have an effect on my weight. I don't diet because I have found that a good, vigorous screw will take it off as well as a sauna.

"Fuck you, Rufus."

"Okay, if that's what you want."

"I don't mean literally. I mean figuratively."

"Which one? The one in the bar where the billy goat is doin' it to the sheep or the one at the landing where the monk is screwin' the nun. You remember that old joke about the priest who raised up this whore's ass by puttin' a Bible under it? She said what the fuck is goin' on, I don't need no uplift from Jesus Christ, he ain't one of my regulars. The priest come back: You sinner, it's for your own good. Then he put it in and he say, the Holy Book is beneath you, the holy man is above you, the holy pole is in your hole so wiggle your ass to save your soul. Hot damn!"

"Rufus, really. That is so gross."

"You know, sometimes I'm sorry I didn't try out for the preacherhood. Big stud like me, lotta charm, I could have fixed up my lips and my nose with the collection money and had me a nice little congregation up on the Gold Coast. Screwin' virgins right and left. Oh yeah, I can see it now. They gettin' right with Jesus Christ the same time they gettin' right with Rufus Rastus."

"Rufus, do you never think of anything but getting laid?"

"No worse than you. What time did you get home last night?"

"None of your business."

"I know you didn't come in before 2 A.M. That's when I woke up, had me a big one, figured I would take it down the hall. What size has Horace got? Little guy, huh? How can you get any fun out of a guy with a small tool when you been screwed by the champ?"

"Listen, yours isn't the biggest I've ever had. Not that it's a matter of size."

That hurt his feelings, I could tell, just crushed him. That on top of everything else. He sighed and slumped, looked really down.

"Geraldine, I feel bad."

"You should."

"What the fuck am I gonna do?"

"I told you. Look for a job."

"It ain't just that. Everybody in town gonna know I didn't succeed in my mission, didn't save the block."

"Oh, come on. You couldn't have been serious. You knew you couldn't win."

"I didn't know that. I thought I could."
"Well, tough, you didn't."
"There is only one way left."
"No, there is no way left."
"Yeah, there is one way, but I hate to use it."
"Don't do anything crazy."
"No crazier than a lot of what's goin' on these days."
"You can't win. Forget it."
"Geraldine, I want to say somethin' serious."

I wondered. Most of the time he's so full of bravado and bullshit you can't believe half of it. Now, though, the supercilious, smartass expression that precedes so many of his pronouncements was gone. He looked vulnerable. Like some little kid about to cry. Like some old man about to kick the bucket.

"Feel free. And it's free. What's on your mind?"
"If anythin' should happen, I want you to know I appreciate everythin' you've done for me. You been a good friend."
"Thanks for the compliment. Can't think of higher praise. If you've finished our lunches, let's be on our way. I've got some paying clients coming in at two o'clock."
"I wish I was one. Cause you deserve it."
"Yeah, I know."
"If I could stay in the bedroom and freeload another couple of days I would sure say 'thank you.' After that I'll be out of your hair."

He looked really down, beat, as forlorn as I had ever seen him.
"Hey, cheer up. Okay, you can stay. Listen, I hate to admit it but I'm sort of sorry for you. You've been shafted."
"So if anythin' happens, I want you to know I ain't forgot you. You see this?" He lifted his hand on which rested the diamond ring I had first seen him wear at one of my parties. "This is for you. Just jerk it off before anybody else gets a chance. Should bring five hundred at least."

I laughed. "Hey, why all the doom and gloom? You're young and strong and the world's got a few more spins. I don't want your ring. Actually, what I would like at the moment is you. You look so down and out, it brings out the sweetness in me. What do you say we get the hell out of here and go home and get in bed for half an hour?"

So we did that, Rufus for a time exulting in the fact that he was a smash success at something and me having a pretty good time, too. Thus doth the Creator provide a solace when nothing else seems to.

14

Howard Baltus here. It is satisfying to know for a certainty that if one is patient and has powerful business allies, things will turn out all right in the end. I'm referring to the house, of course. I suppose you have come to the conclusion that I am fetishistic about it, a real nut, so that nothing in my life—neither my wife nor my job—seems as important. I admit I was consumed by my happy contemplation of moving day. I know you're smiling out there, or jeering or worse, and you find it difficult to understand how I let myself become so obsessed to possess. Possess what? A house? Furniture? A beautiful view of the Capitol and Washington Monument from the upper floor? Is that all? I admit it didn't make a lot of sense and I won't try to convince you because I can't convince myself. I do know that something powerful told me that if I didn't get in the house . . . well, I did, and so it's academic.

The personal effects and the housekeeping items arrived this morning along with the plants, the china and silverware, the books and the other odds and ends from the old place. Hilltop Home Improvements kindly consented to take on the responsibility—dealing with the movers, putting down the rugs, hanging pictures and filling the various closets and nooks and crannies according to a plan drawn up by Vivian and me. Vivian and I have been getting along better though we are still not screwing regularly. We did it for the first time in days last Friday, one of those middle-of-the-night affairs which was prompted by the near miss of a wet dream. If I don't orgasm from sex three times a week, I'm going to have three nocturnal emissions. You will recall that the bed which Vivian and I occupied in the apartment—it has been sold to a *ménage à trois* down the hall and they took possession within an hour of our last usage—was a triumph of space. Vivian and I have rattled around in it lately, what with our temporary coolness, and when I took the right side and she the left there was a great, vast no-man's-land in the middle. She was so far away that if I'd had a wet dream, the ejaculate wouldn't have splashed her a bit. I was on the verge of one on Friday, a crazy dream about me and some woman I didn't even know. Which is the funny thing about sex dreams, you can do it with people you've met only seconds before. Once it tends toward anything intimate—undressing, certainly, but kissing or even touching sometimes—I am likely to come in seconds. What is disappointing is that I never actually get to stick it in; I have erupted and awakened way before. Last Friday, however, I was jerked out of my dream by Vivian's. She is something of a sleep talker and thrasher and had verbalized so loudly I was awakened. It was all groaning and moaning, the kind of sound a sexually excited woman makes when she is working her way toward orgasm. It is a noise which flatters a man enormously, deluding him into thinking he is the only one capable of provoking such passionate abandonment. I used to hear it invariably from Vivian when our love was new and each kiss an inspiration but that was long ago and, as I've complained many times lately, the sexual feeling between us is pretty limp. The way she was carrying on the night in question, however, I had this feeling that something within her was crying out for something in her and that here was a chance for us to kiss, screw, make up and establish a happy mood for the second honeymoon I envisioned for the first night in the new house. So I reached for her and kissed her and put the middle finger of my right hand on her clitoris in the classical, established way and was happy to note that the thing was engorged and slippery and since I was erect from the dream I worked her legs open, got into position and put it in.

"Oh, you brute," she said, still half asleep. "Oh, you great big savage fucking hunk, I want it. God, give it to me."

It's interesting the things women say when they are in the breeding mood, not realizing at the time how it doesn't fit in with reality too well. Because I am not a "brute" or a "savage" or a "hunk". Nevertheless, I put on my usual great performance, prolonging the thing twenty-three minutes and inducing two orgasms in her and letting myself have one only when I felt I had done my duty. "Vivian," I said as I withdrew, "you've made me very happy. What a marvelous way to spend practically our last night here. The next time we do it we'll be in the new place."

That should not be too far off because the housewarming party is running down even as I talk about it into this tape recorder. I'm in the den. The party was all I hoped it would be. Once Rufus Jackson's taxicab was no longer the great attention-grabber in the alley, the picketing and the animosity faded. Some of the neighbors actually smiled when they saw me and with that as an omen I felt I could dismiss the dogs and guards from Capitol Security Corporation. I sent out the invitations ten days ago, which I think is within the protocol limits, and put "Regrets only" and our old phone in the apartment at the bottom. Since Vivian and I don't know a single soul on the block you can imagine how difficult it might have been to decide on the invitation list. My intention was to include everybody in the block on both sides of 6th Street. I didn't exactly feel I could go up to each of the residences to see if there was a name on the door, or knock on it and inquire within, or send an invitation to the "Occupant" as a kind of junk mail. But I realized my official government position could be used to solve the problem in a matter of minutes. All it took was a phone call to the Director of the Census Bureau, which happens to come under the Department of Commerce, and an expression of my interest. The Director first quoted a statute which says that individual census data have the strictest confidentiality but when I explained how the house restoration had enormous sociological and economic significance for the block and my use of the data would be harmless and productive he relented. "If you don't," I told him, "I'm afraid this office will not look too kindly upon your next budget request." I have not flaunted my position heretofore because it was not particularly germane, but through the years I have risen to Assistant Under Secretary of Commerce for Fiscal Affairs and you should realize I am not without resources. Very definitely.

So I got the names and addresses as they were in 1980 and sent everybody an invitation. I realized that the information would not be strictly up to date but I took care of that by putting "or occupant" next to the name on the envelope. Done that way, nobody's feelings would be hurt. At least nobody complained. Indeed, nobody even called to say they couldn't make it so we felt confident that most of the two hundred people we invited would show up. We spared no expense to ensure they would enjoy themselves. I ordered all the liquor from Sixth Street Liquor, down at the corner, making sure of a plentiful supply of favorite brands and drinks—Gilbey's gin and Smirnoff vodka and J & B scotch and Miller beer, both regular and light—plus two cases of champagne and five bottles each of Beefeater gin, Stolichnaya vodka and Chivas Regal scotch and a case of Heineken Premium Light beer for those with slightly more discriminating palates. Ridgewell's did the catering and I gave them carte blanche. When money is no object they will bring in a crew of people in black tie. One man established a raw bar at which he shucked oysters and clams, another did cheese and fruit crepes over a chafing dish and another did beef tartare on party rye and pumpernickel. A waiter type moved around the place with toothpicked shrimp and several other waiter types carved the roast beef, the ham and the turkey and made sure there were always plenty of little hot things here and there. I liked what I had ordered for the dessert table. In addition to the usual French pastries I had them do a crystal bowl of strawberries and a crystal bowl of raspberries, with whipped cream and powdered sugar on the side. Espresso coffee, of course, plus the regular blend for those for whom espresso might be too exotic. In addition to the above . . . well, there is no point in going on. Perhaps the best way to convey the significance and magnificence of it all is to tell you that Ridgewell's charge per person was $37.50, which does not include the liquor and which came conservatively to $8.50 per person. Nothing chintzy there, let me tell you.

Vivian and I met our guests at the door. Both of us were simply dressed. Vivian was wearing pink silk harem pants under a shimmering white top to which five or six hundred expensive sequins had been hand affixed but there were no diamonds at either her neck or wrists and her plain pearl earrings did not seem ostentatious. Had they been, Vivian would certainly have disdained them. As has perhaps been noted prior, she is a woman of impeccable taste in clothes and would not be caught dead in anything the least bit inappropriate. I wore a pair of russet wool trousers, a creamy turtleneck pullover and an understated dark-umber ultrasuede jacket. I had thought of a plaid evening jacket but rejected it as the sort of thing that might make some guests uncomfortable. I mean, me in evening clothes and they in corduroys and blue jeans, it wouldn't look right.

The first guests arrived exactly at the announced time of 7 P.M. At Georgetown and in the other fashionable neighborhoods, nobody shows up at the official starting time. To do so, or to be the first guest, is thought unsophisticated. Someone who determines such things long ago decided that the absolutely perfect time to arrive at a party is a quarter of an hour before what should be the party's middle. The idea has caught on to the extent that most guests descend upon the scene practically *en masse*. That works against making the grand entrance, which is the point of the late arrival, but the custom has long been established and apparently nothing can be done to change it. Denying the bar to anyone tardy in excess of fifteen minutes might possibly be effective but there is always the threat that some of the more thirsty types might wreck the joint.

The first guests were old Mr. and Mrs. Dudley. You will remember that they used to live upstairs. The master bedroom and the nursery have replaced their shabby gentility. I was really surprised to see them because they had not been invited, not any longer being residents of the block. But I gave no hint that I was displeased or that they were not welcome. "So nice to see you," I said. "So happy you could come. I don't believe you know my wife, Vivian." Vivian shook hands and said, "I've heard so much about you. Marvelous you could make it. We'd have been terribly upset if you hadn't." Vivian is good at that sort of thing, lying, I mean, and smoothing over any little social crisis with diplomacy and tact. I try, but I don't usually achieve Vivian's success. I am too honest to be effective. Mr. Dudley wore a grey suit of some double-knit material that showed its age and a white shirt too large for a neck which seemed to have shriveled and wrinkled a good deal since I had seen it last. His tie was a widely striped yellow and red number and I imagine it was something he had bought for the occasion at Dart Drug. Along with the usual line of pharmaceuticals, greeting cards and trashy best sellers, Dart Drug serves as a very adequate poor-man's haberdashery. You can get all the necessary clothing items there at a fraction of what you might pay at some place like Raleighs or Lewis and Thos. Saltz but it is not stylish. I have never quite understood why cheap clothing is so frequently bizarre and ugly. It is as though the designer wanted to punish poor people for the fact that they have such poor taste. Mrs. Dudley wore something nondescript and ill-fitting in blue wool, the sort of frock one often sees on bag ladies as though it were some kind of uniform. Bag ladies do not encumber their necks with imitation pearls or douse themselves with cheap cologne because such extravagances are beyond them but Mrs. Dudley is not a bag lady and she should know bettter. Though I suppose there comes a time in life when one stops caring about constantly upgrading one's appearance and simply continues in the old familiar ways, frumpy though they may be.

A steady stream of guests followed the Dudleys. I shook hands, introduced myself and Vivian and said, "So happy you could come." After that and depending upon what they said, I varied it a trifle, offering "Tell me again which house you occupy" or "Of course I recognize you, you live right across the street" or "Your mother-in-law? Marvelous" or "All these children are yours? I had no idea" or "Would you mind repeating your name? I don't remember it being on the guest list" or "Is it a cash bar? Heavens, no" or . . . Well, you know what I mean, the usual preliminary chitchat that fills the social gap and signifies nothing.

Mr. Sanford Williams, who used to live in what is now the billiard-table-and-piano room with the long bar at the side, came at about the 75-guest mark. Again, I was surprised because he had lost his party eligibility once he was no longer a resident of the block. He seemed not the slightest bit self-conscious about crashing, just saying, "Williams is the name. You got any objection to my goin' down, see do you still have some of my pictures?"

"Pictures? I beg your pardon."

"Yeah, my *Playboy*, my *Hustler*, my tits, ass and cunts. My action shots. You seen 'em?"

"Mr. Williams, I don't know if you remember Mrs. Baltus. Darling, this is Mr. Williams, formerly down below."

"How do you do," said Vivian. "Marvelous you could come."

"Yeah, I remember her," said Williams. "The day she stepped in the dog shit."

"Yes, quite," I said, favoring Williams with a small laugh to help cover his crudity. "So far back. In those days it seemed that cleaning up after the dogs would be the only problem. Little did we realize, heh, heh."

"I took an inventory as soon as I got to my new place over in Anacostia," said Williams. "They is six or seven definitely missin'. You seen 'em?"

"Why, no," I said. "But you should understand we didn't personally clean out the premises after you and the others departed. The renovators did that."

"Uh huh," said Williams. "If that's your story, okay. But there was some really juicy shots in there. The one where two chicks is eatin' this one guy and he's eatin' one of them . . ."

"Believe me, Mr. Williams I haven't seen them. They're not here."

"Those pictures cost me a mess of money," said Williams. "If somebody stole 'em I be really pissed off." He looked at me and Vivian very aggressively. "I could get a search warrant without no trouble."

"Darling," I said to Vivian, "why don't you continue greeting the guests and I'll take Mr. Williams down to his old place and show him how it's changed."

We left Vivian at the door and headed for the lower region. The days when it was a separate entity are long past. The renovation process sealed off the front and rear entrances and now access is provided solely by the circular steel-and-wood staircase that pierces the house from top to bottom. We descended to a scene that I had envisioned as likely but which shocked me nevertheless. First, I was surprised at the intensity of the smoke. It hung like dirty fog, horizontally, an asphyxiating miasma. Why everybody wasn't coughing and choking I don't know. Most were bellied up to the bar and most were drinking beer. With the bar amply stocked with whiskey and the rest of it, it didn't make much obvious sense. I suppose it was explained by the fact that the place was so stuffy and hot that beer was the best thing to combat total dehydration. Not that anybody seemed distressed. There was a lot of laughter, that special kind of high-pitched cackle that seems indigenous to the neighborhood, and the mood it projected was furthered by the zealous dancing in the area between the billiard table and the piano. Just for the party, I'd had disco lights installed. I disco dance a little myself, but I must confess there was litle resemblance between what I do and what I saw. They've got rhythm, no question, and I can understand how they would turn the stereo to a station that specializes in hard rock. I suspect they did not realize, however, that the area they had chosen for their aggressive stomping had been sanded and polished only days before and was not designed to handle seven or eight couples, many of whom were not properly shod for dancing. It is one thing to glide around in Johnston & Murphys or Guccis and it is quite another to attack the floor with high-topped work shoes or sneakers. I could see at a dim glance that Hilltop Home Improvements would be awarded another lucrative contract. And not just for work on the floor. Several cigarette burn marks were evident when I crouched down to take a better look at the carpets, the piano legs showed scuffing, and when I rose I could see that some idiot had put a lit cigarette on the music rack. On a Bosendorfer, can you imagine!

The man I had hired to play innocuous background music was not where he should have been. When I looked around I saw him at the bar, one hand around a beer, the other hand massaging the posterior of one the ladies. I had told him he was not to mingle with the guests and now he had deliberately disobeyed me. My first thought was to upbraid him but then I realized the woman was not in the least distressed and if that is what it takes to make some bitch happy I'm for it. After all it was a party and if the person she came with didn't raise a stink why should I? Seated at the piano was a man I distinctly remember as one of the picketers. He was playing jazz in a very flamboyant and high-powered way and had I observed his performance in a fashionable nightclub I would have been generous with applause and would probably have sent a drink and five dollars over to him at intermission. He had a bevy of admirers. About as many were clustered around him as were dancing and it was interesting in a nerve-racking sort of way to be aware of what came from the piano as opposed to what came contrapuntally from the stereo. It was one big mass of sound as far as I was concerned and I was hard put to distinguish the basic beat of one from the other. The guests were coping with it easily, some at the piano snapping their fingers in time with the disco, some on the dance floor clapping their hands to the beat of the piano. It showed that they could concentrate on two different things at one time and was in a way a kind of laboratory demonstration of the black race's extraordinary ability to excel in the field of music. I must express a certain envy because my rhythmic inability is reflected in my comparatively feeble efforts on the dance floor. Oh, I get around without crippling too many partners and they have been known to flatter me, but my skill comes from expensive lessons, not from any inherent, God-given talent.

"Is everybody having a good time?" I asked. "Is everybody happy?" I raised my right hand over my head to get their attention and then waved it back and forth in a friendly manner so they wouldn't get the impression I was distressed at the speed at which my beautiful basement was being reverted to the condition from which it had so recently been rescued. "Have a drink on the arrival of Mr. Sanford Williams. He used to live here."

"Thank God he still don't," said somebody amongst those massed at the bar, his voice rising from the babble with the intensity of an extra in a mob scene speaking his one great line. "That asshole never gave a party his whole life." That remark generated peals of raucous laughter and made me feel very good because inherent in it was praise for both the party and the fact that I was part of the neighborhood. "That asshole don't deserve to be drunk to," this same somebody said. "Do it for the guy puttin' on the party." And much to my amazement and pleasure those on the dance floor stopped dancing and those around the piano stopped listening and everybody picked up a glass from somewhere and somebody said "Let's hear it for Mr. Baltus, he's all right." The glasses were lifted and emptied in one nearly simultaneous salute and I can't tell you how much that spontaneous gesture pleased me. It really made me feel warm and for the moment entirely inclined to overlook the rapidly deteriorating condition of all my handsome furnishings.

The cordiality of the moment almost prompted me to deliver the little speech I had written for the occasion but I held off because what I wanted to say was meant for everybody and I knew that many guests had still not arrived. So I left the cellar, noting as I did that Mr. Williams was being readily accepted by the others—back slapping from the men and hugs from the women and "hi ya doin'" and "you lookin' good" and "gimme five" and all the rest of the patois—and that he had apparently lost the belligerent mood with which he had confronted Vivian and me. I ascended the beautiful circular staircase, feeling, as I lost the sight and sound of the nightclub chaos which was erupting again as I left it, that these good people could, with the proper example and tutelage, learn to appreciate the value of property and proper conduct. Give it a year.

The main level had filled nicely in my absence. I was happy to note they were people who had more interests in life than rushing down to the bar and carrying on. They were older, more sedate types and while they were not bashful about helping themselves to the delicacies of the buffet, they were careful where they put the dirty dishes and their cigarettes. Beyond that, several impressed me with their interest in the fine arts. A powerful Mark Rapko hangs in the dining room, a new acquisition from the same prestigious Georgetown gallery that had made it possible for me to become owner of the beautiful paintings in the master bedroom. The Rapko is typical of his work, being nothing at first glance and a lot more than nothing when it is given the study it deserves. What one sees superficially is a solid black canvas. But if you stare at it fixedly for the proper amount of time, one can see that it is not solid black at all but *almost* solid black in certain areas and *very nearly* solid black in others and *faintly* solid black in still others. A very cerebral work, indeed, and once we are completely settled and I have more time, I plan on contemplating the thing until I have derived the full benefit. I realize it may take several weeks even if I am willing to spend as much as ten or twelve minutes a day which is a real expenditure in these busy times but I just don't care. That picture cost me a fortune and I intend getting my money's worth out of it no matter how long it requires. Money aside, there is the deep satisfaction that will come from living with and mastering something powerfully inscrutable. Not everybody could do it.

"What do it mean?" This from a gentleman who had been standing in front of the canvas. I had snagged a glass of champagne from a passing waiter—a nice touch, champagne, though very few guests had chosen it—and joined the fellow who was regarding the Rapko. He was about fifty and wore a real suit, none of that blue-denimed leisure crap, and black-framed glasses. Before he spoke I had taken him for an educator possibly or a rug-and-furniture salesman. "Do it mean the guy didn't have no other colors?"

"Sir," I said, "I don't believe we've met. I'm Howard Baltus, the host. So happy you could make it."

"Oh," he said, "you the one. I left my invite at home. Your missus say it don't make no difference, come right on in. Call me Virgil."

"A fine classical name," I said. "A dignified name. It suits you well."

"Well, thank you," said Mr. Virgil. "Thank you. A lot of folks don't know it, but the way it was explained to me by my mama, a Virgil is a male virgin. Did you know that?"

"What? No, I didn't," I said. "Isn't that interesting."

"It might be if it were still true. Only it ain't. That's my wife right over there. She got me when I wasn't more than about eighteen."

I looked. The wife was seated on the good Piotr Pendrecki, not that the price these days of Pendrecki chairs would permit the owner to admit that it was otherwise. She had the chilly appearance of a woman with an enormous ability to communicate a lifelong resentment against life. I nodded pleasantly, raised my champagne, smiled. I definitely wanted to ingratiate myself with her; if I could get her to like me, everybody else in the neighborhood would be a snap.

"When my mama found out," Mr. Virgil went on, "she was really angry because she had me in mind for somebody not so round in the heels and weak in the knees. It was too late then. I was already on my way to bein' an unmarried father. That changed, too, before too long."

It is flattering to have perfect strangers pour out their lives to you at first acquaintence but really . . .

The man turned from me and toward the picture. "Mr. Baltch, that is one goddamned hunk of black paint. I can't make hide nor hair of it. What's it supposed to do, cover the wall safe?"

I chuckled at the witticism, if that's what it was meant to be. "Mr. Virgil, if you will excuse me, I think I had better relieve my wife at the door."

"Okay, I figured you didn't have the answer neither. You get it, let me know."

I left him laughing, an incipient art critic of the sort who likes the pretty and is suspicious of everything else. I must make certain that our Christmas card to him and his formidable wife is nothing more challenging than a print by those two genteel purveyors of the familiar and simple, Mr. Nathaniel Currier and Mr. James Merritt Ives.

Guests were still coming in as I worked my way back to the front entrance, laughing and cackling and more at ease than those who had come just at seven and who had seemed slightly awestruck at the beginning, slightly unsure of what was expected and how they should conduct themselves. The newer arrivals seemed much more animated and as I approached the door I realized why. There— resplendent in a blue blazer of conservative but perfect cut, blue plaid trousers of a striking design, shiny black loafers with tassels, a white shirt with a low-set, widespread collar into which a blue-gourded tie nestled perfectly and a diamond of blinding size on a hand which had the recent benefit of a manicure—was the dominating presence of Mr. Rufus Rastus Jackson, the one person I was certain I would not see on the great night and who I would prefer to never see ever.

For a moment I thought he had just arrived. He stood next to Vivian, along with four women and three men and I supposed they would move on after the amenities. But no, while I waited patiently in the hallway for them to pass, I realized the bastard was practically making a speech—the same speech followers of this story have already heard so many times: RASTUS, the "poor deprived people of 6th Street" and all the goddamn rest I'm sick and tired of. I was bound and determined I wouldn't lose my temper on my night of triumph but had the man no manners at all, no sense of propriety, no understanding of the fact that I had won and he had lost and why the fuck didn't he just stay the hell away instead of charging in and taking my place at my front door with my wife practically close enough to touch . . . Jesus Christ, I mean really!

I coughed ostentatiously after thirty seconds and Jackson turned toward the sound to see who had the nerve. "Howard, old buddy, good to see ya," he said, not self-conscious in the slightest, not taken aback a bit by my righteously indignant expression and responding to it with a smile wider than a watermelon. "How the hell you doin'? Me and Viv was just talkin' about the good old days when you could go to a party in this house without spendin' an hour dressin' up for it. But I ain't complainin'. You lookin' good, man, and old Viv, she lookin' beautiful." He walked right up to me, grabbed my right hand, shook the blood out of it, put his left arm around my shoulders and if I hadn't had the presence of mind to do a quick two-step to the left would probably have drawn me into a bear hug. It's a disgusting habit, this man-hugging, and is an import from a Europe becoming more decadent by the day. Goddamn it, I don't like it and neither do the rest of the few straight men still around. The fact that this Jackson creature tried it is a sad commentary on how his life has changed. I attribute it to his media notoriety. Before that came along, he would have denounced it as queer. Christ, maybe he is . . .

"Oh, hello, Jackson," I said, formally. "Good to see you. Glad you could make it." When good manners have been drilled into one from the beginning, one will say the right thing no matter the circumstances. "I do admit to a certain surprise."

"Hey, man, I'm glad you appreciate it. I could have gone to a couple of Georgetown brawls. Also sweet Geraldine Lance is throwin' a minor bash for those sex fiends she hangs around with. But when it came time to make a decision I didn't hesitate a bit. If I couldn't be with old Harold and lovely Vivian on their big night I didn't want to be nowhere."

I took that part about Geraldine with a grain of salt because I had asked Geraldine to the party and she had declined out of the necessity to go to New York on a legal matter. And as for Georgetown, how could he get to Georgetown now that he no longer had the taxi? Take a taxi? What cabbie would pick him up? A big ugly black guy is a risk damn few want to take. Not that I blame them.

"I know what you're thinkin'," said Jackson. "How'd I get here, seein' as how I have been temporarily deprived of my livelihood by certain unnamed forces of repression. But, hell, I still got a few friends in the neighborhood and a couple of 'em swung around to pick me up on the way over."

"I see," I said. "And where are you living these days?" I couldn't have cared less but the habits of civilized conduct stay with one even when contrary behavior is strongly indicated. "Found something more comfortable than a taxicab?"

Jackson laughed, the sound erupting out of him as though I'd said something hilarious. "Howie," he said, "I'm gonna let you in on a little secret. You're not gonna believe this, but you're lookin' at a big winner in the D.C. Lottery. You wanna know the number I played? 757, the same as this house. Paid off ten thousand bucks. TEN THOUSAND BUCKS! Yeah, man, with that kind of money I can live anywhere." I didn't believe him for an instant and I don't believe it was his intention that I should. He was teasing me, denying me the satisfaction of seeing him grovel. Only I didn't think it was a bit amusing, just the dumb fun-and-games of a born loser and a comedian for life. If he had been a real man he would have said, "Mr. Baltus, I don't have a place to stay more than a night or two and I need all the help I can get. I'd appreciate anything you can do for me." But no, he had to come on as though he didn't have a care in the world. If he had shown a little humility, a little defeat, I would have been generous in victory. I have several staff-car driver billets under my control at the office and as I recall they pay $12,500. That is not bad for someone who is facing the indignity of accepting Government unemployment money. Though in his case I suppose he would consider unemployment money a paid six-month vacation.

"Congratulations," I said. "Glad to hear it. Glad you could come." I knew I was repeating myself but the man had a bad effect on my poise. "I suppose you know your way around. There's food and drink all over the place. Help yourself."

And with that I turned on my heel and strode off toward the staircase—yes, I did, I literally strode—and headed up it. I did not give Jackson the satisfaction of looking back, lest his mockery of expression do further damage to my mood. But I could hear that damnable cackle of his as I ascended and then something he said to Vivian I couldn't quite catch and her reply and I couldn't catch that either. I did not want him stationed at my front door, you can be certain of that, and the moment I reached the upper level and spotted a waiter I described Jackson and told him to approach him with the message that his old buddy, Mr. Sanford Williams, had a chick lined up for him in the basement. The waiter said, "Okay, Mr. Baltus, there isn't much need for me to stay up here anyhow. They've been mostly giving the place a quick look, taking a pee some of them and going on down below. I think there's just one old couple off there in the back."

He pointed toward the room designated to one day be the nursery and I proceeded toward it. Just as I suspected, Mr. and Mrs. Dudley were there. Mrs. Dudley sat on a chaise longue and Mr. Dudley sat on the stool at the dressing table. Both looked awfully sad considering that the dirty dishes piled on the chest of drawers—where the baby's clothes will be one day—showed they had dined well and the glasses they held were still pretty full. Then I realized they were sitting much as they must have when the nursery was their bedroom and had probably been talking about the way things had worked out for them. How they had to move and all that. How I was the son-of-a-bitch that caused it and all that. How it's hard being black folks and all that.

"Mr. Dudley, Mrs. Dudley," I said, "I can't tell you how really happy I am that you could be here tonight."

"Lawdy," said Mrs. Dudley, "I don't hardly recognize it."

"Where did the radiator go?" Mr. Dudley asked. "Noisiest son-of-a-bitch in the world."

"It don't seem it could be the same place," Mrs. Dudley said, her wonder showing. "Seems bigger than the old days."

"Are you happy where you are now?" I asked. "Are you getting along okay?"

"We're makin' it," said Mrs. Dudley, a certain martyr quality evident in the statement. "Lotta folks crowded together but that ain't nothin' new among black people." She surveyed the premises, took a swallow of her drink. "This is a pretty room for the baby. Where you hidin' it?"

I laughed. "It's not here yet. But we're hopeful."

"White folks don't make kids the way black folks do," said Mr. Dudley. "Black folks can make a kid without even tryin'."

"Hush up," Mrs. Dudley said to Mr. Dudley. "Just because Mr. Baltus put out a lot to drink, ain't no reason to forget your manners. You ain't home."

"The hell I ain't. This is my home right here. I lived in this room twenty-five years."

You can understand why I hadn't invited the former tenants. What's past is past.

"Mr. Dudley, if you and Mrs. Dudley would come down to the main floor I'd like you to be near me when I talk to the other guests. I think after you've heard me, you'll understand that what's happened is all for the best."

I got them to their feet. Pulled almost. They would have preferred sitting and getting even more smashed, I knew, but I couldn't leave them. They were practically at the point where another drink or two and they would be out of it for hours. Okay, I wouldn't put them out into the cold unless I was satisfied they could drive (Did they drive here? They just seemed to materialize. The doorbell rang and there they were) but, honestly, I wasn't at all interested in them spending the night. This is not a hotel.

So I herded them toward the staircase and down it. When we reached the ground floor I led them to the sofa in the living room. I signaled a waiter to bring them coffee. "Nothing alcoholic. Tell the bartender." Then I returned to the staircase and the public address system equipment I had installed for the occasion. I would have preferred to address the guests face to face but there were so many—most of them down below but seventy or so in the living room and the dining room and on out in the garden—that it would have been impossible. It was almost ten-thirty and soon some would be leaving though none had so far. At least nobody had sought me out to compliment me on the lovely party and say "Thank you." I turned on the requisite switches and after everything had sufficient time to warm up I picked up the microphone.

"Ladies and gentlemen, can you hear me okay?" My voice resounded throughout, the amplified words coming back slightly delayed as sometimes happens and with the portentous, larger-than-life quality you get from speakers and loudspeakers at national political conventions. I hate it when people begin by saying "Can you hear me okay?" It's dumb. If they can't hear, how can they hear the question? It is the custom, however, and I am careful about not defying custom too many times. It is enough that I am doing the daring thing on 6th Street.

"Ladies and gentlemen, may I have your attention?" Those I could see gave it, and the steady roar from down below subsided and the piano playing stopped and somebody turned off the stereo. It is always satisfying when all ears are focused. "This won't take long. In a few minutes you can get back to whatever you're doin'. Drinkin', eatin' or foolin' around." Notice how I dropped my g's? Just a little touch there, but I get the laugh I had hoped for. A couple of "right on's came from the distance and "Amen, brother, tell it like it is" came from some man who had flaked out on a beautiful Persian rug, a drink in one hand and a hunk of roast beef in the other. I am sure he did not for one moment realize the potential for damage to something that cost . . . Enough of that. You will get the impression I am excessively materialistic. I am not excessive about anything. As the pundit once put it, all things in moderation.

"Ladies and gentlemen, as you can imagine this is a proud day for my wife, Vivian, who is at my side, and me." That was not entirely true because Vivian was not at my side even though we had rehearsed my speech a number of times and she knew what was expected of her. I looked around, hoping she would at least respond to cue, and in a few seconds she did so, emerging from the stairwell as smoothly as a show girl making her entrance at the Miss America Contest. A beautiful woman—and I was terribly proud when she came to me and kissed me. The kiss was what she was supposed to do just as I finished the "at my side" line so it pleased me that we were on schedule again. I was about to go on when I realized that Vivian had been followed up the staircase by the Jackson creature—which may or may not have meant they had been drinking together or eating together or dancing together or . . . no, no, certainly not. Jackson, much to my surprise, stationed himself next to me. So there we were, the three of us, like it had all been planned. That was a development I certainly did not approve of but there was no possible way I could disengage myself without offending Jackson. I don't know why I was so solicitous of his feelings; God knows he has never been of mine.

"First off," I said, "I want to thank everybody for coming. Vivian and I sent out about two hundred invitations and you have more than exceeded the quota. Which proves we have even more friends than we realized." Some laughter, some whistling, some applause, some foot stomping—just the usual polite response to the first part of the speech where the speaker is supposed to say something funny. For almost fifty bucks worth of food and booze it was the least they could do. "If we had any more friends we'd need another house. And you all know how much trouble we had getting this one." Some laughter, etc., and a few boos. I was happy to get the former and wasn't put off by the latter. That was my strategy: lay it on the level and win them with truth. First a few jokes but then turn utterly serious.

"Now that we've got the house and now that you're all in it, I'm certain this is the start of a new spirit and new progress for the neighborhood. I realize there was great objection in the beginning —some from the individuals most affected, some from others who felt threatened, some from outsiders who hoped to capitalize on what seemed to be happening. But I never once despaired of seeing my dream come true. This is where I want to live and this is where Vivian and I hope to raise our family (I leaned toward her and gave her the rehearsed peck) and this is where we intend meeting our responsibilities as human beings and as citizens of the Nation's Capital. It is my fervent hope that you will join with me so that together we can successfully challenge the hurdles that lie ahead and so together we can share the rich rewards that will come from the fruits of our labors."

I paused. If they were going to be difficult I wanted to sense it right away. If they were going to regard it as bullshit I wanted to hear them smell the first whiff. If they were going to puke I wanted to alert the waiters. I heard nothing and I was encouraged.

"There is no need for me to elaborate on the obstacles that lie between the unsatisfactory conditions that have prevailed in the past and the goals of the future. You are just as aware of them as I. But it won't do any harm to list a few of the main items so we understand each other. I think we'll all agree that upgrading the condition of the housing should be our first-priority project. You don't have to look beyond the walls of this lovely house to realize what can be done if time and effort are expended in a productive way."

A small buzzing ensued and I was not foolish enough to misinterpret its significance. They were offended—but that was part of my plan. Better get it out in the open so that what I was leading up to would have even greater impact.

"Now I know what you're thinking. You're thinking it's easy for me and tough for you. I admit I may have been luckier in some ways. And I don't mean just because I was born with a white skin and you were born with a permanent suntan."

That were a few snorts and a guffaw or two. Okay, that is how it is done in Washington these days—call the blacks black as if they weren't aware on their own. People in the know in Washington don't simply disregard color—they emphasize it in the most up-front and forthcoming way. A good thing, of course, when you consider that in the old days upper-strata whites hardly looked at blacks, hardly deigned to notice their existence. These days it's entirely different. These days one looks right at them and they either look right back or right through—which is in itself one of the great achievements of the civil rights movement. The Government, of which I am only a small part, can take credit.

"But the good fortune with which I was blessed is a fortune indeed. I suppose most of you aren't aware of it but my grandfathe- —a poor immigrant from the old country who didn't have it any better than many of you—founded Banner Suits. I'm sure you've heard of it. He made a bundle. My father did even better. He made bundles my grandfather hadn't even dreamed of. And with four or five of those bundles he created the Baltus Philanthropic Foundation. Never heard of it? I'm not surprised. Because the philanthropies have mostly been directed toward Israel to help with hospitals and schools and housing for the poor. It does enormous good and I am proud that my family is making the effort. But I suddenly realized not too many weeks ago, goddamn it, that it didn't make a lot of sense to send all that money to Israel when there are a hell of a lot of people right on this block who could use it just as well. And another thing, people right on this block have been pouring their money into Banner blue jeans and leisure suits and jogging pants all their lives. And if Banner hadn't prospered in the first place there wouldn't be any Baltus Philanthropic in the second place, right? So why shouldn't the people who made it all possible benefit? Friends, neighbors, I asked myself and I've got to tell you the answer was obvious: 6th Street deserves the money as much as Israel."

I could sense guests surging forward all over the house. They knew I was leading up to laying some money on them and that will do it every time. When the mercenary instincts are properly stimulated there is a figurative reaching out of hands for a handout no matter how one tries not to. I understood perfectly and I was terribly pleased that I could make it possible. I just hoped someone among them would have the good sense to signal the piano player, whoever it might be, to be ready with "For He's A Jolly Good Fellow" at the proper moment. I had coached my own man but you will recall he had abandoned his post for some floozy at the bar. His tip will reflect his neglect.

"Effective the first of next month, with the blessing of my father and the others in the family who are directors of the foundation and myself, the sum of $50,000 a month for every month in the indefinite future will be allocated to the rehabilitation of each and every house in the 700 block of 6th Street without regard to ownership or state of repair. Yes, you heard me right. Fifty thousand bucks each and every month until this block is an example for every other block on Capitol Hill. What do you think of that?"

Cheers and catcalls and applause was what they thought of it, the sound sweeping toward me the same way it must have swept toward Marc Antony when he read Caesar's will to his friends and countrymen in Rome. A very satisfying sound, indeed.

"And friends, that's only the beginning. Once the physical aspects of the block begin to be improved we can start concentrating on the moral aspects of our existence. Now I'm not suggesting we're more immoral than anyone else but I'm sure you'll agree with me that having a liquor store at one end of this block is something we don't want and we don't need. It's not the liquor itself that galls me. I like to drink and I like to give my friends a drink as you can certainly tell from the way the bar is stocked. What galls me are the D.C. Lottery tickets. You buy a D.C. Lottery ticket at the liquor store and you're taking your hard-earned money and throwing it right at the politicians down at the D.C. Building who've got better things to do with it than help the people who gave it to them. It's not like the Baltus Foundation, let me tell you that. How do I know? Figure it out. If they cared a rat's ass about the 700 block of 6th Street down at the D.C. Building, they'd never have permitted it to disintegrate into the ghetto it is today. Excuse me for using that word if I've offended you but it's the truth and you know it."

I hadn't intended becoming so exercised because when I do I tend to lose my Harvard polish and revert to the colloquialisms of my father and grandfather. Expressions like "let me tell you" and "figure it out" and "you know it" creep in and I sound only slightly more sophisticated than those of lesser education. If I can't keep my poise when I'm talking, I would be better off not talking at all. Even though what I said came straight from the heart.

"And once the liquor store is kicked out we can work our tails off to get a library in its place. It won't be easy because there will be pressure from the owner of the building to let him lease it to McDonald's. No way. McDonald's sells junk food, which is bad enough, but what about the paper napkins and the bags which McDonald's claims they clean up but are all over the block in no time? It's terrible—and we don't want it around here. A library is the answer. A library is the best thing that could happen and I'm sure it will have a pronounced effect on raising property values."

I went on in that vein for a few more minutes. I brought up the matter of the running dogs and the scattered garbage and the graffiti and all the rest. Okay, it may have sounded presumptuous, but as a neighbor and a friend I felt I should be indulged. And also, and this was the main reason I persisted, it was for their own good. The trouble with our modern society is that people aren't preached to enough. Bleeding hearts say if you tell people they should shape up and also how they can do it, it smacks of paternalism. I don't see it that way. After all, the Baltus Foundation has always been run on a sound business basis and there didn't seem to be any reason why the beneficiaries of the upcoming munificence should not be made aware of their responsibilities. There is no free lunch.

"But those things can wait. Tonight is the night we party. Bartenders and waiters, I want you to fill every empty glass. You piano player down in the basement, let's get those keys plinkin' and will somebody please turn on the stereo and get this place movin' again? I want to hear the sound of people havin' a real good time."

I was about to turn off the public address system and work my way through the crowd to get some individual reaction to my ideas. I expected my hand would be grasped a number of times and maybe a few women would throw their arms around me and possibly one or two would kneel in front and address me as Savior (A joke! I'm just kidding, believe me!). But before I could put the microphone down it was snatched from my grasp by Jackson and before I could protest he had brought it to his mouth and shouted, "Let's hear it for Vivian and Howard Baltus, they're okay!" Jackson was not ignored. The cheers came down on me in a great, engulfing wave and I must confess to one of the most truly satisfying times of my life. Though I am by nature moderately modest I reveled in the praise as what man wouldn't. I reached for Vivian so that our happiness could be shared as a loving unit but she had drifted off. No matter; I'm sure she heard the applause wherever she was.

Right now I'm in the second floor den, putting into the tape recorder the events I've just described. The sound of revelry is diminishing and I suppose the guests are working themselves toward departure, an event which they must approach with distaste considering the contrast between my place and theirs. But not for long. The Baltus Foundation money will make the difference. I wouldn't be surprised if one day fairly soon Vivian and I will be happy to accept invitations from within the neighborhood. Right now my place is at the front door with Vivian, saying goodby to our guests and accepting their thanks for the favors of this evening and those which are promised for the future. Right now I'm pulling the plug on the tape recorder . . .

15

It happened seconds after the last of the guests had had their hands shaken and been clapped on the back if they were men and pecked on the cheek if they were women. We were on the small landing just outside the front door, framed there like a happy couple in *Better Homes and Gardens*, waving, smiling and, in Howard's case, very nearly blowing kisses. Howard was slightly ahead because he is not accustomed to the limelight and had been generously pushed by me to the forefront. He looked so pleased with himself and the world, sure that the party had put us in good favor with the neighbors and that everything he envisioned for the block was well on the way. Only a cynic would have begrudged him his happiness. Okay, Howard had possibly been incredibly naive in saying some of what he said but he intended it to be taken in the most friendly way. He meant so well, which makes it even more horrible. If he had been a mean, insensitive racist who bought blacks out of their homes so he could humiliate them at a profit, what happened might have to a certain extent been rationalized. Not forgiven, of course, but explained away. As it is, what followed was horrible and brutal and unbelievable, the grossest, most cowardly act imaginable and I am not going to be satisfied until some black son-of-a-bitch pays for it in the electric chair.

Down on paper I suppose I sound removed, dispassionate to a certain extent, almost the uninvolved observer. I have chosen to assume such a role deliberately; it is my English nature. The passage of time has helped. At the exact moment I screamed and when Howard fell I knelt over him and saw where the jagged brick had ruptured his skull, saw the blood spurt, saw his eyes roll back, heard the lone agonizing shriek and saw him go in seconds . . . All right, that is enough; I do not intend letting myself get carried away. There was a shout from the sidewalk just before the brick arced through the night. I presume it was a guest though it may have been somebody not invited. The police pointed that out. Possibly, I don't know. What I do know is that I heard somebody yell "Down with Baltus! Up with RASTUS!" seconds before Howard was struck, a warning and a threat and a rebuke to Howard all wrapped up in one. Before I could react, or Howard, the missile flared out of the darkness pointed inexorably at Howard's temple. I know I was conscious of the missile's approach, not that I could do anything about it beyond shouting "Look out!" If Howard had not been waving both hands above his head in the manner of Richard M. Nixon, perhaps he might have gained a split second during which he might have taken evasive action. A head movement of no more than a foot might have made the difference. A difference in trajectory of no more than a degree or so might have made me the victim, not Howard. Thank God it didn't. That may sound callous but you wouldn't believe me anyhow if I said I wish I had died and Howard had lived. Not at all. I grieve his death and I seek the widow's revenge but I'm not sorry that when the brick came hurtling toward us it found Howard and missed me. Self-preservation is stronger within me than any sense of martyrdom. I must be honest.

That same instinct for preservation gripped most of the guests the moment they realized what had happened and they raced off in every direction, fearful of interrogation by the police. A few, either innocent or brazen, rushed to the fallen Howard and to me, crouched beside him. Among them were Jackson and the Dudleys. Mr. Dudley said, "The one that threw that had a good eye on him and a good arm, too. Can't do nothin' about the man on the ground. He be dead." Mrs. Dudley said, "I had a feelin' somethin' like this might happen. Folks should know better than servin' too much rich food and whiskey to folks ain't used to it." Jackson extracted a white handkerchief from his breast pocket and pressed it against the wound. Blood gushed for a minute or so, then subsided, and by the time the ambulance and police sirens became audible Howard had ceased to exist. "I can go to the hospital in the ambulance," Jackson said to me. "Ain't no point in you goin'. You gonna have to talk to the police."

I must say the police were thorough. Within minutes they were everywhere. They blocked off the block, they interrogated witnesses, they carefully put the murder weapon in a plastic envelope and sealed it, they took at least fifty pictures and they tramped endlessly though the newly created front-yard garden. Howard would not have liked that but Howard's wishes are the least of it now. Mine are everything. What became apparent within days of the death is that I am to be a person of impressive means. The will names me as the only beneficiary and as soon as it is probated I am to receive $1,500,000 in blue-chip securities and a yearly income of $110,000. I had no idea. I knew Howard was well off but the strength of the trusts established by Howard's grandfather and father had not been revealed by Howard. It raises interesting questions, not the least of which is why Howard had bothered with working when he and I could have had a perfectly lovely time in the jet set. The answer has been stated a number of times but his demise confirms it more than ever: The good he thought he could do on 6th Street meant more to him than anyone gave him credit.

Howard was buried in the King David Cemetery in Falls Church, a Virgina suburb, after a funeral service at the Washington Hebrew Congregation. It is supposed to be the most fashionable Jewish congregation in the city. I don't know. There is a sameness about funeral services. A few speeches, a few prayers, a few songs, a few tears and it's all over. The service for Howard was conducted largely in Hebrew. I cannot understand why except that it is the tradition. Howard did not speak Hebrew or understand it and God knows I do not. Howard's relatives and his Jewish friends seemed equally unfamiliar and those who looked non-Jewish or who were black were, of course, totally out of it. Not that it made any significant difference to us in the audience. I am certain the rabbi did his best for Howard and got him a nice place to stay in Jewish heaven and any praying in Hebrew by others wasn't really necessary. I *was* called on at the cemetery. The widow is required to pray as the casket is lowered and the rabbi spoke the Hebraic phrases slowly and I repeated after him. I wanted to ask why I couldn't say something in English, like "ashes to ashes, dust to dust," phrases out of the Protestant Service, the point being that if God does exist He should have extraordinary powers, not the least of which is a proven ability in an infinite number of languages. However, I did what was expected of me. I did not weep. Others were not so contained. One of Howard's old aunts was practically out of control. She is an anti-WASP of the first water and we have not been friendly. She did come up to me after the dirt had been thrown down on Howard and spoke a platitude or two, but after she wandered off toward the other relatives I am certain I heard her refer to me as "the shiksa." I am not "the shiksa." I am Howard's wealthy widow and don't you forget it.

Many from 6th Street were at both the synagogue service and the cemetery: the Dudleys and Sanford Williams and Rufus Jackson plus twenty or so others. Statistically, it was a pretty good showing because it was a Monday morning. Howard would have been pleased at the turnout, seeing it as a significant demonstration of respect and admiration if not affection. I looked them over carefully when I had a chance, not knowing but what I was in the presence of the murderer. Geraldine Lance and Lucius DeTroit, the real estate broker, were there, too, and I could not help but think back on the day when Mr. DeTroit had first brought Howard and me around to 757. If only I had protested a little more. It was Howard's idea; I was pefectly content at the FoxDen. There is so much to be said for staying with your own kind.

I was taken home alone in the funeral director's limousine, a black Cadillac. The funeral director wondered if I wanted to ask a few people over and if I did he knew a caterer who was available on short notice. I said no. I needed to be by myself for practically the first time since the tragedy. The police felt they had to interrogate me much of the Sunday following and the newspaper and TV reporters called again and again. It is a distasteful custom but I am a colleague and can understand and was cooperative. "No," I told them, "I haven't the foggiest notion who could have done it. But I will not be satisfied until I see that black son-of-a-bitch pay with his life." Those were my exact words and I can say that with certainty because I had written them down in advance and in anticipation. I was not quoted with precision. The *Washington Post* had it, "I will not rest until the criminal is apprehended and tried." The *Washington Times* said, "I will not rest as long as the perpetrator roams the face of the earth." And the lesser publications did little better, though one did convey my sincere interest in having somebody suffer in the extreme degree. It headlined its story "Capitol Hill Hostess Hails Capital Punishment." Euphemisms for "black son-of-a-bitch" were used freely elsewhere. There was "inner-city citizen" and "a person with a minority background" and "a man tall enough to play in the National Basketball League." For God's sake, whatever became of freedom of the press?

I have requested and been granted a short leave of absence from the station. I have signed many forms brought to me by an attorney I had never heard of before but who surfaced with Howard's will. He assured me he has looked after the Baltus family legal affairs for many years and I can trust him. I do. It has been my limited experience, however, that it is a smart idea to have one lawyer check on another and I have retained Geraldine Lance in that capacity. I have begun to interview prospective maids. I have signed up with a yard-care firm. I have had a number of very serious talks with the black police detective assigned to the case and I have already come to the conclusion that the probability of finding Howard's killer is almost nil. The detective says they will in time interrogate everybody on the party guest list but he is not optimistic. The murder weapon, he says, failed to yield fingerprints, which suggests to him that the assailant acted deliberately and rules out anything spontaneous and unrehearsed. He wanted to know if Howard had any enemies. I told him about our experiences with the purchase of the house; draw your own conclusions. He said a good way to approach the case would be to offer a reward for information leading to the arrest and conviction. I said fine, what did he have in mind? Well, he said, if you could see your way to go that high, a thousand dollars would probably do it if there were witnesses. I said that was an agreeable amount and there had to be witnesses. I said the walk to the sidewalk and the sidewalk itself had had any number of people on it and surely the throwing of the brick had been observed. Not necessarily, he said. It was dark and happened so fast. Well, I said, would it help if the reward money went to fifteen hundred—or higher? No, he said, if we go too high, people will be accusing anybody just on the chance they're right. That way you would stir up a lot of ill will in the neighborhood. Ill will, I said, what do you think caused my husband's death if not ill will? He had nothing to say to that. He did want to know if I intended to stay in the house. Had I thought about selling it? Maybe I would feel safer elsewhere. Listen, Lieutenant, I said, let's get one thing straight. They couldn't scare us out before and they're not going to scare me out now. What's the matter, can't the police force do its job? He said he would assign a few men to keep an eye on the place round-the-clock for a few weeks but he couldn't guarantee anything. Nobody could, not in these times with lenient judges letting hoodlums back out on the street two hours after they are arrested.

Rufus Jackson called on me three days after the funeral. He drove up in a car that looked very much like the Jaguar I believe Geraldine Lance drives. Geraldine filled me in on the details of his Hack Office hearing and the license suspension that had given Howard and me relief from the harassment that had preceded. Rufus rang the bell at five o'clock in the afternoon and I went to the front door, peered through the peephole a second and opened the door wide. I was determined not to act as though I were a prisoner in my own home. He was wearing his standard hacking outfit: white sneakers, blue jeans, brown sport shirt and a greasy black cap. The leering arrogance I usually associate with the man was modified somewhat by a certain expression of sorrow.

"Yes," I said. "What is it?"

"How ya doin', Viv. You doin' okay?"

"As well as can be expected. Was there something you wanted?"

"Can I come in?"

"No."
"I need a drink of water."
"No. Sorry."
"The bathroom? I gotta pee real bad."
"What? Certainly not."
He squirmed a little to emphasize his need.
"I'll pay if that's the problem."
"Mr. Jackson, I'm frightfully busy this afternoon. Would you be good enough to state your business? And if there is none, please go."
"Viv, I ain't really had a chance to say nothin' about poor Howard. I want you to know I feel bad about it."
The nerve of the man.
"Why? You're what caused it. How could you possibly be sorry?"
"No, I didn't. I didn't have any part of it. Others got carried away. Not me."
I looked at the lying bastard, gritted my teeth, scowled furiously and pushed the door to close it. His foot was in the way.
"If you don't go away immediately," I said, "I will call the police."
He thought it over, frowned. "How you gonna do that? You can't close the door as long as I'm leanin' on it. If you move away I could come in. Once I'm in, they is no way I would let you call the cops."
I couldn't believe it. "Are you threatening me? If I want a policeman it doesn't require a phone call. There's a police officer in that car right across the street from yours."
He turned his head, looking at the black Dodge in which sat a man reading a magazine.
"He don't look like no policeman to me. That's some guy probably sellin' dope. You didn't know they sold dope in the neighborhood?"
"You are terribly wrong, Mr. Jackson. The police detective in charge of the murder promised me protection."
Jackson's chuckle conveyed his contempt. "They always do that. Protection for the victim's family in case the bad guys strike again. Protection for the accused's family in case somebody try to get revenge. Protection for the liquor store that got stuck up. Protection for . . . Hell, if they protected everybody needs protectin' they wouldn't have no time to write tickets for double-parkin'."
"We'll see about that," I said, and I began to wave my hands to attract the attention of the man in the car. I was about to shout when Jackson pulled his foot away.
"Okay," he said, "ain't no point in causin' a stink. I'm jus' tryin' to be friendly."

"I don't need your friendship, thank you very much. Now please go."

Jackson stood his ground. "You know somethin', Vivian, you a lot like Howard. You got a real conscience on you."

"A conscience? All civilized people do. All uncivilized people don't. All they care about is taking the easy way through life. You should know about that."

"Hey, Viv, how about holdin' it down? You ain't on the radio. This ain't no TV show."

"My name is Mrs. Baltus. I would appreciate it if you would remember that.

"Oh, I remember it okay. Funny thing you didn't complain when we was knockin' a few back in Bertram's bar."

"I was extremely kind to you. I could have turned you in to the Hack Office for any number of violations."

"Wasn't no need. Others took care of it. Only you didn't because you got a conscience."

"Mr. Jackson, you're repeating yourself. What's on your mind?"

"I need a job real bad."

"Sorry, no jobs here. I have a maid. I have a yard man."

"Yeah, but you don't have no bodyguard. You thought about that?"

I scorned the suggestion. "Why would I need a bodyguard? I'm not a head-of-state, I don't have a million dollars . . . well, not this minute."

"This is a tough neighborhood. Somethin' bad could happen again."

"Listen, you may not realize it, but I am descended from people who fought the Battle of Britain. They didn't surrender and I don't intend to. It wasn't my idea to move to a place where people like you would be the neighbors, let me make that clear. But I'm here and I intend to stay. If necessary I can make this place a fortress. I can hold out until every black on the block has been replaced by a white. I can fight."

He raised his fists in mock dismay, as though I were about to hang a haymaker on him.

"Vivian, can I ask you a question? Some of the RASTUS members has come to me wantin' to know if they still gonna get the money Howard promised from the Baltus Philanthropic. Should I tell 'em forget it? Or is the accident gonna stand in the way?"

Honestly, and I know this strains credulity, the man was serious. After the initial shock of disbelief I could understand why. People who have once been offered a carrot expect carrots in their diet eternally.

"Is that your idea of a joke?" I said. "Howard was murdered and you still expect his money? Are you entirely without decency?"

"Vivian, I don't know who was responsible. Only whoever it was wasn't acting on orders from me, Rufus Rastus Jackson, President For Life of RASTUS. I don't go for that kind of shit. I loves the Good Lord too much to do anythin' like that."

There is an unreal quality about Jackson, as I'm certain you've noticed. The terrible part is that he really believes himself. The man should be put away in St. Elizabeth's Mental Hospital as one who has lost all touch with reality.

"This conversation is approaching the ridiculous," I said. "I suggest we terminate it immediately."

"You didn't answer my question. Are we gonna get the money? See, we realize old Howie just tryin' to buy us off, keep us quiet. The thing is, a promise is a promise. And just because one guy screwed up don't mean the rest of the people should suffer. They was friendly, wasn't they? Come to the party and drank and ate and made old Howie feel good. That kind of hospitality on the part of the guests should be repaid. The fact that Howie is dead don't make a whole lotta difference as far as the people is concerned. They still need everythin' he promised."

A phrase from *Alice In Wonderland* popped into my head. The one where the White Queen—or somebody—says in effect: Don't bother trying to pin me down on the meaning of words; they mean whatever I say they mean.

"Mr. Jackson, if you have a pencil and paper you might want to take notes so there won't be any misunderstanding. This neighborhood will never get a penny as long as I have anything to say about it and I suspect my wishes will be deferred to. If I have any influence in the world it will be to encourage white people to buy houses in this block and rid it of the scum who live here now. You can tell your friends they can bloody well go screw themselves as far as I'm concerned."

Jackson stepped back from the door, pulled his wallet from his hip pocket, extracted what looked like a D.C. Lottery ticket, plumbed another pocket for a pencil, closed the wallet, put it on his raised knee, planted the paper on the wallet, gripped the pencil in the writing mode and looked me over.

"There ain't a whole lotta room on this thing. How about I just say, 'Drop dead,' signed Vivian Baltus?"

I tried to slam the door shut but the man has well-developed reflexes and his foot intruded before I could succeed. The door bounced off his foot and came right back to me. It struck me on the right hand; a well-groomed nail was snapped in the process.

"Goddammit," I yelled. "Goddamn you, you miserable black bastard. See what you've done?"

Jackson took me literally, barging on in and closing the door behind him before I could do anything further. Oh, what a mistake I had made in opening the door in the first place! What a horrible mistake!

"Let me see it," he said, grabbing my hand. "Let me see what this miserable black bastard has done to poor old Vivian."

I wasn't put off for a moment by his solicitude. Everybody knows what Jackson has had on his mind from the very beginning and now, at long last and in spite of my avowed and demonstrated determination to discourage, resist and fight it with all my strength, it had finally come down to his having me where he wanted me. He had destroyed Howard and now he would destroy me. If that sounds melodramatic, so be it.

"Does it hurt real bad?" he asked. "If it does it's your own fault. Those long red nails you wearin' is way too long. Keep 'em neat with a nail clipper and you wouldn't have no problem."

I snatched my hand away. I like my nails long and I like them pointed and I like them vivid. The nail on the third finger no longer matched the others but the others looked strong and sharp and I knew that in not too many minutes their scratching ability would be my only defense.

"You gotta nail file somewheres? I would file that if I was you. Or if you in too much pain to do it on your own I could do it."

"No," I said. "I don't need your help. And now for the last time will you please go?"

"If it's in the bedroom I could get it."

"No, please, please go."

"If you ain't sure we could go hunt it down together. The first one finds it gets a reward. How about it?"

"Mr. Jackson, honestly, I appreciate your concern but I can cope with the problem on my own. It's only a broken nail. It hurt for a minute. Now it's stopped hurting."

"Damn. And I was hopin' for an excuse for us to go upstairs."

"Why? Why would you want to go upstairs?"

"You know why. The bedroom's upstairs."

I mean, really, what sort of talk is that? Does the man expect me to give him an invitation? If he intends attacking me, why would he require a bedroom? A bedroom is for seduction. For what he had in mind, any place at all would do. The beautiful rug in front of the fireplace or the exquisitely modeled dining-room table or the infinity of the massive bar or the baby grand not far away . . . God.

"Mr. Jackson, you've got it all wrong. I have no intention of going into a bedroom with you or going to bed with you or doing anything at all that might suggest I have some interest in physical intimacy. Let's get that straight. Just because I was kind enough not to report you for that sophomoric hanky-panky in your taxi doesn't mean I intended it as a prelude to something more. I certainly haven't encouraged you. But be that as it may, your feelings are all one-sided. I must assure you I am not reciprocating."

"Reciprocating, what's that?"

"What? Well, back and forth in one sense. In the sense I'm using it, it means you may want me but I definitely don't want you."

"Back and forth? How about in and out? Hey, it sounds like screwin'. You like to screw, don't you?"

I gasped, I flushed, I gave him the sternest possible look and I turned away. If I could gain the kitchen without being too closely pursued I might escape out the back door. I headed for it.

"I am not going to dignify the crudeness of that question by a reply," I said over my shoulder. "If you'll excuse me, I must talk to the maid. I'm having a few people in for dinner." Christ, what a line! If I couldn't come up with a better line than that what hope was there?

Jackson saw it the same way. "The maid? They ain't no maid. If they was a maid she would have answered the door and seein' as how I'm a brother she'd have let me take a piss and I'd be on my way by now. Vivian, you shouldn't tell no lies. How come you to say they's a maid? They ain't no maid. Unhuh."

I stopped and turned to face him—and to make one last try.

"I'm not going to debate my conduct with you. I've told you again and again to go. Why do you persist?"

"Oh, shit, Viv," he said, "knock it off. I come over here thinkin' I could give you some consolation on your loss with a little you-know-what. Help you over the rough spots with somethin' take your mind off the bad side of life. I figured it was the least I could do for an old friend."

It is disgusting that so many men think sexual intercourse is the answer to all the problems of the day. Not that it doesn't soothe when it's done properly and not that I hadn't been deprived for what seemed like ages and not that this great ape didn't have an animal something that appeals to one's hormones if not one's better sense. But, my God, he was black and ugly and I have never done it with anyone black and very few that weren't terribly good looking. How could I possibly?

"Look at it this way," Jackson said. "You owe me somethin'. Took my home. Took my job. Took my pride. You just about destroyed me. If you gonna live with yourself, if you gonna live on this block, if you don't make amends you ain't gonna be able to make it at all. You got a conscience on you, Viv, I already said it. You feelin' guilty about the whole thing. Now you got the opportunity to prove to the world you ain't no red-necked racist. Oh, yeah, you called me a miserable black bastard but that's only to hide your true feelings, which is the other way round one hundred percent. It's something you got mixed up with from hangin' around with your former husband, Howard. A lotta that do-goodin' baloney has rubbed off on you and you gotta follow in his footsteps. Otherwise, you be talkin' about gettin' outta here quick as possible, takin' a loss on the property if need be and movin' your sweet ass back to the FoxDen. But you ain't. So how about us gettin' on with it?"

I have been propositioned more convincingly by university sophomores, who, of course, have had the advantage of courses in logic and debate and so could muster something vaguely plausible if not compelling enough to convince me. Argument has never been that important, anyhow. I would rather respond to my natural instincts than to a studied appeal to my reason.

"If you touch me you will regret it to your dying day."

Help! I need help! That vapid line truly doomed me.

"Viv, baby," Jackson said. "we gotta quit wastin' time. We're gonna do it, we gotta do it. If we don't do it, a lotta people put down their hard-earned money is gonna bitch all over the place. We don't want that."

What's the use? He was right. Further resistance would be pointless. If some salacious sex scene had now become inevitable, I could at least take refuge in the dictum that has steadfastly served so many Englishwomen: Grit your teeth and remember it is for the good of your country. I would submit—hopefully with a certain grace. "Grace under pressure" is the expression our beloved Winston Churchill might have used. But we're not talking about Grace under Pressure, are we? What it has come down to is Vivian under Jackson.

"If you ain't got no particular objection" said Jackson. "I'd like to do it down in the basement, in the back part, over beyond the stereo and the furnace room."

"I couldn't care less," I said. "But why there?"

"Sentimental reasons. A former friend of mind got gangbanged down there. I don't go for that. So you don't have to worry about takin' on a mob."

At this juncture Rufus—I believe you will agree it has finally come to the time when the use of his first name is acceptable—put his great hands on my shoulders and turned me toward the circular staircase. It was in no way loathsome or intolerable. Gentle, really, and in a way polite, almost as though he were ensuring I would be first through a door. I went to the staircase, I descended it, I turned and waited.

"One of the great things in life," said Rufus, "is seein' a woman with a good ass on her go down the stairs. You ever noticed it? The way the cloth breaks one way like it's gonna stay broke and then it reverses and breaks the other way? Prettiest thing in the world and I wanna congratulate you because you do it as good as anythin' on 14th Street. Straight ahead if you don't mind."

Straight ahead took us past the bar and the baby grand, past the small dance floor where the disco lights had flickered only last week, past the billiard table and the stereo, through the door of the utility room, past the furnace, the washer and drier and the ironing board—the same one upon which Howard and I had attempted a tricky maneuver inspired by a painting we had seen at Geraldine Lance's—and thence to the maid's room. Its door was open, the room was empty. I had interviewed but I had not engaged. Had I done so . . . well, it was much to late for regretful pondering.

"Yeah, this is the place," said Rufus. "Sanford's bedroom not too long back. It looks better now."

I hadn't the foggiest idea of how it had been before. Now it was routine maid style on the order of a room in a cheap motel: a chest of drawers, a table and chair, a bed and a good-sized mirror. I had added a large but inexpensive reproduction of a painting of Christ on the Cross. I had purchased the thing in the hope that its presence in the maid's room would discourage her from permitting her boyfriend to spend the night. The effectiveness of such a nostrum has never been statistically determined and yet there is the persistent belief that it is a deterrent as effective as the threat to dismiss her straightaway if she get's pregnant. Speaking of that calamity, I hadn't taken my birth control pills for months. Do you suppose I should have explained that to Rufus?"

"This is it," said Rufus. "Let's get it on."

That blunt instruction was capable of only one interpretation: that I should get it off. I sat on the edge of the bed and removed my sneakers and my white wool socks. Then I rose and took off my pale blue cashmere sweater, my simple white silk blouse and my designer blue jeans. That left only my brassiere and my panties—what we call knickers in England but had I used that term *you* might get the impression I was dressed for golf.

"Will you feel deprived if I continue?" I asked Rufus. "I mean, this is very often where the man wants to undo the snaps and finish the job."

Rufus looked me over. He had shed his shoes and his socks and his shirt and his slacks. He still retained his undershirt and his shorts, which meant we were more or less even.

"Viv, in the interests of time, why don't you just go ahead on your own?"

"All right," I said. "Only would it be asking too much if the lights were turned off? It would help me get through it."

"No problem," said Rufus. "I seen you naked so many times in my mind, the real thing ain't gonna be much different."

So Rufus extinguished the light and I took off my top and dropped my bottom. We were not in complete darkness by any means. The basement does not have full-length windows, only those short versions that help cut the subterranean gloom. Their venetian blinds cast prison-bar shadows against the two inmates. Against me, I must say, the effect was startling, the shadows contrasting in a very dramatic way with my fair English skin. Not so for Rufus. His body is intensely black and dusky and it devours sun so completely that the shadowed and non-shadowed areas appeared almost identical. He came toward me presently and tweaked my nipples with his thumbs and forefingers for a minute or so. Both rose in accordance with the commands of a properly functioning nervous system. To check, I suppose, the condition of the magic wire, he parted my middle with the middle finger of his right hand. It was gooey, but not terribly so, and when I saw the size of Rufus' member I realized something more was required than a probing finger. In the interests of comfort I suggested a stimulation procedure likely to be more effective. Rufus demurred slightly but with my encouragement went ahead. Soon I was very gooey, very pleasantly gooey, even excessively gooey and climbing rapidly toward . . . All right, that is quite enough. I have gone much further with the graphic aspects than should be expected from one of my tender sensibilities and I put my foot down Well, not exactly down, because in a very few minutes my foot, my feet, were way up indeed. In a way that was the worst of it, the gross indignity of the situation, this great stud screwing me blind and all I could think of was, my God, how undignified for the feet.

16

My name is Rufus Rastus Jackson all you assholes out there and don't you forget it. Not that there is much chance you goin' to, seein' as how I have come out on top when it looked like I didn't have no chance at all. You gotta admit the cards was stacked against me and everybody was thinkin' old Rufus was down and out so bad he ain't never gonna get on his feet again no matter what. It just proves that this is a great country we live in, full of opportunity if only you smart enough to take advantage of everythin' comin' your way. No matter what went on, I knew if I kept my faith and said my prayers everythin' would turn out okay by The End.

As you know from the previous speaker, Viv and I made out down in Sanford's old bedroom, same place where Celia got gangbanged. Vivian is kinda shy about describin' exactly what went on but since you is the kinda folks want everythin' you got comin', it looks like I'm gonna have to spell it out. Okay, here we go. Viv strips right down to her bare ass; I strips down to mine. I look her over as good as I could considerin' Viv called for lights out and there wasn't much comin' through the slats except this little bit make Viv look like a zebra. Reminded me of what the guy zebra said to the chick zebra: "Wait'll I get you out of those funny striped pajamas, baby, and I'll show you a thing or two." Does a zebra have two? Anyhow, I notice a couple of disappointin' things about Viv right away. First off, her tits ain't all that great. When she's wearin' those tight-fittin', low-cuttin' call-girl numbers her knockers push out just like Marilyn Monroe when she was posin' for those calendars down at the grease rack at Charlie's Garage and Radiator. Close up—and I was close enough to touch 'em, which I did—they wasn't no better than what those models got in Garfinckel's window. Kinda on the skimpy side and when I put my hands on 'em to jiggle 'em a little, see how much they weigh, they wasn't any heavier than a coupla jelly doughnuts. Also they was a little droopier than you get in a really first-class boob and if I'd had a quarter on me at the moment, if I had shoved it up underneath her left tit and her ribs it would have stayed there. Same with the right tit.

Okay, Vivian ain't no spring chicken any more than the rest of us and you gotta expect a little slop takin' over the bod when you climb into the thirties. I was willin' to overlook it even though I am used to much better. Celia, for instance, who you may recall wasn't nothin' more than a down-south darky not too far back, has got a pair on her that got more spring in 'em than a foam-rubber cushion. As for Geraldine, about whom we ain't heard a lot lately sexually speakin', her knockers is deservin' of a centerfold spread in Playboy. I ask her once, "Geraldine, with tits like that, you ever thought of posin' for the porno magazines? You and me together, we could make us a lotta money." She said the D.C. Bar would take a dim view. A dim view? Those suckers must be queer every fuckin' one of them if they puttin' on dark glasses to look at Geraldine. All right, you don't wanna hear about no Celia and no Geraldine right at the moment. Vivian is the one. As I was sayin', her tits has got a little sag but I ain't gonna criticize her for somethin' for which she ain't personally responsible. The hair on her pussy is another thing entirely. With all that blond stuff she showin' up on her head, you think she gotta be that way all over. The truth is, ladies and gentlemen, she is a livin' lie! The hair on her snatch is just plain old pussy hair, kinda tan and brown and there is a hell of a lot of it. Chicks with a lot of pussy hair usually got hair on their faces and some damn near moustaches and it is a sure sign they may be lesbo. Well, Vivian's face was smooth as a baby's ass up until now but when I realize she been buyin' her goldilocks at the beauty shop I look at her real close to see if she is showin' some five o'clock shadow. She ain't, but for all I know she may have given it a once-over with the electric razor not ten minutes before I arrive. A woman who will dye her hair blond when the hair God gave her is brown as a mouse is not to be trusted. My mama told me that.

Okay, I pinch her nipples a little bit, see if they is in workin' order. They seems to be, risin' up after a while as nice as warts on a water buffalo. They is the usual color, pink, and they don't have any hair around the edges, which is another sign you may be dealin' with a woman who is a female faggot. After I check out her points I run my right hand up and down, here and there checkin' out the rest of the body work. No real problems. Her belly don't stick out too much and there is this sharp angle where her waist stops and her hips begin and her ass is strong as a new mattress. The only thing not as good as the rest of it is her pussy. Yeah, I put my finger in and I gotta tell you it ain't no wetter than a week-old oyster. I rub it here, I rub it there, nothing happens. What with all the hair and everything closed down tight I can't even find her love pimple. I figure, pussy must be takin' a nap.

"Vivian," I say, "what is goin' on? We can't screw with you closed up about as tight as Fort Knox. I know what's up there is awful fine, but it ain't gold. How about gettin' with it?"

"Rufus," she say, "honestly. I am not accustomed to being penetrated so bluntly. Have you never heard of foreplay?"

Of course I've heard of it. Only I don't call it no foreplay. I call it diddlin'. Which I thought I was doin' pretty good with my finger. I try it a few wiggles more.

"I'm frightfully sorry," she say. "I'm still very dry. It needs to be lubricated."

"Well, goddamn," I say, kinda peevish like, "you mean I got to go all the way upstairs for the Vaseline? How come you didn't think of it before?"

"Not Vaseline," she say. "There's a better way."

Okay, I know what she is talkin' about. But, Jesus, askin' me to do that on the first date shows she don't respect me at all. The second date, maybe, or the third, okay, but askin' a man to do a kinky act like that right outta nowhere—just who the hell does she think she is?

"No way," I say. "I ain't gonna do it. If I have to do that, I just as soon forget the whole thing."

"Oh, come on, Rufus," she say. "Don't be shy. Haven't you ever done it before?"

"Of course I've done it," I say. "I've done it a hundred times. Only I don't hardly know you. What did you say your name was?"

She laugh. "Rufus," she say, "are you a real man or not? Real men don't eat quiche, it's true. Real men eat pussy."

Okay, right after that she put her right hand on my left hand, give me a little tug, kind of fall away on the bed, slither around and spread her legs. Jesus Christ, it's Sanford's dirty pictures all rolled up in one! It's a cunt lookin' at me straight in the eye! It's a cunt wantin' to know what I'm gonna do about it! God almighty, what a cunt!

Well, I don't have no choice seein' as how my manhood been insulted and it was nibble the nooky or nothin'. I get down on my knees, work up to the bed, sling her legs over my shoulders and go to work. I gotta say old Viv must have planned the whole thing because her pussy has a good smell on it, not like some of those pussies ain't had a bath in a week. I tongue around here and there until the lips give up on goin' steady and I inch my way up until I make contact with her you-know-what. I get my hands on her tits, diddlin' the nipples and the same time I start nibblin' on her to get her attention.

"No teeth, please," she say. "Not yet, at least."

Hell, I know how to do it. I don't need no coaching. I mean, here I am doin' her a favor and already she is tryin' to take over. These women libbers think they know everything. Only there is no way I can explain my position on the matter unless I am some kind of a ventriloquist, all my normal speakin' equipment bein' buried about up to my ears. There is no call to spell out what happen in the next five minutes, except from the past I realize you is a bunch of perverts out there and if you don't get plenty of lurid details you gonna complain. Well, it ain't no big deal, just Vivian moanin' and groanin' and carryin' on in the usual way and when she finally comes, beggin' me to stick it in. Not quite yet, baby. She is still vibratin' all over the place and scratchin' my back with those of her fingernails which is still in workin' order and shoutin' out her wishes. That's when I give her her you-know-what a really sharp bite, let her know who is in charge. She can't take it and she squirm and break loose and kinda collapse and I figure if I don't put my cock in her soon she gonna be so worn out she can't move a muscle. So I shove it in. "Fuck me, baby," I say. Waste of breath. She about dead. Well, I give it a coupla in-and-outs and in no time at all my cock has worked up to your standard frenzy. I let it shoot. I hope you're satisfied. Viv and I sure was.

After that we rest, maybe snooze a few minutes, get up outta the bed. I know what you're wonderin', how come a great stud like me don't do it again, don't do it right up to dinner time? Friends, if that's the main thing on your mind, go buy Harold Robbins or one of those other porno trashers because I do not believe in talkin' in detail about something private just so you can get yourself all aroused, maybe go out and commit a sex crime on somebody on the way home from work.

We put on some clothes and go out to the bar. We have us a coupla small double scotches on the rocks. I fix 'em at the request of Vivian. It ain't strictly right I should be tendin' bar because I am a guest, but I ain't one to quibble about standin' on ceremonies.

"You want that cheap stuff left over from the party," I ask her. "Or Johnny Walker Red? Or Chivas Regal?"

"Whatever you suggest," she say. "I hardly know the difference."

I take the Chivas for myself and pour the cheap stuff for Vivian. I figure there is no point in wastin' good scotch on somebody can't appreciate it. Howard, may his cheap Jew heart rest in Heaven, would have said "Right on!"

I'm pretty sure he'd say "No way!" to what Vivian and I talk about after we settle down with our booze. Because a lot of it is about Howard's money and the best way to use it. It ain't right to discuss what you gonna do with everythin' he left behind for his poor defenseless widow when you ain't twenty minutes from givin' the widow a bangin', but there ain't a lotta time left in this fairy tale and there's some things gotta be worked out.

The first thing I tell Vivian is she is makin' a real mistake thinkin' she can live in the place without protection, pointin' out that she would have to put on a party once a week to keep the neighborhood from hatin' her as much as they did when she and Howard began bustin' the block. I say there is only one person capable of beatin' up on the burglars if anybody should try somethin' along those lines and there is only one person could be a calmin' influence on the powerful political movement still smartin' from the fact it lost one battle but ain't give up the fight and there is only one person who could be counted on to take care of any horniness problems should they rear their ugly heads at any time, day or night. The answer is Me. Vivian agrees all the way and without further ado we draw up an informal, unwritten, no-cut contract right on the spot and effective immediately. I will take care of all of the above and for said services will be compensated in the amount of $20,000 per annum, such sum to be incrementally distributed to me every two weeks not later than noon on Friday. Fifteen percent penalty for late payment, the contract subject to review in six months and I has the right to abrogate the whole thing on thirty days notification. (I'm still on good terms with Geraldine Lance, remember, which explains why I can spout all that legal crap.) We drink to that, feelin' good as we go along. Pretty soon we gettin' the urge to get it on again but I ain't gonna tell you anything about what happened except we climb all the way up through the circular staircase, gettin' dizzy from all those dammed circles, and when we come out on the top floor we turn left and head for the Master Bedroom. You heard about it? Got all those mirrors and I gotta tell you they is worth whatever they cost because it is almost more excitin' watchin' yourself doin' it than doin' it. We horse around a bunch of different ways and I am sorry as hell we don't have no camera because I can see how some of the scenes would be great for them personalized Christmas cards. The next night I say goodbye to Geraldine and bring all my things over. I tell Geraldine I am tired of her constant bitchin' just because I am always in her goddamned refrigerator once in a while. I tell her from now on I won't be usin' her goddamned hot water neither and sharin' the shower to save a few lousy bucks would have to be done with somebody else's body. I tell her all my charms and assets is committed to a long-term contract and comin' into my room when she is hard up and expectin' me to perform whether I'm in the mood or not is a thing of the past. She took it very well, I gotta admit. "Free at last," she say. "Free at last, thank God almighty I'm free at last!" That is just her way of funnin'. Deep down I know she is sorry to see me go and in a way I am, too, because Geraldine worked hard on my behalf when I was havin' a struggle but I figured she got enough out of me in trade because she don't say one single word about any legal fees. When I return her car after usin' it to truck my stuff to Vivian's, I say "Geraldine, baby, I guess this it. Unless you care to drive me back over to Viv's. It would save me the cab fare." Geraldine say she would forgo the pleasure.

"But come have one final drink, you rogue, you worse than peasant knave," she say. So we cozy up to her bar and I take on a little Johnny Walker Red, the Chivas not bein' out in the open and I don't want to look bad pokin' around where she hid it. "You know, Rufus, you've changed a lot over the year. You're almost literate, you've learned a good deal about personal hygiene and you have displayed an amazing talent for coming out on top. Congratulations. I didn't think you had it in you."

Now if this were your ordinary tearjerker scene I would mumble somethin' about how grateful I am, how I couldn't have done it without her support and how I would never forget how much I owed her (glidin' right over the last so she wouldn't bring up no legal fees) and all the rest of that crap. I'd practically be shufflin' from embarrassment, my hat would be all crumpled up like some old darky can't speak from the emotion of it all and my eyeballs would be mistin' up so bad I'd be askin' for the loan of a handkerchief. The hell with that. What I say is, "Geraldine, I won't be seein' much of you from now on. But I ain't gonna forget you because you was the fifth best piece of ass I had in my whole life. But it's over now. Try to understand. If you ever in a jam, feel free to write and I will get back to you just as soon as I can squeeze it in. Ciao."

What is this "ciao" shit? It is something I pick up over in Georgetown at a party. "Ciao" is what high-class Italians say to each other and it means the same as when Americans say "Let's get together some time soon and do lunch." In other words, how about chow? Geraldine was speakin' the truth when she said I had changed in the last year and that is a good example. Geraldine is right to be proud of me, a one-time ghetto rat well on his way to bein' conversant in a foreign language.

I put my clothes and my typewriter in the maid's room at Vivian's but it is only a formality because I ain't sleeping down there any more than I used to sleep in the cab. I take my new duties seriously, tryin' to be professional and everything, not casual like at

Geraldine's when I was a hard-workin' stud without no pay. Workin' for nothin, that's all in the past. Speakin' of the past, another person from out of it, Celia by name, come around after I been settled in a week or so, knock on the door. Vivian is at the studio where she has returned to work. I tell her it's better than lyin' around the house cryin' for old Howard and screwin' the balls off old Rufus.

"What's on your mind, girl?" I ask Celia through the microphone. That is somethin' Viv had installed at my suggestion and also the TV camera so we can see who's out there before we let 'em in. "Whatever it is, we don't want any."

"Rufus," she say, "open the door. I got somethin' I got to tell you."

"My ears ain't sick. What is it?"

"I can't talk out in the air. Lemme in."

"No."

"If you don't let me in I'm gonna go to the cops."

"You want the address? Wait a minute and I'll get it."

"You better not push me, man. What I got to say you better listen."

"How you know I'm here anyway?"

"It's all over the neighborhood."

"You don't live in the neighborhood."

"I got friends."

"Friends? I'd be careful about gettin' friendly with anybody lives around here. They ain't to be trusted."

"Listen, Rufus, you better let me in, you hear?"

"Listen, your own self. I got an important position in this house. I can't screw it up by lettin' in just anybody. Get lost."

"You don't let me in, you ain't gonna stay there very long."

Okay, I let her in. I could hear she was gettin' worked up and when she gets mad she will kick and scream over nothin' at all. If she started kickin' the door and bangin' it, Vivian would give me hell for not protectin' the property and she'd be talkin' about takin' it outta my pay.

This Celia woman waltzes right in, give me a big smile, puts her arms around me, ooches her pussy right up underneath my belt buckle and say, "Hey, lover, you lookin' good."

I snatched her offa me like she has the contagious poison ivy. "Now don't start that," I tell her. "I don't mess with the likes of dumbchicks like you. I got a contract with the lady of the house and she find out I'm messin' with you, she gonna shake me out of this place like I'm a loaded dust mop."

When Celia realize she couldn't turn me on, she backs off, gives me a dirty look, at the same time tryin' to stomp on my foot.

"Celia, you is toyin' with death. You be careful, girl, are you gonna be the second one around this place in the last two weeks."

Celia say, "Well, if I am, you gonna be the third. I'll kill you with my dyin' breath."

"How? You got halitosis? There is things you can buy for halitosis."

"Rufus, don't you be funnin' me. Just because you're shackin' up with the rich widow, don't make you better than everybody else."

"How you know I'm shackin' up?"

"Hell, everybody knows it. It's all over town."

"So what? It ain't against the law."

"Maybe so. But what made it possible sure as hell is."

"I didn't have a thing to do with it."

Celia poohed.

"Who you kiddin'? Ain't you ever heard of incitement to riot?"

"Of course I heard of it. I used to have a lawyer chick. She taught me a lotta that law talk."

"Well, you better go see her, see can she help."

"Now why should I do that?"

"Rufus, there is a reward out for information on the killer. Didn't you know?"

As a matter of fact I didn't. Who would put up the money? Who would have the interest? I turn it over in my mind a second. Vivian, of course.

"I didn't do it. It don't concern me."

"The hell it don't. Accordin' to what I've heard, somebody is about to spell out the name of one of your old buddies. It just so happens this old pal of yours ain't exactly a good friend of mine."

"I got lots of buddies. Which one you talkin' about?"

"Sanford. The one that just about raped me to death not forty feet from where we standin' right now."

"Sanford? They sayin' Sanford did it?"

"That's right. Threw the brick. If he'd had any luck he'd have missed but it didn't work that way."

"Sanford? You're sure it's Sanford? I never thought he had that kinda arm."

"That's what they sayin'."

"Nah, Sanford didn't do it. I don't think."

"The talk is Sanford."

"So who's gonna turn him in?"

"That's the problem. Some folks out there are claimin' they heard him yell 'Up with RASTUS' about the time he let the brick fly. RASTUS, that's your scam, ain't it?"

I do not like to hear RASTUS referred to as a "scam." It was and is a legitimate enterprise all the way. If I had taken the trouble back at the beginnin' I am certain I could have gotten a tax-exempt status for it without no trouble.

"RASTUS lives," I say. "RASTUS ain't give up the fight. The only thing is, RASTUS is resortin' to different tactics."

"You mean you sell out on your friends? Gone over to the other side? That's what it looks like." We was still standin' at the door but Celia look around and see the place ain't nothin' like the old days. "Looks like you got it made."

"I'm doin' all right."

"Out on the street they ain't exactly sure. That bullshit you give 'em about stoppin' the block bustin', most of 'em still believes you was on the straight and level. That's why they ain't rushin' down for the reward money. If they do, they know you gonna be in a jam—you and Sanford both. Him for doin' it, you for eggin' him on."

"I didn't egg him on. Who say I egged him on?"

"Maybe you didn't in so many words. But he was in RASTUS and RASTUS is resistance and you is the leader. It ain't gonna take a jury five minutes to give you twenty years in the penitentiary."

"Now way. My mouthpiece could get me off."

"You can't count on it. Better pack your bags and get out of town right now. You lie low somewheres, it may be three or four years before they catch you. Maybe not even then. Maybe you be dead by then. A chance you gotta take."

This Celia can be goddamn sarcastic at times, you know that?

"Listen up, Celia, I ain't gonna run. Howard Baltus been dead over two weeks. If the neighbors was gonna finger Sanford how come they haven't done it?"

"I just said. To protect you. And for another reason. Sanford may not be as popular as you but he's got one good thing goin' for him. He's black. And I do believe if most folks around here has to choose between helpin' a white chick get her revenge and some down-and-out black brother, they gonna side with the black guy."

I show her my smile. "Well, you makin' it sound awful simple, like I don't have a thing to worry about as long as Sanford ain't picked on."

"Oh, you got plenty to worry about. You and Sanford both."

"How come?"

"How come? Didn't you hear what I said a minute ago? Sanford was the one damned near killed me. Him and those other bastards."

"So what? That was a long time ago. Nobody hardly remembers it."

"I remembers it. Oh, yeah, it made a deep impression." Her voice gets all quavery when she say that. Next thing she starts bawlin'. "I ain't never gonna forget it as long as I live. I want my satisfaction."

"Baby, you can't do nothin' about it now. Remember, we talked about it and I give you good advice. Told you to keep your mouth shut and go on about your business."

She stopped her bawlin' right quick, give me a tough expression. "Listen, I wasn't nothin' but a hayseed back then. I didn't know any better. I know better now."

"So what? It's too damned late. Statue of limitations. Something else I learned from my mouthpiece."

"Oh, I know that," she say. "Gettin' him for rape may be askin' too much. But murder . . . oh, yeah, I'm gonna get the son-of-a-bitch for murder. And also the reward money."

"Un huh," I say. "And when you get him you gonna get me, too. Is that what you got on your mind?"

"Right on, man," she say. "You was givin' me a hard time back then. It's why I left. You don't remember you was batterin' the hell out of me?"

"I was? And you gonna go to the police because of a little thing like that?"

"Yeah," she say, "I am. I got to stand for the principles of women's liberation."

"Celia, there is one damn important thing in all this you have not mentioned. Who was it rescued you from Sanford and the others? Don't that count for nothin'?"

"Right," she say. "It does. And when the judge is about to sentence you for aidin' and abettin' I will rise up in the court and ask that he be merciful on account of what you did. You probably end with no more than fifteen years, with time off for good behavior and the nine months you been in jail before the trial."

Well, we argue about what good would it do if Sanford do time and I do time and what's done is done and Howard Baltus deserved whatever he got and back and forth until we reach some kind of agreement that she would let sleeping dogs snooze and before I fully realize what the hell is goin' on we is driftin' down the circular staircase, past the bar and the piano, past the stereo, past the washin' machine and the dryer and into the maid's room. What happens then ain't none of your damn business because if I admit I screwed the chick to keep her quiet I would have to tell you she was anythin' *but* quiet when we was doin' it. Okay, I think we about ready to wrap this mother up except for one more thing. The doorbell rings one afternoon about the time Celia usually comin' by to get some of what it takes to keep her mouth shut. Only it ain't Celia pushin' the button this time. You know who? You wanna guess? The mailman? The paper boy? Delivery man with a package? Hell, no. You ain't gonna like the answer. It is none other than that creep we been spared lookin' at for a coupla months, that famous pervert and faggot, that well-known cocksucker from Georgetown, Mr. Lucius DeTroit, the man with the extra-stretch lips and the no-bone lower jaw. I like to throw up from the sight of him even though it is only on the TV.

"Go away," I yell at him through the mike. "Get lost. I got the clap. I got the syph. I got the crabs. I can't get it up. Nothin' here for you."

The TV screen don't show color. Don't make no difference. You could tell Lucius is turnin' red, blushin' like he'd been caught in the men's room with his pants down and a cock up his ass by some cop just come in to take a well-earned shit. Lucius is the kind of queer so damned eager he'd forget to throw the bolt. For a second it look like he gonna turn and run but his kind don't give up so easy. No matter how humiliatin' it might be for people like us, a faggot who's had a taste can't never be satisfied with less than the whole meal. It's like a man-eatin' tiger gettin' a sample from a big-game hunter with a nose bleed. A very sad situation, let me tell you.

"Mr. Jackson," he say, "would you be kind enough to turn that loudspeaker down? People on the street can hear you."

"Lucius Deepthroat eats cock three times a day," I yell into the mike. "When he ain't eatin' cock he eatin' shit."

Old Lucius just about pass out and die right then and there. I could see his eyes buggin' and the tears comin' and the sweat start fallin' off his head. He's a complete mess, worse than a baby-raper had the finger pointed at him at the police line-up.

"Mr. Jackson, sir," he say, whimperin' like a dog, "please let me in. It's about business."

"Business?" I come back. "I ain't doin' no business with you. Not after the last time."

"It'll only take a few minutes," he say. "I promise."

The snivelin' son-of-a-bitch. On the other hand, Celia be comin' along directly and I sure don't want this mother doin' his number when she come swingin' her sweet self up the front steps.

"Okay," I tell him. "But if this gonna be more than five minutes I'm gonna kick your ass outta here worse than the time before."

"I promise," he say, not that I believe him. Anybody who'll believe a homo is askin' for it. That's why it is so bad when the homos get to be teachers. You believe 'em when they tell you the world is round and the next thing you know they tellin' you it's okay to take it in the mouth. Lucky I stayed away from teachers as much as I could when I was young and didn't take no chances. Which is why I am all stud today and got a clear conscience. What the Good

Lord wants is for me to fuck chicks and I am a follower of the Lord. Somebody say Hallelujah. Somebody say Amen.

I let the mother in. Aside from his face bein' all worked up, he don't look bad. Got him a nice tan suit and a blue shirt with those white buttons at the collar in case you can't afford starch and a blue tie sprinkled with baseball bats like he is some kind of sports fiend. Hah! You know what them bats stand for and so do all the other fags. Puttin' it on ties is advertisin'. But I don't say nothin' because I'm hopin' the creep will get it off his puny chest and disappear before Celia show up.

"Okay, man, let's hear it," I say all gruff and tough. "I ain't got all day."

Lucius take a few deep breaths, unbutton his jacket, push his shirt front down his pants, hitch up his trousers, fuss around with his tie, rebutton his coat and pat his pretty hair. Then he run a comb through it. God almighty! Queers is always concerned about their personal appearance, no matter how bad they just been humiliated. They is absolutely without pride!

"Mr. Jackson," he say when he all tidied up, "what you just said to me out on the front landing was inexcusable. I think you owe me an apology."

"What?" I come right back, jumpin' on him hard. "What the fuck you talkin' about? I ain't apologizin'. Every word I said was true."

"No," he say, "I don't suck cocks. What I do is make love to a man I love."

Right there I knew I had been had again. Because what happened in the next ten minutes was practically what the French call "didja view." It is a shorthand way of saying "Didja see what happened the first time? It sure as hell looks like I'm gonna have to mess with that mother again." The son-of-a-bitch had lied all the way about wantin' to talk business. That was just his trick to take advantage of my trustin' nature. What he wanted—well, you know what he wanted. What he *said* first off was, "Mr. Jackson, I came by to pay my respects to Mrs. Baltus and to tell her how sorry I am about Mr. Baltus. And to see the house. And to thank her for leading the way." That ain't business; that's bullshit. "I was surprised to find you here."

"Well, I am," I say. "It don't concern you. I'll tell Mrs. Baltus what you said. Now git."

"Uh, now that I'm in, would it be too much trouble if I looked around?" He is cranin' his neck toward the front room. "I haven't seen it since the Baltuses moved in."

"No way. Mrs. Baltus find out I'm lettin' strangers in she'll give me hell."

"Remember the first time I was here? What a difference."

"Yeah, I remember. The toilet was busted. And so was you. You couldn't have paid off the neighborhood muggers. Now go on."

Lucius pass his hand over his face, pat his hair, fuss around with his tie, take a deep breath. "Mr. Jackson, I, uh, honestly didn't know you were here when I knocked. But I would be lying if I didn't say I'm glad to see you. I've been trying to find your whereabouts ever since the death of poor Mr. Baltus."

"How come? I didn't do it. You tryin' to get the reward money from turnin' me in? Forget it."

"Oh, not at all. I know you didn't do it. I know you couldn't do a thing like that. But I know who did."

"Great. Everybody I talk to knows who done it. Who'd you talk to?"

"Well, according to my sources, it was old Mr. Dudley, the one who used to live on the upper floor. Is that what you heard?"

"Old man Dudley? You gotta be kiddin'. Who gave you that dumb idea?"

"The neighborhood. It's been mentioned more than once."

"Shit, old man Dudley didn't have the strength to bend over. How the fuck could he pick up a brick and throw it?"

"I don't know. I'm just saying what I heard."

"Well, goddamn, if everybody is pointin' at Dudley, how come they ain't took him down to the police station, beat the shit out of him 'til he confesses?"

"Mr. Jackson, I don't know if you quite realize it but you are something of a hero to the people around here. You didn't win but you fought hard."

"Yeah, yeah, I know all that. So what?"

"If Mr. Dudley is arrested, you'll be linked to him. You'll be accused of encouraging him"

"I didn't do no such a thing. How come everybody blamin' everything on me?

"They're not blaming you. If they were, you'd probably be named as the murderer. You had more reason than any of the others."

"Listen, dumbass, where do you get that shit? I don't have more reasons, just the same. We all been crapped on in the neighborhood. If anybody should be blamed it's guys like you."

Lucius nod his head. "Right," he say. "You have something there. I didn't think so before, but now that poor Mr. Baltus is gone, I realize this whole business of disturbing the block was a terrible thing. I wish I could undo the past."

I just about laugh out loud. Poor dumb bastard don't realize you can't go back once progress is taken hold. You livin' in the past, you livin' on your dreams. You gotta get on with it, no matter how tough it is on some folks ain't seen the light.

"Lucius," I say, "just what in the hell do you want? You come over here to pass the time of day about the block, all I can say is 'Screw the block'."

"No," he say, "that's not what I really want to do, talk. What I want to do is make love."

He said it right out loud, just like that, not a bit of shame.

"Man, what the hell is goin' on with you? You know I don't go for that. You don't remember last time?"

"Oh, yes, sure. I'll never forget it. At least some of it."

"You don't remember how I kicked your ass down the front steps? You want to go through that again?"

"No, certainly not. But maybe you've forgotten what I said before you did it. What happened back in your bedroom was proof that you're not as straight as you think, Mr. Jackson. You should realize you're permanently tainted. You may not have done it since and you may never do it again but in the eyes of the Lord you're gay. You may have only sinned once but once is enough."

"You son-of-a-bitch, Lucius," I say. "I ain't no queer. So what if I did it once? I ain't never gonna do it again. Can't you get that through your thick skull?"

"Oh, yes," he say, talkin' the way a white man talk when he's holdin' all the good cards. "I think you will."

"I said no, man, no."

"You will," he say, this shit-eatin' grin formin'. "If you don't do it, I'll tell Mrs. Baltus. I can guess your role in Mrs. Baltus' house. If she knew about our incident of last fall I don't imagine she would regard you as kindly as she now does."

Now that was blackmailin' a black man, pure and simple. Or tryin' to. Personally, I ain't convinced. Vivian ain't no chick from the country—unless you mean England, which ain't no real country, bein' about the size of Connecticut wrapped around Rhode Island—and she would realize that a man with a body like I got is gonna attract all types: women, men and hard-up sheep. She would laugh it off. "Well, Rufus, let's give it a whirl straightaway. If you can't get it up you're fired." And I would swell up real good, of course, passin' any test she wanted to give me with flyin' colors. On the other hand, Lucius could maybe plant some doubt. Just supposin' I have a small problem one night and Vivian say, "What's wrong, stud, your mind on somebody else? Lucius DeTroit, for example?" Where would I be then? If she said that, somethin' bad would be established between the two of us and she would start lookin' around for somebody else's body. She ain't gonna find one better but she might not find that out for months. I can't take no chance.

Okay, I want everybody to understand I'm doin' this under protest. I walk the mother through the front room—his eyes gogglin' at how good it looks—right along to the circular stairs, down the stairs, past the bar and the piano and the stereo, past the furnace, the washer/drier combination, the ironin' board and on into the maid's room. The way we is usin' the maid's room you might think it has the best bed in the house. Anyway, Lucius and I go in and Lucius shut the door and give me this look, all lovey-dovey, goo-goo eyes and just about slobberin' at the mouth.

"I know this strikes you as terribly crude," he say, "being so deliberate about it," his coat comin' off and his shoes and his pants and his tie and shirt and his shorts and his T-shirt. "But I've only got my lunch hour and I'm sure you have your assignments regarding the maintenance of the house and there is no point in wasting time."

"Hey, wait a minute," I say. "What the hell you doin' takin' your clothes off? You wanna eat me, I guess they ain't no way I can get out of it. All I gotta do for that is wheel it out. You takin' your duds off to show me what you got, I ain't interested."

Which ain't exactly the truth. Any man start exposin' himself in front of another man, the other man gonna look, see how does he compare. In the shower after the basketball game (did I tell you I was the star forward at Eastern High many years ago. I did? Oh), while you're skinny dippin' in the Potomac River and even if you and your buddy are only takin' a sociable leak up against a brick wall. It ain't no faggoty thing like Lucius did a year ago when I was makin' a play to get the toilet fixed but it happens and they ain't no point in sayin' it don't. So I look the fucker over. He ain't bad. Considerin' he ain't more'n about five feet nine, he got him a nice build. A little too skinny, maybe, but his muscles stand out good and you can tell one from the other. If he has any speed on him at all he could easy make third-string cornerback in a pickup game on 6th Street. His cock . . . Well, I gotta admit the thing surprised me. Nothin' like my monster, but it's thicker than a three-dollar sausage and it's archin' out over his balls instead of droopin' the way some of 'em do. His balls is big as hens eggs and I figure he has a combination that could do a pretty good job on a chick with a small pussy. Not that the cocksucker ever would. A chick could go nuts from horniness before a faggot would use his.

"Rufus," he say, "it's much better when both parties are bare. Friendlier. More trusting. More like we cared for each other."

Well, shit, I don't care for him more than a rat cares for a cat but I've gone this far might as well give the guy an extra thrill. So I take 'em off and hang 'em up. Not like a year ago where I was puttin' on a fast strip tease, but kinda turned away and hidin' because all the time Lucius was watchin' me like an eagle watchin' a newborn baby in case the mama turn her back. Made me nervous, made me self-conscious, him starin' at me like that and breathin' harder and harder as the number of things protectin' my fine brown frame from the eyes of the pervert become fewer and fewer and I become nakeder and nakeder. Finally I am bare as a polar bear except I ain't polar at all. Yeah, I figure by the time I get everything shed, what with Lucius just about droolin' at what he's gonna get, my cock would be standin' up ready for Lucius. As I said once before, a cock ain't too discriminatin'. Cock is blind as a beggar sellin' pencils. When he knows he's gonna get into something warm and wet and tight he don't care if it's cunt or mouth as long as it don't bite.

Only the funny thing is, cock is lookin' as limp and shriveled as it did when I was about nine years old. Back then, the best thing about it was that I didn't have to do what girls do to take a leak. I don't exactly remember when I found out it can carry pee and come both, but I figure a lot of chicks still ain't realized that the thing that gives them babies is also used to pass piss six or seven times a day. I don't know about them, but I sure as hell wouldn't want to be fucked by somethin' that had piss pourin' out of it maybe minutes before.

"Something wrong, Rufus?" say Lucius. He lookin' at it. "What's wrong?"

"Not a damn thing wrong," I say. "I was screwin' a chick ten minutes before you got here." That is a lie. "He just takin' a little rest. You go right ahead and he be standin' in no time."

So Lucius gets down on his knees and puts his mouth around it and gives it some back and forth, round and round, up and down, this and that. Nothin' happens. Cock is like dead. He don't get big, he don't get long, he don't get hard. Cock ain't respondin' any more than if he is takin' a cold shower in February. If anythin', he collapsin' and shrinkin' all over the place and lookin' like he wanta settle down in his nest and go to sleep. The son-of-a-bitch is definitely not in the mood to be the plaything of the pervert, no doubt about it.

"All right, Lucius," I say after about two minutes, "you has failed the test. Cock don't like the way you doin' it and if cock don't like it there is no way in the world he can be forced. Excuse me, I got to get dressed. Company is comin' any minute."

"Wait, wait, wait," Lucius say, drawin' back from his work and pantin' hard and rollin' his eyes and blinkin' he so upset about his failure. "Give me a few minutes more. I know I can do it."

"No," I say. "I'm gettin' a headache."

"Well, what about me?" he say. "What about that?" and he gets up offen his kness and I be go to hell if he ain't got him a hardon bigger than an eighty-cent cucumber. One advantage white studs have over us black guys is the red shows up better on white skin and the head on it is bright as lipstick on a downtown whore. Throbbin', too, and higher than level, which is a sign a cock gives when it's ready for combat. "Who's going to take care of that?"

"Don't look at me," I say, even though they both was, Lucius and his thing eyin' me like I was responsible for them gettin' so worked up when the truth is I been forced against my will.

"Now wait a minute," Lucius say. "You practically promised. If I don't get some satisfaction, I'm going straight to Mrs. Baltus."

Well, straight as he was right then, Vivian might figure on doin' some missionary work and start makin' a man out of him. It is supposed to be impossible to change 'em once they are set in their ways but I wouldn't count on it.

"Nothin' I can do," I say. "My cock ain't interested. Forget it."

"Well, mine is," he say. "And if I can't do it to you, is there any reason why you can't do it to me?"

This is where I have to lower the curtain and take the amnesia defense. Otherwise I gotta tell you how my cheeks got red (even though you can't exactly tell it on a black man) and my jaw dropped out of shock and I was screamin' "No way, man, I ain't gonna eat you! I don't give a shit what's gonna happen! You can tell Vivian, you can go to the police about Howard and you can cut off my balls! It won't make any difference, I won't do it!" That's what I say and that's what I mean but if that's what I do I ain't sayin'. I got a right to my privacy and the Fifth Amendment backs me up right to the hilt. The fact that Lucius left ten minutes later lookin' like the cat that swallowed the canary don't necessarily mean some cat swallowed his. You can draw your own conclusion but I ain't givin' you a pencil.

Okay, about a month has passed since Lucius came around and everythin' is nice and quiet. Things has settled down to a routine in the Baltus household, my paycheck is comin' in regular and I don't see no clouds on the horizon. It is now finally time for what Geraldine calls the summation, the summin' up and the meanin' of it all. One thing at a time.

The Killin' of Howard. I'm afraid this has to go in the books as one of those unsolved crimes of which the Metropolitan Police has had more than their share. Those things happen. The papers hit it good for a week or so but they got new murders comin' on practically every day of the week and they got to keep up with the latest. Same with the TV. Same with the radio. The reward money got a few folks to go down to the police but the police can't accept it when it's nothin more than "a black guy with a short haircut" or "an old black man with a cane" and nobody has been arrested. I sure as hell don't know who did it and I don't want to. It's over and done with and the guilty party is sufferin' enough from the knowledge of what he did. Geraldine told me that. She said it is an argument she has used many times in the court and I could believe it all the way. So I do.

RASTUS. The strategy of RASTUS is to lay low for a while, let things cool down. I has had a few talks with Vivian after her ashes has been hauled and she is relaxed and in a good mood about what the Baltus Foundation is gonna do. I have this feelin' in time she will go along with the wishes of the dead Howie, may he rest in peace. These things can't be given a swift kick in the ass to get 'em movin' and I don't want to upset any apple carts when I am eatin' as many apples as I want. As it is, RASTUS has to be given credit for raisin' what Celia would call the "conscience level" in the neighborhood. Before RASTUS they knew they was bein' crapped on. Now they realize they got the power to make whitey strain some when he about to shit. Another good thing to come out of RASTUS is the fight song. Remember how it goes? "RASTUS is your leader 'til the day you die." Oh yeah, a good fight song can give a lotta hope to the common people, the people who need it most.

Lucius Deepthroat and Celia. They got me by the nuts the both of 'em. Celia a coupla times a week on her lunch and Lucius when he's in the neighborhood once or twice a month. I can handle it without no problems and it is the least I can do to protect my old friends Sanford and the Dudleys and also not upset Vivian, who is goin' through her mournin' period as strong as the Battle of Britain durin' World War II. As she herself would put it, "We must carry on, all of us, and make the very best of a situation not of our own choosing."

Rufus Rastus Jackson. I come out on top all the way. I'm wearin' nice clothes every day and eatin' regular and it ain't no junk food like before. Vivian and me go to parties in the Mercedes and to the Kennedy Center for the culture stuff I never had no interest in once upon a time. It ain't easy but I'm learnin'. The other night, to give you an example, there was this symphony by a fellow named Brahms. I look around, I'm the only black guy in the audience. That put the responsibility on me and though I almost doze off a coupla times I has to uphold the honor of the black race and look like I'm enjoyin' it as much as the honkeys. As a matter of fact, a lot of it I did. If only they'd had a good sax man I'd have liked it even more.

Some of it had a good beat and was catchy and I was whistlin' little bits on the way out. "Don't whistle," says Vivian. "It's not cultured." Okay, I quit. I don't know everythin'.

What I *do* know is that most of the time I'm feelin' like the American Dream. Nobody can say how long it will last and I ain't countin' on no heaven on earth forever. But most everythin' I prayed for has come to pass. I'm still livin' in my old house except it ain't an old house any longer. It is as fancy as anything up on Massachusetts Avenue and I can understand how much it meant to Howie. How he wanted to live in it with Vivian and screw her and have kids. I'm doin' a great job on the first part and Vivian is bein' damn careful about the second. That is the main thing right now and it is enough. Maybe one day down the road we can get it all together, start really likin' each other, Vivian and me, maybe even fall in love, get married. Before that could happen I would have to get my rough spots smoothed down and talk better and stop stayin' "you know" so much. Accordin' to Vivian, white guys with a good education and an important position in life never say it. But not many of them are doin' any better than me. Me and my great body and my charisma took like, you know, a short cut, right? We got it made, right? And havin' said that, there is only two more things to say:

THE END